Invisible

Lindsay Woodward

For Beverley and Matthew.
My favourite siblings. I love you very much.

4

ONE

Alice pounded the delete key as she muttered her usual mix of profanities, which then became more audible when the doorbell chimed.

'Now you bloody come!' she hissed as she desperately tried to find the error in her coding. She was on the cusp of resolving the issue but she needed to concentrate.

The doorbell dinged again. With a huff, she yanked off her glasses and marched out of her home office. She stomped down the stairs, but as she reached the bottom she took a calming breath. Steadying her irritation, she slowly and carefully opened her front door.

'It's just your Ocado delivery, Miss Bloom,' the smiley man shouted. Alice was standing right in front of him but he couldn't see her.

She stepped away so her voice was in the correct location. 'Can you leave the bags in the hallway as usual, please.'

'No problem. I'm doing it now.'

Alice watched as the attractive man carried her ten bags of shopping across the threshold and into her spacious hallway. Then he picked up the bags from last time that she always left ready by the door.

'Thanks for the return bags,' he shouted, as if Alice could be anywhere.

The delivery team had always handled her anonymity well. But Alice had never been sure if it was English politeness and they were actually desperately curious, or if, in fact, they just didn't care. Like everyone else in her life.

You see, Alice Bloom was invisible. She had been now for four and a half years. Totally invisible. And not one person knew.

She closed the door as the man got back in his van, and she carried the bags through to her large kitchen. She started searching for the frozen items (mainly her precious salted caramel ice cream) when she heard her mobile phone ringing from upstairs.

She didn't even flinch. It had to be a work call. No one else ever bothered to phone her. And even her work calls were few and far between.

As she carried on packing away her groceries her eyes became fixated on the box of doughnuts. She really wanted a sweet treat. She made the quick and satisfying decision that as soon as everything was packed away, she was going to have a cup of tea and a doughnut.

Her phone rang again. Cursing the person calling her and their total impatience, she darted up the stairs.

But the second she saw her phone, her whole demeanour lightened.

'Hi Dan,' she said, swiftly answering the call, her voice a melody of delight. They'd already spoken that day so she wasn't expecting to hear from him again. It was a lovely surprise.

'I can't be long, I've got to be back in the meeting in a few minutes, but I had to call. We've just been told the news.'

'News?'

'The award nomination.'

'Oh,' Alice sighed, rolling her eyes.

She headed back down the stairs, still with that doughnut

fixed firmly in her mind.

'I'm really happy for you,' Dan said.

'It's not exactly a nomination is it. Not like the Oscars. The Marketing department strategically put the new release forward for an award to help promote it.'

'It's still recognition of your work.'

'It's a popularity vote! We're obviously *definitely* going to get shortlisted as we're one of the biggest companies in the UK, therefore they'll want to sell us lots of tickets for the ceremony. And then it's all down to how many customers vote for you.'

'Well, there you go then,' Dan replied. 'If you take our market share-'

'Don't give me the market leader spiel. Size should not be relevant as to whether we win the award, but it absolutely will influence the outcome. So in that sense it's all a load of crap.'

Dan sighed. 'Congratulations anyway. It doesn't matter how you win, the important thing is that you deserve to win. The new software blows the competition out of the water, and it's all down to you.'

Alice tucked the now invisible phone under her chin before she picked up the kettle and filled it with water.

'The whole team worked on the development,' she insisted. 'Have you congratulated them as well?'

'It was your baby. Just take the compliment and shut up.'

Alice did as he requested. She didn't say another word about it. But it wasn't a cold silence. Dan never failed to make her smile.

'Anyway, that wasn't the only reason I called,' Dan added. 'I completely forgot to say it earlier, but happy birthday.'

Alice stopped moving, the kettle still gripped in her hand. 'What did you say?'

'Happy birthday,' Dan repeated.

Her heart started to thump. 'How did you know it was my birthday?'

'I have my ways.'

'Seriously, how did you know?'

'I just happened across the information.'

'Tell me, Dan!' she virtually yelled.

'It's all right.'

'Nobody knows. How did you find out?'

'I haven't been spying on you or anything.'

'Dan!'

'Okay. It's quite simple. A few months ago it was the anniversary of your dad's... passing. There was a tribute to him. Apparently they do it every year. As part of it they mentioned you, and in the depths of the information handed out, I saw your birth date. I remember stuff, what can I say.'

'The whole company knows it's my birthday?' Alice gasped; panic exploding through her.

'If they'd bothered to look.'

'That's illegal! They can't give out that sort of information without my permission.'

'Alice, stop it. It was a tribute to your family. Besides, I don't think anyone else cares.'

Alice lost her breath for a second as his words stung her. It wasn't a new pain, but it still didn't stop it hurting.

'I didn't mean it like that,' Dan quickly added. 'It's just that people listen to your dad's story, but you're never here. It was only because I happened to look that I noticed. Has anyone else wished you a happy birthday?'

The sharp stinging morphed into an ache. The word "no" was just too sorrowful to utter.

The kettle that she was still holding slowly started to vanish. Anything Alice touched for longer than a minute or so always vanished along with her. It was never permanent. Items always reappeared as soon as she let them go, but it was like her anonymity was contagious.

She placed the kettle down on the draining board, knowing she'd never be able to switch it on if she couldn't see it.

'I haven't mentioned to anyone else that it's your birthday.' Dan's voice was soothing. 'If you don't want me to, I won't tell a soul. But at least reassure me that you'll be celebrating tonight.'

Alice glanced down at the bottle of Prosecco poking out from one of the Ocado bags. That was her celebration tonight. At least she was acknowledging the day.

'Fizz and friends,' she said, telling herself that Sammy her teddy bear was as good as a friend. 'What better way to celebrate.'

'Are you going out?'

'We're just going to see how things go.'

'Because if you are in town, we'll be out tonight. You could join us.'

'Who's we?'

'The sales team. As we're all up for the monthly meeting, we're heading into Starley Green tonight for dinner and drinks. We'll probably end up at Strikers if you want to join us. Bring your friends. It would be great to finally meet you.'

'I'll chat to the girls, see what they want to do,' Alice said. 'My main friend, Sammy, she's usually got things already planned, though.'

'It is your birthday.'

'I'll see what Sammy says.'

'I hope you can make it. Look, I'd better go. Perhaps I'll see you later?'

'You never know. Enjoy the rest of your meeting.'

'All right. Bye.'

'Bye.'

Alice slumped over the sink. Her need for a doughnut had subsided and she left the kettle where it was. Now all she needed was a hug from Sammy.

She headed up to her bedroom and wrapped her arms around her giant cuddly bear. Her dad had given Sammy to her for her fifteenth birthday. She'd asked for a pet – a cat or dog would have sufficed – but instead she got a giant stuffed toy. Alice hadn't been best pleased at the time, but now she was very grateful for her closest friend in the world.

'I am curious what Dan's like,' she told Sammy as they curled up together on the bed.

Alice had been chatting to Dan for several months. It had started not long after he'd first joined Blooms Security Solutions as their newest salesperson. When she'd seen the office number calling her that day, she'd immediately assumed it was the Head of Product Development, but instead a polite man apologised for disturbing her and asked for her help.

Dan had been having problems with his first big customer. Their software wasn't working properly, and the support team had been less than forthcoming with useful advice. Dan had managed to track down that Alice was the brains behind most of the products, and he'd used his cunning to get her number.

She'd been so surprised by his call, she'd willingly offered him all the help he needed. And then he'd made a point of calling her several times after in an attempt to take her out for a thank you lunch.

Through her steadfast declining of his continued invitations to meet, a friendship blossomed. Alice's one and only friendship for many years.

Well, except for Sammy.

'I don't even know what colour his hair is, or how tall he is,' she said, placing Sammy next to her as if they were in an important consultation.

She imagined Sammy talking back to her, pointing out that Alice had every right to treat herself on her birthday.

'That's what the Prosecco is for,' Alice argued.

She imagined Sammy telling her that she'd had Prosecco at Easter, and during the August Bank Holiday weekend. Her birthday needed more of a celebration.

'But I haven't been out in a really long time,' Alice said, feeling the nerves of Sammy's suggestion. 'You really think I should go into town?'

She could almost see Sammy's enthusiastic nod.

'I supposed there's no harm in just having a quick drink and seeing what Dan looks like. That might be nice.'

Sammy was still nodding.

'Okay. All right. You win. I'll go out.'

TWO

Alice swayed back and forth on her decision for the next few hours, until eventually Sammy put her foot down and Alice felt compelled to go.

It wasn't the first time that Alice had gone out for the evening since she'd become invisible, but it was hardly a regular occurrence. That being the case, coupled with the fact that it was her birthday, Alice decided to make an effort with her appearance. Even though no one would ever know.

She pulled her very long hair back into a pony tail, put her favourite jeans and a smart T-shirt on, shoved her keys and phone in her pocket, and as soon as her clothes had adopted her contagious invisibility, she went on her way.

It was a beautifully warm early September evening. So warm in fact that even though the sun had set, the sound of laughter and family enjoyment could still be heard through open windows.

Alice dodged her way into town, avoiding people at every opportunity. As it was only a Thursday night she'd been hoping that it might be quiet, but it seemed the warm weather had encouraged socialising.

She headed straight for Strikers. She'd frequented the bar quite often before her invisibility had struck, but since then she'd been just twice, when the cabin fever had become too much for her. The last time had been a Friday night and the venue had been packed. She'd had to pin herself up against the wall just so she wouldn't bump into anybody. It had always been far more awkward than amusing to Alice when someone bumped into her. The look on their faces was alarming, as to them they'd struck nothing but air and air had fought back.

This time, thankfully, the bar was quieter. Plenty of seats had been taken but very few people were standing around.

It was dimly lit inside, with a purple and red hue, and the music wasn't too overpowering at this still early hour of partying.

Alice scanned the room for potential Dans when she spotted someone she recognised. It was John, Head of Sales. He'd been the company's first ever sales employee and he'd been a good friend to her dad for many years.

He was sitting with four other people: three men and one woman. Alice headed on over, eager to find out which one Dan was.

She stood next to the long table they occupied and she studied the faces of the three men she didn't know. Dan had told her that he was thirty during one of their many chats. That day was Alice's twenty-sixth birthday, so she was expecting to see someone who looked about her age (whatever she actually looked like now). However, two of the men must have been in their forties and the only other man there was far too young. He only seemed about eighteen. Maybe Dan appeared young for his age?

'Here you go,' a man said, placing a tray of drinks down on the table.

'Thank you, Dan the man!' John said, and Alice had her answer.

For the first time ever, Alice set her eyes on Dan. He had a lovely warm smile on his round face. He was tall and slim, but not skinny; and he looked incredibly smart, like he'd made a huge effort even though it was just work drinks.

'Right, I need to know: who are you waiting for?' John asked Dan as he took his pint off the tray.

'What do you mean?' Dan replied, taking a seat at the end of the table, which just happened to be closest to Alice.

'You keep looking at the door. Or are you just desperate to escape?'

'It's always good to know where your nearest exit is.'

'I think you've checked it out sufficiently now,' John said.

'Checked what out?' the youngest man asked.

'Nothing,' Dan replied.

'Haven't you seen him?' John asked the man. 'Dan has been watching that door for most of the night. I want to know who he's waiting for.'

'I don't know what you're talking about,' Dan said, shrugging. 'I'm just looking around. You lot are all boring me.'

'That may be the case,' John replied with a smirk, 'but you're still looking for someone. Are you dating someone locally? You've got that look in your eye.'

Alice stared into Dan's brown irises, trying to work out what John meant. Was Dan seeing someone? She suddenly felt put out that he hadn't mentioned anything to her.

'What look?' Dan asked.

'A mixture of hope and disappointment.'

'Do you spend a lot of time looking into my eyes?'

'No, I just recognise that look all too well. I had it when my ex-wife used to frequently stand me up.'

'I'm not waiting for your ex-wife, if that's what you're worried about.'

John sniggered. 'I should hope not, but you are waiting for someone. Who is she?'

Alice's chest tightened as it dawned on her who Dan could be waiting for. She could see in her peripheral vision that all of his colleagues were now equally staring in curiosity.

'Will you just drop it,' Dan asked.

'No, I'm happy to keep this going all night,' John stated with a grin.

Dan sighed. 'You're not kidding, are you?'

'No.'

'All right. It's not a big deal. You've made it a big deal but it really isn't. It's work drinks so I invited someone else from work. That's all. I just wanted to make sure they knew where we were sitting if they joined us.'

'Okay. Who did you invite?' John's voice was now full of intrigue but Alice still couldn't take her eyes off Dan.

'If you must know, it's Alice.' Alice stopped breathing. She wasn't sure how she felt.

'Alice?' the youngest man asked. 'Who's Alice?'

'Don't you mean who the fuck is Alice?' one of the older men asked, laughing. Alice saw Dan roll his eyes. She liked that.

'Why would I mean that?' the younger man asked.

'The song, you know,' the older man explained, but the younger one just shook his head blankly.

'Alice Bloom,' Dan clarified, firmly.

'Alice Bloom?' John virtually spat.

'She works for the company,' Dan stated.

'I suppose. Not that anyone ever hears from her. I think maybe Glenn talks to her every now and then.'

'I talk to her,' Dan said.

'What do you mean you talk to her?' John asked.

'We talk,' Dan shrugged. 'On the phone.'

'And she said she was coming out tonight?'

'I invited her.'

'Why?'

The tightness in Alice's chest converted into sharp stabs as she turned to see John's mystified face.

'Why not?' Dan replied. 'Besides, today's her-' he stopped himself and Alice once again held her breath. 'She lives close and we're all out tonight. I thought it might be nice to meet her.'

'What do you talk about?' John asked, his face screwed

up as if he was querying the strange behaviour of an alien.

'What does who talk about?' a woman insisted to know as she took a seat at the table, seemingly having come from the toilets. She had short straw-like hair that flopped around her face, and big bulging eyes that suggested she never missed a thing. She was young, perhaps in her early twenties.

'Do you know who Alice Bloom is?' one of the men asked.

'No,' she said, as if not knowing was a cause for concern. 'Bloom? As in Bloom's Security?'

'Daughter of Norman Bloom,' John confirmed. 'His one and only child.'

'What about her?' the woman asked, determined to know more. Alice couldn't believe how unapologetically nosey she was.

'She works for the company,' another man said.

'Where does she sit?' the woman asked.

'She works from home,' Dan said.

'I've never met her,' the woman remarked, like it was a personal insult.

'Very few people have,' John replied.

'Why? Why would Norman Bloom's daughter never be in the office?'

'It's complicated,' John explained. Alice bit her lip.

'How so?' the youngest man asked.

'Long story short, when her father died, his shareholding got passed down to Alice, but she was only young. Still at uni. She wasn't ready to take on anything that big. She's still technically the major shareholder, but she only seems to take an interest in product development. Apparently she sent an email to the board saying she'll agree with the majority on everything, and all they have to do is email her the minutes of meetings. That's about the height of her contribution.'

'I bet the board loves that,' the quieter woman stated, but Alice was more interested in the nosey woman. She was remaining very quiet, listening intently to every word, as if she were absorbing knowledge to later use to her advantage.

'The board was willing to do anything Alice wanted,' John said as he shook his head.

'Why do you say it like that?' Dan asked, curiously.

Alice felt her heartbeat quicken as she awaited the story she hated to hear. 'Do you know what happened with her parents?' John asked.

'I don't,' the nosey woman declared.

'Wasn't it a plane crash?' Dan queried.

'Yeah, but do you know the full details?'

'Not really, no.'

'She's never told you?' John enquired.

'We mainly talk about work stuff,' Dan replied. Alice didn't know whether to feel hurt or not that he was downplaying their friendship so much.

'It wasn't just as black and white as a simple plane crash,' John explained. 'Basically, her parents had gone to Taiwan for business, but the company had cocked up with the return flights. When Norman and Julia got to the airport they found they'd arrived at the right time, but the flight had been booked for the next day. So they had to wait around for twenty-four hours while the flight they had expected to get sailed home with no issues.'

'So they should never have been on the flight that crashed?' Dan asked, his face whitening.

'It was an accident.'

'Both her parents were on it?' the nosey woman checked.

'Yes. Her mother was a freelance photographer,' John detailed, 'so whenever she could she'd tag along on the international business trips to get some good shots.'

Dan sat back, a melancholy expression on his face.

'What's that got to do with the board?' the nosey woman asked.

'They blamed themselves for getting the flights wrong,' John replied. 'No one knows exactly who booked them. Or at least we've never been told. But that one error cost the company owner his life. It's pretty sobering.'

Alice's eyes were locked on Dan. She was desperate to know his thoughts. He now knew the truth. She wondered if he'd ever tell her.

No one spoke and Alice felt the sting of tears threatening as the faces around her absorbed her sad story.

She needed a drink. She took one last look at Dan before she escaped to the bar. She located a quiet spot right at the end, away from the other punters.

On her first night out after her invisibility had struck, she'd devised a plan to get a drink, knowing she couldn't feasibly pay. She'd wait until the staff were all busy, and then she'd sneak back behind the bar and grab a bottle of beer. Or wine if the night was that bad. She had to keep it low towards the floor in her hand for about a minute until her contagious disappearing act took over the bottle, then she was free to happily swig away unnoticed.

As she was eyeing up which drinks were closest to her, ready to put her plan into action, a smell hit her nose. She noticed it was emanating from the man that had just appeared next to her. He had a musty whiff about him, like he'd been left in the back of a cupboard in a really old house for years.

He was short and plump with badly greased up hair, as if he'd attempted some sort of trendy spiky look and then someone had sat on him just as the gel was setting.

'Who's next?' the barman asked. Alice returned her focus to the fridges, whittling down exactly what she could liberate with ease.

'She is,' the whiffy man said, pointing in Alice's direction.

She looked behind her, assuming she was standing in someone's way, but no one was there.

'What can I get for you?' the barman asked, looking directly at Alice. She stayed very still and quiet, trying to work out exactly whom he was speaking to. 'Come on, love, I haven't got all night.'

She felt his eyes pierce into her. 'Are you talking to me?'

she asked quietly.

'I don't see anyone else standing there. What do you want?'

'You can see me?' she asked. She turned to the whiffy man who was also staring at her. 'You can see me too?'

'Yeah,' he replied with confusion.

Her jaw opened wide as a fizz of excitement shot through her. Could this really be happening?

THREE

'Oh my God!' Alice yelped as she raced to the toilets. She burst through the door, the smile achingly wide on her face. She jumped in front of the row of mirrors, but all she could see were the cubicles behind her and a slightly disturbed expression on the woman's face next to her.

She looked down at her hands. Nothing. She couldn't see them. She was still invisible.

'Can you see me?' she pleaded to the woman, who was now wide-eyed with fear. The woman momentarily froze before dashing out of the toilets without drying her hands.

Alice shook her head with disappointment. Someone must have been standing behind her. It was just a freaky coincidence. She had to get a grip. She headed back over to the bar to sort herself out with a drink.

'You're back!' the whiffy man said.

Alice stood agape. She looked down and for the first time in years she saw her hands.

They looked dreadful. All that time chewing her nails had left them wrecked, and the skin seemed older and dry. But they were there.

'You can really see me?' she asked the man.

'And I like what I see,' he said.

'Do you want a drink now?' the increasingly irritable barman asked.

Alice went to say yes when she realised she had no money. She hadn't seen cash in years, and her cards were safely tucked away in her office drawer at home. She hadn't thought there was a need to bring them out.

She never saw herself as a thief, more that the world had punished her for her loss and so she was owed a few freebies here and there to make things equal.

'I'll buy you a drink,' the whiffy man said. 'Anything you like, babe. What can I get for you?'

'That would be very kind of you,' Alice said, enjoying the strange sensation of interacting with someone. It had been a long time since anyone had bought her a drink. 'I'll have a glass of white wine. If that's okay.'

'Make it a large,' he said to the barman. 'It's her lucky night.'

'It certainly is,' Alice said as she studied her hands again.

The whiffy man moved in closer. 'You come here often? I don't think I've seen you here before. I'm sure I'd remember such a pretty face.'

Alice hesitated, uncomfortable by his close proximity. 'Very rarely,' she muttered.

'Who you here with?'

She hesitated again. 'Work friends,' she said. 'They're sitting over there. But I'm getting bored with all the work talk.'

'I can think of lots of things that we could talk about.'

Her white wine was placed before her and the whiffy man kindly paid. 'Thank you very much,' Alice said, picking up the glass.

'No problem. Where do you live?'

'Not far. Nearby. You?'

'Not far either. How have we never met before?'

'You'd be surprised.'

'I think you're really sexy.'

Alice pondered this. Her hair was swept back

haphazardly in a ponytail, her face hadn't been touched in years, she wasn't particularly dressed up, and as she looked down she saw her belly poking out of her T-shirt in a way it never used to. She felt anything but sexy.

'Can I kiss you?' the man asked as saliva started to eke out the corner of his mouth. Alice tried not to heave as he edged closer to her.

'We've only just met,' she said, pushing him gently away. 'I'm a lady.'

'I bet you're an animal,' he replied, his eyes alive with lust.

Alice didn't know what to do. She wanted to be talking to Dan and getting her life back, not standing with this drooling, smelly man who only came up to her chin; as she could now very clearly see.

'I'd better get back to my friends,' she said. 'They'll be starting to worry. I've been gone for a while.'

'Yeah, of course. I understand,' the man said taking a step back. 'I'm with that lot over there, in the corner.' He pointed to a group of people all in their twenties huddled around a table. They were sat at the other end of the room from Alice's colleagues. 'Come and find me later. I'll walk you home.'

'You'll walk me home?' Alice checked, feeling her skin prickle.

'I want to make sure that a beautiful girl like you gets home safely. There are very few of us gents left in the world.' He took a step closer to her again and grinned in her face.

'That's very kind of you,' Alice said, backing away. 'Bye then.' She walked off quickly, making a beeline for the safety of Dan and John.

Halfway there, she halted. She must look a right mess. She couldn't meet Dan looking the way she did. She had to at least tidy her hair up.

She scuttled over to a dark corner, ready to do a little preening, when she noticed her glass of wine slowly starting to fade away. She was disappearing again. What was going on!

She took a gulp to steady herself as a horrifying thought came to her. As much as it sickened her to even consider it, the only constant in both of her appearances had been that creepy little man. It was like he had anti-invisibility power. And she'd really liked it. She'd forgotten how nice it was to be spoken to; to actually interact with someone. Even if it was a smelly weirdo.

She needed to test her theory. She downed the rest of her wine for a bit of Dutch courage, placed her glass discreetly on the floor out of sight, and then she yanked the band out of her hair. She tried to scoop it all back again as neatly as possible, really taking her time. She knew it wasn't going to be perfect, but at least she could try to make it less bumpy, as she was sure it had looked before.

She patted her clothes down, checking for pockets sticking out and curled up ends, and when she felt a tad more confident, she walked over to Dan and John's table.

'How can you possibly say that's the best film of the twenty-first century?' the nosey girl said, her eyes still bulging.

'Because it is.' Dan was firm in his response and Alice detected that he didn't particularly like the nosey girl, although it wasn't hard to see why.

Alice gave them a minute, deciding it was possible that they'd just not noticed her yet as they were too engrossed in their conversation.

'It's so not. It's long and boring,' the girl argued.

Alice knew straight away that Dan was referring to The Lord of the Rings. It was one of his favourite films, just as Game of Thrones was his favourite TV show. And Alice was absolutely in agreement. They'd wasted many an evening discussing the particulars of both in great detail.

'What then, I dread to ask, do you think is the best film of the twenty-first century?' Dan enquired.

'It's easy. There's no competition.'

'Never heard of it. When was it released?'

John chuckled and Alice smiled.

'No, I meant there's no competing with what is obviously the best film... well, I think ever made.'

'Now I am curious,' Dan replied. 'Because I think the best film ever has to be *Blade Runner*. I can't wait to hear what you consider to be better than *Blade Runner*.'

'Good call,' John agreed, but Alice shook her head. She loved sci-fi and fantasy but she'd never been able to see why he was such a fan of *Blade Runner*. There were so many better movies out there.

'It's *The Greatest Showman*,' the nosey girl stated.

Dan looked shocked and then he creased up laughing. 'Are you serious?'

'It's brilliant. It's so well done with incredible music. I've seen it like a hundred times.'

'*The Greatest Showman*? Have you ever actually seen *Blade Runner*?'

'I watched half an hour of it and was bored senseless. No one ever says they get bored watching *The Greatest Showman*.'

Alice was becoming tetchy. She needed to know for sure whether they really couldn't see her or whether they were just too deep in their argument.

Zoning out the nosey woman's attempts at singing some of the tunes from her favourite film, Alice moved to stand behind Dan's chair. She carefully placed her hand on his shoulder. He jumped and turned around.

'What was that?' he said to the man next to him.

'What?'

'I just thought... I felt something.'

'Wasn't me.'

Dan shook his head as he looked directly at Alice, but he couldn't see her. Just as she feared.

She had her answer there, so next stop was the whiffy man.

She slowly walked over, happily moving away from the

nosey girl's continued efforts at showcasing her terrible singing voice.

The whiffy man was sitting with his own bunch of loud people, all who seemed to be a few steps beyond tipsy. She stood next to him but he didn't react.

'Oi, Bladder,' a lad nearby said as he pointed to Alice. 'You got company.'

The whiffy man looked up and his eyes seemed to instantly sparkle with delight. 'Hello, babe,' he said, attempting some sort of lusty purr.

'Hello,' Alice said, her heart troubled by the mix of ecstasy at being seen, and sheer disappointment of the company she found herself in.

'I knew you'd be back.'

She shrugged. 'There's only so much work talk a person can bear.'

'Of course.' Alice found the smugness on his face quite disturbing. 'Take a seat, take a seat. You want to sit on my lap?'

'Karl!' the woman next to them shrieked, her voice loud and animated. 'Give the poor girl some dignity.' She stood up to greet Alice. She was tall, big boned, and probably not that attractive under the slabs of make-up, but it was hard to tell.

'You'll have to excuse him,' the woman said. 'He rarely gets pretty girls talking to him. Or any girl for that matter.' She guffawed, taking Alice by surprise, it was so flamboyant. 'Anyway, babe, you can have my seat. We're off. I would have loved to have chatted to you. Are you on a date with Karl? It would have been great to get to know you better. I do love to meet new people. It's one of my things. I'm a people person. Everyone says it about me. Isn't that right, Ethan?'

'What are you going on about now?' a male voice said from behind them.

Alice turned around to see the most beautiful man in the world approach them. He was about six foot tall with dark hair, and eyes so chocolatey, Alice wanted to lick them. His chiselled features and toned physique were almost too good to be true, and Alice couldn't help but be in awe of how his muscles flexed beneath his T-shirt as he grabbed the animated woman by the waist.

'This is Karl's new girlfriend,' the woman virtually sang. 'I was just saying how we have to go, but it would have been lovely to get to know her better.' The woman clutched Alice's hand. 'We'll have to have a girls' night one night. I'll get the Prosecco. I love Prosecco. Do you love Prosecco?'

Alice opened her mouth to answer, but the woman didn't give her the chance.

'Of course you do!' she continued. 'Who doesn't like Prosecco? Oh, we're so similar. I can see us being besties, you and me. Or like sisters. I've always wanted a sister.'

The woman hugged Alice warmly. Despite how peculiar it all seemed, Alice felt waves of comfort wash through her. It was the first human contact she'd had in years and suddenly she realised how badly she'd missed it.

'We need to get going,' Ethan said.

'We've got to be in London tomorrow,' the woman informed Alice.

'A weekend away?' Alice asked.

The woman cackled. 'Oh honey, you're so funny.'

Alice smiled, hoping that the woman would elaborate, but she didn't.

'Grab the seat,' Karl said to Alice, pulling the woman's chair stiflingly close next to his. 'Come and sit down.'

Alice didn't move. All the eyes around her were staring at her and she didn't feel at all comfortable. Talk about an entrance after being blanked from the world for so long.

'I think she wants to come to London with us,' the woman cackled again.

'Shame we couldn't get to know you better,' Ethan said with disinterest slapped across his face. He was clearly very eager to leave. 'I'm sure we'll see lots more of you.'

Alice couldn't take her eyes off him. She was genuinely

gutted he was going. It was the one time she wanted to be invisible, so she could follow him all over the place and feast her eyes on his body at her leisure. Invisible eyes could go anywhere and everywhere.

She could feel the lust for this man emanating from her body. Anyone close to her was surely going to get intoxicated by her dopamine high, it was so potent. The overwhelming urge to be touched consumed her, and voluptuous thoughts of how he could resuscitate her libido flooded her brain.

'I'm Alice,' she said, holding out her hand. It was far too formal, but she was desperate for his touch in whatever way she could get it.

'Lovely, babe,' the woman butted in, hugging Alice again, much to Alice's severe frustration. 'I'm Felicity. But all my friends call me Flick. You can call me Flick. We are practically sisters after all.'

'Ethan,' the Adonis said. He turned to Flick. 'Can we go now?'

'Okay, babe. Bye everyone!' Flick waved to the table, but most people just ignored her, and then Ethan practically dragged her away.

Once they were out of sight, Alice turned to the empty chair and the eager Karl sitting very closely next to it.

Alice hesitated but she knew she couldn't just leave. If nothing else, she wanted to know more about Ethan.

'Are they a couple?' she asked as she carefully sat down.

'Who?' Karl asked.

'Ethan and Flick.'

'Is that what she told you?'

'No. It just looked that way.'

Karl shook his head. 'I don't think so.'

'Why are they going to London together?'

'London?'

'They just said they were going to London tomorrow.'

Karl shook his head again. 'They're just going home.'

'Together?'

'I doubt it. They're just sharing a taxi.'

Alice hesitated. 'Does Ethan have a girlfriend at all?'

Karl shrugged. 'Sometimes.'

'At the moment?'

Karl shrugged again. 'No, I don't think so.' Then his face lit up. 'So I've got a girlfriend and Ethan hasn't? How about that!'

'You've got a girlfriend?' Alice asked, feeling her skin prickle again.

He placed his hand on her thigh. 'You and me, babe. We're going to be good together.'

She gently pushed his hand away. 'Let's not rush things.'

'No, of course not. I'm a gentleman.'

'Right.'

He sat back, staring at her. She wasn't used to being so conspicuous.

'So your name's Karl?' Alice asked, trying to think of something to say.

'Yeah. Did I hear you say your name was Annie?' he asked.

'Alice.'

'Oh, Alice. Cool. Like the film.'

Alice hesitated. 'I suppose. And the book.'

'Did they make a book of it too?'

Alice smirked. 'Yes. I think so.'

'Cool. You're like famous. Do you sing too?'

'Sing?' Alice asked, confused.

'What was it? A hard knock life and all that. The sun will come out tomorrow. I never saw it.'

'No, that's...' Alice stopped herself. It didn't matter.

'So when are we going out?' he asked.

'Out?'

'On a date.'

'You want to go on a date?' she asked.

'You are my girlfriend.'

Alice didn't know whether to laugh or cry.

She looked at his face. His hazel eyes lacked all depth,

his lips were rough and small, and she was quite sure he had a bit of mud on his cheek. At least she hoped it was mud. However, all that aside, she wasn't having the worst time. And it was the most human contact she'd had in years. That was something.

'All right. Let's go out.'

'Brilliant!' he said, kissing her square on the lips. His rough mouth scraped at hers, and she held her lips tightly together as he pushed hard, as if force and affection were somehow interlinked. He pulled away sporting a grin from ear to ear. 'Can I have your number, then?'

'Where are you going to take me?'

He shrugged. 'Where do you want to go?'

'Dinner perhaps?'

He shrugged again. 'They're doing two for one at The Royal Oak if you want?'

Alice had to look down to stop her giggles. She took a breath and glanced back up at him. 'Sounds wonderful.'

'Shall we go tomorrow?'

'You want to go out tomorrow?'

'Yeah. It's Friday!'

'Okay. I don't suppose I have any other plans. Shall I meet you there?'

'Nah, I'll come and collect you. Like a proper gentleman.' He paused. 'You live local, right?'

'Yes. How about we swap numbers and I text you my address? Or actually, you were going to walk me home?'

'Yes, of course. Can't have my girlfriend walking home on her own.'

'Great. Actually, I'd better go soon. I've got an early start tomorrow.'

He pulled a face. 'You want to go now?'

'Is that a problem?'

'It's just... I haven't seen my mates all week.'

Alice felt compelled to laugh again.

'That's fine. You stay. You have a good time. I'll get home on my own.'

'No. That's not right. Stay out. Come on, I'll get you another drink.'

Alice smirked. 'I really have to go. Do you have your phone?'

He handed her his sticky, cracked phone and she typed in her number. Then she rang herself so she'd have his number too.

'There you go. We're all sorted.'

'Do you want me to walk you home?' he asked, reluctantly.

'No. Please, stay. I'll be home in no time.'

'All right, but at least text me to say you got home okay.'

'Of course. That's sweet of you.'

'I'll pick you up about half five, then.'

'Half five?'

'Yeah, the two for one finishes at seven on a Friday.'

Alice's lips were shaking, she had such a desire to laugh. 'A frugal and organised man. I like it.'

'Love you babe,' he said, slapping a kiss on her lips one more time. 'See you tomorrow.'

'See you tomorrow.'

Alice stood up. She glanced across the room towards where her colleagues were sitting. They were all still deep in conversation, so she darted quickly outside making sure not to be seen. The second she left the bar, her body instantly vanished from sight. Although, for the first time, Alice wasn't bothered. She was laughing too much to care.

What a night!

So strange was her encounter with those people, she didn't for one minute think that Karl would actually turn up to collect her for their date. But she'd certainly had fun.

A long needed birthday to remember. For many different reasons.

FOUR

At half past five on that Friday night, Alice had one eye on the clock as she sat trying to decipher her next move on her online chess game with Dan. She'd finished work bang on five pm, jittery with the idea that Karl might actually show up. But at the same time she kept telling herself that there was no way he'd be coming.

She'd texted him her address earlier that day but he hadn't replied. A sure sign he wasn't going to appear. Karl was probably sitting in the pub with his mates at that moment, having completely forgotten who Alice even was, let alone that they had a date. Hence the reason she was lounging on the sofa with her iPad next to her, proving to herself that it was just any other night.

She pushed her glasses up her nose as she focused on her game - her glasses that were becoming less than useful every day as she was desperate for an eye test. It had been six years since her last eye test. Still, they were better than nothing.

Her doorbell rang. She jolted up so quickly, her iPad trampolined off the sofa and landed face down on the soft carpet. She grabbed it quickly, too edgy to check for scratches, threw it back on the sofa, and then stared at the doorway with apprehension. Would it really be him?

Convincing herself that it was probably a salesperson, she placed her glasses on the coffee table and scuttled over to the door. With a deep breath, she opened it a crack, and instantly she saw Karl, sporting a huge smile on his unattractive face.

'Hello Annie,' he said.

She laughed, opening the door fully to greet him. 'It's Alice.'

He didn't bat an eyelid. 'I know. That's what I said. Hello Alice. Are you ready?'

She couldn't quite believe it. He was there. He'd turned up.

She studied her hands; her actual flesh in sight. This was all like a really bizarre dream.

An idea clicked in her head. 'Actually, I'm not quite ready. But would you join me upstairs while I finish off?'

His grin became wider and his eyes twinkled with lust. 'Upstairs?'

Alice felt her stomach churn but she refused to let his unpleasantness ruin things. 'Will you just sit with me while I put my make-up on?'

'Oh. All right.'

She wanted to cartwheel. It hadn't even occurred to her until that moment that she would be able to see her face and actually apply make-up. She couldn't remember the last time she'd worn make-up. Her products were probably way past their best now, but it didn't matter. It was better than nothing.

Karl stepped in, automatically taking his shoes off. Alice spotted a hole in his sock and a stench hit her nose. She started to giggle. This was both liberating and awkward. But she was determined to focus on the positives.

'It's this way,' she said, leading him up the cream carpeted stairs and across the landing to the third door along.

'Where are your parents?' he asked her.

'What?'

'I'm guessing this is their house?'

'It was. They left it to me.'

'You lucky bitch.'

Alice stopped. She didn't know how to respond to that. She felt like she should say something, but nothing seemed appropriate. Instead she just decided to carry on.

She opened her bedroom door to reveal a pink paradise. Her room was exactly as it had been in her late teens. She hadn't really been in the best position to redecorate.

'Cool room,' Karl said as he started nosing through her things, mostly toys and knick-knacks from her youth.

She left him to it, not wanting to waste a second more. She needed to see her face. She sat down at her dressing table and her jaw dropped open.

Her face was different. Not massively different, but a little bit older and she had a few spots. But it was so good to see it again.

She quickly freed her light-brown hair from its lumpy ponytail. It looked ridiculous. She grabbed her brush and groomed herself. She used to love doing her hair. She tied it neatly back in a bun, hiding her split ends, and then she concentrated back on her face.

She yanked open her drawer, ready for action. She dug out her make-up bag from the back where it had been left untouched for years. Her mascara was far too clumpy to use, but her eye-shadow and pencil would do, and she had a bit of foundation and powder to bring back her fresh, youthful skin.

'You girls make me laugh,' Karl said, sitting on her bed. He bounced up and down and smiled, as if he approved of its springiness.

'Why?' Alice enquired as she drew black pencil across her eyelids.

'How long have you been getting ready for? Two, three hours?' He rolled his eyes and shook his head. Alice watched him in the mirror, but he didn't seem annoyed. Actually more delighted to have a girlfriend who was so vain.

She almost went to tell him the truth, but then she decided to play along. This was all such nonsense anyway. She might as well enjoy it.

'About three hours,' she said. 'I already have several layers of make-up on. It takes time to build up.'

'I don't know why you bother,' he said. Alice waited for a compliment to follow but he just shook his head and rolled his eyes again and that was that.

'Nearly done now,' she said. 'We can't be late for those two for ones, can we.'

'No. It's bloody expensive otherwise.'

Alice smiled as she dabbed at her brown eye-shadow.

'You got any beer?' he asked, bouncing up and down again.

'Yes, in the fridge,' Alice replied, then she cursed under her breath. She couldn't have him going down there. She'd lose her ability to see herself. 'I'll get one for you. You stay here.' She jumped to her feet. 'I bet my boyfriend has had a hard day at work. Can't have you exhausted before our date.'

'Nah, I don't work Fridays,' he said. 'But cheers.'

Alice nodded before shooting down the stairs to get them both a can of lager. She was never short of anything. She had a lot of disposable income as she never went anywhere, so she made the most of online shopping and bought lots of food, drink, books, computer games and anything else that a person needed for solitary entertainment.

No wonder her flat stomach was a thing of the past.

She raced back upstairs and handed Karl one of the beers before she cracked open the other one. Then she sat down and began preening herself once more.

Half an hour later, they were walking down the road, this time away from the town centre, and Alice felt alive. It didn't even bother her that Karl kept trying to hold her hand. She was enjoying evading him by running off and pretending to be interested in trees or flowers, or anything else they passed.

The Royal Oak was a pub on the edge of a retail estate outside of the town centre. Alice had never been in there. It had been a bikers' pub when she'd last ventured out this way, but now it was a family friendly eatery and couldn't be more different.

They grabbed a table not far from the door, taking the first one they came across on this busy Friday night, and they both grabbed a menu to see what they fancied.

'Sorted!' Karl announced proudly.

'Sorted?'

'I'm having garlic mushrooms to start and then the blazing burger with extra garlic bread. It's my usual. They know me here.'

Alice regarded him before glancing at the menu to see exactly what the blazing burger was. It was a beef burger with extra chillies. What a romantic date she was having – chillies and garlic. She stifled her giggle as she studied the menu once more.

'We're having starters then?' she asked.

'Fuck yeah. I'm starving.'

Alice hid her face behind her menu to mask her smirk.

She hadn't eaten out in so long, she knew she'd have to have chips. Oven chips were never the same.

'Right, I'll have the same as you,' she said.

'What?' This seemed to throw Karl.

'I'll have what you're going to have.'

'It's a really hot burger.'

'I can see that. It has four mini flames next to it on the menu. That's seriously hot.'

'You can handle that?'

'Let's find out!'

'All right. I'll go to the bar. What are you drinking?'

'Do you want some money?' Alice said, although the only thing she had on her was her debit card.

Karl touched her hand and she noticed his dirty nails.

'When I take a girl out, I take a girl out. You'll want for nothing tonight. I did an extra shift this week, so there are no issues.'

'Are you sure?' she asked.

'We're going to have a great night.'

'Thank you.'

'So what are you drinking?'

'I'll have whatever you have.'

'I'm having beer.'

'Sounds good to me.'

Karl hesitated. 'Cool.'

He walked off to the bar and Alice tidied the table, placing the menus back and neatly lining the condiments up against the wall. After that she gazed around the pub.

It was packed full of drinkers and families; some people obviously just having left work but everyone seemingly ready to enjoy a luxuriously hot weekend.

After a short while, Alice realised she was staring. The filthy looks being sent back in her direction were the biggest give away, and it made her snap back into the reality that she was no longer invisible. She looked down at the table, keeping her eyes focused on the wood, remembering that her actions now had consequences. Karl might not be next to her, but he was still in sight at the bar just a few metres away and that made Alice very visible.

Karl was gone for about fifteen minutes but finally he arrived back with two pints of lager. He smacked them down on the table, spilling both drinks. He took his seat and swiped the liquid from the table onto the floor with not a care in the world.

'You were ages,' Alice said. She was very glad he was back so she had something else to look at.

'Huge queue. Oh babe, did you miss me?' He touched her hand again and Alice couldn't help but study his dirty nails. They were black, like he'd been playing with coal and had just sort of half washed them afterwards.

'What do you do for a living?' she asked.

He took a huge gulp of his pint. 'I'm proud to say that I've had the same job since leaving school.'

'You didn't go to uni or anything then?'

'Ugh, no. I wanted to work. I come from a family of workers.'

'Fair enough. What work do you do then?'

'You know the supermarket in town?'

'Asda?'

'No. The little one. Dobson's.'

'You mean up by the library?'

'That's the one. I work there.'

'Great. Doing what?'

'Customer liaison.'

'Wow. Like customer services, that sort of thing?'

'Absolutely. And my till is always balanced at the end of every day. I've never even been a penny out.'

'You work behind the tills?'

'For six years now.'

'And that's called customer liaison?'

'That's what Ethan calls it.'

'He works there too?'

'He's the manager. Well regional manager. Well actually I think he's just been promoted or something. They've got a meeting somewhere today.'

'In London?' Alice asked.

'How did you know?'

Alice went to reply but stopped herself. It was too much like hard work. 'Does Flick work with you as well?'

'No.'

'Then why did she go to London with Ethan?'

'Did she?'

Alice took a sip of her drink as she shook her head.

'Do you know Flick?' Karl asked her.

'No. I'd never met any of you before yesterday.'

'Oh right. You just seem to know a lot about her.'

'I guess I just pay attention.'

'Cool.'

Karl took a sip of his drink as the conversation dried up. Alice expected him to ask about her in return, but he clearly wasn't going to.

'Did they say how long the food would be?' Alice asked after a few minutes of silence.

'Yeah, like forty minutes or something. But don't worry, we got our two for one.'

'That is a relief.'

'Tell me about it! You women spending ages on your make-up, you could have cost us a bargain. Anyone would think you had a hot date!' He grabbed her hand from across the table, squeezing it tightly, and Alice bit her lip to stop herself from grimacing. She really couldn't work out why a customer liaison assistant would have such dirty hands. What did they sell? She'd have to pay the store a visit.

'Do you want to know what I do?' she asked.

'Sure,' he shrugged, removing his grip and gulping at his pint again.

'I work for a security company helping them to develop products.'

'Like security guards?' he asked.

Alice snorted a laugh. 'Yes, I help to invent robotic security guards. They're terribly popular.'

Karl's eyes widened with fascination. 'Really?'

'No, you idiot! Security like CCTV, access control, intruder alarms, that sort of thing. I'm a programmer. I develop the software.'

'Why does CCTV need software?'

'To make it work. To make it clever. I've actually just helped to develop a new form of proximity monitoring. It's set to change the industry. I hope.'

'Cool.'

Alice had expected Karl to be more interested, but he didn't seem that bothered at all.

'Maybe we will have robotic security guards one day,' she said, trying to lighten the mood.

'Do you think?' he asked, his eyes captivated again.

'Shall I pitch it to the R&D team and see what they say?'

'Yeah! What's R&D?'

'Research and development.'

'Wow! You work with them?'

'Every day.'

'You must earn like mega bucks. Is that how you can afford that big house? You don't live with your parents do you?'

'No. My parents have both... passed on. They left me the house.'

'Wow! I mean sorry. But wow. Cool.'

'Do you live with your parents?' Alice asked.

'Yeah. It's the best way.'

'Oh?'

'So that means we'll have to go back to yours.'

'Back to mine?' Alice asked, hoping he didn't mean exactly what she thought he did.

'Yeah. When we want to do it.'

'Do it?' She started to chuckle, but this time it was more from horror than humour.

'Yeah. You know. Do it.' He began thrusting his arms back and forth as if to demonstrate. 'You are my girlfriend.'

'Have you had many girlfriends?' she asked.

Karl shrugged. 'Loads.'

'Seriously. If we're going to start something, we need to be honest with each other. That's how this works.'

Karl studied her, as if calculating whether to trust what she was saying.

'How old are you?' she asked.

'Twenty-four.'

'A toy-boy then.'

'I am not!'

'I'm twenty-six. I just meant you're younger than me.'

'You're like a cougar!'

'No. No I'm not. Tell me about your past.' He just glared at her. 'How about I start? I had a boyfriend at uni. We were together for two years. But when my parents died, I sort of just cut everyone out of my life. It's hard. Harder than you think.' Alice paused. It had been a long time since she'd talked about such things. Her only real friend was Dan and she'd actually revealed very little about herself to him. 'You're the first date I've had since then,' she admitted, feeling a strange sadness about how much time she'd lost being invisible. Maybe letting people in wouldn't be so bad.

'So you've not been out on a date in ages?' Karl asked, deeply interested.

'No. Now it's your turn. Tell me about you.'

He shrugged in his usual way. 'Like I said, loads of girlfriends.'

Alice shook her head and exhaled before sipping at her beer. She feared this was going to be a long night.

After more strained conversation, their food eventually arrived. But Alice could only pick at it as she had full view of everything in Karl's mouth at all times and it made her feel quite sick. It seemed as soon as the food arrived he found a million things that he desperately needed to talk about, and a mouth full of sloppy burger wasn't going to stop him.

The burger was indeed very hot, but Alice enjoyed what she managed to eat of it. It was something different from the same home-cooked things she'd had week after week, year after year.

Karl bought them another pint after the meal and they sat in relative silence again, just about managing agonisingly small small-talk. Karl had definitely saved his best bits for the food.

'Shall we head off then?' Karl asked the second he'd finished his drink.

'Where do you want to go?' Alice asked.

'Back to yours?'

Alice hesitated. The image of him thrusting his arms back and forth flashed in her head. That was the last thing in the world she wanted. 'You know, Karl... although we are obviously boyfriend and girlfriend. I mean obviously. We have only just met. This is technically our first date. If you don't mind, I'd like to get to know you better first before we... we... tackle the bedroom.'

Karl seemed surprised. 'You want to be my girlfriend? Like really?'

The word 'no' was screaming around Alice's head, but she knew she couldn't give up this new found liberation. She was out. She could see her body. She felt alive again. Although she'd willingly pushed everyone away five years ago, she hadn't up until now realised just how lonely she'd been. If Karl was her only way of alleviating that loneliness, even for a little bit, then she owed it to herself to carry on.

'Of course,' she said, quickly following up with, 'but if we're going to start a proper relationship then we need to do things... properly. Take our time. Sleeping with someone too soon can cause issues. If we want this to last for the long term, then let's cement the emotional relationship before we move on to the physical one. Does that make sense?'

'Relationship?' Karl asked, his eyes aglow. 'You're really hot.'

'Thank you,' she said, looking down at her chewed nails. She definitely needed to sort them out. 'How about for our next date you come round my house? I could cook for us! Then we could spend some quality time together, like proper boyfriend and girlfriend. I could be painting my nails while you watch the football or something. We could do it tomorrow!'

'Villa are playing Sunday.'

'Then a film. You pick the film. But we'll be together, spending quality time together, like an old married couple. Building up to the physical stuff. In due course.'

Karl seemed to love this idea. His smile was warm, actually touching his eyes for the first time. 'What time do you want me round?'

'Early afternoon?' Alice suggested. 'Whenever you're ready.'

'Brilliant.'

'How about we call it a night for now, so I can get my beauty sleep for you tomorrow.'

Karl chuckled. 'You don't need beauty sleep. You're already beautiful.'

Alice smiled, but it didn't touch her eyes.

Alice let him hold her hand on the way home. It seemed only polite. Especially as she was riddled with guilt. She told herself over and over that she wasn't using him. This was good for him. He clearly hadn't had many girlfriends. This would be good practice for him, getting him ready for when he was actually going to meet the love of his life.

They arrived back at her house and he didn't hesitate in kissing her on the doorstep. She kept her lips firmly shut, not enjoying the rough sensation at all. It got even worse when he pushed her against the door, his force once again being confused with sentiment.

Alice gently nudged him back, trying to smile. She could see drool in the corner of his mouth where he'd clearly delighted in the kiss. Her stomach turned over.

'I want to be honest with you,' he said, holding both of her hands. Alice once again became fixated with his dirty nails. 'You love me, don't you? I can be honest?'

Alice shot her head up to look him in the eye. She wasn't sure how to respond. 'Yeah,' she said. 'I mean, if we're going to grow into a loving relationship then we need to be honest.'

'You're right. You've been honest with me, I need to be honest with you.'

Alice's stomach turned over again but this time with guilt. She wasn't feeling like a good person at all.

'I haven't had loads of girlfriends,' he admitted. 'Sorry I lied.'

'It's fine,' Alice replied. 'It doesn't matter. It's who you are now that I'm interested in.'

'Good. Because...' He shifted on the spot awkwardly. 'I'm also a virgin.'

Alice's jaw dropped open. That was all she needed.

'I've been waiting for the right woman. I'm so glad I waited for you.' Karl kissed her again, and this time the tip of his tongue broke through her barrier. She stepped back, actually revolted by the touch of him. He didn't seem to notice, though. He threw his arms around her, hugging her tightly, his head nestling into her shoulder.

'I love you,' he said.

Alice stood still, gently placing her arms around him in return. Life truly was unfair.

FIVE

The doorbell chimed the next afternoon and Alice practically skipped out of the kitchen where she was preparing a feast. Gone were her concerns from the day before. Now all she could focus on was the fact that she was going to have a whole day of seeing herself.

'Hello, Karl,' she said as she opened the door with a huge smile. 'It's so good to have you here. Come in, come in.'

'Hi babe,' Karl said as he entered. He slipped off his shoes like a well-behaved boy and Alice couldn't help but notice more threadbare socks.

'You want to watch Netflix? Sky Movies? Amazon Prime? A Blu-ray? Take your pick.' Alice led Karl into her large living room. Just as they stepped through the doorway, Karl halted in awe.

'This is all yours?' he asked.

His eyes widened as he absorbed the sixty inch TV hanging on the wall. Then Alice saw him check out the slick unit nestled below it that housed her games consoles and Blu-ray player.

'Yeah. I need to keep myself busy. I don't go out much. Or at least I haven't been. I've got about five hundred games in that cupboard over there if you want to look.'

Karl didn't move. He was now staring back at the TV.

'It's like being at the cinema,' he uttered. 'Do you have *Star Wars*? I'd love to watch *Star Wars* on a TV like that. No, hang on, *Indiana Jones*. Yes. It would have to be *Raiders of the Lost Ark*. No, any of the *Marvel* films. Watching *Endgame* on that TV would be immense. Can we do that? Do you have that?'

Alice picked up a remote from the coffee table.

'Why don't you just watch them all. Here.' She handed over control. 'I have all the *Star Wars* and *Marvel* films in UHD in that cupboard.' Karl's eyes widened even further as he followed her finger to the other side of the room where a large black unit stood. 'But I only have *Indiana Jones* in HD.'

'You own all those films?' Karl walked over to the cupboard in question. He slowly opened the doors to find hundreds of neatly stacked Blu-rays all staring back at him. 'Wow.'

'Can I get you a drink?'

'Can I have a beer?' he asked, hesitantly.

'You can have whatever you want.'

'I love this place!'

Alice skipped off to get Karl and herself a beer, and then she returned to find Karl already slotting *Star Wars* into the Blu-ray player.

'Are you hungry?' she asked as she placed the beer on the coffee table.

'I am a bit.'

'Good.'

She darted off again and returned with platefuls of sandwiches, crisps, chicken legs, sausage rolls, salad, pizza and Indian snacks. 'You're in luck as Saturday night is normally my binge in front of the telly night. I always have a few yummy snacks in. Help yourself.'

Karl's amazement and joy became visibly enhanced. 'I can eat all this?'

'Eat as much as you like. I'm going to have a few bits, then I've got a face mask to do, and I need to paint my nails.

I'll just be over there keeping myself busy. You work your way through the films and the food and enjoy yourself.'

'Okay!'

Alice was in heaven as she preened herself for the first time in years, and Karl didn't bother her at all. His eyes were glued to movie after movie.

After the third film, she asked him to take a break and she convinced him to join her in the bathroom while she shaved her legs. She said she was worried about cutting herself and made out she had a phobia of razors. The idea just came to her and Karl seemed to go along with it, willingly sitting on the edge of the bath as she shaved away in her shorts. It felt so good.

As soon as she was done, they returned to the living room for another 4K treat.

Karl finally pulled himself away from her TV at about midnight. As he said goodbye, the pair were both smiling from ear to ear. Even his attempts at kissing her didn't break Alice's good mood.

It had been the perfect date. She'd managed to do all the simple things she'd longed to do for years and he'd been spoilt rotten in the laziest of ways.

The next day, during her Sunday regime of cleaning, Alice sent Karl a text asking if he'd join her for a date night out in Birmingham that coming Thursday. She really wanted to have her hair cut, so she implied that as she was out anyway, if he joined her for her hair appointment then dinner would be on her at any place of his choosing. She hadn't been to Birmingham in years. It was all so exciting.

His positive response was almost immediate, and then he followed that with suggesting that they go out for a night of drinking the following Saturday and get pissed together. Alice was so thrilled to be going out anywhere, her reply was just as swift.

By the time Monday came around, Alice was virtually drowning in her smile.

It was mid-morning and she was working through some

bug fixes. She normally hated that sort of task. Whenever the software development team couldn't solve a problem (or couldn't be bothered), it got escalated to her. She resented every second of having such menial jobs being pushed her way. She knew either laziness or lack of training were to blame, and she also knew that the generously paid head of department should be dealing with the issue. But she'd never said anything. She didn't want to get dragged into office politics and management problems. So instead she ended up cursing her way through simple tasks that distracted her from the things that would actually make the company money.

Not today, though. Today she just felt happy to be alive and she was actually enjoying herself.

Her phone rang and she saw it was Dan calling.

'Hi Dan!' she sang.

He hesitated. 'You sound uncharacteristically chirpy. Good weekend?'

'The best, actually.'

'So you had a good birthday then? With the girls? Sammy was it?'

Alice smirked, thinking of her cuddly bear that was asleep on her bed. 'Yeah. It was good birthday.'

'What did you do in the end?'

Alice took a breath. Her natural instinct was not to talk about herself. She hated sharing. But she felt like she needed to tell someone about this. About her weekend. She couldn't tell him the absolute truth; the thing that was really making her happy. But if she didn't mention anything then she feared she might explode. It was a new and wonderful feeling.

'I ended up meeting someone,' she practically blurted out. 'I had a date. Two actually.'

There was silence on the other end.

'Dan? Are you still there?'

'Sorry,' he said. 'I went through a tunnel. I'm driving. What did you say?'

'I said, I had a date. I've got a new boyfriend.'

There was a small but noticeable pause before Dan said, 'Wow! That's great news. Brilliant. Did you say you met him on your birthday?'

Alice was the one to pause this time, but she didn't have a moving vehicle to blame. She had the thought that she'd met Karl just metres away from Dan when he had no clue that she was there.

'You went out?' Dan probed. 'I thought you were going to have a night in with fizz and friends and all that.'

Alice tried to think quickly. She didn't want to hurt Dan's feelings. How could she say she was out but she didn't bother coming to see him?

'We went into Birmingham,' Alice said. 'Up Broad Street. I told Sammy that you were in Strikers and we should pop by. That's right, isn't it?'

'Yeah. We were there most of the night.'

'But Sammy had... she'd booked a taxi. And a table. A booth. In one of the bars.'

'Oh right, which bar?'

Alice stopped. She hadn't been to Birmingham in years; not since her days at the University of Birmingham. She couldn't remember which bar was which, and it had all probably changed anyway.

'What's it called?' Alice said. 'You know. The one at the end.'

'Sorry, I don't know. I don't really go into Birmingham much. I do live in London, you know.'

Dan was one of two sales people covering the London area. He was from the south and Alice had always detected a home counties accent more than a cockney one. That was her only indication that he wasn't London born and bred, as they'd never talked much about their backgrounds.

All she knew was that he now lived somewhere in the Capital. He did tell her once what area it was, and for some reason she had Wembley stuck in her head. Although she was pretty sure the only reason for that was because

Wembley was one of the few places she was actually aware of. Truth be told, she wasn't sure if people even lived in Wembley or whether it was just a location for football. London was such a confusing place.

All in all, Alice's geography outside of the West Midlands was pretty much non-existent.

'Where are you driving to?' she asked, trying to get off the subject of her birthday.

'I'm just on the edge of Richmond. You'd love it, it's beautiful here. I was with a client. I have a question actually, if you've got a second?'

'Of course. I always have time for you.'

'This client was sold a very budget system,' he started to explain. 'It's not meeting their needs and they want to know what add-ons they can get to protect them better.'

'What do they mean add-ons?'

'Basically there was a break-in down the road. It's got them shook up. Now they're talking about getting twice as many cameras to cover every inch of their land, and they want infra-red thrown into the mix too.'

'Is their land not covered already?'

'It's a shocking system. I can't believe we sold it to them. Fewer, higher end cameras would have given them a much better solution, but they were sold ten ton of rubbish. I don't think their needs were ever even assessed. The whole job's a mess. Not unlike others from my predecessor.'

'And that's why he was sacked.' Alice knew very little about Dan's predecessor. He'd been the only London salesperson at the time. He'd brought in a wealth of sales, but every single one had been problematic. It seemed he was great at the selling but very poor with the product knowledge.

Dan was completely different. He'd worked for an access control company before, so cameras, lighting and alarms were all new to him. But he worked hard, asked lots of questions and cared about his clients. Alice didn't know how successful he was on paper, but she knew he put in maximum effort and she admired him very much for it.

'So we sold them something that didn't truly meet their needs, and now – surprisingly - it's not working for them?' Alice said.

'That about sums it up.'

'How do they want to use the IR?'

'I don't know. They were panicking. But I can't see how sticking a few extra bits in here and there is going to solve their problem. They need a proper spec. We need to do it right. The only issue is how do I handle it? It's going to cost and I don't think it's fair that it only costs them.'

'I agree. Perhaps we can cut a deal. Like give a very generous discount. Take a hit on our margins just this once.'

'I thought that. But how do I broach the subject with John?'

'Are they a big client?'

'Middleish.'

'Long term potential?'

'Definitely. And they're growing.'

'Well, there you go. Make John see the investment.'

'I suppose. Thanks. Sorry, I shouldn't be speaking to you about sales issues, but I needed to know my instincts were correct before I spoke to John. He'll have me finding a way to charge them extra if he has his way.'

Alice smirked. 'Well, I'm all for maxing out sales, but ultimately we have to put our customers first. I completely agree with your instincts on this.'

'I appreciate that.'

'And you can speak to me about anything. I mean anything. Please don't just talk to me about technical issues. That would be so boring.'

'All right. On the subject of other issues then, when are you going to play your turn? I don't like it when you overthink your move. It's dangerous.'

'Getting nervous about losing two on the trot are we?'

'It's never happened before and I won't be letting it happen now. Have you been too busy with your new boyfriend? Is he distracting you?'

'Nothing distracts me from chess.'

'What's his name?'

'My boyfriend?'

'Yes.'

'Karl.'

'Local?'

'Yes, he lives right by me. He took me out for dinner on Friday and then... I cooked for him Saturday.'

'Wow, two consecutive nights. Must be serious.'

'It's exciting at the minute.'

'You've never talked about boyfriends before.'

'No.' Alice decided to be honest. 'I haven't had a boyfriend in years. In fact, after my parents died I kind of shut myself away. It was good to be out enjoying myself again on my birthday. It felt nice.'

She waited to see if Dan would tell her that he now knew the whole story about how her parents died and why she wasn't actively on the board of the company. But all he said instead was, 'Are you happy?'

'I can honestly say I'm the happiest I've been in a long, long time.'

'Good for you, then. Good. I'm glad to hear it. Anyway, I'd better go. I have to have that chat with John now. Wish me luck!'

'Yes, good luck. I'll be thinking of you. Let me know how it goes.'

'Will do. Bye then.'

Dan hung up quickly, but Alice was too busy smiling to read anything into his abrupt ending.

The time in the corner of her screen caught her attention. It was approaching one o'clock and she decided to break for lunch. Unlike normal, she was going to have a long, leisurely lunch that day. Life was good, and nothing was going to bring her down.

SIX

Dan pulled into the car park of a supermarket he'd just spotted and he stopped his car in a space towards the back, out the way.

He took off his seat belt and rested his head on the steering wheel, disheartened. She had a boyfriend. They'd been on two dates in just one weekend. She must really like this guy. Why couldn't the sales team have gone into Birmingham instead of staying in crappy Starley Green last Thursday?

Dan was dying to meet Alice. He'd liked her since their first conversation together. He'd been desperate for answers that day. No one had been willing to help him, and then Glenn, the department head, had joked that maybe he should speak to the person who designed the damn product, never expecting for one second that Dan would take him seriously.

Dan had prised Alice's number from Glenn's very reluctant fingers. Glenn had been insistent that she wouldn't speak to him. In fact, in the end he'd only given up Alice's phone number out of morbid fascination to see what would happen.

Dan hadn't hesitated in pacing back to his desk to call

this mystery woman. He'd been expecting some obnoxious, unhelpful witch, when a lovely, surprised voice answered.

She sounded genuinely delighted to be hearing from him. Not at all grumpy, cold and difficult as the rumours had suggested. She couldn't have been more willing to assist him, and it ended up putting him on a course to reaching his first target. Not only did he manage to solve the client's problems after one call with Alice, but they'd also bought extra products that he'd offered them following Alice's advice.

From that moment, he knew he had to meet her. He'd never so much as seen a picture of her, but he knew if her looks were anything like her voice and personality, then she'd be stunning.

He'd tried for months after that to take her out for lunch, whenever he was up at Head Office. He spent most days working from home or travelling to see clients, but at least once or twice a month he had to be in the office in Starley Green and he always made a point of inviting Alice out somewhere. But for reasons he'd never been able to fathom, she was never available. She always had other plans, too much work or some other excuse.

It didn't stop him from calling her regularly, though, and over the past few months they'd become quite friendly. He actively tried to find things to talk to her about. Whatever the reason, however small the excuse, he'd call her number to ask her about something and she never failed to answer. She was an incredible woman. A beguiling woman. And her playing hard to get had driven Dan insane. He was now thinking about her on a daily basis, fantasising about this gorgeous brunette with big beautiful eyes and soft curves.

He sat back with a sharp exhale of frustration. She had a bloody boyfriend. Two dates in one weekend. Was that Dan's fantasy over with?

Dan's phone rang. He saw it was John calling and he knew he should take it.

'All right, boss,' Dan said.

'How's it going?'

'Been better.'

'It didn't go well with Hitchins, then?'

'No, they're not happy at all.'

'Well, it's your job to make them happy.'

'I don't think we did a proper specification last time. I think we need to start from scratch and do it correctly for them.'

'Is that why they asked to meet with you, so you can requote them for everything? Are they asking for a new spec?'

'No, they're asking for IR and a few extra cameras.'

'Then give them that,' John said, as if it really was that simple.

'But it's not going to meet their needs. It's not doing right by them.'

'Okay, so how are we going to do right by them?'

'We messed up. I think we owe them.'

'How do we owe them?'

'Is there any way that we can cut a deal?'

'You mean like a discount?'

Dan could sense the disapproval. 'Like a big discount.'

'Not a chance.'

'But-'

'I need those margins to be healthy, Dan. I appreciate what you're saying, but ultimately they placed the order. They weren't forced into it.'

'We gave them bad advice.'

'Do they know that? Are they challenging that?'

'No, but-'

'If the system they bought doesn't meet their needs, that's on them.'

'You know it's not as simple as that. You know that's not fair.'

'But do they?'

'This is wrong.'

'This is business.'

'Are you saying you want me to go in there, blame them for our mistakes and then sell them loads of new equipment? As really that's the only way we're actually going to meet their needs.'

'If they want a better system, they'll need to pay for it.'

Dan gripped the steering wheel with irritation.

'I can give it to Emily if you want?' John said and it stabbed Dan right in the chest.

'No.'

'She's closing, Dan. She's closing a lot. I don't have to remind you that she's smashing her target and you've barely scraped through for the past few months. Last month was bad, Dan. You need this. This job alone could set you past the mark.'

'Okay. You're right. I'll put together a proposal for them.'

'Good lad. Let me see it first. Before you send it to them.'

'Seriously?'

'I want to help you, Dan. You try hard but something's going wrong. I don't want to see your efforts wasted.'

'Fine. No problems,' Dan said through gritted teeth. 'Give me a couple of days.'

'Good lad. Speak to you soon.'

Dan let out a huge breath as he hung up. He knew "I don't want to see your efforts wasted" meant "I don't want to sack you" and it seriously aggravated him.

Dan had been the star salesperson in his last job. He'd smashed every target and had been promoted twice in a very short space of time. He hadn't even found it hard. Sales had always come naturally to him. Then one day Blooms, a major player in the market, had contacted him and offered him a job. They were offering a better salary with a huge commission, and he was supposed to be the senior salesperson in the territory. He couldn't turn it down. It would be a dream come true if only he could bloody sell something.

He couldn't figure out what was going wrong. With virtually every job he came across, Emily already seemed to be working on it. Emily was his fellow salesperson within the London territory. After the disaster that was his predecessor, they'd decided to get two sales people to cover the one area, but it was like she had her slimy hands all over the city all the time, not giving Dan any room to breathe.

He'd speak to a prospective client and the next thing he knew she was putting in a quote, saying that she'd been working on them for weeks. John had backed her every time. She was putting in the quote whereas Dan had just had a conversation. John was far more impressed with the former.

John kept calling her "the closer", like it was some sort of super power. The only revenue Dan was bringing in was from his existing clients; the ones that had been handed to him. The clients across London had been split fifty/fifty between him and Emily, but as far as he could see she wasn't paying them much attention. Instead she was bringing in relentless amounts of new business and closing every lead imaginable. Dan was just left with a bit of scrappy upselling and it seemed there was nothing he could do about it.

He was a Business Development Manager not an Account Manager. When he'd started the job his goal had been to make all of London's businesses safe and secure with a Bloom's solution. But instead he was making no mark at all.

Dan grabbed his wallet from the pocket in his car door and stepped out. The humidity was noticeable after the coolness of his air con and he unbuttoned the top of his shirt. He was off to see another client in an hour, so just time to grab a quick sandwich. And maybe something easy that he could throw in the oven for dinner. Dan loved to cook normally, but he now had a long night ahead working on that proposal. A proposal that he desperately didn't want to have to put together.

All in all, the week was starting off pretty crap for Dan.

SEVEN

Alice finished the last of her stretches in her home gym. It was Saturday afternoon and she'd had quite a week.

Her date on Thursday with Karl had been fantastic. He'd sat quietly in the corner playing on his phone while she'd had her hair cut (which now bounced joyfully around her shoulders) and then she'd dragged him around the shops while she bought the first new clothes she'd treated herself to in years.

After about twenty minutes of shopping he'd become bored and whingy, but Alice had joked about what a proper relationship they had. She painted a stereotypical image of him as the bored boyfriend who was being forced to go shopping, and the notion seemed to delight him. Any guilt she might have been experiencing vanished as he began blissfully playing the role of the suffering partner with the shopaholic girlfriend. He even rolled his eyes and tutted at the lady in the fitting room, muttering about how Alice was terrible when it came to clothes.

The evening then ended just as Alice had promised and she'd bought him dinner at the place of his choice. Given a city with a multitude of cuisines on offer, Alice had been woefully disappointed at his selection of pie and mash.

She'd been craving something special after having nothing but the same home cooked meals for years, yet she found herself stuck with a chicken pie and crappy mash potato. Karl, however, couldn't have been more thrilled.

As much as Alice had enjoyed her night out, it had also been quite revealing. She was far from chubby, but trying on clothes had forced her to see how the years of staying at home had taken their toll.

Since becoming invisible, Alice had been careful not to become too lazy. She'd put together her home gym after the first six months, determined not to fall into a vegetative state. And she'd used it at least twice a week. But now she could see herself again, it was obvious she was far from the fit, skinny Alice she used to be.

That afternoon, as she struggled through her sit-ups, she had to admit that her weight gain was perhaps not totally due to a lack of exercise, but the exorbitant amount of food she'd been eating was probably also a main contributor to the problem. An hour in her home gym a couple of times a week hadn't really been counterbalancing the boredom munchies. Food was comforting. As was wine. But whereas both might have been kind to her soul, she hadn't considered the damage to her waistline.

Now she was very aware of it, she was determined to reverse that damage, and reverse it quickly.

She wiped down her exercise bike and treadmill and headed to her bathroom. She was feeling good after her workout and she was looking forward to the evening ahead. She was going out, she had a brand new dress to wear, and she was ready for some fun!

Karl rang her bell shortly after seven o'clock and Alice jumped up from the settee where she'd been waiting eagerly for the past twenty minutes. She was showered and dressed and she'd blasted her hair dry. All she had to do was style her hair and apply her brand new make-up. She dragged Karl up the stairs and he once again delighted in having a girlfriend who took ages to get ready.

Not half an hour later and they were walking together to the centre of Starley Green for a night of drinks and dancing.

They headed straight into Strikers again, obviously one of Karl's favourites, but Alice didn't mind. First stop was the bar. Karl ordered Alice a large glass of wine, as requested, and he had a pint of lager for himself. Then they turned and spotted his friends, in the same corner as where they'd sat before. As if it were their special corner that they owned.

'Shall we go say hi?' he said.

'Sure,' Alice said, feeling butterflies at the prospect of meeting Ethan again. She couldn't see him, but she hoped he'd show up. This time she looked good.

Karl grabbed two spare seats from across the room and they sat down at the table with his friends. He didn't say hi to anyone, nor did anyone particularly acknowledge his existence.

'How do you know these people?' Alice asked.

Karl shrugged. 'I went to school with most of them.'

Alice scanned the faces of the dozen or so people around her. 'They look older than you.'

'Yeah, they weren't in my year. But Ethan invited me out for drinks one night after work and we sort of became mates.'

'Oh right.' Alice noted how they seemed like anything but mates, but she also acknowledged that she wasn't au fait with the etiquette of "guy mates". Maybe they did just sort of exist together without speaking. Maybe that was what guy friendship was all about.

'Who. Are. You?'

Alice looked up quickly, surprised by the sudden male tone that came from above her. Her heartbeat doubled in intensity when she saw it was Ethan.

'Hi,' she said, unsure if he was annoyed or captivated. It could have been either.

'This is Alice. My girlfriend,' Karl said.

'We met the other day,' Alice said, standing up to greet Ethan. Her eyes followed the length of his toned physique, the outline of which was erotically visible through his tight trousers and short-sleeved shirt.

Her skin began to tingle at the need to be touched. He had this beguiling effect on Alice in a way she'd never known before. Her body seemed to crave him, as if one night with him could make up for half a decade of celibacy.

'No we didn't,' Ethan replied. 'I'd remember you.'

Alice decided not to correct him. Partly because she was too flustered and partly because she reasoned that she did look incredibly different now with make-up and shorter hair.

His eyes became fixated on her, as if he were consuming every inch of her with just his irises. The fizzle it sent through her seemed to explode across her lips in the way of an enormous smile that she couldn't contain.

'You're Bladder's girlfriend?' Ethan asked, incredulously.

'Bladder?' Alice queried.

'Yeah. He pisses himself a lot,' Ethan responded, quite matter-of-factly. Alice glanced down at Karl who didn't seem to bat an eyelid. She suspected that he might just be happy to have a nickname, regardless of how horrible it was.

'Are *you* taking the piss?' Ethan stated, grabbing Alice's attention again. 'There's no way you're Bladder's Mrs.'

Alice coughed, as if to clear her throat. She was full of regret about what she was going to have to admit. 'No. I am indeed Bladd... Karl's girlfriend.' She took a deep breath. Without Karl she wouldn't even have met Ethan, let alone actually be having a conversation with him. She needed to be thankful for what she had.

'Lucky son of a bitch,' Ethan muttered. 'Well, can I get you a drink?'

'A drink?' Alice didn't know what to say. She was fluttering with flattery at the same time as apprehensive about the awkwardness of Karl's mate so obviously flirting with her. Even worse that Karl was sitting right next to them. 'I've already got one, but thank you.'

'No, you want a cocktail. Let's have the most expensive cocktail. What about a Zombie? Do you like them?'

'I've never had a Zombie.'

'Then I have to get you one.'

'Karl?' she said, feeling as if she should include the man she came here with.

'What?' Karl asked, looking up from his phone that he was now scrolling through.

'He can get his own bloody cocktail!' Ethan huffed before swaggering off to the bar.

Alice watched him walk away, enjoying the sight of his perfect body. It was then that she noted how she wasn't the only person in the room to be looking in his direction. Heads were turning all over the place, captivated by his commanding presence. Both men and women seemed to be in awe of him, and Alice decided they must either be mesmerised by his beauty, just as she was, or jealous of their own relative inadequacies.

Whatever their reasoning, Alice was enthralled by the notion that the eyes of most of the people in the room were on the man that she'd been speaking with. The man that was now buying her a drink. The man that had, in all intents and purposes, been chatting her up.

Did he fancy her? Alice couldn't believe it. She felt wobbly with excitement.

What was more, Karl seemed to be okay with it. He was looking quite happily at Twitter on his phone.

Alice's jubilation paused for a second as she considered a dark side. Were they into girlfriend swapping?

Instantly she realised that she didn't care. She'd gladly swap Karl for Ethan!

She took a deep breath and decided to think no more about it. She knew if she started to dwell on it, she'd ruin the fun. It was much better just to enjoy every minute as it came. This was far too brilliant to over-analyse. Logic would surely only ruin her buzz.

Alice sat down and waited for Ethan to return. Karl ignored her, swiping up and down on his phone, watching videos and liking Tweets.

Maybe it was going to be that easy. Karl would lose interest and she could sail off into the sunset with Mr Perfect. Maybe life was finally rewarding her after being so nasty to her for so long.

'There you go, babe,' Ethan said, placing a tall glass filled with a shiny red liquid into Alice's hand.

'Thank you. It looks lovely. What's in it?'

'You tell me.'

'Okay.' Alice giggled before she sucked up some of the cool concoction through the straw. The burning smack of a spirit hit her throat. 'Woah, that's definitely rum.'

'It's one of my favourites,' Ethan said before sucking up a quarter of his glass in one mouthful.

'Oh, sorry,' Alice said, looking around the table and noticing all the seats were taken. 'Do you want to share my chair?'

'It's fine. Someone will move for me in a second,' Ethan replied. 'Besides, I like to stand. I can keep a better eye on what's going on. It's good to always be aware of your surroundings. Remember that.'

'Okay,' Alice said, sipping on more of her drink.

'So tell me about yourself,' he said. 'I'd like to know more about what makes Alice tick.'

'Oh,' Alice said, deciding it would be better to stand up and join him. She glanced across at Karl again, but he was now playing a game on his phone, not at all interested in either of them.

'What do you want to know?' Alice asked. Her choice of heels meant that although she towered over Karl, she was now just an inch or so shorter than Ethan. In every way she felt far more comfortable with him.

'I work in management,' he said.

It wasn't what Alice had been expecting but she assumed it would lead somewhere. However, after a few moments of silence she realised that he wasn't going to elaborate. That really was all he was going to say.

'Karl said you work for Dobson's?' she said, trying to keep the conversation going.

'Yes. As a manager. I was running the local store, but they recently promoted me to senior buyer.'

'That's amazing!' Alice said. 'That's why you were in London?'

'It certainly was. That's where the head office is. I had to go down, meet the team, get trained up. Train other people up. The Starley Green branch has been one of the most successful stores in the country since I took over. That being the case, they wanted me to go down and share my story with other branch managers. Tell them how to do the job well.'

'That's incredible. I bet the branch will be sad to see you go.'

'I was only gone for a day. It was a day's training. That I gave to other people.'

'So where are you based now?'

'In Starley Green still.'

'As a senior buyer?'

'That's not technically the title.'

'So what is your title?'

'Senior manager.'

'Of what?'

'Of the Starley Green branch. It's complicated. Basically, they wanted me to be the senior buyer, but, as you rightly say, the branch didn't want to let me go. So I agreed to stay on as the promoted senior manager.'

'So you're not a buyer?'

'I now consult as a buyer. I give head office the advice they need, when they need it. But the most important place to be is with the customers. That's where the action is.'

Alice's head was spinning. Ethan had said a lot but she

wasn't really sure what on earth he'd actually told her. She felt no wiser about what he did for a living, other than the fact that he worked for Dobson's supermarket. She thought it best to change the subject.

'Tell me about Flick. Is she your girlfriend?'

'You know Flick?'

'Yes. Last week, when I was here. I met both of you.'

'I wasn't here then.'

'No, you were. That's when I first met you. You left early with Flick as you had to go to London.'

'Is that what she told you?'

'You both told me.'

'I wasn't here then.'

Alice sighed. 'I look really different tonight. I guess you don't remember me.'

'I'd always remember you,' he said, his voice soft and sultry, but it did little to dissolve Alice's confused frustration.

'I was here. You left with Flick,' she insisted. 'Remember Flick saying how we were like sisters?'

'You're Flick's sister?' he asked, shocked.

'No.'

'Oh, I remember! Yes, she was raving about you. Saying what a nice girl you are. Yes, Bladder's girlfriend. I remember.'

'See! So is Flick your girlfriend?'

'No. Is that what she said?'

'No, you just left together and I did the maths.'

'Because we left together you thought that something was going on between us?'

'Yes.'

'Oh baby, no. Of course not. You have no reason to be jealous.' Ethan stroked Alice's thumb. It sent a rush of electricity through her. 'Believe me, babe, you have nothing to worry about. Flick and I live in the same street. We just got a taxi together.'

He continued to stroke her thumb gently, and Alice

relished in the long needed touch. It might have been small but it was heaven. They stood staring at each other in contented silence until Alice's head took over and the need for more information became too much for her to bear. 'Does Flick work with you? Why was she going to London with you?'

Ethan smirked. 'You are a jealous one, aren't you? I can see I'm going to have trouble with you.'

'No, it's not like that.'

Alice was a woman of detail and logic, and since she'd met Karl and his friends the two elements had been drastically lacking. But she could see she was starting to appear a bit possessive so she decided to back off.

'Sorry. It's just fun learning about new people,' she said.

'No, I should be apologising,' Ethan said, releasing her thumb, much to Alice's disappointment. 'Things have been hard ever since I got back from London. There's a lot of pressure with my new job. Being in management is very difficult. Not everyone is cut out for it. I mean, I was born to do it. I take it in my stride. It's not the job that gets to me, it's the extra pressure of having to train everyone else. Being the best is a huge burden.'

Alice took a sip of her drink. She wasn't sure how to reply.

Ethan came close to her ear, so only she could hear. 'You see everyone around us. Not just at this table, but the entire place.'

Alice scanned the room before nodding.

'They all either want to be me or they want to be with me. They're all jealous.'

Alice stood back. She didn't know how to react. Although she wanted to accuse him of being arrogant, she had seen with her own eyes the attention he'd received from the people around them.

'It's a curse,' he said. 'I mean, you think I'm good looking, right?'

Alice still didn't respond.

'I'm not trying to be funny,' he said. 'I'm being serious. I'm trying to make a really serious point. I didn't choose to look this way. Yeah, I work out at the gym four times a week, I wear designer clothes and I only use the best products. But am I not allowed to do that? Who doesn't do that? We all try to look our best. I just happen to have a really outstanding basis. It's a curse.'

Alice was dumbstruck.

Ethan focused on her intently. 'I don't want to look like this. I don't want to look like a model. I don't want to have the abs and the guns. Feel this.'

He grabbed Alice's hand and pressed it against his stomach.

'No seriously, feel,' he said, lifting up the bottom of his shirt and inviting her to touch his flesh.

Her mouth dropped open as she caught her first glimpse of him. He was perfect. He had an absolutely perfect body. She couldn't resist. She slid her hand onto his silky skin. It was like a warm, smooth brick wall and her body throbbed with desire. It was a deep, intimate desire that she'd been denied for far too long.

She turned her gaze towards Ethan's chocolate eyes. They were staring back at her with a lustful hunger. How she wanted to be his breakfast, lunch, dinner, supper and midnight snack.

He pulled her in closer to him and her hand automatically slid to his back. The sensation of him was so intoxicating it was almost having a psychedelic effect. She was lost in a state of lasciviousness, which only intensified further when he pushed his torso against hers. She thought she might actually explode.

He whispered into her ear. 'People have expectations when they see someone attractive. I have expectations thrust upon me all the time. Do you know what it's like to be so...'

'Visible?' Alice finished, breathlessly.

'Yeah. Visible.'

Alice stared into his eyes. How she longed to be that visible. Everything about this man before her was enchanting and wonderful. She tightened her hold of him, yearning for him in both body and spirit.

'Be visible,' she muttered back to him. 'It's wrong to be anything but visible.'

'You think so?' he asked, seeming so vulnerable to her. He pushed against her again, their bodies now firmly locked together and their lips just millimetres apart.

'Excuse me!' Karl said, ramming into their embrace. 'I need a piss.'

Alice quickly backed away from Ethan's hold. She'd completely forgotten that Karl was even there.

'Sorry,' she said, letting him past. The sight of him seemed to free her from Ethan's spell. As reality took hold, she could feel herself hurtling back towards earth, and as she watched Karl make his way through the crowds, the situation finally hit her with a thunderous smack.

'Wait!' she said, running after him. 'Don't leave me.'

The sexual charge from Ethan had almost made her forget that she wasn't totally visible. But she wasn't, and the truth was she needed Karl nearby.

'What do you want?' he asked

'Don't leave me. I came here with you. We need to stick together.'

'You seemed to be sticking to Ethan.'

'I was just chatting. Getting to know your friends better. Isn't that what you want?'

'You were practically snogging.'

'I couldn't hear him very well. We were just standing closely. Don't read anything into it. Trust me, Karl, the only man that I need to be around is you.'

Karl's eyes slowly softened and it made Alice feel sick. Not because Karl had horrid hazel eyes that always looked somehow glazed over and clogged up, but because she knew she was a horrible, using liar and Karl deserved better.

'You really like me?' he asked.

'I'm your girlfriend.'

'You like me more than Ethan?'

Alice paused. 'I'm your girlfriend.' It was all she could think to say.

'Come on then, babe.' Karl grabbed her hand and led her towards the toilets. In her heels, he only came up to her shoulders and she felt quite embarrassed by how silly they must look together. 'Do you need the loo as well?' he asked as they arrived down the side corridor where the toilets could be found.

Alice considered her options. 'Yes. I'll go now too. But please don't go back without me. Promise me. You go to the loo and then you wait here until I appear. Okay?'

'Okay, babe. I won't leave you. Don't worry. I love you. I'm never going to leave you.'

Alice felt the urge to sit on the floor in a heap. This literally couldn't get any worse.

She made her way into the toilets knowing that she would instantly disappear from view the second the door closed. Thankfully there wasn't a queue and most people were drunk anyway. She swiftly locked herself in a cubicle when no one seemed to be looking and she planned to slowly let it fall open again when she was done. That way she could make her escape quickly while everyone tried to figure out what was going on with the eerily opening door.

As she sat down on the toilet, she took a second to contemplate Ethan's confession. He felt visible. He was totally visible. He was visible to everyone in the room, like a beacon of gorgeousness.

Alice had only ever felt the complete opposite. She'd never felt like she'd mattered at all. But talking to Ethan had given her a boost. The most visible man in the room only had eyes for her, and that was a startling sensation. A startling yet invigorating sensation.

In that instant she felt like she'd wasted so much time.

She knew her parents would never want this life for her. She found herself suddenly longing to be very visible. To be very visible with Ethan. She wanted the burden of that expectation. Of his expectation. She wanted to live in the world again. She wanted what Ethan had, and she wanted to be with him, so very, very badly.

It all became crystal clear: Ethan was the man that was going to give her everything.

Life was finally slotting into place. She'd met Karl so she could be with Ethan. This was her destiny.

She reached out to flush the toilet with a renewed sense of purpose, when she stopped.

Her arm was there. Her arm was in sight. Well, some of it anyway; from her elbow to her hand.

She blinked a few times in case the power of the Zombie was confusing her brain, but when she focused again, it was still the same.

Her arm hadn't turned totally invisible. Her arm was still there even though Karl wasn't.

That could only mean one thing: she was coming back to life!

EIGHT

Alice waved her hand in the air with a delirious smile. She could see her fingers and she was all alone. It was like a dream.

Her brain started to calculate what could have happened. Why this was now the case. She had to process it. If she could make sense of it, then she might be able to work out a way to bring her whole body back. There was something in her new relationship with these people that was springing her back to life.

Ethan had to be the key. She'd been around Karl loads over the past week and nothing had changed. It had to be Ethan. Maybe Ethan was at the centre of everything. His extreme visibility was making her visible again.

She considered how it could be working. Perhaps Ethan's association with Karl had rubbed off enough to make her visible at times, but actually touching Ethan had been the final trigger.

She felt that rush of adrenaline again at the thought of touching Ethan.

She slipped into a fantasy where Ethan was waiting outside the toilet for her, desperate to be with her. He'd thrust her back into the cubicle and his lips would devour her. Before she knew it she'd be unbuttoning his shirt and exploring every inch of that perfect torso. And with every touch of her fingers, a new part of her body would reappear.

Her smile vanished as she realised that if Ethan was to whisk her off her feet and join her in this cubicle for a fiery embrace, then he was going to have a bit of a shock when all he could see of her was the end of her arm. That might be a passion killer.

Her skin began to crawl when it dawned on her that the only chance she was going to have of an intimate moment with Ethan at present, was if Karl was going to be watching. That was far too disturbing for words.

She flushed the toilet knowing that she should get back before Karl got bored and wandered off.

She turned to the cubicle door, listening to the many voices outside. She guessed there must now be a queue. Great! It was one thing to carefully let a door swing open apparently all of its own accord and disappear out when no one could see you, but a floating arm was going to cause quite a stir.

She contemplated what to do. She needed a distraction.

She looked around her. About the only thing to use was the toilet roll.

Right. She grabbed it and yelled, 'Look everyone!' Then she threw it over the top of the cubicle into the corner, away from the exit. She yanked open the cubicle door, happy to see that all eyes were on the mysterious flying toilet roll, and she bolted out of the toilets as fast as she could.

The second she opened the door and Karl set his eyes on her, she reappeared. He certainly had quite a startling effect on her visibility.

'Thought you'd got flushed down the loo,' he said.

'There was a queue,' Alice said. 'You know what us ladies are like.'

'Yeah,' Karl replied, rolling his eyes.

She pulled her antibacterial hand gel out of her bag. She'd not left the house without it ever since her first visit to a public toilet since turning invisible. It seemed that taps mysteriously turning themselves on and off was quite an alarming sight for ladies also using the facilities. Hand gel rendered far fewer shrieks.

After she'd finished, Karl grabbed her hand and led her towards the bar.

'Another drink?' he asked.

'I've still got some of my wine. But thank you.'

'Do you prefer cocktails? I can get you a cocktail.' There was a reluctant tone to his voice.

'It's fine. But thank you, Karl.' All Alice could think about was Ethan. She wanted to head back over there. She wanted to be rid of Karl. It was so irritating that she was well and truly stuck with him.

'You know what, why don't I buy you a drink,' she said as the guilt of her thoughts pecked at her.

Karl's eyes lit up. 'Yeah?'

'You want a pint?'

'I'll have one of those Zombie things.'

Alice paused. Pie and mash and a Zombie cocktail. Karl was anything but predictable.

'Are you sure? It went straight to my head. What was in it anyway?'

Alice grabbed the drinks menu from beside her and she flicked to the rum section, at least sure of that ingredient. Before she even had a chance to read the contents, she saw the price. £12.50. £12.50!

Ethan had spent £25 on two drinks for them. That was so sweet.

And now Karl was expecting her to do the same. Bloody cheek!

'Do you know the price of these?' Alice asked him.

'Yeah, I know. We normally only have cocktails in the two for one. But that's before six.'

Alice shook her head. Then she sighed. She supposed she owed him a lot for everything he was doing for her. A cocktail or two was the least she should give him.

'Two Zombies it is then. I can't have you drinking on your own, can I.'

'Brilliant!'

Drinks in hand, the pair headed back to the table. Their seats had now been taken and Ethan was sitting on the other side, wedged in the corner, talking to someone else. He didn't even notice that Alice had returned.

'What game were you playing on your phone?' Alice asked Karl as she kept one eye on Ethan. She paid no attention to Karl's reply. 'Great. Tell me all about it,' she added, letting Karl ramble on.

She laughed out loud, taking Karl by surprise, hoping desperately that it would grab Ethan's attention. But he'd become oblivious to anything else in the room. He was just speaking, relentlessly, to that other lad.

Eventually, after about half an hour of asking Karl a ton of questions that she barely heard any answers to, and reacting in far too elaborate ways, Ethan looked across.

As their eyes met, she instinctively turned away, feeling like she'd been caught out. Even though that was kind of the point.

'I got a C in Maths. That was definitely my best subject,' Karl said as she turned to face to him.

'Fancy that,' Alice said, pretending to be completely engaged with the conversation. 'Maths was my favourite too.'

'Did you get better than a C, though?' Karl challenged.

Alice casually glanced over in Ethan's direction again. He was still looking and a small thrill zipped through her. He held his glass up as if to say "cheers" and nodded in her direction, flashing his stunning smile.

She nodded back, holding up her now empty glass. She'd downed that cocktail far too quickly and she was starting to feel a little tipsy.

She focused back on Karl who was now glaring between her and Ethan.

'He's a nice lad, isn't he,' Alice said. 'Friendly. Anyway,

what were you saying?'

'What grade did you get in Maths?' Karl said.

'Oh, A star. I got all A stars at GCSE, A's at A Level and a First in my degree. I guess I'm a bit of a nerd!' She chuckled, mainly through the giddiness she felt from the alcohol buzz.

Karl's jaw dropped open. 'You're a genius!'

'Not really.'

'What job did you say you did again? Make CCTV cameras?'

'No, I develop the software to support our security products. It was my dad's company. He was good with the hardware, but I've always been more interested in what makes things tick.'

'Do you run the company now?'

'No.'

'Why not? Didn't your dad hand it over to you?'

A sickening sadness pulled at Alice's stomach. She wanted to give Karl a very good reason as to why she wasn't currently running the company, but her new found lease of life was making her feel dreadful about her past decisions. She suddenly wanted to cry.

She turned her attention to Ethan. He was back chatting to that lad again. He was gorgeous. He was absolutely gorgeous and he'd been flirting with her. She shouldn't feel sad. This was a new start. The past was the past, there was nothing she could do about that. But she could change her future and stop wasting her life.

'Do you want another cocktail?' she asked Karl.

Karl shifted awkwardly on the spot. 'I can't...'

'I'm buying.'

His eyes widened with delight. 'Are you rich?'

'No,' Alice replied, shaking her head. 'I've just not been out enjoying myself in a really long time. Let's make up for that right now.'

'If you're sure.'

Alice grabbed Karl's empty glass from his hand and she

marched on to the bar.

Two more cocktails later and the pair were on the dancefloor, trying not to fall into other people under the influence of the Zombies. Alice was definitely drunk, but she was having a fantastic time.

As she danced, she still kept one eye on Ethan who was now keeping both eyes on her, enjoying the spectacle of her moves. In her mind she was sexy and alluring, and the reality really didn't matter. She felt good. That was all she cared about.

It was approaching two am when Karl told her he was ready to leave and he'd walk her home. Alice was far from ready for the night to end, but she could see how tired Karl was.

'Okay,' Alice said, regretfully. 'But can we just say goodbye to your mates first? I do hate to disappear without saying goodbye.'

Karl shrugged and they headed over to the table where about half of Karl's friends were still happily drinking and chatting.

Alice made a beeline for Ethan.

'We're going now,' she slurred, slipping into a gap right next to him on the banquette.

'Have you had a good night?' Ethan asked, his gentle tone warming Alice all over.

She leaned in. He smelt so good. He smelt of musk and manliness. She closed her eyes so she could focus on his scent. 'I've had the best night. Thank you for introducing me to Zombies.'

Ethan laughed. 'That's no way to talk about my mates!'

Alice leaned back, opening her eyes. She hadn't got a clue what he was talking about, and her inebriated brain couldn't be bothered to work it out.

'I haven't met your mates,' she said. 'I was only interested in meeting you.' She smiled. It was a grin so large and real.

'See,' Ethan said. 'It's my curse. I can tell you want me. You've been undressing me with your eyes all night.'

'I have not!'

He moved in closer to her ear and whispered softly. 'Believe me, whatever you've been imagining, the reality is far more impressive.' He grabbed her hand and put it on his arm, gesturing for her to squeeze his muscles.

She squeezed. It wasn't the muscles in themselves that made Alice's heart throb faster. Sure, he was very fit, but Alice had never been blown away by vanity. What made Alice purr with delight was the feel of his skin. It was the feel of his hand over hers, stroking her softly.

'You feel so nice,' she mumbled in a drunken haze.

'Oh baby, there's plenty more where that came from.'

Their lips became tantalisingly close and Alice could feel the heat from him.

'Alice, are you ready?' Karl asked, once again ruining the moment.

She looked around. 'Sure! Ethan was just showing me his muscles. He's very proud of them.'

Karl didn't say anything, but Alice recognised sadness in his eyes and she felt awful. Awful for treating Karl so badly and awful because it meant she couldn't get to see more of Ethan's muscles.

'Let's get you home,' she said, going to stand up, but she was halted by the sensation of Ethan caressing her arm.

'Come and see me at work tomorrow,' he whispered. 'I'll be there all day.'

'In the shop?'

'You know where it is?'

'Yeah. Okay. See you then.'

Ethan kissed her on the cheek before glancing at Karl. 'I like your girlfriend, Bladder. You lucky bastard.'

'Yeah,' Karl replied, dimly.

Alice was giddy with happiness as she stood up. Well, happiness and rum. Karl clasped her hand tightly, virtually marking his territory, and they walked out of the bar.

The cool air was instantly refreshing as they stepped outside. As they started to head towards Alice's home, that's when she noticed the burn on her feet. Her heels had looked fantastic, but now she was being punished for dancing too much.

'You'll have to slow down,' she said to Karl.

'Are you okay?'

Her elegant walk from earlier had now been replaced with a painful hobble. But it wasn't ruining her high. She was seeing Ethan tomorrow!

Was it like a date? I couldn't be. Could it? You can't date someone when they're at work. Can you?

She hoped Karl wouldn't be there. She wanted Ethan all to herself for a change.

She stopped. Stopped dead still in the middle of the pavement.

'What is it?' Karl asked.

Karl had to be there tomorrow. She could see Ethan whenever she wanted, but the only way he was going to see her in return was with Karl in sight.

Alice wanted to scream. Karl was both her saviour and her encumbrance. She wanted to hug him at the same time as pushing him off a cliff.

She studied her arms, hoping that by the time she got home they'd both have reappeared along with the rest of her body and she'd need Karl no more. But that didn't seem likely. If there was one thing she'd accepted over the years, it was that life was not fair.

'Are you working tomorrow?' she asked Karl, seeing it as her only option. She didn't want to not visit Ethan as that might give him the message that she wasn't interested.

'Yeah. Which is why I need to get home. Come on.'

'You're working?' Tingles of joy returned. All was not lost.

'Yeah.'

'What time are you working?'

'Not until midday. But still.'

'Can I come and see you at work tomorrow?'

This made Karl stop. 'You want to see me at work?'

Alice shrugged. 'I've had such a nice night. I know I'm going to miss you tomorrow. I thought perhaps I could drop in and say hello. Would that be okay?'

'Of course it would! I'll miss you too. I'd love to see you.' Karl hugged Alice tightly. 'Then I could come to yours after work. Maybe then we could do it, you know. We have waited ages.'

'Karl, it's been a week. I don't think we're quite ready yet. Do you?'

'Yes! If you like me, what's the problem?'

'Trust me, sex is emotional. If we rush it, it may tear us apart. You don't want us to break up, do you?'

Karl's shoulders slumped down with disappointment. 'No.'

'Good. All in good time. We need to make it special.'

They started to walk on again.

'How do we make it special?' Karl asked. 'What can I do?'

'We need to plan a weekend away. That's what we need. Just the two of us. But somewhere really special. Romantic. Like one of those cottages. They're only a few hundred pounds. We could split it fifty fifty.'

Karl hesitated. 'I can't really afford that.'

'It's fine. We'll save up. It will make it more special then.'

'But that could take ages.'

'If it's what we really want, it will be worth it. It is what you want, Karl, isn't it? You want to be with me?'

As Alice said those words she felt like such a bitch. She knew she was a terrible person, but she couldn't help it. There was no way she was going to sleep with Karl. She knew she'd never be able to go through with it. Part of her felt like she really owed it to him, but as soon as she saw his weirdly dirty hands and the way his mouth foamed up when he was excited - despite the fact that his lips were constantly bone dry - it made her want to heave. He was so far from what she wanted, it was unreal.

'It is what I really want,' Karl said. 'I really want you.'

'Good. That's settled then. Let's start making plans. We can research where we want to go and then save up. It won't take long. And it will be a weekend to remember forever. How about that?'

'Something we can tell our grandkids?' Karl asked, his eyes full of hope.

Alice couldn't meet his eyes. 'I'm not sure if any grandkids would want to know about this story.'

'Oh right, yeah. We're gonna do it!'

Karl was almost skipping when they returned to her house. He kissed her on the doorstep and she battled against his forceful tongue that tried to prise her firm lips open.

'It's late, you'd better be going,' she said, pushing him away. 'I'm worried as you have work tomorrow.'

'It's fine. I can stay the night if you want.'

'No, you'd better go.'

'My mum and dad don't mind if I stay out all night.'

Alice couldn't believe he'd just said that. 'Good to know. But for now, you get home. Get your sleep. I'll see you tomorrow.'

'All right. See you tomorrow.'

With one last kiss that nearly knocked her flat against her front door, Karl hopped off down her driveway. He was on top of the world and Alice felt like she was digging a huge hole for herself in completely the other direction.

As she fumbled with her key, she found herself desperately hoping that this mess wouldn't get any more complicated.

NINE

Alice woke up late the next morning. She rolled over feeling groggy from her hangover, but a smile was plastered to her face. She glanced at the clock on her bedside table and saw it was approaching eleven.

Remembering that Karl started work at midday, she decided not to leave it long after that before she went to see Ethan. She didn't want him to think she wasn't bothered.

She pulled her duvet back, ready for the exciting day ahead, when she got the most wonderful surprise. Virtually all of her right arm had now returned and some of her left hand. She was turning back to normal at last!

She skipped out of bed with joy. She might be in the middle of a ridiculously complicated mess, but at least it was having a positive effect. That made it all worth it.

She cooked herself a soothing fried breakfast to help with the hangover and downed three glasses of water. The skipping about wasn't any good for her headache, but she couldn't help it. The hangover was not going to win. Her happiness would prevail.

Breakfast eaten, she then showered and chose a lovely flowery dress to wear. It was another warm day, as if September was mirroring her good mood and clinging on to summer.

It was then that the issue of her hair and make-up hit her. How was she going to spruce herself up for Ethan if she couldn't see her head?

She made some quick decisions, determined to stay positive. She could tie her hair back and slip some basic make-up into her bag. If she remembered correctly, the tills at Dobson's were by the window, so she could slyly groom herself in the reflection of the glass while Karl was serving customers. Not perfect, but it would do.

One problem solved, she then had to find a way to deal with the new issue of her non-disappearing arm and hands. It had been fine walking about before - she'd been totally invisible. As long as she'd avoided walking into people, she could quite happily get about. But now she was scary floaty arm and hand person.

She sat at her dressing table, absorbing the eerie sight of some of her body in the mirror. She had to find a way of covering it up.

She jumped to her feet and grabbed her cardigan. She figured that if her clothes became invisible like normal then it would hide her arms.

After about a minute of wearing her black cardigan, it slowly disappeared, being engulfed into her non-existent state. And, as she had hoped, it completely masked her arms. Now she just had the issue of weird floaty hands.

She looked out the window. It was a lovely warm day, but she had no choice. She'd have to wear gloves.

She was sweating before she left. It was very uncomfortable. But being hot and sweaty was a far better option than being arrested and experimented on for being a random arm that wasn't attached to a body.

She took her time on the walk. Although she couldn't wait to get to Dobson's, both to see Ethan and to strip these clothes off, she knew if she walked too fast then she'd be a complete dripping mess by the time she got there.

Thirty-five minutes later, she stopped just around the

corner from the small supermarket. Although the chain was quite large, this was a smaller, mid-town branch that just stocked the essentials.

She knew she'd have to wait until the outside of the shop was clear before turning the corner completely. If Karl really was working on the tills, and they were by the window as she'd remembered (and was really hoping for), then the second she stood outside the front she would surely reappear in a flash. That could be quite a shock to an unsuspecting shopper.

After a few minutes it fell quiet and Alice seized her chance. She paced around the corner and immediately spotted Karl who was serving a customer. He looked thoroughly fed up, clad in his official red shirt and customary black trousers, just like all the staff.

She yanked off her gloves and cardigan and shoved them in her crossbody bag, before studying her reflection.

She almost gasped. Her face was all red and sweaty.

Not wasting a second, she tidied up her ponytail and then dabbed a bit of powder on her cheeks in an attempt to calm the scarlet. She then whipped out her mascara and a bit of eye-liner for definition. It would have to do.

As she was finishing off, something caught her attention. She focused through the window to see Karl waving at her. His boredom now all replaced with the pleasure of seeing her.

She waved back as her eyes caught another figure right at the end of the aisle ahead of her. It was Ethan.

Whereas Karl looked like he was wearing his dad's clothes, Ethan worked his uniform in a whole different way. The shirt wrapped around his muscles, accentuating his toned physique, and the trousers complimented his strong legs, as if they'd been deliberately tailored to showcase his perfection. Alice's mind boggled at how he could make that dull outfit so sexy.

Her ogling was distracted by Karl's eager gestures, calling her inside.

She tried to smile. Why was it only he had the power to make her be seen? Life wasn't just unfair, life had a sadistic sense of humour.

She entered into the refreshing air-conditioned shop and she caught her breath.

'Hi,' she said to Karl, approaching the tills. 'It's a lovely day, isn't it.'

'I wouldn't know. I'm trapped in here until seven.'

A customer approached and Alice stepped aside. 'I'm just going to have a little look around,' she said, edging away.

'Okay,' Karl said before greeting the customer.

Alice made her way towards the back of the aisle where she'd seen Ethan. She was as casual as she could be, trying so hard not to make it look like she was desperate to place her eyes on him.

'Hello baby,' Ethan said, tidying shelves at the back. 'I thought I saw you outside. I'm glad you came.'

'I'm glad you invited me.'

'You want to step into my office?'

Alice went to agree enthusiastically when she realised she couldn't. She couldn't even step out of the aisle. As soon as Karl was out of sight, so she would be. She had to make sure she stayed in this aisle, around all the sweets and alcohol.

'I don't want to go to your office,' she replied, in what she hoped was a sexy voice.

'Why not?'

'I don't know if I'm safe being alone with you.'

'Oh,' Ethan grinned. 'You definitely won't be. But you'll have a fucking good time.'

'Why don't we stay here?'

'Here?' Ethan asked, the light dimming from his face.

'Here. Where Karl can see me.'

Alice felt a punch in the stomach from her own sense of decency. She was becoming a horrible person. But when she lost herself in Ethan's eyes, she couldn't help it.

'You want Bladder to see you?'

'Yes. That way he won't get jealous. How can I be up to no good if I'm standing right before him?'

'You are such a player,' Ethan said with a satisfied grin. 'And here's me thinking you were a good girl.'

'You're not disappointed are you?'

'I love it. But how am I going to kiss you if we can't be alone?'

Alice scanned the area around her. No one was in sight. In fact, the shop was very quiet. She pushed Ethan back, just enough so their heads were out of sight - around the top of the aisle - whilst at the same time sticking her leg out behind her so it was still in Karl's eyeline. Thankfully it seemed to work.

'Like this,' she said, and then she placed her lips onto Ethan's and kissed him quickly.

'You're a crazy bitch, you are,' he said, and then he took her cheeks and kissed her properly. It was deep and fervid, and Alice's leg dropped down as she got lost in Ethan's hold.

Her body was aglow with lustful energy as Ethan devoured her with his lips.

'Excuse me,' a male voice said. Ethan immediately pulled away and turned to greet the old man standing behind him.

'Can I help?

'What's that?' the customer said, pointing to Alice. She looked down and gasped as she saw her unattached arm floating about.

She took a large step back into Karl's line of sight as Ethan turned to face her.

'What?' he said, looking around for a problem.

'I just thought...' the customer said. He shook his head and rubbed his eyes. 'Nothing. Must be the light.'

'It's dark in here, isn't it,' Alice said with a sweet smile before she checked that Karl was still safely tucked away behind his till.

'No,' Ethan said, seeming quite confused.

'Did you want help with something?' Alice asked, getting

the customer back on track.

'Oh yes. I can't find the newspapers. They're not by the door. They're always by the door.'

'No, they're by the tills now.'

'I don't know why you insist on moving things all the time,' the man said as he trundled off towards Karl.

'To piss people like you off,' Ethan mumbled before taking a big breath and focusing back on Alice's face. 'Now, where were we?'

'Right about here,' Alice said, pulling him closer to her.

'You're not really Bladder's girlfriend, are you?'

'We've been out a few times.'

'You know he's an idiot, don't you. He's not like me.'

'He's not an idiot.'

'He is. When he first started working here, he spelt his own name wrong on the application form. Instead of Karl Blade with one D, he spelt it with two D's. He spelt it B-L-A-D-D-E. That's why we call him Bladder. Because he's an idiot.'

Alice paused as she realised that she hadn't known Karl's surname before. She felt bad as she hadn't even been bothered to find out. She knew so little about him.

'I'm sure he didn't spell his own name wrong,' she said.

'He follows me around like I'm a god. We don't even know him but he started joining us for drinks. He's like a bad smell that won't go away.'

Alice suddenly felt quite protective of Karl. He may not be perfect – far from it – but he didn't deserve to have his so-called friends speak about him like that.

'Don't be nasty,' she said, pushing Ethan away. 'Karl's been good to me.'

'I'm sure he has. But can he give you what you really want?'

'And what is it you think I really want?' Alice said, her irritation levels rising.

'To be treated like the goddess that you are.' Alice's annoyed stance relaxed. She hadn't expected that answer.

'To feel such ecstasy that it takes your body weeks to come down afterwards.' Alice couldn't resist the smooth exhale as his words stirred her. 'To be pleasured in ways that you never knew existed.' Ethan came in close so his lips were practically touching hers. 'To be with me,' he finished in a breathy whisper before kissing her again. This time it was slow and soft to begin with, before his urgent desire for her took control.

She fell into his arms, their embrace needy and desperate, like they'd both been starved of human contact for far too long. She pushed against him so she could feel his body, and, as she did, she once again completely disappeared out of Karl's sight. She melted further into his kiss, blissfully oblivious to the fact that it now looked like Ethan was kissing fresh air.

She pulled away to take a breath, meaning it to just be for a moment. But as she opened her eyes she couldn't see Ethan in front of her. That only meant one thing: she had turned invisible and he'd been infected. Horrified, she took a large and urgent step backwards, and, as Ethan opened his eyes, they both popped back into view.

Her lips were raw and tingling from the kiss and they were both a little breathless.

'You need to get in my office. Now,' Ethan demanded.

'I can't,' Alice said, trying not to show how much she'd enjoyed the firm tone he'd taken with her.

Her mind flashed through ideas like blindfolding him, but it would never work. If he pulled it off at any point and saw just half an arm in front of him, that would definitely be the end of any future romance. She took him for an open-minded individual, but that might be one step too far.

'Are you turning me down?' he asked.

'I can't do it to Karl.'

'You can get me all aroused, though. That's okay.'

'I shouldn't have done that. I do really like you. But... As it stands, Karl is my boyfriend.'

'I don't give a shit about that. I've been with married

women. It doesn't matter.'

'It matters to me.'

'You're one of those cock teasers, aren't you. Is that what you're doing to Bladder? Are you playing us off against each other?'

'No! Of course not. I would never do that. Look, I like Karl and I said I'd go out with him. But you... you have this effect on me. I don't know what it is. I really want you. But I can't cheat on Karl.'

'Then break up with him, we'll shag, and you can get back together.'

Alice felt deflated. 'Is that all you want?'

'Isn't that all you want?'

Alice didn't know what to say. For the first time in her life she was seeing herself as nothing but a selfish user. She was using everybody.

If only she could get her body back then she could sort it all out.

'I really like you, Ethan. I really do. I want more than just some shag in your office.'

'Oh, I see. You want romance. Is that what Bladder's giving you? Dates and flowers and chocolates and all that? Look, I'm not into that soppy shit, but if you want to be with me then you'll have the time of your life. You need to decide what you want and stop messing everyone around.'

Alice didn't move. What could she say? She'd made her decision. She knew what she wanted. Life just wasn't letting her have it.

'I tell you what. Why don't you let me know when you've grown a pair?' With that, Ethan turned away and walked off, right through a door that led behind the scenes of the shop. No doubt to where his office was.

Alice caught her breath. How she longed to follow him, but she was stuck in a worse state than before. She couldn't even be invisible anymore, she was now limb lady.

She turned to Karl, who was busy sorting out an issue with the self-service machine. He was bending over and, because his trousers were so loose, his bum was on display to the world. In every way she found him revolting. But she was also starting to pity him.

She slowly walked down towards him, biding her time until the shopper had gone.

'Where have you been? What were you doing up there?' Karl asked, heading back to his place behind his till.

'I was looking at the wine. Trying to find a nice bottle for tonight.'

'Tonight? You mean a bottle to share?'

Alice glared at him, feeling like all the light had been sucked out of her. 'Sure, why not. But you're not staying over. I'm not ready for that yet. Can we just have dinner?'

Karl shrugged. 'All right. Can we watch something on your big TV again?'

Alice closed her eyes. She knew that the day had peaked and it was going to be a full downhill slide from now on.

'I'd better make that two bottles of wine.'

TEN

At exactly the same time as Alice was choosing her wines, Dan was finishing off the last of his beer in his parents' back garden in Hertfordshire.

'Steaks are always better well done,' his father said as he flipped the five slabs of beef over that were sizzling on the barbecue. 'I don't know what this rare nonsense is about. They moan the meat is chewy, but it's barely been introduced to any heat.'

Dan was relaxing in one of the garden chairs with just half an ear on his father's ramblings. His parents loved to host barbecues and his dad loved to lecture everyone on how everything should be cooked, as if he were some sort of barbecue MasterChef.

'Do you see how I've seasoned these chickens?' his dad continued.

'I know,' Dan said. 'Cajun.'

'You can't drown them. Too much olive oil is where most people make the mistake.'

Dan closed his eyes as he enjoyed the warmth of the sun on his face. He acknowledged how it would probably be the last time he'd sit in his parents' garden that year. Before he knew it, he'd be visiting them for Christmas and it could be snowing.

He loved their garden. It was enormous, but suitably so as it backed onto their large detached house. This was the house that Dan and his two sisters had grown up in. He'd lived there from birth right up to when he was eighteen, when he'd left to study Business Management at Greenwich University.

That had been his first step into living in London and he'd never wanted to leave.

'Get your old man another beer, would you?' Dan's dad said, jolting Dan from his slumber.

'Same again?' Dan asked, collecting the empty bottle from his dad's hand.

'Whatever you can find.'

Dan headed into the kitchen to find his mother and two sisters arguing over the best way to cut tomatoes.

'Daniel,' his mother said the second he came into view. 'What are you up to?'

'I'm getting a couple more beers.'

'You mind how much your father has while he's cooking the food. I don't like him drinking when there are open flames.'

'It is his birthday, mum.'

'That's why I'm allowing him to have a beer at all. But you tell him it's limited until after the food has been eaten. I won't be driving him to A&E if he has an accident. He'll have to live with the burns.'

Dan nodded and rolled his eyes as he opened the fridge.

'We were just talking about you,' Mary, Dan's older sister said.

'Oh yeah,' Dan said with disinterest as he pulled out two bottles of Peroni.

'Daniel, be a darling and fill our glasses up too while you're there.'

Dan grabbed the Prosecco before he knocked the fridge closed with his foot.

'We were wondering what the future Mrs Daniel is going

to be like and if we're ever going to meet her,' Mary explained.

'You might. On my wedding day,' Dan said as he topped up the three glasses before him.

'Do you even know who she is yet?' Clare, his younger sister asked.

'Oh, it could be one of many.'

'Oh for goodness sake, Daniel,' his mother huffed. 'Why are you so secretive? Do you have a girlfriend or not?'

'Why are you so interested?'

'Because in the thirty years of your existence, you've only brought home one girl, and that was when you were fifteen.'

'And that's why I've not brought another girl home since!' Dan stated.

'Have you even had a girlfriend since you were fifteen?' Mary asked. 'You're not gay are you?'

Dan shook his head. 'Because I choose not to share the details of my love life, it means I'm gay now does it?'

'It doesn't matter if you are,' his mother said.

'Where's that beer?' his dad said, poking his head through the French doors.

'Sorry, I'm being interrogated,' Dan said before he grabbed a bottle opener from one of the kitchen drawers.

'We're trying to work out if Dan has a secret girlfriend,' Clare said.

'Or if he's gay,' Mary added.

'I don't want to know,' his father said, holding his hand out for the beer.

'At least someone respects my privacy,' Dan said as he popped the tops off the two beer bottles.

'That's your third beer,' Dan's mum said to his father.

'Don't start,' his dad replied.

'I'm not taking you to A&E. I refuse to. I've already had two glasses of Prosecco.'

'I'll keep my eye on him,' Dan said as he swiftly left the kitchen and joined his father again in the garden.

Dan enjoyed the afternoon with his family. They ate lovely food, got tipsy together and played board games in the garden until the early evening. It was then that he and his sisters needed to head home.

They shared a taxi to the local train station and they all headed off to London together. They reached St Pancras station and all got on the London Underground, continuing their journey on the Piccadilly Line.

'You got a busy week at work?' Mary asked Dan as they stood huddled closely by the doors of the train.

Dan hesitated. He hated it when his family asked him about his job. His sisters were ridiculously intelligent and hugely successful. Mary – who was three years older than him - was a lawyer working for a massive legal firm in the city. More than just working for them, she had been the youngest ever partner and was regularly making waves in her field.

If that wasn't bad enough, Clare - just a mere twenty-two - was studying to become a doctor. She'd excelled at pretty much everything she'd ever done, and was the pride and joy of his parents.

Dan felt like the disappointment in the middle. His parents had never said anything like that, but he was just a crappy salesman who worked for companies that no one had ever heard of.

Even when he'd won prizes for his sales achievements, his parents had only ever given him a small smile and a weak 'well done.'

He didn't even have the sales achievements anymore.

To add to that, he was actually dreading the day ahead. He had to go and visit that client again who'd been given all the wrong equipment for their needs, and he was going to have to encourage them to accept his proposal to start the specification from scratch. With no discount. He wasn't looking forward to it.

'The usual,' Dan replied with a small shrug. 'You?'

'Oh yes. Because my client work is clearly not enough, I've been roped into planning a trip to Africa as part of our extended Corporate Social Responsibility. At least the PR should be amazing. Then I've got that mentoring on Thursday, and then on Friday I'm supposed to be seeing Georgina. It's her birthday, but I need to spend some time with Laurence this week or he'll go mad.'

'You'll see him at work,' Clare reasoned.

'Thank goodness I do, because at the minute we're both barely at home.'

The train slowed down as it made its approach into Gloucester Road station.

'See you soon, Dan,' Mary said kissing her brother on the cheek.

'Behave yourself,' Clare grinned as she hugged him.

'You too.'

They got off the train and waved goodbye, and the doors closed swiftly behind them.

Dan let out a breath of relief. He loved his sisters very much but he always felt exhausted after they left. He was now looking forward to a quiet night at home.

About half an hour later he was letting himself into his lovely little flat in Wimbledon. It was minimally decorated and impeccably tidy. Dan was nothing if not organised and neat.

Before he could relax, he sorted out a suit for the morning, making sure to iron his shirt and get himself all prepared. He hated being late for anything so he always got himself ready the night before, no matter what was happening.

He poured himself a glass of water from the filtered jug in his fridge, enjoying the cooling sensation as it slipped down his throat, and then he flopped down in front of his TV.

Within seconds of flicking through his Freeview channels, Dan's mind had started to wander. And it wandered to the same place it always did: his image of Alice.

He hadn't spoken to her in days now. The news of her boyfriend had upset him quite a bit.

Dan had been single for two years, after having a string of short-lived relationships with women he'd met online. Women that he was never going to tell his family about as they were all wrong.

Dan wanted a companion in his life but he was incredibly picky. Having two sisters who were clever and well-presented but also good fun and family oriented had set Dan's expectations very high. He became quickly bored by any woman who couldn't stimulate him mentally, and he'd surprised himself by how fussy he was about their looks.

It wasn't that he wanted them glammed up and special. Quite the opposite. He had simpler tastes. He liked girls that cared about their appearances but weren't too vain. At bit of make-up on a night out, but could happily go to the shops without feeling the need to coat on layer upon layer of foundation and whatever else girls plastered on.

He hoped Alice was like that, because he loved everything else about her. She was the most challenging woman he'd ever spoken to (outside of his family), but it was a challenge that he was fast becoming addicted to. So much so, he was starting to believe that he could never not find her attractive regardless of how she looked – if he ever actually got to meet her.

He'd backed off from speaking to her this week in an attempt to protect himself, but now he was missing her a great deal.

He had to meet her soon. He just had to. He couldn't let her slip through his fingers. He'd never felt this way about anyone before. As he sat flicking up and down through the channels, he made the decision that he was just going to have to be honest. He had to tell her how he felt. He had to demand that they meet to discuss it. It was time to be brave.

Or maybe that was just the alcohol talking.

Dan flicked the TV off. He was restless. He decided to

make himself a decaf coffee and then call it a night.

As he stood up, he closed his eyes. He brought up his perfect image of Alice again.

He wasn't going to lose her. He couldn't. One way or another, he was going to have to meet her soon. He was going to have to.

ELEVEN

It was Monday morning and Alice was sitting at her desk, digesting the minutes from the previous week's product development meeting. The ideas were uninventive and lacked any sort of innovation. But then they always did. She usually just ignored the management's discussed product roadmap and instead devised her own. And no one ever challenged her. She had her father's flair for creativity and problem solving. Alice sometimes suspected that their ideas were deliberately boring in order to encourage her to do better.

She'd been feeling irked anyway that morning and now reading the minutes had made her even more tetchy. Even the fact that both her arms and shoulders were now in sight still couldn't brighten up her day.

The night before had been difficult. She'd cooked Karl and herself a scrumptious Sunday roast before he'd settled on the settee to watch one of his beloved action movies. Alice didn't mind his taste in films. She much preferred car chases and murder mysteries to romance. She hadn't got the patience for slow-moving character pieces. They didn't interest her at all.

She'd been fine with the movie choice and she'd made

peace with the fact that Karl was going to be a part of her life, but what she hadn't been able to deal with were Karl's repeated attempts at snuggling up.

As soon as dinner had finished, he'd made a beeline from the kitchen table to the sofa, where he'd stretched himself out, as if it were impossible to be comfortable unless your body was touching all three cushions.

Alice had left him to it while she'd tidied up and then she'd joined him in watching *Guardians of the Galaxy*. Although she'd deliberately sat away from him on an armchair.

Five minutes later and she could feel his eyes burning into her.

'Come and sit with me,' he'd said, shuffling so there was a gap next to him.

'No, you look so comfortable.'

'Come on. We could cuddle up.'

'I don't think *Guardians of the Galaxy* is a cuddle up movie, do you?'

'We could watch something else.'

'No! I love this film. Definitely let's keep watching this film. Definitely. And I'll sit here.'

Another few minutes passed by before Karl's eyes were staring at Alice once more.

'At least come and sit next to me,' he'd said. 'It's cold here on my own.'

'I could turn the heating on. It is approaching autumn.'

'No, no. Don't do that. I'm just lonely on this huge settee all on my own.'

'You have so much room. Don't you like it?'

'I'd prefer it if you were sitting next to me.'

'I can't. I'd love to but I can't. You see... I have a bad back. Sitting on the settee really aggravates it sometimes. I'm better propped up on this armchair.'

'Oh no. That's shit. Are you okay? I could give you a back rub.'

'No! I'm fine as I am just sitting here.'

Karl's eyes drifted back to the film, but it didn't last long.

'If you can't come to me, then I'll come to you,' he'd said, standing up and then sliding in as best he could next to Alice.

He put his arm around her and he was practically sitting on her lap.

After about three minutes of breathing in his musty scent and not once being able to take her eyes off his dirty hand, Alice had stood up, perhaps far too urgently, claiming that she had cramp in her leg.

Karl's attempts to rub her leg then started a spiral of ailments that rapidly had Alice feeling close to death with a violent fever. It had become so bad she'd told him she'd have to go to bed.

Even that didn't get rid of him, though, as Karl insisted on tucking her in.

'You should go,' Alice had said as Karl pulled the duvet up around her and stroked her hair. 'You don't want this. Trust me. It's best that you steer well clear. Whatever I've got, it's nasty. I can tell.'

'It's come on really quickly.'

'Hasn't it just. It's awful. You'd better go home.'

'Will you call me if you feel any worse?'

'Of course. Of course I will.'

'I can stay if you want. I don't mind.'

'No! Please. Please go. Please leave. I'm worried I'll make you sick. I'll feel terrible if you're ill. Will you just please leave.'

'Okay. Okay. Take care.'

He placed his dry, cracked lips on her forehead and kissed her goodnight. She tried not to grimace.

He finally left her room, waving goodbye, and when she heard the front door shut, she got straight out of bed to finish watching the movie. She'd been enjoying it. She'd forgotten how funny *Guardians of the Galaxy* was.

She sighed as she read through the notes from the meeting again. She felt anything but motivated. Just the thought of having to endure Karl's lips anymore was sickening. But without Karl she had nothing. No Ethan, no life, no enjoyment. He was both her liberty and her curse.

A new email flicked into her inbox. It was from the Marketing Manager, someone whom she rarely got emails from.

She opened it up to see it was addressed to the whole company.

Hi

I'd like to share some fantastic news. Our new PXK Proximity Sensor has just been nominated for Product of the Year in the upcoming Cor-Sec Awards.

This nomination is a testament to the hard work that the product development team has put in and demonstrates to the industry how Blooms Security continues to stand at the forefront of innovation.

Voting is now open. Please could you all vote for our product using the link below and encourage any customers, suppliers, peers, contacts, friends and family to also vote.

If you have any questions, please do let me know. Let's hope we're successful at the Awards Ceremony being held in two weeks' time in London.

Kind regards
Natalie

The second Alice's eyes reached Natalie's sign off, her phone rang. It was Dan.

'You've just seen the email too, huh?' she asked with a smirk.

'Congratulations. I'd say you must be delighted but I remember our previous conversation.'

'I told you we'd be shortlisted. It was like a given. Now it's all down to who can get the most votes in their wide-reaching, completely manipulated marketing strategy. The actual quality of the product is in fact quite redundant at this stage. It should be called "the award for who can get the most votes for any old product they want to put forward", as essentially that's what it is.'

'Has anyone ever told you you're a cynic?'

'Yes, you. On several occasions if I recall.'

'Then I'm very wise.'

'I may be cynical but it doesn't mean I'm wrong. Life is not about having great things thrust upon you. Life is about how you handle the shit you're dealt with. And those who can polish a turd will always excel.'

'Woah, someone's having a bad day. You're usually grumpy, but this is negative, even for you. Things going badly with the boyfriend?'

Alice paused. Over the past few months she had spoken to Dan about almost anything and everything. They'd shared views on the company, politics, popular culture, their particular likes and dislikes and just plain gossip. The only thing Alice had never spoken about was her family or anything deeply personal. She had her secrets and Dan didn't need to know.

Dan was the light in her otherwise drastically humdrum existence. She didn't want to share harsh truths with him. When she was talking with him she felt alive; she felt happy. He made her forget about her troubles and he caused her no grief. Unlike the new men she'd met.

So Alice had to decide. She'd enjoyed sharing the news that she had a boyfriend. That had been fun and exciting. But did she want to divulge all the nitty gritty? Albeit leaving out the core of the issue. Her invisibility, after all, was not exactly a normal problem one shared with friends.

But she could talk about a love triangle and not knowing what to do. How do you choose without hurting someone? She could ask for advice on what men really wanted and gauge Dan's opinion on Ethan's abrupt exit the day before?

She was ready to start just that conversation, when she stopped. Something in her wouldn't let her. Something in her told her that she didn't want to share all that with Dan. She didn't want their fun, friendly conversations to become ruined by her ridiculous problems.

Instead she found herself saying, 'When does life ever run smoothly when men are involved? But it's nothing that this girl can't handle.'

'I'm sure. I hear you're good at polishing turds.'

'Are you calling my boyfriend a turd?'

Dan laughed. He had a lovely, joyful laugh. 'Of course not.'

'Anyone would think you were jealous.' Alice chuckled, but there was no response on the other end. 'Dan? Dan? Are you there?'

'Sorry, I'm back. What were you saying? I got distracted. Got another call coming through.'

'Do you need to go?'

'No, it can wait. I'm not going anywhere until I convince you to attend the awards dinner. I know we've got a table booked for the night and I know for a fact that they'd never deny you a seat. After all, if it wasn't for you we'd have no product in the first place, let alone an award nomination.'

Alice was stunned to silence. It would never have occurred to her to attend the awards, but the idea was appealing. She could wear one of her new dresses. She could get to schmooze at an industry event; the type her dad used to hate going to, but she'd always loved the sound of. She could meet her colleagues.

Hang on, could she?

'Who else will be there?' she asked.

'Well me, for starters,' Dan replied. 'I'd love to finally meet you. It's crazy that we haven't met yet. I don't even know what you look like.'

'Don't worry, most people don't,' she said.

'But do most people speak to you a few times a week?'

'Not lately, you haven't. I was getting worried. If it hadn't been for the fact that you've still been playing chess then I would have been calling out for the search party.'

'Missed me did you?'

'Of course I did. I haven't been able to feel superior to anyone for a week.'

'Oh!' Dan laughed. 'That's hilarious. Especially as I know you really enjoy our chats because you're so in awe of me.'

'In awe?' Alice was properly giggling now. Her sour mood had completely evaporated.

'Yes. I am awesome.'

'Yes. Yes you are. I can't deny it. You know I love you, Daniel White.'

Alice was still giggling but Dan had gone quiet again.

'Dan? Dan? Are you still there?'

'Yes. I'm here.'

'Okay, what aren't you telling me?'

'What?' Dan's voice was now far more serious.

'What aren't you telling me?'

'Why am I not telling you something?'

'You've got that tone in your voice.'

'Tone in my voice?'

'Yes. You have a tone when you're avoiding something. I hear it all the time but I normally just go along with it. But now I haven't heard from you in a week and I'm starting to think something's up. What's going on?'

'When do I have that tone?'

'Like whenever I ask you about the Sales meeting. You go weirdly quiet, and then when you do start talking you go all high pitched.'

'High pitched?'

'Well, it's not that high. Your voice just goes a bit higher than normal. You pretend like there's nothing to talk about, but I always know there's something you're not telling me.'

'Are there any other times you've noticed a tone in my voice?'

Alice knew the answer was yes, but she didn't know whether to say. She didn't want to open up the conversation of why she never left the house. But maybe it was time to. Her body was returning, so maybe it was time.

'Yes,' she said slowly. 'I heard that same tone when I repeatedly told you I couldn't come out for lunch. And last week when I said I'd been out for my birthday in Birmingham. I really am sorry that we didn't come to Starley Green. Really. Is that why I've barely heard from you? Are you mad with me?'

'Of course not. Don't be silly.'

'I know me not ever seeming willing to see you has annoyed you.'

'I wouldn't say annoyed.'

'You have to understand. I went through a lot when my parents died. It's taken me a long time to get back on my feet. But I'm getting there now. And I'd really love to meet you. I consider you a good friend, so we should meet up.'

After a small pause, Dan said, 'Definitely.'

'There's that tone again! What aren't you telling me?'

'What? No! No. Nothing. I was just thinking about what you said. I consider you a good friend too. I'm always here if you want to talk. You must have been through a lot.'

'Thanks, Dan. And it goes both ways. For example, if you ever want to share what's so bad with the Sales meetings, I'm a good listener.'

Dan sighed. 'It's not the Sales meetings themselves that are the problem.'

'What do you mean?'

'Alice, it's such a mess. Have you got a minute? It would actually be really good to talk.'

'I've got all the time in the world.'

'Do you know Emily? The girl who shares the London territory with me?'

'Only from what you've told me about her.'

'Well, she's burying me. It doesn't matter what I do, she is always one step ahead in terms of sales. And just when I think she can't possibly get her claws in, she slices me from behind.'

'Sounds painful.'

'She's getting all the new business that's out there. Even when I've been chatting to companies, she'll send a quote to them the next day claiming that she's been working with them for weeks.'

'But surely there'd be a data trail if she had?'

'She only updates the CRM periodically. No one ever knows in real time what she's working on.'

'Do you update the CRM?'

'Religiously. I have to. We get ten percent of our commission deducted if our movements aren't logged in the sales system. Emily is the only person who gets away with this "I'll do it when I have time" crap because she's blowing everyone else out the water. She's untouchable.'

'Is she really that good?'

'The only way she could do what she's doing is if she's psychic. Nothing else makes any sense.'

'There's always a logical explanation.'

'Whatever the explanation, she's making me look like a fool. Remember that client I asked you about last week? The one who'd had a break-in and was panicking?'

'Oh yes. What happened there?'

'I was supposed to see them today but John called me first thing to say it's being handed over to Emily.'

'What?'

'On somehow hearing about what had happened – and I don't know how she could have. The first I'd heard about it was last week. Anyway, at some point between me visiting the client a week ago and this morning, Emily has made a visit to both them and their neighbour and has pitched a joint venture. By going in together they're getting a brand new high-end solution but it'll cost them only fifty percent each. And I mean they're looking at all the works. They pretty much share the land so it's an obvious win. I don't know why I didn't think of it. I'm kicking myself.'

'But they're your client.'

'Were my client.'

'She can't do that.'

'She can and she has. John was thrilled with her. It makes her the top selling BDM for the third month in a row.'

'But it's your client,' Alice repeated, beginning to feel

rage.

'The company next door is now her new client, and as my client is going in with that quote, I effectively lose them to her. There's nothing I can do about it. I just don't know why I didn't think of it. It's such a good idea. I was too focused on the problem that I'd inherited rather than finding the best solution.'

'Did you even know that the company next door was looking for a new system?'

'I don't even know who the company next door is. Maybe she is that good.'

'No, good would have been to talk to you about it rather than snatching your client from under your nose.'

'She doesn't operate like that. Maybe that's my problem: I'm not ruthless enough.'

'So effectively John has praised her for undermining you.'

'All John can see is that she's reached two hundred percent of her monthly target and I'm only at fifteen percent.'

'I'm so sorry, Dan. I had no idea things were that bad.'

'I thought I was good at sales, but this is-'

'You are! Don't say that. You are. You speak the truth and you know your stuff. I don't know who this Emily is, but I don't get a good feeling about her at all.'

'If you come to the awards night, you'll get to meet both of us. There's no chance she'd miss the opportunity to suck up to potential customers.'

Alice was convinced. She had to find a way to go. 'Do people bring a plus one with them to these things?' she asked.

'What do you mean?'

'Like, could I bring a date with me?'

'Erm... No. I don't think so.'

'You see I really want to go, but... I'm not good with travelling. I know the awards are in London, so I'll need a chaperone.'

'A chaperone?'

'Yes, like a plus one.'

'You want to bring your boyfriend?'

'Exactly. Do people normally bring their partners to these things?'

'No. There will be loads of us there. You won't be alone.'

'But you live in London. You won't be travelling down.'

'No, but-'

'You know what, let me speak to John. It's been a while; it's time we had a good catch up. I'm sure I can be persuasive.'

Dan paused. 'Sounds good.'

'You're doing it again!'

'What?'

'That tone. You do want me to go, don't you?'

'Of course! It was my main reason for calling.'

'That's settled then. I'm going to find every way I can to make this happen. Fingers crossed, Daniel White, I will see you in two weeks.'

TWELVE

Alice and Karl were back at The Royal Oak, enjoying another two for one super hot, garlicky meal. Alice had invited him out with the sole purpose of asking him to come to London with her for the awards ceremony, but she had made the decision to wait until after they'd eaten to discuss it to avoid any unnecessary viewings of the burger being chewed up in his mouth as he responded.

They were taking their last bites and she began to feel the nerves. The awards were such a big moment for her. She would rather be going with anyone but Karl. She wasn't at all bothered about whether the company won or not. It was the anticipation of seeing her colleagues that was playing on her mind. Or, to be more precise, the notion of meeting Dan for the first time.

She had her outfit all planned out. She was going to wear her new stunning black dress with the perfect accompanying sexy stilettos. She also knew exactly how she was going to be styling her hair and make-up. Everything was focused on making a striking impression after she'd been out of the picture for so long. She wanted to be a visible force and make people take notice. She didn't want to be forgotten about anymore.

She was excited about absolutely everything except for one major issue: going to the awards was only possible if she factored in Karl. She had to turn up with him. And to make it look not entirely bizarre, she had to pretend that he was her boyfriend.

The sexiest shoes in the world wouldn't distract from the impression that Karl was no doubt going to make. It wasn't exactly how she was hoping to be remembered.

She looked over at him. He was smiling to himself with food stuck between his teeth, and he'd had some sort of weird yellow gunk on his ear all night. She'd avoided even attempting to figure out what that was.

Talking to John had been the easy part. Getting her two places at the table had been a breeze. Finding the strength to actually ask Karl was proving to be a whole other situation.

'Hi, it's Alice Bloom,' she'd said to John two days ago with extreme confidence.

'Alice?' he'd asked down the phone, clearly not able to believe it.

'How are you?'

'I'm good, thanks. How are you? Is everything all right? It's... It's lovely to hear from you. Just... not what I was expecting.'

'I have a question to ask and I thought you might be the right person to help me out.'

'Of course. What do you need?'

'I've been told all about the upcoming award that my new sensor has been nominated for.'

'Yes, it's great news isn't it. Well done.'

'Obviously this gives me great pride. Having my work recognised is something I know my father would be immensely supportive of. As such, I feel that I should break the silence that I've assumed for too long - since my tragic loss - and take my step back into the world at the awards presentation. Don't you agree? Don't you think my father would really like that?' There was no hint in Alice's voice at all that she was spouting out any old crap to get what she wanted.

'Erm...'

'I take it there will be room at the table for me to join you? After all, without me there would be no nomination in the first place.'

'Erm... yeah.'

'We can think of it as not only me joining you, but also me being there to represent my father. As we well know, without him there would be no company, therefore no products, and ultimately, again, no award.'

'Of course. Of course you must be there. We were struggling to find customers who were free anyway, so there's plenty of room on the night. It will be great to see you, Alice. I'll arrange it with Marketing to get you a place.'

'Fantastic. And it's great to hear that there's plenty of room as I'll be bringing a plus one with me.'

'What?'

'I haven't left the house in a long time. I've been through a great deal. You can't expect me to just suddenly travel all the way to London on my own, can you?'

'Well, I'll be travelling down.'

'I haven't seen you in years, John. That would be a bit awkward, wouldn't it. Thank you for the offer, but if you want me to attend the award ceremony, to be there to help celebrate our potential win - of the product that I developed virtually all by myself - then it's a two for one deal. I'll need my friend there with me. Besides, it saves you all that effort of finding extra customers, doesn't it. It gives you more time to make those sales. My dad would be so happy with that time efficiency.'

'Erm, yeah.' Alice wanted to laugh. John sounded so uncomfortable. But she deserved this. The company owed her.

'So you'll speak to Marketing for me?' she encouraged. 'Would that be all right? Get them to email me the details?'

'Erm, yeah. I suppose.'

'But tell them I'll book my own train. The company doesn't have a strong track record of getting bookings right, does it?' She enjoyed that dig very much.

'Leave it to me. I really look forward to seeing you and your friend in a couple of weeks.'

'Thank you, John. That's very kind of you. I look forward to catching up then too.'

That had been Monday afternoon. It was now Wednesday evening and Alice was waiting for her moment to ask Karl.

Their plates had been cleared away and she felt safe to start the discussion.

'Do you remember I told you that I develop security products?' she started.

'Yeah, the robots.'

Alice opened her mouth to explain the truth, but it seemed futile. Instead, she just nodded. 'That's right. Anyway, one of my solutions has been nominated for an award.'

'That's great news. Well done!'

'Thank you. The ceremony is the week after next, in London, and I've got two tickets to go. Would you like to go with me?'

'To London? I can't afford to go to London. It's well expensive down there.'

'Have you ever been to London?'

'No. It's too expensive.'

'Even more of a reason to go, then. Not only will you be helping me to celebrate a potential award win, but you'll get to visit the Capital for the first time. And it's all expenses paid, meaning you won't have to pay for anything. How does that sound?'

Karl's mouth opened wide but Alice wasn't sure whether it was with delight or shock. Or perhaps both.

'So everything would be paid for?' he asked.

'Everything you need, like travel, accommodation and sustenance. Yes, that would all be paid for.'

'Accommodation? Like a hotel?'

'Yes, we'd have to stay overnight in a hotel.'

'When is it?' He now seemed fully engaged with the idea.

'Two weeks tomorrow. It's a Thursday night. We'll have to travel down on the Thursday afternoon and we'll come back late Friday morning. We'll go by train. Does that sound okay?'

'Yeah, easy. I don't work Fridays anyway, and I can swap my Thursday shift. The others do that all the time.'

'So you'll go with me?'

'Yeah!'

'That's fantastic news.'

'I can't believe it.' He seemed far too excited about a trip to a corporate awards evening.

'We could fit in some sightseeing on the Friday morning if you like?' Alice offered. He was obviously thrilled to be going to London.

'Sightseeing as well?'

Alice hesitated. 'As well as attending the awards, yes.' Did he mean that?

'And the other thing,' he said, nodding as if to gesture something important.

Alice definitely wasn't following. Not that that was unusual with Karl. Or any of his friends for that matter. 'What thing?'

'This is the weekend, isn't it?' There was something about his eager smile that made Alice's blood curdle.

'No, it's two weeks tomorrow.'

'No, I meant this is like *the* weekend?' He winked and then started to thrust his arms back and forth in that cringeworthy way he'd done before.

Alice was horrified. She wanted to scream. She opened her mouth to forthrightly object and tell him that he'd got it all wrong, when she realised she had absolutely no comeback. She had promised that on a getaway together they'd consummate their relationship and this very discussion was about a trip away. They were going to share a hotel room. She hadn't felt it right to ask the company to pay for two rooms when technically she was bringing her boyfriend along.

Alice's heart sank further when it dawned on her that they would be staying in a swanky hotel. It would be all lovely and romantic, and in any other relationship it would be the ideal opportunity to make love.

'We're going to do it!' Karl almost squealed. 'Are you excited?'

Alice's eyes landed on his dirty fingers - his inexplicably, constantly dirty fingers – and her stomach knotted.

'I guess so,' she smiled. 'I can't think of any reason why this trip isn't the perfect time for us to connect physically. And believe me, I've tried.' She laughed, as if it were all a hysterical joke, and then tears started swelling up in her eyes.

Now she was the one backed into the corner and she couldn't see any escape.

THIRTEEN

The next two weeks flew by and Alice worked her way through a jumbled mix of emotions. Firstly, she was dreading the idea that Karl might actually try to touch her. She shivered every time she even thought about it.

She'd come up with a plan to get him blind drunk. That way he'd be too intoxicated to do the deed, it would be all his own fault so he couldn't blame her, and he'd still have a good time. Free alcohol was, after all, the next best thing to sex, right?

It hadn't all been negative though. Despite feeling sick about Karl and his dirty hands, Alice had also been given plenty to smile about. For example, her state of invisibility had been dramatically changing for the better. Now both of her legs and arms were in full view.

Although to anyone else it would have been a hugely unnerving sight, Alice had spent hours in front of the mirror entertaining herself. Unattached limbs seemingly floating about of their own accord were hilarious. Especially dancing around after a few glasses of wine.

Then there was Dan that had made her grin broadly every single day. Ever since she'd confirmed her attendance to the awards and they knew they were finally going to meet, their friendship had flourished. They were speaking more often and for longer, and talking about more personal things. They were even getting more competitive in their online chess matches, adding a fiery touch to their relationship, which Alice had adored.

Whereas before she'd looked forward to their calls, now she was getting butterflies in her stomach every time the phone rang. She couldn't wait to chat to him in person, breaking down the barrier of the phone line.

After two weeks of emotional highs and lows, the day finally arrived. It was a Thursday in late September and the sun was still prominent in the sky.

Karl knocked on her door an eager twenty minutes before the taxi was due, and she finished packing while he sat on the sofa catching up on Twitter.

Soon they were on their way.

As they sat on the train, he tried several times to hold her hand or squeeze her knee, and she came up with every excuse imaginable as to why it wasn't comfortable for her. His elbow was in the way, it was too hot, she had cramp, she needed the loo. She'd gone to the onboard shop twice to get refreshments, just to avoid the sticky touch from his ever so filthy hands. She was dying to ask him why they were so dirty, but she was just too scared about what the answer could be.

They eventually arrived in London Euston and Alice insisted that they get a taxi to the hotel. It was all the way over in Chelsea and she wasn't feeling confident about using the tube. It wasn't the underground system in itself that bothered her - it was that it might be busy. Lots of people meant a crammed space, and she didn't want to be any closer to Karl than she absolutely had to be. The last thing she wanted to do was encourage more attempts at touching.

The traffic was surprisingly light for mid-afternoon London and they arrived safely at the hotel within half an hour.

They entered the lobby and Karl's jaw immediately

dropped open.

'It's so posh!' he blurted out.

The interior possessed the majesty of a castle but with a highly modern décor. It had somehow captured the grandeur of historical stateliness through twenty-first century architecture and smart technology. It really was a place to be in awe of. But maybe with more subtlety than Karl was showcasing, as he kept repeating over and over how posh it was, as if there were no other words to suffice.

Alice checked them in at the sharply efficient yet wonderfully friendly reception desk, and then she swiftly marched them on to their room.

She opened the door to the surprisingly large area and Karl raced in.

'Wahoo!' he said, leaping onto the bed and bouncing up and down. 'It's so comfortable. Are we going to do it, then?'

Alice tried not to outwardly grimace.

'That's not very romantic,' she said, unpacking her dress and carefully placing it in the wardrobe. 'You need to woo me first.'

'What does woo mean?' he asked, finally sitting still on the bed.

'It means we need to relax. How about we go to the bar for a little drink or two? Start the night off as we mean to go on. It is a night for celebrating, after all.'

'So woo means get drunk? I need to get you drunk?'

'No,' Alice laughed, perhaps too hysterically. How close to the truth he was. 'Woo means to charm me first. Build up the romance. Feel comfortable together. Have a drink or two to relax. Especially because it's free. I mean the alcohol will be free all night. Did I tell you that?'

'What!' Karl looked like a kid on Christmas day who'd received everything he'd added to his list.

'Shall we go and have a tipple, then?'

'What's that? Is that a cocktail?'

'What?'

'Does a tipple have rum in it? Like a Zombie? I like rum.'

Alice hesitated before deciding it was easier to play along. The whole situation was just plain ridiculous so she might as well join in the madness. 'Yes. Yes it does. So let's go and have two tipples. With rum. Lots of rum.'

Alice led the way to the bar. She knew she'd never be able to get away with expensing all their drinks all night. She intended on giving Karl absolutely everything he asked for (in a beverage sense only) and so she would pay for most of it. It was worth it, after all. She'd gladly pay a couple of hundred pounds not to sleep with him. It was awful but true.

She ordered two rum and cokes and took them to the table where Karl was still staring around, gaping at the chandeliers and the beautiful art on the wall.

'This place is so posh,' he said.

'I suppose so,' Alice replied.

'Thanks for my drink. So this is a tipple?'

'Some call it a Cuba Libre, but whatever floats your boat.'

Alice sipped carefully. As much as she wanted to get legless to survive Karl's repeated attempts at seduction, she knew she needed to be at her best for meeting her colleagues. Especially Dan.

Alice was also curious about meeting Emily: the woman who appeared to be Dan's arch-nemesis. The more Dan told Alice about Emily, the less Alice liked her. She might be securing sale after sale for the company, but something didn't add up about her technique. Nobody can come from nowhere and suddenly be that good at their job. Alice was suspicious and she was ready to suss out this Emily once and for all.

She successfully managed to make her 'tipple' last for an hour and a half, whereas Karl had managed to down three rum and cokes in that time. But she was more than happy to buy him whatever he desired.

By the time they got back to the room, there was sadly

no time for sexual activity as they needed to get ready for the evening. Alice insisted that a full ninety minutes would be required to glam herself up, so she left Karl scrolling through the TV as she happily started her grooming.

The first step was to lock herself in the safety of the bathroom. Sadly, all she could achieve in there was a shower, though. As soon as the door was shut, her head and torso disappeared from sight.

After a leisurely hot shower, she dried herself off and then wrapped the snuggly complimentary hotel robe around her. She opened the door, letting the steam free, and her body instantly appeared the second Karl was back in sight.

He didn't look up from his phone as she began to apply her make-up and style her hair.

He still hadn't said a word by the time she'd finished perfecting her look. All she needed now was to get dressed.

She took her dress from the wardrobe and locked the bathroom door again. She squeezed herself into the tight but flattering outfit, struggling a little with the zip at the back but refusing the let Karl's dirty fingers touch it. And then she watched it fade away with her invisible contagiousness. She was desperate to see how she looked. She couldn't remember ever trying so hard with her appearance before. If she didn't look good now, she knew there was no hope for her.

She dashed out of the bathroom, grabbed her sparkling silver stilettos from nearby the bed where she'd placed them, and then she posed in front of the full length mirror by the door.

She was extremely pleased with herself. Her black sleeveless dress tucked everything in nicely, and her shoes boosted the glamour of the dress just as she'd hoped for; even more so with the silver clutch bag by her side. Her hair flowed in large curls around her shoulders, and her make-up was fresh and bright but with an elegant subtlety.

She turned to Karl who was still sitting on the bed, absorbed in a game. She held out her arms, expecting him to react, but it was like he'd forgotten she was even there.

She cleared her throat to get his attention.

'Are you done?' he asked. 'It's taken you like forever.'

'How do I look?' she nudged.

'Yeah, nice,' Karl replied, still with half an eye on his game. 'It smells of girls in here now.'

Alice slumped her shoulders. 'Are you going to get ready?'

'What time we got to leave?'

'Just before seven. The Champagne Reception starts at seven.'

'Cool. I'll get ready about ten to then.'

'Are you not having a shower?'

'Why?'

Alice shook her head. 'If you want one, you can.'

'Cool. I'll just get to the next level and then I'll put my suit on. You said bring a suit, didn't you.'

'Is it black tie?'

'Yeah, my mum bought me a new black tie, just like you said.'

'As in a dinner jacket?'

Karl laughed. 'What's a dinner jacket? Sounds like some sort of bib to stop you spilling food over you.'

'It's a tuxedo. Do you know what a tuxedo is?'

'Yeah.'

'Well, have you brought one of them?'

'No, I've brought a black suit with a black tie. That's what you said.'

'You said you knew what black tie meant. You said you'd get it sorted.'

'I did! I got my mum to buy me a black tie.'

'Great. You'll look like you're going to a funeral.'

'Won't everyone have black ties if it's – as you say – a black tie event?'

'They'll all be in tuxedos.'

'Then it should say a tuxedo event. It's not my fault if it's not clear.'

Alice took a deep breath. 'Quite right,' she said, realising, as usual, it was best just to give in. 'Quite right. I'm sure half of the men there will look like they're attending a funeral. So be it. Let's just get you lots of Champagne.'

'Is that free too?'

'Every drink you want tonight will be free. Please, don't hesitate. Have as much as your liver can bear. Please.'

'Cool. This is gonna be great!'

Alice caught up on her work emails as she waited for Karl to complete his game, and then, at just before five to seven, he finally put his suit on. At least he could manage a Windsor knot, far more than she'd expected.

'What do you think?' he said, mirroring her stance from earlier to get her approval. At least she was willing to give him the time.

She placed her phone back in her bag and she gave Karl her full attention. The disappointment couldn't have hit her harder.

His suit was creased from where he'd scrunched it in his backpack and his shoes had scuff marks all over them. This couldn't be further from the impression Alice wanted to make, but she had no choice. It literally was go with Karl or don't go at all.

So this was it. She was about to meet Dan - and lots of her other colleagues. And she was about to introduce this scruffy, slightly whiffy, short, naïve man as her chosen partner in life.

Alice stood up with determination. Every cloud had a silver lining, she was sure she'd find hers at some point that night.

FOURTEEN

Dan sipped nervously on his bubbly. He'd arrived early at the Champagne Reception held in one of the function rooms at the hotel in Chelsea. He wanted to make sure that whenever Alice appeared, he was there to meet her. But it seemed most of the other guests also had reasons for arriving early, and at five to seven there was a sea of black around him.

Since it was a black tie event and that a good proportion of his peers happened to be male, virtually all Dan could see around him were people dressed in dinner jackets, almost like a mirror image of himself. Although Dan's suit was perhaps a little bit more expensive than those in his proximity.

Dan had made extreme efforts to look his best that night. He was determined to make a good impression. He couldn't remember any woman ever stirring up his emotions like Alice did. He'd never felt this way about anyone before, and he hadn't even met her yet.

He hoped that she was attractive, but he was pretty sure that unless she had three heads or was a complete, drooling slob (which he believed was highly unlikely) then he was probably going to fall in love with her right on the spot. This notion both terrified and delighted him.

She might have a boyfriend, but Dan had made a firm decision that this was merely a hurdle to get over, not a blockage. After all, Dan had known Alice for longer and they got on very, very well. He also hoped that his expensive cologne, gelled hair, moisturised face, slick, three piece suit and shiny black shoes would all help persuade her away from the competition. His plan was to cast a very dark shadow over this new man in her life, and up until that point he'd been feeling quietly confident. But now the nerves had really kicked in.

Dan scanned the room to see if he could spot someone who could be Alice. A benefit Dan was finding of it being a black tie event was that the few females in the room stood out like beacons. Even the ladies who were dressed in black were noticeable with the flesh of their arms or their flowing hair.

He may not have a clue what Alice looked like, but he was sure he could whittle it down quite easily. She would be a young, probably (hopefully) beautiful woman with a man in tow.

He spotted a potential fit entering the room in a bright scarlet gown that left little to the imagination. She seemed about the right age and she was with another similarly aged man. But Dan couldn't believe that Alice would wear something so loud and coquettish.

Then she cackled. Alice didn't cackle. That couldn't possibly be Alice.

Dan scanned the room some more, unconsciously knocking back his Champagne as his agitation intensified.

Women started popping up all over the place but he hadn't seen one yet that fitted what he knew about Alice.

He turned back to the door as a beautiful lady entered. She was wearing a stunning black dress that shimmered against the light of the chandeliers and elegantly flattered her gorgeous figure.

That had to be Alice.

Dan didn't move. He watched her as she grabbed two glasses of Champagne, handed them both to the man next to her, and then took another one for herself.

Dan focused on the man next to her. He was short and podgy without any particular style to him. He was just sort of there, totally at odds to this woman's glamorous appearance. He didn't even have a dinner jacket on. He looked like he was going to a funeral. Could that possibly be her boyfriend?

Maybe it wasn't Alice?

She was staring around the room. It wasn't a general glance. It was obvious that she was deliberately searching for someone.

Her eyes landed on Dan and for the first time their gazes met. She smiled at him. It was a warm, sexy smile and Dan prayed that it really was Alice. He very much liked what he saw.

His stirred up emotions became more forcefully passionate as she approached him, with the little man following.

'Dan?' she enquired with a huge grin.

'Alice?' he replied with hope.

'I knew it was you! Everyone else was lost in conversation, but I knew you'd want to meet me as much as I've been looking forward to meeting you.'

Dan's heart began to throb. Nerves? Exhilaration? Relief?

Confusion? Was that really her boyfriend?

'It's great to finally meet you.' He wanted to hug her. He wanted to kiss her and hug her, but all he found himself doing was holding out his hand. Everything else felt inappropriate with the little man next to her watching their every move.

Alice seemed surprised by his hand, but she shook it anyway. 'I know. At last. Sorry it's taken so long.'

'It's worth the wait.' Dan didn't mean to stare, but he couldn't resist taking her all in. She was so beautiful.

'I like your suit. You look really nice,' Alice said.

'So do you. You're stunning.' Dan stopped himself. Could he say that in the presence of her boyfriend? He turned to the little man. He was a very scruffy little man. Maybe Dan had got it all wrong. How could such a gorgeous, intelligent woman be with someone so ungroomed and vacant?

Maybe after being single for so long she was a bit desperate?

'Thank you,' Alice replied before a short moment of awkward silence. Dan wanted to speak, but he was too busy trying to put all the logic in his head, while breathing in Alice's sublime scent. She really was gorgeous.

'So fill us in on the plans for the night,' she said. 'You're a seasoned corporate event-er, or so you keep telling me. Do we just mingle? Where do we eat?'

'We'll get called in to sit down for dinner shortly. Have you seen the table plan?'

Dan had checked it straight away. He'd begged the Marketing team to ensure that he was sat next to Alice. He'd told them he had important client business to discuss with her, but the last thing he wanted to do was talk about work.

All he could think about was how much he wanted to be alone with her.

'No. So we don't get to choose where to sit?' she said.

'No. But we have good seats, don't fear. Blooms are major sponsors, so we're right at the front. We won't have far to go to collect that award.'

'Will I have to go up if we win?' Alice asked, concern slapped across her face.

'No, don't worry,' Dan chuckled. 'You're not one for the spotlight, are you?'

'Just being here is a big step for me. As you well know.'

'It's fine. We had to state who was collecting the award in advance. Glenn's going up.'

'Glenn will be here as well?'

'Yeah. You speak to him a bit too, don't you?'

'Once a month, maybe. He is the Head of Product Development. I kind of have to. Will be nice to put a face to the voice.'

'It certainly is.'

Dan knocked back the remainder of his Champagne. He could feel his voice shaking. What was happening to him?

His eyes caught the little man again. This strange fellow was now working his way through his second glass of Champagne, and he seemed quite content in just gaping at Dan and Alice, not feeling any need to contribute to the conversation.

Dan had to know.

'I'm sorry, who's this?' he asked Alice.

Alice flushed. Her chest and face became instantly red. It was so cute.

'This is Karl.'

'Oh right. Hi,' Dan said.

Karl swigged on his Champagne before nodding to Dan. 'Hi.'

'Is Karl the boyfriend you've told me all about?'

Alice cleared her throat. 'Yes.'

'Oh.'

How is he Alice's boyfriend?!

Dan glanced between Alice and Karl over and over, trying to work out where the mutual attraction might be found. But he couldn't see it. Karl must be the luckiest guy on the planet!

'Can I get you another Champagne?' Dan asked Alice.

'Are we allowed two?'

Dan couldn't stop his eyes from turning to Karl who was happily downing his Champagne like he was glugging beer.

'Who's going to know?' Dan shrugged.

'Okay then. One more for all of us.'

'One more for him too?' Dan checked, pointing at Karl. 'Definitely.'

Dan fought through the crowd to reach the Champagne table that was placed right near the entrance. He grabbed three glasses and then carefully headed back to Alice.

'There you go,' he said, handing out the drinks.

'I need a piss,' Karl said.

'Okay. Let's go together,' Alice said.

'You need to go as well?' Dan asked. He was hoping for a minute alone with Alice. It was terribly awkward with the little man hanging around.

'I do,' she said. 'Would you mind holding my Champagne while Karl and I track down the facilities?'

'Of course not.'

Alice passed him her glass, and then Karl followed suit and shoved his glass too in Dan's hands.

'I know how much is left,' Karl said, without so much as a pinch of irony.

'Okay,' Dan stuttered with bewilderment.

Dan watched the pair about to leave when Karl skewed off to the left. He headed straight for the wall and placed his two empty Champagne flutes right on the floor near the skirting. Then he grabbed Alice's hand and dragged her off out of sight.

Dan took a breath. None of this was playing out how he'd imagined. Alice seemed incredibly uncomfortable, and her odd little boyfriend had no personality at all. What was she doing with him?

Dan waited on his own for about ten minutes, unable to drink any of his own Champagne as he was awkwardly holding three glasses. Finally the pair reappeared, still hand in hand.

'Thank you so much,' Alice said, removing her glass from his hold.

'Cheers,' Karl said before he checked the level of the liquid. He actually checked the level of the liquid.

Dan took a gulp of his drink.

'Oh, it looks like we're heading in,' Alice said. She pointed to a door that had opened to the side of the room.

'Good, I'm getting hungry,' Dan said.

'Me too,' Alice nodded. 'Shall we just follow you? Do

you know where you're going?'

'I certainly do. This way.'

Dan led the way slowly behind the crowd into the much cooler main function room. It was dark with sparkling lights in every direction and a main stage at the front with two podiums.

Each of the thirty tables were decorated with a black table cloth, twinkling confetti and a huge vase in the middle sporting a large black feather.

They tracked down table two, right at the front, and they located their allocated seats. Dan was delighted to be sat next to Alice, although she had Karl on her other side. Thankfully Emily was on the opposite side of the feather, as far away as she could be.

'That's Emily,' Dan whispered in Alice's ear as Emily began greeting everyone loudly.

She had a gold, far too tight dress on, which did nothing to flatter her large hips. But what she lacked in style, she certainly made up for in confidence.

'That's Emily?' Alice asked. The look in her eye suggested that she was putting a name to a face she already knew.

'Have you met her before?' Dan asked.

'No,' Alice replied. 'Of course not.'

'You must be Alice!' a voice boomed from next to them. Speak of the devil. Emily threw her arms around Alice as if they were old friends reunited.

Alice pushed her gently away. 'And who might you be?' Alice asked.

'I'm Emily.'

Alice studied her. 'Do you work for Blooms?'

'Yes. Surely you've heard of me? I'm currently your top salesperson.'

'No,' Alice said, quite dismissively. Dan couldn't help the small smile that crept up on his lips. Just when he thought he couldn't like Alice more.

'Really? I've been working hard to boost sales within the

London area. I've had a great deal of success. Haven't I, Dan?'

The smile dropped from Dan's lips as he fought the urge to slap her.

'You work with Dan?' Alice asked. 'Oh, that's great. You're so lucky. There's a lot you could learn from such a talented Business Development Manager.'

Dan's smile quickly returned.

'Erm... Oh yes. Absolutely. And you're the daughter of Norman Bloom. Such a tragedy what happened. But I'm sure he'd be delighted to know that his company is in such good hands.'

'Whose hands are you referring to?' Alice asked.

'Well, yours for starters. Look at this award nomination.'

'A mere popularity vote. My father would see right through it. Who else?'

Emily appeared uncharacteristically thrown. She wasn't used to not having her way. Everyone else seemed to adore her. Dan was so glad that Alice was on his side. 'I suppose sales people like me too,' Emily had the audacity to say. 'And Dan,' she quickly added. 'And John. We're all working hard to make you and your dad proud.'

'Did you know my father?' Alice asked.

'No. Such a shame. I would have loved to have known him.'

'Then with all due respect, could I ask you not to speak about my father as if you know what would and wouldn't have made him proud.'

'But...'

Dan really had to stop himself from laughing.

'I didn't...' Emily continued. 'I just meant... I'm sure he'd be proud of a successful company.'

'He liked honest, straightforward, respectful people. There's working hard and then there's working honestly and smartly. Which category would you say you fall into?'

'Erm... I work hard. And I'm honest and smart. I guess.'

'I look forward to getting to know you better, Emily.'

With that closing comment, Alice turned her whole body to face Dan, leaving Emily staggering behind her. 'Dan, you were telling me about what you've got planned this weekend.'

'Oh yes,' Dan began as he tried to control his jubilation. 'I'll be back in London...'

'And who are you?' Emily asked. Her words made Alice immediately spin around.

'I'm Karl, Alice's boyfriend,' Karl said, his mouth full of bread, and crumbs all down his shirt.

'Alice's boyfriend. How lovely!' Emily said, shaking Karl's hand.

'We'd better get you a drink,' Alice said to Karl, pushing Emily aside and taking the bread from his hands. She gestured for him to wipe away the mess and then she turned back to Dan.

'Do we just order drinks from the bar in the other room?'

'We have wine at the table,' Dan replied.

Alice scanned the table. 'Not a lot of it.'

'We normally get about half a bottle each.'

'Beer. I think Karl needs beer.'

'Oh right. Doesn't he drink wine?' Dan asked.

Alice paused. 'Where can we get beer from?'

'The waiters will be around in a minute. You can order from them.'

'Perfect.'

'Jeremy!' Emily was off, hugging one of Dan's ex-clients at a nearby table.

'I don't trust her,' Alice whispered to Dan.

'You make me laugh. You certainly gave her a hard time.'

'I don't like being hugged by strangers and I certainly don't like my dad being used as a technique to get on my good side. I've got my eyes on her.'

'So has everyone else. But everyone else seems to have a rose tinted filter. I'm so glad you're here.'

'You can count on me to see things as they are.'

Dan spotted Karl out of the corner of his eye pouring a huge glass of wine.

'I think he does like wine,' Dan said. Alice swiftly turned around just as Karl was brimming his red wine glass with wine white.

Alice turned back to Dan, smiling. 'He likes to sample all that's on offer and then make a discerning choice.'

'Sample?' Dan noted with a smirk as he watched Karl delicately pick up his overflowing glass. 'Does he know he's supposed to share?'

'I'll get another bottle. It's fine,' Alice snapped. She'd had her moments of snappiness on the phone, but Dan could tell this was more. Something was wrong.

'Are you okay?' he asked with concern.

'What beers do you have?' Alice said, ignoring Dan and grabbing a waiter that walked by.

'Budweiser or Corona. We only have bottles. We do a mixed bucket for twenty pounds.'

'Brilliant. We'll have a mixed bucket please. And can I charge it to my room?'

'Yes, no problem.'

'Is that for the table?' Dan asked as the waiter walked off.

Again Alice paused. 'Do you want beer as well?'

'I'm happy with the wine.'

'Help yourself if you want. I just want to keep Karl happy. Saves keep bothering the waiter, that's all.'

'Oh right.'

'Alice?' John said appearing beside them. He looked like he'd seen a ghost.

'John,' Alice replied.

'You look so different.'

'You have no idea.'

'I'll leave you two to catch up,' Dan said, optimising on this perfect moment to step away. He needed a second to clear his head.

As soon as he was in the relative peace of the toilet he

took a huge breath. This was turning out to be one very weird night. Alice was everything he'd hoped she'd be, but he couldn't get his head around that boyfriend.

Casting a shadow was easier than he'd anticipated. He only had to stand next to Karl and he was superior in every way.

But maybe Alice liked small, strange men?

Whatever was going on, there was no way Dan was giving in. Whether he wanted to admit it or not, he was head over heels in love and he couldn't let Alice slip through his fingers.

FIFTEEN

A few minutes later and Dan returned to his seat, only to find the introduction speeches had started. He smiled at Alice and she grinned back. She had such a lovely face.

Dan didn't listen to a word of the speech. He didn't even know who the speaker was. All he could think about was Alice.

He wanted to talk to her. He wanted to touch her. He wanted Karl to be on an ejector seat so that he could catapult him out of the building, and then Dan would swoop Alice up in his arms and kiss her lovingly, making her forget that Karl ever even existed.

The applause around him snapped Dan from his daydream.

'That was quite an introduction, wasn't it?' Alice said. Dan really couldn't comment, but he sensed her wonderful cynical tone so he knew he didn't have to say much.

'It certainly set the scene for the evening.'

'You'd think we were curing cancer or something. It's only bloody security products.'

'Don't knock it. We save lives in our own way.'

'Oh for goodness sake.'

Dan saw her lips trying to hide her smile. He wondered

if she had that same beautiful look on her face every time she was being grumpy.

The starter appeared before them and they picked up their cutlery to finally begin eating.

'I'd ask what your opening speech would entail but I'm guessing it would be along the lines of informing everyone how pointless these awards really are,' Dan said.

Alice laughed. 'But I'd add in how nice it is that we're all here together as an industry and I'd encourage everyone to have a good old knees up after the rigmarole of the pointless award giving. It wouldn't all be negative.'

'No. That's inspiring.'

'I think so.'

'Ugh! What is this!' It was Karl's voice. Dan looked past Alice to see Karl letting bits of chewed food fall out of his mouth in disgust.

'Karl!' Alice said. 'Don't do that.'

'What is it?' Karl groaned. 'I thought it was ham.'

'It is. It's Ham Hock Terrine.'

'Ham doesn't taste like this. This tastes like shit!'

Dan watched as Alice took a deep breath. Everyone on the table was staring at Karl's actions but Alice was keeping her cool. She evaded all the eyes around her as she pushed Karl's plate aside.

'Never mind,' she said. 'We can't all like everything. How boring would that be? Have my bread roll. And have another beer.'

'Is everything all right?' Dan asked.

'Of course. He's a man of simple tastes, that's all. I should have known. I should have warned him.'

'It says beef for mains,' Karl whined, looking at the menu that had been placed on the table.

'Yes. You like beef don't you,' Alice said.

'Will it really be beef? Because that's not really ham. When my mum buys ham it doesn't taste like that.'

'Yes, it will be beef. It will probably be very tender, not like the steaks you normally eat. But I'm sure you'll enjoy it.'

With a screwed up face, Karl necked back more of his beer before breaking up the bread roll and spreading crumbs everywhere.

Alice calmly returned to her food.

'I like it,' Dan said. 'I never have terrine at home. It's a nice change.'

'I agree,' Alice nodded. 'I actually don't think I've ever had terrine before. I don't eat out very often. But I think it's delicious.'

'Yes, you're always cooking something, aren't you?' Dan said. 'It's very disciplined. I wish I could be more like you. Ordering in is far too easy. It's not good.'

'Isn't it funny how the grass is always greener,' Alice mumbled.

Dan opened his mouth to ask Alice to elaborate on what she meant, but Glenn, who was sitting to Dan's right, suddenly asked Dan a question and Dan was drawn away from his conversation.

The mains had arrived before Dan could get back to speaking to Alice again. They talked some more about their favourite foods, while Alice kept one eye on Karl.

Thankfully he seemed to like his beef and mashed potato. Karl didn't say another word, he just sat quietly eating every last morsel. He didn't make a sound during the apple pie dessert either, letting Dan and Alice happily continue their chit-chat.

After the coffees had been served, the music kicked in and the ceremony finally commenced.

There was a comedian hosting the awards and he began with some general stand up. Everyone else was laughing along, but Karl was doubled up with hysteria.

'This is the funniest thing I've ever heard!' he yelled at Alice.

She seemed too controlled. Dan couldn't believe how embarrassing that little man was, but Alice just took a deep breath and appeared to let it wash over her. It wasn't like she saw Karl as amusing or cute. It was like she was tolerating him. For reasons that Dan couldn't fathom.

Dan had stopped laughing as his attention turned completely on to her. He was desperate to know what was going on in her head.

Out of nowhere, Alice stood up in shock. She quickly bent down and Dan could see that Karl was lying on the floor, grasping his stomach with tears pouring down his face.

Dan had a moment of hoping that it might be appendicitis. Then he saw that Karl had just fallen off his chair because he was laughing so much. Dan was at first disappointed before the awkwardness of it all made him quite uncomfortable. The comedian really wasn't that funny.

When Alice had Karl back in his seat, she grabbed him another beer. That's when Dan noticed her hands were shaking. There was something very wrong but Dan couldn't work out what it was.

'Please just be quiet and drink your beer,' she said to Karl. It was like she was babysitting an alcoholic.

Maybe he was an alcoholic.

But why was Alice with him?

After the stand up routine had finished, the first award was announced and Karl started to clap and holler loudly.

'We're going to kick the night off with a biggy,' the comedian said. 'It's Apprentice of the Year.'

'Is this your one?' Karl asked Alice.

'No. Not this one. We're in Product of the Year.' She passed Karl the brochure for the night that detailed all the awards and nominees, but Karl didn't even look at it.

Dan wanted to chat to Alice. He wanted to play that game where they would guess the winner of each category and see who could score the most points at the end of the night.

But all Dan could do was sit and watch in fascination.

As every award was announced, Karl would ask Alice if this was hers. And every time she replied, Dan could sense a little dent in her cool exterior.

Finally, nine awards in, Product of the Year was announced.

'Is this your one?' Karl asked again.

'Yes,' Alice said with a big sigh. 'Yes it is.'

'Woo!' Karl shouted, applauding ferociously.

'Best of luck,' Dan whispered in Alice's ear. He wanted to hold her hand so much.

'Luck has nothing to do with it,' she said with a wink.

God he was in love.

'The nominations are for CKW Control...' the comedian said.

'Is that your company?' Karl asked.

'No. We're Blooms Security,' Alice replied.

'How does he not know that?' Dan had to ask. It was starting to border on the ridiculous.

'I don't like to talk about my work,' Alice replied. 'You know I rarely talk about myself.' It was true. It had taken Dan a long time to get anything personal out of her. But then again Karl was sitting at the Blooms Security table. How could he not know whom she worked for?

'Is that you?' Karl asked as another company was announced.

'No, we're Blooms,' Alice replied with ever growing aggravation.

'Is that you?' Karl asked as the final nomination was announced.

'Yes,' she sighed. 'That's us. That's my product.'

'Go Blooms!' Karl shouted, raising a chuckle from everyone seated around them.

'And the award goes to...' The envelope was opened and Dan noted that he actually felt nervous. As cynical as Alice might be about the award, he really wanted her to win. He wanted her hard work to be officially recognised.

He wanted an excuse to kiss her.

'Blooms Security Solutions for their PXK Proximity Sensor.'

'Is that you?' Karl asked as everyone on their table burst into cheers and applause.

'Yes,' Alice said.

Music pumped through the speakers as Glenn rose to his feet to accept the award.

'Congratulations!' Dan said. He put his arm out to hug Alice, seizing this amazing moment. His lips were tantalising close to kissing her cheek when suddenly Karl stood up, knocking his chair behind him.

'Woo!' he cheered. 'That's my girlfriend's award! For her robot!'

'Will you sit down!' Alice demanded, pulling away from Dan. She grabbed the chair and then grabbed Karl, yanking him back to his seat. Karl kissed Alice hard on the lips and she almost fell over herself, clearly not expecting it.

'Your robot won!' he said, laughing. 'You're so clever!'

'Did he say robot?' Dan asked.

Alice turned to face Dan. She hesitated before smiling. 'Yes. It's a joke of ours. He says I'll be making robotic security guards before long. He's very proud of what I do. It's his strange wit.' Alice was now laughing but the humour hadn't reached her eyes.

'I thought you didn't talk about work,' Dan noted.

Alice stopped laughing. She sat very still, looking almost beaten.

'I have to ask,' Dan said. 'Is everything all right?'

Alice paused before whispering, 'If I told you it's complicated would you accept that?'

This time Dan didn't hesitate. He took her hand in his. She had such lovely soft skin.

'I'll accept anything you tell me,' he said, now sure that something was very wrong. 'Just know I'm here for you. Always. Whenever or however you need me.'

'It's fine. I'm fine,' Alice said, letting his hand go and acting breezily. 'Life just has ups and downs, doesn't it. But don't worry. This is the happiest I remember being in a long time. Believe me.'

'Are you sure?'

'I promise.'

When all the awards had been given out and the ceremony had formally closed, the party continued in the bar.

Alice had bought Karl a pint of beer, although he looked absolutely wrecked. He was propped up on a stool near the bar while Alice was talking to Glenn.

As people started heading to bed and things got quieter, Dan decided to take a moment to chat to Karl. He was eager to find out what was really going on.

'Hello Karl,' he said.

'Hello.'

'Have you had a good night?'

'Yeah, it's been brilliant.'

'And we won the award. That was great, wasn't it. For Alice's robot.'

'I know! She's so clever.'

'Have you seen her robot?'

'Yeah, it's amazing.'

'You've seen it?'

'Yeah,' Karl nodded. 'I mean not in real life. But Alice told me all about it. She tells me everything. She's very clever. And she's rich. She has such a big house.'

Dan didn't know whether to laugh or punch him.

'You spend a lot of time with Alice, then?' Dan said.

'Yeah. Sometimes. She's hot, isn't she,' Karl slurred.

Dan glanced over to where Alice was standing nearby. She was absolutely stunning.

'We're going to have sex tonight,' Karl stated and it churned Dan's stomach.

'Really?' Dan replied.

'We've been waiting for a hotel.' Karl's eyes were drooping as he sipped on his pint.

'What does that mean?' Dan asked.

'We've been bonding so we can be together forever. You

see physical relations are better after people wait and bond first. We're going to be together forever after we have sex.'

Dan took a moment as his brain computed Karl's rambling. 'Are you saying you haven't had sex yet?' Dan felt full of hope.

'We're doing it tonight. To cement our phys... phys-cal relationships... and be together forever.'

Dan's face twisted with repulsion. 'It sounds like you're joining a cult.' He didn't know what to make of any of this bizarre conversation. He was both relieved to hear that this Karl was yet to touch the woman he loved, but also horrified by the notion that it could happen tonight. Not that Karl seemed in any fit state to rise to the occasion. And not that Alice seemed in any rush to get to bed. It was half past one in the morning and she was still in deep conversation.

'I like sex,' Karl said and then, much to Dan's horror, he started thrusting his arms around like he was doing a drunken Locomotion.

'Right.'

'I think I want to have sex now,' Karl said.

Dan followed Karl's gaze back towards Alice. Dan very much wanted to have sex with her too.

'Yeah! I want to do it now,' Karl said, practically falling off his stool. He downed the remainder of his pint and staggered over to Alice.

Dan moved a few steps closer so he wasn't in the way but he could still hear what was about to happen.

'Can we go now?' Karl said, interrupting Alice's conversation.

'Karl, I'm talking.'

'I want to go to bed.'

'Okay.'

'You said we could have sex.'

Dan watched as Alice's face turned bright crimson.

'Excuse me,' she said to Glenn as she pulled Karl aside. She said something to him but Dan couldn't make it out. It was so frustrating.

Alice then led Karl back towards the bar.

'Is everything all right?' Dan asked.

'Yes,' Alice said, returning to her calm, controlled state. 'Karl is going to have one more drink and then I think we'll have to retire. To sleep.'

'Oh right,' Dan said, utterly perplexed by what was happening.

'Shall I get us all a nightcap?' she said.

'I don't want a nightcap. I want a tipple,' Karl moaned.

Alice rolled her eyes but before she could say anything, Karl was waving for the barman's attention.

'Can I have a tipple, please?' he ordered.

'You're going to have to be more specific, mate,' the barman said.

'A tipple!' Karl demanded.

'We'll have three rum and cokes, please,' Alice said.

'See,' Karl said to the barman. 'It's called a tipple.'

'You do like rum, don't you?' Alice asked Dan.

Dan much preferred brandy at the end of a night, but he wasn't going to disagree. Alice needed all the support she could get.

'Dan?' she nudged as he was contemplating his answer.

'Perfect,' he said.

Karl could barely stand up straight as they sipped on their final drinks.

'Have you had a good night?' Dan asked Alice, partly out of politeness and partly to see how she'd respond.

'Yes. I really have,' Alice said with sincerity. 'Glenn's lovely, isn't he. It was so nice to talk to him about something other than work.'

Dan looked over at Glenn who was now being talked at by Emily. He had no doubt that she'd be the last to bed, selling and networking until everyone was exhausted or she'd exhausted every opportunity.

Glenn was a gentle man in his fifties. He had a soft demeanour, floppy grey hair and thick rimmed glasses that perfectly suited his round face. Dan knew there was no way he'd tell Emily to shut up, but he could see Glenn wasn't at all engaged with her endless yammering.

'Do you think we should save him?' Dan asked, nodding towards Glenn.

'No,' Alice said. 'If we save him then he might not remember how irritating she is. Surely it can't just be us that sees it?'

'Fair point,' Dan smirked.

'Have *you* had a good night?' Alice asked him.

'I certainly have,' he replied. 'Firstly I want to say congratulations again for the well deserved award win.' Dan clinked his glass against Alice's. 'You can be as cynical as you like, but I think it's a great achievement.'

'I suppose it's a testament to how well established my father's company has become. As we know, unknown businesses have no chance of winning as the people giving out the awards would have nothing to gain from it.'

'Would your father have really thought the same?' Dan asked.

'Oh yes. He hated these events. Don't get me wrong, I've had a wonderful night and I've loved the company, but I still believe it's all a load of nonsense.'

Karl's head flopping towards the bar caught Dan's attention.

'I think your boyfriend might have fallen asleep,' Dan said.

Alice turned to see Karl resting against the bar like it was a comfy pillow. She took the drink from his hand and Dan could swear a look of relief washed over her.

'Do you want me to help you get him to bed?' Dan asked.

'Would you mind?'

'Not at all.'

'Come on, Karl. Time for bed,' Alice said, waking him up. Karl sort of groaned a bit but he wasn't fully conscious.

Dan took one of Karl's arms as Alice steadied the other, and they helped Karl move. He could stand but he was far from stable.

They propped him up as they headed to the lifts and made their way very slowly to Alice's third floor room.

As soon as they got in, they placed Karl on the bed.

'I'll leave you to undress him,' Dan said and Alice scrunched up her face. She actually looked repulsed.

'What is going on with you two?' Dan asked. He couldn't resist. He had to know.

'What do you mean?'

Dan paused for thought. He had hundreds of questions that he was dying to ask. Although he knew none of it was really his business, he was desperate to find out just what Alice was doing with this man. She didn't even appear to particularly like this Karl yet she was openly calling him her boyfriend.

They hadn't had sex. Dan knew that now. But Karl had believed tonight was going to be the night to change that. However, he'd got himself far too drunk.

A notion wedged itself firmly in Dan's head. Alice had encouraged Karl to have three glasses of Champagne, she'd bought a bucket of beer especially for him and she'd plied him with drinks after the ceremony.

'Dan?' Alice nudged.

'Were you trying to get him drunk tonight?' Dan asked.

This time Alice took her time to reply. Her face was clearly searching for the right answer and Dan could tell she wanted to say something. He could tell she was ready to explain everything. But then she looked at the floor and shook her head.

'It's complicated,' she said. 'Would you mind if I just left it there?'

'Of course,' Dan said. 'It's none of my business anyway. I'm just worried about you. Things don't add up. Not that I... I'm just saying...' Dan took a breath. 'I only want you to be happy. I care about you. I want to know you're all right.'

'Oh I am,' Alice said. 'I really am. For the first time in a long time, I'm happy.'

Dan knew, without any question, that Alice meant that. She really had just declared true happiness. But why did she then seem so awkward with Karl?

Dan had to concede that he may never know, so he stopped trying to work it out and instead he focused on the fact that they were finally alone together.

Dan had felt the urge all night, and he knew at last he was being blessed with his moment.

'Hug goodnight?' he said.

The smile warmed Alice's face. 'Definitely.'

He placed his arms around Alice and pulled her in against him. She nestled into his shoulder and Dan felt his heart start to throb again.

'I've loved spending time with you tonight,' Dan said, his voice low to make sure he didn't wake Karl.

'Me too,' Alice replied.

'You truly are an amazing woman.' He shifted his head and she turned up to meet his eyes. Their vision now locked, he could feel his attraction to her stirring up inside of him. 'And you're incredibly beautiful.'

'You think so?' Her smile was humble and cute. He wanted to kiss those lips so badly. He wanted to run his hands through her thick, hazelnut hair.

He wanted to kick Karl to the floor and then place her on the bed and make love to her. Or better yet, leave the drunken idiot there and carry her to his room where they could properly explore each other's bodies.

'Very beautiful,' he said, his lips now just centimetres from Alice's. She closed her eyes and he was ready to kiss her. She wasn't fighting him. Surely she must feel it too.

Suddenly the room started to vibrate through a terrible noise.

It was Karl snoring. It cut through the moment like a tractor burrowing between them.

Alice stood back. The magic had all gone and she seemed engaged with reality once more.

'Thank you for helping me with Karl,' she said, signalling

an end to the night.

'It was my pleasure. What are friends for.'

'You're the best friend a girl could want.'

Dan felt a stab in his chest. Those were not words he wanted to hear.

'I'd better let you get some sleep,' he said, making it almost a question so he could leave it open for her to disagree.

'Do you want to meet for breakfast?' she asked, putting the brakes on his burgeoning proposal.

'Sure,' he muttered. 'That would be lovely.'

'It's already nearly two. Shall we meet at nine thirty?'

'Sounds good. Well... Goodnight, Alice. It's been great to meet you at last. I've had a really good night.'

'Me too. Sleep well.'

'Any problems with Karl, give me a call. I'll keep my phone on.'

'I will. Thank you.'

'No problem.'

'Goodnight.'

Dan hovered by the door, hoping she'd say something more. Perhaps there was still a chance that she'd kiss him.

But she stood back and waved goodbye and he knew it was all over with.

'Night.' He closed the door behind him and stood in the brightly lid corridor.

He was head over heels in love and he hadn't got a clue what was going on.

SIXTEEN

As Alice watched the door close behind Dan, she felt both elated and deflated. She'd had a brilliant night. It had been wonderful to finally meet so many people. Especially Dan. But Karl had tried her patience more than she'd ever expected.

She knew it was partially her own fault. He wouldn't have been quite so embarrassing had she not thrust alcohol down his throat all night. But if she hadn't have got him so hammered then he might have been trying to have sex with her right at that very moment.

She shivered at the thought. She really felt nothing but irritation when it came to Karl. Well, irritation and gratitude. He'd made it possible for her to be out. He'd set her free in so many ways. But life had put a warped condition on that freedom.

She went to the bathroom and got changed into her thick pyjamas. It was nowhere near cold enough for such wintry nightwear, but she wanted every bit of defence possible to ward off any of Karl's romantic ideas.

She came back into the bedroom and carefully rolled Karl over onto one side of the bed, still on top of the covers, and then she curled up under the duvet on the other side.

She could feel the power of his snores through the mattress and she knew she wouldn't get any sleep. But there was no way she was going to wake him. No sleep was better than his dirty hands touching her.

She closed her eyes and her thoughts turned to Ethan. As Dan had hugged her, she'd immediately remembered the last time that she was in a man's embrace, and it had given her goose bumps. That kiss with Ethan had been the best moment of her life. But it had ended so sourly.

She replayed that kiss at the back of the aisle in Dobson's over and over, smiling to herself. His firm, toned body and gorgeous face. The way he looked at her with such deep desire. Alice couldn't remember anyone ever looking at her with such desire – almost hunger – and it made her feel alive. He'd churned up feelings she'd missed having and she really wanted his eyes to undress her once again. She wanted to be with a man so badly. Well, she wanted to be with a man she found attractive. And Ethan was like some sort of god. All she could think about was having sex with him. Her thoughts had become locked onto that single idea, as if her animal instincts had taken over.

She finally managed to doze off, but she was frequently woken by Karl's snorts and farts. He was far from an ideal bed companion.

At eight o'clock she decided enough was enough and she got up. Besides, she knew she'd need plenty of time to wake up Karl and get him ready for breakfast. He was still in a deep sleep.

To combat any advances he may make that morning, Alice decided first that she'd have a shower and get herself ready. If she was fully clothed then it would be harder for him to suggest they have sex.

She headed into the bathroom and closed the door. She reached across the bath to turn the shower on, not surprised by the sight of her arm.

She started to take off her pyjama top when suddenly she stopped.

Her torso was still there.

She could still see her torso.

She ran to the mirror to check it wasn't her imagination. She could see her face. She could see her face still!

She waited patiently, staring at herself, waiting for bits to slowly vanish, but everything remained perfectly in view.

She was whole.

She was whole!

She was back.

She sat nervously on the edge of the bath, believing it was too good to be true. She waited and waited, but her whole body and her pyjamas remained fully visible. And Karl was locked away on the other side of the door.

Alice jumped to her feet and punched the air. At last! She was finally free! She had finally battled her demons and she was ready to be launched into the world once more.

Wasting not a second more, in case it was all a temporary lapse of invisibility, she swiftly showered, dried herself and then grabbed her clothes. As soon as she was dressed, she flicked on a bit of make-up and tied back her hair. She was ready for the world and she couldn't wait.

She texted Dan to say she hadn't slept very well and she was going for breakfast early, and she'd love him to join her if he was awake; but not to worry if not. And then she left Karl still snoring away and she stepped out into the corridor with a beaming smile.

She got in the lift and made it all the way to the restaurant, all on her own and in full view. It was so exciting, and utterly liberating.

As she waited to be guided to a table, her phone vibrated.

I'm up too. I'll be with you in a few. x

It was Dan texting back. Even better. She could actually have a proper conversation with her lovely friend without Karl embarrassing her.

'Table for one?' the waitress asked.

'No, my friend will be joining me in a second,' Alice replied.

The waitress led her to a table towards the back of the restaurant and Alice ordered a coffee. Her head was slightly sore from the wine and rum, but she wasn't going to let a small hangover ruin her high.

She headed over to the hot buffet. It had been a very long time since Alice had eaten a fried breakfast that someone else had cooked and she was determined to pile her plate high.

'Morning,' a voice next to her said as she chose three sausages. It was Dan. He looked tired but full of smiles.

'Morning. How are you?'

'I'm good. Very good.'

'Could you not sleep either?' Alice asked.

He shrugged. 'It's always hard when you're away from home. But I had a great night, so it's worth it.'

'Yeah, me too.'

'Where's Karl?' Dan asked, searching around the restaurant as he grabbed a plate.

'He's still in bed. I thought it best to let him sleep. He was in a state last night.'

'Yes, he was.'

'I thought he might be nervous,' she explained. 'I wanted him to relax. I thought a few beers might help him.'

'Oh they did. He seemed very relaxed by the end of the night.' Dan had the glimmer of a smirk.

'And I'm happy to leave him in that relaxed state until we have to check out.' Alice knew she'd have to go home with Karl, but she didn't need him anymore. As awful as she felt for completely using him, she was relieved that she didn't have to see him ever again. There had been times when he'd made her skin crawl.

She did feel terrible. She wasn't proud of her behaviour. But Karl had got something out of it too. He'd now been to London and he'd had a completely free night out. She'd given him some attention and his confidence seemed boosted. Surely Alice hadn't been completely selfish?

She led Dan back to their table and they sat down and devoured their delicious breakfasts.

'Do you live far from here?' Alice asked Dan.

'I live in Wimbledon.'

'Wimbledon! Not Wembley.'

'Wembley? Where did you get that from? That's the other side of London.'

Alice shrugged. 'So where's Wimbledon? It's not just a venue for tennis then?'

Dan chuckled. He had such a lovely smile. It always seemed so genuine and it warmed Alice's heart. 'No, it is. I've got a tent on the Centre Court. It's the most expensive court, I'll have you know.'

'I don't know! People only ever talk about Wimbledon with regards to tennis.'

'Where do you think the Wombles come from?'

Alice paused. She sang the theme tune to the Wombles in her head.

'Oh yeah! Is there really a Wimbledon Common?'

'Yes, it's a nice area.'

'Well fancy that. You learn something new every day.'

'You know, for someone so intelligent-'

'Shut up!'

Alice's smile was radiant. No matter what her mood, Dan always made her feel better. Even though she'd already been walking on air, sitting with Dan made her feel like she was flying through the stars. He was amazing.

'You still haven't told me how far away Wimbledon is,' Alice noted.

'A few miles. It's this side of London, but it'll still take me a good half hour or so to get home. Hence why I stayed over last night.'

'I'll have to come and visit sometime. If you don't mind?'

Dan grinned broadly. 'I'd love that. You're welcome anytime. Perhaps you could come for the weekend and we could see a show or something? Whatever you want.'

'That would be fantastic. And when you're next up in the Midlands you could come round mine. I'd love to cook for you one night.'

'It's a date.' Dan seemed to hesitate before he said with that tone that Alice knew oh so well, 'Karl was telling me you live in a big house.'

There was a second before Alice replied as she tried to work out what else Karl might have said that Dan wasn't telling her. 'It's my parents' house,' she explained. 'The mortgage was paid off so I've been very lucky. Well, maybe not very lucky.'

'There's good and bad in everything,' Dan said.

'Isn't there just.'

The pair fell quiet as they carried on munching through their breakfasts.

'Did you chat to Karl a lot last night?' Alice enquired.

'A bit. He seems...'

'I don't think it's going to work out between us.' Alice felt such a relief saying it out loud.

'Oh,' Dan said with that high pitched tone again.

'Last night got me thinking about how different we are. I was in a bad place and he kind of gave me a confidence I hadn't had before. He helped me get back out into the world when I'd been too afraid to face it. Like literally. But... We're very different. Does that sound awful?'

'Not at all,' Dan replied. 'Lives cross all the time, it doesn't mean you have to get tangled up with them. Sometimes you need something for a short while, but needs change. There's nothing wrong with that. As long as you're honest.'

Alice shoved half a sausage in her mouth so she didn't have to respond. She'd been anything but honest recently, but she'd also had an enormous situation to deal with. That mess had now sorted itself out and so it was time to be honest again. She'd always prided herself on being straightforward, and so she was determined to lose the complications and get her life back on track.

'I'll have to tell him,' she said after she'd finally swallowed the sausage. 'I'll wait until we're back home. He's not going to be in the best state today. I don't want to be unfair, but it's time to move on. And believe me, Dan, I'm very ready to move on.'

'Really?' He raised his eyebrows, clearly eager to know more.

'Oh yes!' Alice grinned inanely as she conjured up images of Ethan. She thought of that kiss again and her whole body started to tingle.

'Deal with Karl first, though,' Dan said, wisely. 'Then you'll be ready.'

Alice bit her lip to stop herself from smiling. She was going to get exactly what she wanted. She was going to have sex with Ethan. All she needed was to find a way to apologise to him for her behaviour last time they met. But she was sure it wouldn't be difficult. She was going to offer him sex on a plate. What man would turn that down?

'You look ecstatic just thinking about the future,' Dan commented, a smile catching his lips, as if Alice's euphoria were infectious.

Alice wanted to tell him. She wanted to share the news about Ethan – a man that could actually be her boyfriend and who wasn't deeply embarrassing. But she couldn't. She didn't want Dan to think poorly of her. She needed to appear to be doing the right thing. The respectful thing to do was to break up with her boyfriend before deciding to get into bed with someone else.

'Who knows what the future may hold,' she said. 'It's exciting.'

All Alice could think about was her yearning sexual drive and how she wanted to place her hands all over Ethan and explore all of his hidden areas.

'You can't stop smiling,' Dan said. 'Stop it!'

'Dan, you're such a wonderful friend,' Alice said. 'Thanks for your support last night. And always.'

Dan's grin started to waver. 'I love you, Alice.'

'Aww, I love you too. So tell me, what plans have you got for the rest of the day? You got much work to do?'

Dan seemed to sigh as he concentrated on the remainder of the baked beans on his plate.

'Sorry, the last thing you probably want to talk about is work,' Alice said.

'No, it's fine. I've only got a couple of things to follow up on. I met a couple of people last night that are worth me keeping in touch with. I'm going to head home in a bit. I think I might actually sit in bed with my laptop.'

'I don't blame you. I was going to start working on a few bug fixes this afternoon, but to be honest I don't feel like much at all. You got any exciting plans this weekend?'

'No, not much. Catching up with my sisters and I'm going out with a few mates tomorrow night. That's about it.'

'Sounds nice.'

'Morning you two. Can I join you?' John said, appearing next to their table.

'You could have done,' Dan said, knocking back his coffee very quickly. 'But I was about to go. I've got some clients to speak to.'

'And I've got bugs to fix,' Alice said, not relishing the idea of having breakfast with John alone. She hadn't known what to say to him last night. He was too much like her dad's friend. It was weird.

'Oh right.'

'Sorry, mate,' Dan said as he stood up.

'Nice to see you again,' Alice said as she followed Dan out of the restaurant.

'What floor are you on?' she asked Dan as they reached the lift.

'Same as you. But at the other end of the corridor.'

'Oh right. I wonder if we're all on the same floor?'

'I hope not. The last person I want to see right now is Emily.'

'I bet she's even more of a nightmare with a hangover,'

Alice chortled.

'No, what are we saying? She'll already be off around London, stealing all my clients. There's no time to spare.'

As they waited for the lift, Alice thought about Emily. She'd remembered her straight away. Emily had been the very nosey girl that had been asking lots of questions about Alice and her family when Alice had first seen Dan in Strikers that night.

She hadn't been very impressed with Emily from what Dan had told her, but when she realised this horrible woman was the irritating, interfering busy-body from the bar that night, Alice's defences immediately went up.

She felt protective of her close friend, and protective of herself. Emily was clearly one to use anything to her advantage and Alice was not going to make it easy for her.

The lift doors opened and Dan pressed for the third floor.

'Maybe I'll see you soon?' he asked. 'Whenever you're ready. I don't want to rush you.'

'Don't be daft. We'll see each other soon, I'm sure. And don't be a stranger on the phone. Keep me up to date with Emily.'

'I will. I'll need someone to rant at.'

'You know I'm a good listener.'

They exited the lift and headed down the corridor. They reached Alice's room first and stopped.

'Hug goodbye?' Dan said.

'Definitely.'

He placed his arms around Alice. She enjoyed the feel of his warm embrace. He was a well groomed man and he smelt divine. Even casually dressed in his jeans and a T-shirt, he still looked smart and sexy. She enjoyed being with him very much, and something about having to say goodbye to him made her sad.

'Text me later?' she asked as she broke away from his hold.

'Of course. You're always in my thoughts.'

'You're so sweet, Dan. You mean the world to me, you know that.'

'As do you, Alice. You really do.'

Alice kissed him on the cheek. 'Speak to you soon.'

She noticed him flush and she instantly regretted the kiss. Maybe she'd judged that badly. She hadn't had a close male friend before. Maybe they should have punched fists or something cool like that.

'Sorry,' she mumbled before fiddling to open the door.

'What? No, it's...'

He moved in to kiss her back but she hadn't seen it coming and instead he caught the side of her head.

'Sorry,' she giggled, now feeling incredibly awkward. What must he think of her? 'Look, let's... I'll see you soon.'

'Definitely. You take care, Alice. And good luck with...' Dan pointed to inside the room where Karl was still in bed.

'Thanks. I'll let you know how it goes.'

'Please do.'

'See you then.' Alice waved her hand as she closed the door, leaving Dan to get on with his day. And probably laugh at how silly she was.

She sat on the edge of the bed where Karl was now quietly breathing still on top of the duvet.

She felt totally mixed up. Weird feelings were sparking through her entire body.

Was it nerves about breaking up with Karl?

Relief?

Perhaps excitement about Ethan? Or fear that he may reject her?

Or maybe embarrassment at having kissed Dan who had clearly been thrown by her unintended advances?

If this was the mess she got into after an hour of being visible, Alice dreaded to think what lay ahead. She needed to get a grip. She needed to stay in control.

This was the start of a new life and she had to start properly getting on with it.

SEVENTEEN

'Wake up!' Alice demanded as she shook Karl. 'Wake up!'

'Five more minutes, mum,' he grumbled as he turned over.

She noticed him dribbling and immediately a rage enflamed inside of her.

'I'm not your mother. Now wake up!'

He opened his eyes with surprise. 'Annie?' He shook his head, realising his own mistake. 'Alice.'

Her muscles clenched. They made a terrible couple. Why was he even with her?

He sat up, the imprints from where he'd slept on his hands distorting his face, and his hair sticking up making him look like a rooster.

'Are we going to have sex?' he asked and Alice actually felt like gagging.

'No, we are absolutely not going to have sex.'

'But you promised.'

Entering this hotel with Karl had ignited the fuse of irritation within Alice, but she'd tried her best to keep the flames at bay. Seeing him in this state, though, recalling the humiliation he'd caused her during the previous night and contemplating how many times his dirty little fingers had touched her skin, Alice could hold back the fire no longer. She exploded into a blazing frenzy that made hell itself seem cool in comparison.

'Sex? With you? You should have thought about that before you got absolutely wasted and fell asleep. What a huge let down you turned out to be. In every conceivable way.'

Karl seemed completely blindsided. 'But... I didn't mean to. You kept telling me to drink. You were drinking too.'

'A real man takes responsibility for himself. You failed miserably. You completely embarrassed me with your drunken behaviour. Just because alcohol is free, doesn't mean you have to guzzle down every last drop like the world's resources are depleting and you need beer to sustain your life. You should be ashamed of yourself. What an utter disgrace you are.'

Karl couldn't say anything. He was stunned.

'Get in the shower,' she ordered. 'Clean yourself up and then we're going home.'

'Aren't we going sightseeing?'

'You're lucky I'm not just leaving you here.'

'What about breakfast?' He seemed properly sad and regretful, and this sent Alice's rage into fluctuation.

She knew he'd actually done nothing wrong. Everything that had happened was totally her fault. However, her wrath was on the loose and logic was not going to get a say.

'I've had my breakfast, Karl. I couldn't wake you up. But if you're quick I'll allow you to have something small and then we're going straight home. I do not want to go sightseeing with you.'

When Karl was dressed, she left him to breakfast while she enjoyed a cappuccino in the lobby. Then they checked out and made their way back towards Euston.

This time Alice didn't mind getting the tube as she was very sure that Karl wasn't going to try anything. He was clearly cursing himself for the way he'd acted. It hadn't occurred to him at all to blame Alice.

They got on the train back to the Midlands and she played chess on her phone while Karl silently played one of his games. It was such a relief.

They got a taxi from Birmingham New Street station straight back to Alice's house in Starley Green. She asked him to join her inside. It was time for a talk and Alice was eager to get it over with.

She let them into her home and Karl sat like a berated child on her settee.

'It's not going to work out between us,' she said, standing over him.

'What?' Karl seemed devastated and Alice felt the sting of guilt.

'You really hurt me last night, Karl.'

'But... I didn't mean to.'

'I'm sorry, but I need to be with a proper man.'

'Like Dan?' he threw back at her.

'What?'

'He was all over you last night.'

'He was not.'

'He was. He kept saying how stunning you were and saying how amazing you were.'

'Dan and I are friends. Good friends. He could probably see that my boyfriend was failing to pay me any attention and so he felt like he should step in. You didn't tell me once that I looked nice.'

'Yes I did!'

'You did not. It's what gentlemen do. They compliment ladies when they make an effort. Dan was being no more than a polite friend. I can't believe you have the audacity to throw jealous remarks my way because you couldn't cut it.'

'Whatever. He fancies you.'

'Well, Karl, I don't fancy you. It's over between us. Can you please leave.'

Karl sat still on the settee, staring at the carpet. Alice wasn't sure if he was going to cry. He didn't move for what seemed like an age.

'This has got nothing to do with Dan,' she said, keen to move things along so he'd go. 'I was friends with Dan a long time before I met you, and I'll be friends with him well into the future. But that's all we are.' Alice bit her lip. If only Karl knew the truth about where her affections really lay. He was bound to find out. But it was her choice.

'Have you ever fancied me?' Karl asked, much to Alice's horror.

Her skin prickled just at the sight of him, but she knew she needed to give him something. She needed to throw him a lifeline. She owed him that much after he'd set her free.

'Honestly?' she asked, knowing that she was about to be anything but honest.

'Just tell me the truth.'

'Well, truthfully, I wasn't sure at first. We just sort of ended up on a date together out of nowhere. But I really enjoyed our time together. I could see a future with us being together. But I think we're too different. Be honest, Karl, you were out of your depth last night. You spat out food, you nailed the wine, you didn't even know what a tipple was.'

'I do now,' he shrugged and Alice wanted to laugh.

'Yes,' she said.

'I think you're hot,' he muttered. 'Thanks for trying.'

He grabbed his bag and without turning back he left her house.

Alice waited for a moment to check that he'd really gone. She half expected him to run back and declare his undying love for her.

But no, he was gone.

She exhaled deeply, letting the relief sink in. She was totally free in every way now.

And she was very ready for the next thrilling instalment of her life.

She looked at her watch. It was approaching half one and she realised she hadn't done any work that day.

She scurried upstairs to check her emails, deciding that she'd have lunch after she'd caught up with anything urgent. However, within five minutes all she was doing was staring inanely at her monitor while she daydreamed about Ethan.

She conjured up images of turning up at his work. He'd smile at her, clearly delighted that she was there. She'd apologise and he'd say it wasn't necessary. She'd say that she'd made up her mind and he'd... look over at Karl who would be serving someone behind the tills.

The fantasy vanished. She couldn't reconnect with Ethan if Karl was watching her.

But no, Karl didn't work Fridays!

Her moment of glee was cut short again as she realised that if her fantasy was to properly play out, then she'd end up having sex with Ethan in his office. That was far too sleazy. This was her re-emergence back into the world of relationships, she at least wanted to go on a date first.

She needed to bump into Ethan on neutral ground. A casual encounter where she could suggest they meet for drinks sometime. She could flirt with him and apologise for how she'd left things. She could make sure that he knew she'd broken up with Karl, in case Karl had been holding back on the truth.

If only she knew where he'd be. Like definitely. She didn't want to keep turning up at Strikers on the off chance he'd be there. She needed a concrete plan.

She sat back in her chair and chewed on the arm of her glasses as she considered what she knew about him.

Nothing. Other than the fact he worked in Dobson's, she knew absolutely nothing.

Surely he must have hobbies. He went to the gym, but there were several in the area. Did he support a particular football team? Anything would help.

She could Google him!

No. She didn't even know Ethan's full name. She was sure "Ethan Starley Green" wasn't going to be hugely helpful.

Worth a try, though.

Just as her fingers were poised to start typing, another idea popped into her head. She may not know a lot about Ethan, but she knew enough about Karl. What if she could track down Ethan somehow through Karl?

Of course! Social media!

It was the perfect stalker platform.

Alice hadn't been on Facebook since her parents died, but she still had an account floating about.

She put her glasses back on, opened up the web page and typed in her email and password.

She couldn't believe how different it seemed. Her eyes caught a red number at the top telling her how many notifications she'd missed. It was huge. Maybe she hadn't been as forgotten about as much as she'd thought.

That didn't matter now, though. She was on a mission.

She typed in Karl's name and then she searched through his friends. A smile instantly grabbed her face when, sure enough, she found Ethan.

Ethan Moody. What a name.

She clicked onto his profile. His picture was of him on the beach in just his shorts, posing like someone out of a catalogue. He had the most gorgeous body.

She felt her legs quiver as she flicked through more of his photos. She had to get him back in her life.

Her phone pinged. It was Dan.

Hope you got home okay. I'm currently in bed catching up on some admin. Don't think I'll be doing much else today. Still smiling about how great last night was though. x

Alice pressed reply and typed out a message.

Got home a short while ago. I ended it with Karl. I thought it best not to prolong the agony. He was sad but took it well. We weren't right for each other. Thanks for being such a great friend. I loved meeting you. Enjoy your relaxed admin day! x

She placed her phone down and continued to ogle over photos of Ethan. Very sexy Ethan.

She clicked back to his profile page. It was mostly locked down except for a few photos and comments here and there. But then, a short way down the page, Alice saw something that grabbed her attention.

Ethan had posted an event he was going to. It clearly said he was going. A band was playing at a local pub in town that coming Thursday night.

That had to be her chance. He was going to be there. He was definitely going to be there. She could casually drop in, as if she were big fan of the band herself, and get chatting to him.

She halted her excitement. What sort of a loser would turn up to see a band all on their own? She could hardly ask Karl to go with her.

Oh God, what if Karl was there too? He'd think that she was there on her own in an attempt to get back together with him.

No, she needed a friend to go with.

Sammy immediately popped into her head and she quickly brushed away the ludicrous idea. It might be sad to go to a pub to see a band on your own, but it was bordering on the insane to take your giant stuffed teddy bear.

She hated the fact that she knew no one. She'd shut herself away for so long, she'd literally got no one left in her life. She was starting to change that now, but it made it very difficult to make new friends when you had no friends to go out with in order to meet new people.

Life was so complicated.

Her phone pinged another message from Dan.

I'm glad it went well. You were far too good for him. I hope we can meet up again soon. You're all I can think about. xx

Alice smiled. Dan was so sweet. He was a true friend.

Maybe he'd come and see the band with her?

But he lived in London.

She sat up straight as she toyed with the idea of inviting Dan. He did come up to Birmingham fairly frequently. There might be a chance.

Alice opened up the shared work calendar on her computer and searched for Dan's name.

She instantly saw his busy working week laid out in front of her. All the sales team were forced to keep their diaries up to date. What a blessing.

She flicked across to Thursday. In the morning he was with a client in Watford and then in the afternoon he was free. And then on Friday he wasn't busy until eleven am.

She opened up the details and saw that it was a call with John. John, Head of Sales. John who was based in the Midlands.

This could all work out.

She grabbed her phone. Could she really ask Dan to join her?

Of course she could. If nothing else, she was thrilled at the idea of spending more time with him. It wasn't just about Ethan.

As she dialled Dan's number, she made a note to herself not to mention anything about Ethan. She was worried it might look a bit heartless trying to date another man just minutes after she'd broken up with her boyfriend.

'Missing me already?' Dan said as he answered.

'I must be,' Alice said, the grin on her face spreading wide. She did love to hear his voice.

'That's good to know.'

'Quick question. I won't bother you for long. I know you're working.'

'You can call me anytime. You know you can.'

'Well, what about we do more than speak on the phone next time? In fact, I know you live in London and everything, but would you happen to be in the Midlands this Thursday at all? Or could you make it up?'

'Thursday?' Dan said.

'Yes. One of my favourite bands is playing at a local pub in town and I thought maybe you'd like to join me?'

There was silence on the other end of the phone.

'Dan?' Alice nudged.

'I'd love to. Really? This Thursday?' He sounded genuinely excited.

'If you can make it.'

'Hang on, let me check my diary.'

Alice waited quietly as Dan checked exactly what she was looking at on her screen.

'We're in luck,' he said a few moments later. 'I'm in Watford on Thursday, so could easily shoot up the M1 after that. Then even better, I have a call with John on Friday to go over a proposal, but I could suggest I come to the office to better discuss it. That way I can expense the night too. How good is that!'

'I can't believe it. It's like it's meant to be.'

'It really is.' There was a weighted pause and Alice didn't know what to say. 'So tell me more about this band,' Dan said, moving the conversation on again.

Alice hesitated. 'The band?'

'Yeah, would I have heard of them?'

Alice flicked back to Facebook and scrolled through Ethan's page. She really hoped that Dan hadn't heard of them.

'They're called Grave Annihilation.'

'What?' Dan asked as Alice pulled a face. What a terrible name for a band. 'Don't they sound cheery. What sort of music do they play?'

Alice was typing furiously into her keyboard to find out anything she could about Grave Annihilation. 'Hang on,' she said to buy her time. 'Work email. Just give me two seconds.'

She scanned Google and saw a description of them. Her heart sank.

'Sorry, what were you saying?' she said, as if it had been

a terribly important work email that had completely distracted her.

'What sort of music can we expect from Grave Annihilation?'

'Erm... Metal,' she said, as confidently as she could.

'Metal?' Dan enquired with surprise. 'Like heavy metal?'

Alice had deliberately left out the word that came before "metal" on the web page she was viewing. It was becoming quite obvious that Grave Annihilation was not going to give them an evening of light entertainment, and she now deeply regretted telling Dan that it was one of her favourite bands.

'Actually, it's death metal,' she said. She had no choice but to sound like she totally understood and enjoyed whatever death metal was. Even though it didn't sound fun at all.

'Death metal?' Dan asked. 'You like death metal? This is your favourite band?'

'One of my favourite local bands,' Alice corrected. 'It may sound weird, but they always put on a great show and the atmosphere is electric. I've never had a bad night listening to them.' Well, that was true so far.

'Right then,' Dan said. This time she completely understood his pause. 'I really do have so much more to learn about you, Alice Bloom. You certainly are full of surprises.'

'Oh, you have no idea.'

'I can't say I've ever listened to death metal. Honestly, I normally like chart stuff. Maybe a bit of rock thrown in. I'll have to look up death metal so I won't show you up. If nothing else, I'm sure it'll be an eye opener for me.'

Alice smiled. Dan was so kind and she loved that he was supporting her very unexpected taste in music. It really didn't sound appealing at all.

'Dinner's on me as well,' she said.

It all went quiet yet again. 'Dan? You still there?'

'Sorry... erm... work email for me this time. What did you say?'

'Dinner's on me. It's the least I can do with you travelling all this way.'

'Whatever. We can work that out. I'm just happy that I'll be seeing you again so soon.'

'You're very sweet. I'm sure we'll have a great night.'

'I'm sure we will.'

'See you Thursday, then.'

'See you Thursday. But speak to you before then, I hope.'

'Oh yes. Definitely. Have a good weekend.'

'You too. Bye.'

Alice hung up the call and she returned to her Ethan ogling.

She couldn't say that Grave Annihilation was a band she was particularly looking forward to seeing, but if it meant she could be with Ethan then it would all be worth it.

Now she had to figure out what to wear.

EIGHTEEN

At seven o'clock the next morning Dan was wide awake. He was staring at the ceiling and fantasising about his upcoming date with Alice.

He'd had the odd moment of doubt through the night as to whether he really should consider Thursday's get together with Alice a date. Maybe she was just being friendly. But then he thought through the logic and realised that it had to be a date.

Within the same twenty-fours that they'd met, she'd broken up with her boyfriend and had invited Dan to go out with her. What else could it be if it wasn't a date?

Full of excited energy, Dan got out of bed. He shovelled some cereal down his throat before gathering his things and heading out of the flat.

He got in his car and made the five minute journey to the gym. He tried to go to the gym at least once every weekend. Well, that was the plan anyway.

He jogged on the treadmill for half an hour and then finished with some weights, before hitting the shower and heading back home.

He was still like a ball of liveliness as he dropped his car off and made his way to the tube.

He was meeting his sisters for lunch in Kensington, but he decided to make a stop at Oxford Street first. He wanted a new shirt to wear for the date. He had to look his best.

He wasn't sure what a person generally wore to see a death metal band. Black was presumably going to be a dominant colour. So he thought maybe a navy shirt might work well. He didn't want to go full on black, but he didn't want to stick out too much. He wasn't sure how friendly death metal fans might be.

It had been quite a shock to learn that Alice was such a fan. But he loved that she constantly surprised him. Maybe he needed to branch out more in his taste of music.

He was so early reaching the shops that he had to wait for them to open. Dan was often an early riser, but this was ridiculous.

At nine thirty on the dot, the doors to John Lewis were unlocked and he made his way straight to the men's department.

After an hour of shopping (just about as much as he could bear) he located the perfect shirt in Selfridges. It wasn't cheap but it fitted him well and it was soft to the touch. Any way he could encourage Alice to touch him was welcome.

He paid for it and then saw that it was only ten thirty-five. He had loads of time to kill. He decided to grab a drink and spend some time playing chess.

As he sat in a coffee shop near Bond Street Underground Station, he contemplated his next move against Alice.

Ever since Dan had first seen *Blade Runner* he'd been obsessed with both the film and the game of chess. But until Alice had come into his life, he'd never met another person who loved the game just as much as he did.

He'd played against many people online over the years. It was when he was struggling against a particularly strong player one day that he let it slip to Alice that he had been up far too late the night before deliberating over his next move.

He'd stopped himself quickly, sure that she was about to call him a mega geek for obsessing over such a silly game. But instead she'd been thrilled. She admitted that she was a huge fan as well and insisted that they start a game against each other immediately.

She was tough competition. She played extremely well. Dan could never play anything other than his absolute best if he wanted a chance of beating her. And how he loved beating her. Because when things became competitive, she became chattier. Their mutual love of the game had brought them close together, but their equally competitive natures had made their relationship bloom.

Dan played his move on his phone and then sipped on his coffee.

Not minutes later, he received a notification telling him that Alice had played her turn. He opened up his app to find that she'd taken his queen. How had he let that happen?

Clearly his happy state was making him lose concentration.

The message notification flashed up in his app.

Either your eye is off the ball, White, or you're luring me into something I can't see. I hope it's the former, but either way, that felt good. x

Dan laughed. His move had been poor but he was never going to admit to it. He replied to Alice.

I'm glad it felt good because you won't be enjoying the rest of the game quite so much. x

Dan sent the message and then had a small moment of panic. He had to find a way to live up to his fighting talk now. He couldn't let her win after saying that.

He analysed the board, determined not to make the same mistake as before, but his tired eyes were letting him down. He may have been full of vim physically, but he had barely slept now for two nights. His mind was being relentlessly dominated by thoughts of Alice. As much as he was relishing in thinking about her, a tired brain was not good for winning chess matches.

He put his phone away and decided not to rush into a move.

He'd finished his coffee but it was still only eleven o'clock and he wasn't meeting his sisters until half twelve.

He thought it might be best to take a walk. Freshen up his mind and burn off some of his excitability.

He made his way to Hyde Park and he strolled around aimlessly for the best part of an hour until he finally reached the bistro on the south side.

He and his sisters tried to meet once a month for lunch. They always met in their favourite little restaurant away from the tourist spots. They'd enjoy the tasty food whilst sharing a bottle of wine and all their latest news.

Or in Dan's case, he could listen to his sisters go on and on before they'd bombard him with questions about his love life. That was how it usually went.

'Is it still fashionable to be late?' Clare said as he approached their table. How she loved to stir things up. It was only twelve thirty-four.

He kissed both his sisters before taking his seat.

'Or perhaps shopping's more important than meeting your sisters?' Clare stated, acknowledging Dan's Selfridges bag.

'Oh most definitely,' Dan replied. 'And I don't even like shopping.'

'What have you bought?' Mary asked.

'Just a shirt. Work stuff.'

Losing interest quickly in his purchase, Mary passed her brother a menu.

'I think we should have red wine today,' Mary announced.

'I'm easy. Whatever you want,' Dan replied.

'I don't mind, but can it be a light red,' Clare said. 'We

had that Shiraz last time and it didn't sit well with me. It's too much for lunch.'

'I think it was the steak that didn't sit well with you,' Mary replied. 'It was practically mooing on your plate. You know dad wouldn't approve.'

'What about a Pinot Noir for today, if you insist on red?' Clare suggested.

'Sounds good to me,' Dan said.

'They don't have a Pinot Noir,' Mary said, scanning the wine menu.

'They did have. I swear,' Clare replied.

'I'm happy with whatever,' Dan said, checking his phone for messages. It was always the same. It wasn't that his sisters really cared what wine they had, it was just an ongoing battle of wills all the time.

All three of them got on extremely well. They rarely ever fell out. But when it came to his sisters, they had this secret game between them of who was best. Dan knew better than to ever attempt competing.

As they continued to debate the wine, Dan took a moment to text Alice.

How's your day going? I was at the gym this morning and now I'm out with my sisters having lunch. Hope you're having a good weekend so far. x

'What's it to be then?' Dan said as he tucked his phone back in his pocket.

'We're having the Tempranillo,' Clare said. 'Unless you have an issue with that?'

'Perfect,' Dan said, nodding. He really didn't care.

'I feel now is the time to tell you that I won't be drinking next time we meet,' Clare announced. 'At the end of this month I'm going teetotal. Except for maybe Christmas day.'

'Why?' Mary asked. 'Is everything okay?'

'It's better than okay. I'm doing the London Marathon next year. I got a place with a charity through the University.

I'm really excited.'

'The London Marathon?' Dan asked with total surprise. 'Since when do you like running?'

'You know I run.'

'On the treadmill.'

'I've actually been running in Hyde Park three times a week for the past month. I have a personal trainer who's developed a rigorous training plan for me.'

'And he told you to go drink free?' Dan asked.

'*She* hasn't said anything about my diet. But I want to be ready in both mind and body, and going sober will definitely help.'

'You mean you want people to ask you why you're not drinking so you can tell them you're running the Marathon without it sounding like you're showing off,' Dan said.

'We're not all obsessed with appearances,' Clare bit back.

'I'm so proud of you,' Mary said and Dan's senses spiked. It was coming. 'We need challenges in life to keep us stimulated.'

'Because studying law and medicine isn't challenging enough,' Dan mumbled, preparing for it.

'I've been considering a skydive,' Mary said and Dan checked his phone again. He knew that Mary had just that second decided to do this. He also knew that by the Spring they'd all be sitting in a field somewhere waiting for her to land.

He quickly managed to block out the details of Mary's impending skydive as he saw that Alice had replied.

Sounds like you're having a nice weekend. I'm in Birmingham shopping. I can't remember the last time I actually had a day just for me around the shops. It's fantastic. I've even booked myself in for a spa day tomorrow to get pampered properly. It feels so good to be out and about treating myself like this. x

Dan smiled. Clearly Alice was getting ready for their date too. He wondered if she'd also bought a new outfit. Maybe a really sexy dress. She did have a gorgeous body.

He texted her back, gladly ignoring his sisters as they compared who would have more work to do in preparation for their feats.

It's always good to treat yourself. I can't wait to hear all about it on Thursday. x

'Are you having your usual?' Mary asked Dan, pulling him back to reality. He looked up at the waiter who seemed to have appeared from nowhere.

'Yes, the burger please,' Dan said. 'Can I have it well done?'

'Certainly. Will that be all?'

'Have you ordered?' Dan asked.

'Yes. Who are you messaging? What's so important?' Clare asked.

'That's everything, thank you,' Mary said to the waiter.

'It's just work stuff,' Dan shrugged.

'You're working on a Saturday?' Clare asked, dubiously.

'You both work at the weekend.'

'I'm a student,' Clare stated.

'And I...' Mary started. 'Have a very different job to you.'

Dan knew that meant "have a more important job" but he didn't rise to it.

Instead he decided to change the subject. 'Do either of you know what death metal is?'

This silenced them. It made Dan smirk.

'In what context?' Mary asked.

'Music. I'm going to see a death metal band next week with a mate. I'm not sure what to expect.'

Both of his sisters hesitated. 'Where is this concert?' Mary asked.

'Up in Birmingham. It's a mate from work.'

'Who is this mate? You're not going to be doing drugs or anything are you?'

Dan rolled his eyes. 'Are death metal and drugs

interconnected?'

'You tell me,' Mary replied.

'I don't know anything about death metal. Hence my asking.'

'It does sound dangerous,' Clare chipped in.

'Oh Daniel. Why can't you meet a nice girl and go to nice concerts?' Mary said. 'Like go and see... I don't know... Westlife or something.'

'Westlife? What are you talking about?' Dan knew that both of his sisters rarely listened to music. Nor did they particularly watch TV. Asking either of them about popular culture was like asking a country bumpkin about the intricacies of city life. That's often what made it so enjoyable though.

'Have you had any dates recently?' Clare asked.

'No,' Dan replied, quite to the point.

'Would you tell us?'

'No,' Dan followed up with.

'We only want to see you happy,' Mary added.

'What's the latest with Laurence?' Dan asked Mary. Laurence was her boyfriend. They'd been together for two years and she was desperate for a marriage proposal. He knew this ought to keep her going for a while.

As she wittered on about her love life, Dan subtly checked his phone again. No message from Alice. She was probably trying on clothes and getting her nails done. All ready for their date.

He couldn't help but smile to himself. He couldn't wait.

After surviving another lunch with his sisters, Dan headed home where he had about two hours to relax before meeting his mates at the local pub. The mates consisted of two old work colleagues and then two of their friends that Dan had always got on very well with.

Dan was normally the beating heart of any party. He was usually the first to buy a round, he could chat very easily to just about anybody, and he was virtually always the last one standing when everyone else was ready to go home.

But that night was totally different. After a couple of pints and a few games of pool he realised he wasn't in the mood for socialising.

His mind was, of course, still thinking about Alice. He had never shared much about his love life with his mates either. They'd met a couple of his short term partners who just happened to be local girls, but generally Dan was a private person. It was far easier that way. The less people knew about him, the more he could control what they thought.

In fact the only person who Dan could say really knew him was Alice. He hadn't expected to be so open with her, but she always sounded truly happy to be hearing from him. She took a genuine interest in his life. And when he'd confessed to her about problems at work, she hadn't given him useless advice such as work harder or don't be so sensitive. Instead she'd got angry for him. She'd supported him instead of lecturing him. It was a breath of fresh air for Dan.

That's why Alice was also the only person who knew how much Dan was hating his job. Emily was obviously at the core of his issues, but the knock on effect was humiliating. Not only was Dan losing sales all over the place, but John was seemingly blaming Dan rather than seeing that something unfair was happening.

Dan's call with John that coming Friday - that was now a meeting as Dan was coming up to Starley Green – was a mentoring session so that John could help Dan better put together proposals and improve his sales tactics. It was the most mortifying prospect for Dan. But if he wanted to keep his job then he had no choice.

Part of him was desperate to tell John to stick the job, but Dan couldn't be out of work. He also couldn't bear the thought of not working with Alice.

As the beer hit his tired mind, the joyful thoughts of Alice became blurred with his worries about work. That's when Dan made the decision to call it a night. He had another beer when he got home, flicked through the telly without actually watching anything, and then he went to bed and counted down the days until his date.

NINETEEN

As Dan drove up the motorway the following Thursday afternoon he was seething. His fingers snapped at the buttons in his car to activate his Bluetooth.

'Call John Snaddow,' he ordered.

All in all, the week had been a very bad one for Dan. Not only had it dragged on while he eagerly awaited his date, but he'd suffered the loss of two more potential clients. And both of them could have been big.

'Dan, all right?' John answered.

'No, not really,' Dan said.

John sighed. 'What is it?'

'I've just got off the phone with your beloved Emily. She's screwing me over, John. Totally screwing me over.'

'You mean she's performing better than you.'

'No, she's screwing me over. I came out of my meeting earlier to find an email from Paul Lavender – as in Head of Security at the Waves Shopping Centre – saying that the second quote is much better and so he's going to go with that. I called him back to find out what he was talking about and he said that Emily, my colleague, had sent the correct quote through and they were much happier with it. She's stolen my client. Again.'

'Hang on. Emily told me on Tuesday that she was speaking with Paul Lavender.'

'I've been speaking to them for weeks.'

'So has she by all accounts.'

'It's in the CRM! You can track what I've been doing. Where are her detailed notes?'

'Look Dan, she's not happy with you either.'

'What?'

'She's agreed with me that she's not going to put things in the CRM from now on as she's claiming that it's you who's trying to steal her leads. Not the other way around.'

'Are you joking? That's bullshit. If that were really the case then why when I speak to these people do they not tell me they're already dealing with someone at Blooms?'

'She's saying the same thing.'

'This is absolute bullshit. I'm doing all the work and she's sending in quotes to my prospects at the last minute and undercutting me.'

'Right, if that's so then do you have any evidence?'

'Why don't you phone up the clients and ask them?'

'I'm not doing that. We'll look ridiculous. Dan, get a grip. As far as I can see, Emily is working extremely hard to win some great deals. All I get from you is moaning about how she's stealing your work. Well, she can't be everywhere, Dan. She can't be bringing in her own work and managing your clients too.'

'She's not managing anybody. I'm doing all the ground work and then she's swooping in and undercutting me right at the last minute to win the deal.'

'And how is she doing that? How does she know what you're quoting?'

Dan paused. He really didn't know.

'You're the one who's been asking for a proper quoting system,' John said. 'But as we don't have one then there's no way she can see what quotes you're sending out.'

'If we had a proper quoting system then at least you'd see that I've been sending out the quotes first.'

'That still doesn't prove anything. It's not about who sends out what quote, it's the fact that she's the better closer and you know it.'

'Anyone can close a deal that's been handed to them on a plate.'

'I'm getting tired of this now, Dan. If you can come to me with evidence that Emily is doing any of the awful things that you're accusing her of, then I'll listen. But the fact is we both know no such evidence exists. You've hit issues, Dan. You're struggling. I don't know what's gone wrong but maybe when we meet tomorrow we can find a way to get you back to the man you were when you arrived.'

'You mean the man I was before Emily was hired. Doesn't that strike you as a coincidence?'

'She's got into your head, Dan. I've been there. Us sales people like to perform, and when things go bad it's a very slippery slope. I know it's hard working with such a high achiever-'

'A high achiever! My sisters are high achievers. Emily isn't even in the same universe as them. She's a lying piece of-'

'Dan! Stop it. Don't say something we'll both regret. Let's talk about it tomorrow. It's not the end of the road, but you need to find your own prospects. You can't keep blaming Emily.'

Dan exhaled sharply. He knew there was nothing else he could say. John was clearly hypnotised by Emily's venomous charm, just as everyone else seemed to be.

Everyone except for Alice. Thank God for Alice.

'Fine, let's talk tomorrow,' Dan said. 'I'm not lying, John. Something funny is going on here.'

'Then it'll sort itself out. Don't worry. Just drive safely.'

'Fine. See you tomorrow.'

'See you then.'

Dan hung up and then spent the rest of the journey ranting to himself about how bad things were.

By the time he arrived at the hotel in Starley Green he

was hugely aggravated and very ready to be in good company. He was looking forward to a beer and some death metal to help blow his frustrations away.

He set himself up at the desk in his room and carried on with a bit of work before he had to get ready.

At about forty minutes before he had to leave, he showered, carefully ironed his new blue shirt, put it on with his favourite jeans, sprayed his new, expensive cologne, lightly gelled his hair and took a deep breath.

This was it. Nothing else mattered now. This was his date with Alice. A moment he'd dreamt about for months and it was finally happening. Everything else would have to wait.

The smile burst back onto Dan's lips as he picked up his key card and left the small hotel.

It was a ten minute walk into town and he felt a chill around him. Things were cooling down and summer was becoming a distant memory, but it wasn't affecting Dan's mood that night.

They were meeting at a pub for dinner before heading to The White Hart where the band was playing at nine o'clock.

He headed into the eatery but he couldn't see Alice anywhere. He took a seat by the window and perused the menu. It was very typical pub grub and that suited him just fine.

'Good evening,' Alice said. He looked up to see her beaming smile. She looked gorgeous. Although she hadn't opted for a sexy dress, her tight T-shirt and jeans flattered her figure and Dan decided that she was perhaps even sexier with a more casual look.

'Good evening to you too.'

'Good journey up?' Alice asked as she took a seat and grabbed a menu.

'Not bad. How's your day been?'

'Very good, thank you. I've been so looking forward to tonight.'

'Me too.' Dan wanted to control his smile. It was starting to ache his face.

'Have you been here long?'

'No, just a few minutes.'

'I've never eaten here. I hope the food's okay.'

'The Steak and Ale Pie is sounding particularly tempting.'

'Good choice. I think I'm just going to stick with the Caesar Salad, though. I'm not that hungry.'

'Is everything all right?'

'Yes, of course. It's just a big night isn't it. It's been a while since I've seen Grave Annihilation. I hope they don't disappoint.'

'I'm sure they won't.'

'Right, what can I get you to drink?' Alice said, standing up.

'No, what can I get *you* to drink?' Dan replied, standing up too.

'I said dinner was on me.'

'And I don't care. Look, I'm all for equality. I'm constantly surrounded by women that are better than me in every possible way. I know full well that men are far from superior and females need anything but looking after. However, I do think there is still a place in this world for chivalry and tradition, and when I go out with a girl I like to pay. Call me old fashioned, but that's how I like it. Please let me have my pride. Don't take it away from me. It's all I've got.'

Alice smiled warmly as she sat back down. 'You are the best man I know. If it means that much to you, I won't argue. I don't think I could argue with that speech. So thank you very much. But I have my pride too, so I'll be paying next time. Okay?'

Dan grinned. 'Okay, you've got yourself a deal.' She was already thinking about their second date. He didn't think he'd ever be able to stop smiling.

Dan ordered the food and drinks and then he returned

to the table. He really wanted to touch Alice's hand and somehow make it feel like a date, but he was too nervous. He didn't know how slow she'd want to take things.

'I don't know how you managed to win that game in the end,' Alice said, snapping Dan from his deliberation.

'When you've got the skills.'

The truth was that after Alice had taken his queen and he'd sent her that message with the fighting talk, Dan had focused more intently than ever to ensure that he won. He'd never put so much effort into a game of chess in his life. So much so, he'd ended up having late nights on both Monday and Tuesday just trying to work out his killer moves.

'I was so sure I had that game in the bag,' Alice said.

'Talking about chess, I have something to tell you,' Dan said.

'You look excited. What is it?'

'Guess what I recently acquired?'

'I don't know. What?'

'A *Lord of the Rings* chessboard.'

'What?' Alice seemed as thrilled as Dan felt.

'It's supreme. You should see it. You'll have to come and see it one day.'

'Have you played on it yet?'

'No. I'm dying to but I need someone to play with. You're the only one privy to my little secret.'

'Our little secret,' Alice giggled.

'I don't know why people have to give you that look when you say you play chess, like there's something wrong with you.'

'I know!'

'It's so much better to play someone you know than a random stranger online.'

'I quite like that we share a naughty little secret,' Alice said with a sly grin.

Dan couldn't resist his laugh. 'Do you have many naughty little secrets with men?'

'Only the men I like.'

'Oh right! That's how it is!' Dan laughed again. How he loved their banter. He had never enjoyed any conversation as much as he enjoyed them with Alice.

Their food arrived and they tucked in. The chatter moved on to stories of their childhood and interesting memories, all the time making each other laugh. Dan was having the best night he could ever remember.

'We'd better get moving,' Alice said looking at her watch as she pushed her plate aside. 'They'll be on stage soon.'

Dan was perfectly happy where he was but he could tell that Alice was eager to see the band.

'Let's go then. Where is this other pub?'

'The top end of town. I've never actually been there, but I know where it is,' Alice said.

'Lead the way.'

They walked side by side still happily chatting as they headed away from the high street towards a quieter end of town. Stuck down a small side alley was The White Hart.

As they entered through the stiff wooden door Dan couldn't believe how big it was inside. It was almost TARDIS like. The outside seemed so hidden and tiny.

Dan could see instruments set up at the front and the place was heaving with what was generally quite a young crowd. And, as Dan had suspected, most of them were dressed in black. It brought quite a dark feel to the atmosphere.

Dan had to fight his way to the bar where he ordered two pints from a very tattooed barman and then they spotted some space where they could stand right in the corner towards the back. It was quite a distance from the band, but Dan didn't think that was a bad thing.

'Cheers,' he said, clinking glasses with Alice. This was anything but a romantic setting, but Alice seemed overjoyed so that was all that mattered.

'Are you looking for people you know?' Dan asked as he noticed Alice scanning the room.

'Yeah. I usually see a few people I know at these gigs.

Always nice to say hello.'

'Will your friend Sammy be here?'

Alice turned to Dan, laughing.

'What's so funny?' he asked.

'It's just... I think Sammy would stick out like a sore thumb in a place like this.'

'I know the feeling,' Dan mumbled.

He watched her as she scanned around for her friends once more. She seemed nervous and excited, exactly as he was. They'd known each other for about eight months and they'd slowly built up an incredibly strong friendship, but Dan was now very ready to take it to the next level.

He wanted to kiss her but it didn't seem like the right place or time. He had most definitely fallen in love with her and he couldn't wait to be with her physically, but he also knew he had to take it slowly. She'd been through quite a lot and she was just getting out and about again.

He knew it was too soon to tell her that he loved her, but he wanted to get his feelings out in the open. They were on a date after all. He should at least be able to say how beautiful she was and how much he liked her.

'I've got to go to the loo,' Alice suddenly announced. There was a real sense of urgency. She thrust her pint into Dan's hand and she pushed her way through the crowd.

The band was coming on soon. Dan just presumed she really didn't want to miss the action.

He scanned the room himself. The place all looked a bit bashed in, as if it wore the scars of many a drunken brawl and no one had considered mending the wounds. Coupled with the fact that the air felt charged with adrenaline, Dan sensed that absolutely anything could happen at any time. This was far from a place that he would normally visit. It had certainly been an eye-opener that Alice would frequent such an establishment.

Dan turned back towards where the toilets were to see if Alice was returning, when he noticed her chatting to a man. He was a good looking man who seemed far too polished to be in such an edgy pub.

Alice's glowing smile lit up her face as they chatted. He must be a good friend.

After a few minutes, Alice fought her way back over to their corner.

'Who was that?' Dan asked as he handed her pint back to her.

'Just a friend,' she said, still smiling. 'Actually, I met him through Karl.'

'Oh right. How is Karl?'

'He didn't know. He didn't even know we'd broken up. But I was sure to set him straight.'

'I'm glad to hear it.'

Whooping and applause rattled through the pub as bearded men appeared at the front and took their instruments. But Dan was concentrating on Alice. He had to tell her how he felt.

'Thank you, Starley Green!' the singer yelled. 'Let's make some fucking noise!'

The cheering intensified but all Dan could think about was telling Alice exactly how he felt.

'Alice,' he said, bringing her attention away from the band.

'Yes?'

'I've...' his words were suddenly blasted away by the most alarming sound. It was like being pummelled by music. And then the singer (if you could call him that) started to scream down the microphone in an unnervingly deep voice, as if it were Satan himself on stage.

'What?' Alice said. Not that Dan heard her, but "what" was easy to lip read.

'I've liked you since that very first phone call we had,' Dan shouted.

'What?' Alice practically screamed, fighting against the agony of the drums and guitars that were being battered on stage. There was definitely some sort of a tune but it was fierce and relentless and it made Dan quite uncomfortable.

The singer began to bellow what must have been actual words, but Dan couldn't make out any of what he was saying. Although Dan thought that might have been a blessing. He didn't look like he was singing about his latest love affair.

'I'll tell you in a minute!' Dan shouted back but Alice just shook her head to indicate that she didn't understand. Dan pointed to the band to tell her it was fine and she should listen to the music that she very strangely liked.

The guitar solo kicked in and Dan had to acknowledge how talented the player was. His fingers were moving quite skilfully, but the sound was intense. If music could be violent, this was a brutal war.

As the microphone took its final bashing, Dan wanted to confess all. This could be an extremely effective form of torture. There was nothing Dan wouldn't do to stop this punishment.

And then it did stop. Almost as quickly as it had begun. Dan sighed with relief as the rest of the room exploded with appreciation.

'What were you saying?' Alice asked, but Dan decided maybe it wasn't the right time for a declaration of his feelings.

'Just that I'm having a good night.'

'Good!'

The ferocious drum beat began to shake the floor once more as another melody kicked in. It didn't really sound much different to the first tune. The singer was banging his head, his long hair flying up and down, before he grasped the microphone and once again barked his gravelly, disturbing tones into it.

Alice put her fingers into her ears. Dan couldn't believe it. He'd wanted to do the same, but he hadn't wanted to seem rude.

Then he noticed her laughing. She was actually laughing. He shook his head as if to query what the problem was and she began laughing twice as much.

Dan couldn't help but laugh in return, but he still wasn't sure what the joke was.

She pointed to the door and mouthed, 'Do you want to go?'

Dan had never nodded more in his life. He gulped back most of the remainder of his pint and then he followed Alice out towards the door.

As they fell out onto the dark street, Alice was bent over with laughter.

'What's the matter?' Dan asked through his own chuckles.

'I am so sorry. That was dreadful!'

'What do you mean? I thought you were a fan?'

'God no!' Alice could barely breathe she was laughing so much.

'What?' Dan was now too in hysterics. 'Why did we come here, then?'

Alice took a few breaths to control her giggles. 'I just saw there was a band playing and I thought it would be a good excuse to invite you up. I thought it might be nice to spend some time together. I didn't know what death metal was. I had no clue it would be so deafening.'

Dan's giggling subsided as he felt the power of Alice's words.

'You didn't need to invite me to a band to get me here,' he said, moving in closer to her. 'I would have come up to stare at a wall with you.'

'That might have been less damaging to our hearing.' Alice was smirking but Dan wasn't finding the humour anymore.

He took another step closer so that he was just millimetres away from her. He looked down at her face. Her beautiful face. And then he focused on her lips. All he'd wanted to do all night was kiss those lips, and finally the right time had arrived.

'Babe, are you leaving?' The door opened letting the din pour out onto the street and a man approached them. Dan recognised him as the man that Alice had been speaking to earlier.

'Yes, I think we'll have to,' Alice replied. 'Sorry. We thought we'd give Grave Annihilation a try but it's not for us.'

'Yeah, they are noisy aren't they,' the man replied. 'I'm only here because I know the lead guitarist.'

'Yeah, you said.'

'But don't go. They get better. They've got some good songs coming up.'

'I think we'd prefer somewhere a bit quieter,' Dan said.

'Oh right,' the man said, seeming to acknowledge Dan for the first time.

'I'm Dan, by the way.'

'Sorry, yes,' Alice said. 'This is Dan, a friend from work. Dan, this is Ethan.'

'All right,' Ethan said and Dan just nodded. 'So are you two on a date or something?'

'No!' Alice immediately replied. She couldn't have emphasised it more. Dan felt winded. 'Dan's up for the night for work so we thought we'd catch up. That's all.' Alice's words were like harsh blows striking at Dan's core. He instinctively stepped away from her.

'Just mates then?' Ethan asked.

'Yes. Totally. Just mates. Like I said, it's over between me and Karl. I'm not seeing anyone else.'

Alice couldn't take her eyes off Ethan and Dan wanted the world to swallow him up.

'So I'm free and single, if you wanted to go out sometime?' Her proposition was aimed very much towards Ethan.

Ethan started to smile. Dan didn't like that smile at all. It made his skin crawl. 'I'm up for that,' Ethan said to Alice. 'Give me your number.' He handed Alice his phone and she typed her details into it. All Dan could do was watch. He had never felt so hurt.

'Are you sure you're not going to come back in?' Ethan

asked.

'You go if you want,' Dan said. 'I'm actually not feeling too well.'

'Are you all right?' Alice asked him, finally remembering that he existed.

'Must be that pie. I don't think it agreed with me.'

'You've gone really pale.'

'If you're going to puke, mate, mind the shoes,' Ethan said.

'I think I'll head back to my hotel.'

'Come on babe, I'll look after you,' Ethan said, grabbing Alice's hand.

Alice stared into the windows of the pub, and then she looked between Ethan and Dan.

'I should go with Dan,' she said. 'Make sure he's okay.'

'It's fine,' Dan said. 'Please, stay with Ethan. Enjoy the band. I'll speak to you soon.'

With that, Dan turned on his heels and marched right off.

'Dan!' Alice called but he pretended not to hear her.

Alice ran after him. 'I'm really worried about you. Are you sure you're going to be okay?' she said, stopping him.

'I just feel a bit sick suddenly. You've got a friend, so why not stay here. Seems a shame to cut the night short just because I'm not well.'

'Do you want me to come back with you?'

'I just want to be on my own.'

'Are you sure?'

'Go and enjoy the band with your friend.'

'But you know I can't stand Grave Annihilation,' Alice said with a smirk.

'Then why did you invite me to see them?' Dan snapped. He had never been so serious.

'Babe, come on, I'm getting cold,' Ethan shouted. 'I'm going in.'

'Please, go with him,' Dan said.

Alice hesitated. 'Are you all right?'

'Go and have a good night,' Dan said.

He looked into Alice's eyes and felt more pain than he'd ever imagined possible.

'See you soon.' With that, Dan left Alice standing on the street. She didn't follow him this time and he was both relieved and devastated.

He didn't even know where he was walking. He walked around the streets of Starley Green for about an hour, the events playing over and over in his head. Why had she invited him up if it wasn't a date? Did she have any feelings for him at all?

He eventually made it back to the hotel. He ordered a pint and took it up to his room. He sat on the bed and felt stupid, alone and absolutely grief-stricken.

Had he just lost the only woman he'd ever loved?

TWENTY

Alice watched as Dan marched off. She considered following him, but he seemed so mad. She reasoned that when she'd felt sick in the past, she'd just wanted to get to a toilet. She hadn't wanted people fussing over her. Maybe it was best to leave him to it and then she could check up on him later.

'Babe, come on!' Ethan shouted as he held open the door to the pub. Dan was out of sight now. It was too late to follow him. Alice hoped he'd be okay. Had she done the right thing leaving him?

She followed Ethan back into the pub, telling herself that Dan would want her to be happy. She should just enjoy the rest of the night and then check on Dan later.

Ethan signalled to ask if she wanted a drink and she nodded. She pointed to the lager pumps and smiled. Any would do. It was impossible to communicate properly against the enormity of the music, so she decided any drink she got, she'd be grateful for.

He handed her a pint, for which she acknowledged her gratitude with a bow of the head, and then she followed him to where his friends were standing, closer to the stage.

The relentless blasts of music carried on for what felt

like hours, with Alice and Ethan standing side by side barely able to say a word to one another against the racket.

Finally the singer announced they'd be taking a short break and Alice almost collapsed with the liberation of this respite. Similar noise was piped in through the speakers around the room, but it was nowhere near as deafening.

'They're good, aren't they?' Ethan said.

'They certainly get a lot out of their instruments,' Alice replied. It was the only good thing she could think to say.

'Babe, sorry I'm late!' A loud, animated voice came from behind them. Alice turned around just as Flick was throwing her arms around Ethan. She kissed him on the lips. 'Have I missed much?'

'They're just on a break,' Ethan replied.

'Oh well, I'm here aren't I? He can't be too pissed at me.'

'Hello again,' Alice said, catching Flick's attention.

Flick glared at her. 'Who are you?'

'I'm Alice. Remember? I was dating Karl.'

Flick shook her head.

'We met in Strikers,' Alice clarified. 'I looked a bit different then.'

'Alice?' Flick said, as if it were all coming back to her. 'As in my Prosecco sister?'

Alice shrugged. 'I guess so.'

'Babe! It's so lovely to see you!' Flick kissed Alice wetly on the cheek. 'Where's Karl?'

'We broke up.'

'She dumped him,' Ethan chipped in.

'Oh no!' Flick moaned, like it was some sort of tragedy. 'Although, I suppose not a surprise really. Come on, I need the loo.' Flick grabbed Alice's hand and pulled her towards the toilets. Alice had just seconds to shove her drink into Ethan's grasp before she was dragged away.

Flick headed straight for a cubicle but Alice didn't need to go. She waited by the grotty sinks that stood beneath cracked, yellowing tiles, not really sure what she was doing there.

'Are you with Ethan now? Is that why you're here?' Flick called through the cubicle door. There were other ladies in the area and Alice hated having to shout back an answer.

'I was here with a friend but he had to go home. I just bumped into Ethan.'

Alice heard a flush and the door sprung open. Flick strode out like she was auditioning for the catwalk.

'Ethan's gorgeous, isn't he,' Flick said as she washed her hands. 'Or do you like them little and fat like Karl?'

'No. I mean yes. Ethan's very attractive. Are you here to see Ethan?'

'No, I'm shagging one of the band,' Flick explained as she took her lipstick out of her jacket pocket. 'That's why Ethan's here. We're all sort of friends now.'

'Oh right. Is he like your boyfriend? The band member?'

Flick guffawed and it seemed to echo around the toilet. 'You're so funny.'

'Am I?'

'I'm far too young to settle down. Yeah, he's like a total sex god, but I can't say he's marriage material. So we just hook up every now and then.'

Alice thought about the hairy, heavily tattooed, rather intimidating band members. They weren't her cup of tea, but then again Flick was under the impression that Alice had fancied Karl. She wasn't in a position to question anyone's tastes.

'That's nice,' Alice said, unable to think of anything else to say.

'They'll be starting again in a minute. We'd better go. He'll bloody kill me if he thinks I've missed the gig. I won't be getting any for weeks.' Flick examined her face and hair one last time and then she grabbed Alice's hand and led her back out of the toilets.

'Had fun?' Ethan said as he handed Alice her drink

191

back.

'Oh yeah. It's always fun in the toilet.'

'Stop it, you'll get me jealous.'

The applause and cheers shook the room as the band reappeared, and Alice knew she'd had enough. She wasn't enjoying herself, she knew she wasn't going to get any time to chat to Ethan, and she was still fretting about Dan's sudden sickness.

'I'm going to go,' Alice shouted in Ethan's ear just as the next tune started burrowing through her brain. She saw Flick run to the front, waving her arms about to make sure that she was seen. It was definitely time to go.

'What?' Ethan shouted back.

'I'm going!' Alice pointed to the door.

'Going?' Ethan mouthed back to which Alice nodded.

She knocked back the rest of her drink and Ethan signalled that he would follow her.

Once outside, Alice felt like she could breathe again.

'You're really going this time?' Ethan asked.

'I've got work tomorrow,' she replied.

'Are you sure?'

'Yeah, but thanks for a nice night. I'm glad you've got my number now. I'll see you soon, maybe?'

'What are you doing tomorrow night?'

'Nothing,' Alice replied as joyful anticipation danced through her.

'Well, you've got plans now. You're coming out with me. I'll text you some details.'

'Okay. Sounds good.'

Ethan moved in to kiss her goodbye. The second his lips touched hers, Alice's sexual drive sparked into action. It was like he was a magnet drawing her in, and she couldn't resist pressing her body against his as he devoured her mouth.

'See you, babe,' he said, pulling away, leaving Alice most definitely yearning for more.

'See you tomorrow,' she replied, her lips tingling with

an uncontrollable smile.

Alice waved goodbye and then she headed up to the main high street to where there was a stream of taxis waiting.

Within minutes, she was home. She let herself in and she flopped straight on her sofa.

Everything was now deathly quiet and she became horribly aware of the ringing in her ears. She dreaded to think what damage had been done. The band had been unnecessarily loud.

She took her phone out of her pocket to check on Dan. She decided a message might be best, in case he was asleep.

Just got home. Wasn't the same listening to Grave Annihilation without you. How are you feeling now? I hope you haven't been too sick. We won't go back to that pub, I promise! Thanks for a lovely night. Sorry it ended so suddenly. Thinking of you. xx

Alice waited a few minutes to see if he'd reply, but he didn't. Feeling tired from the beer and the music, she plodded upstairs and tucked herself into bed. She rested her phone on her bedside table and checked again to see if Dan had replied. He hadn't.

TWENTY-ONE

The next thing Alice knew, her alarm was going off. It was seven thirty am and she felt quite rough.

Her ears were still ringing and her head was pounding. Maybe she'd caught Dan's bug too.

Dan!

She quickly grabbed her phone from the bedside table to see if he'd replied, but nothing had come in overnight.

She sat up as an image of him all alone in his hotel room shook her. What if he'd been violently sick all night? Someone should be there to look after him.

She decided to message again.

Hi, how are you today? Any better? If you'd like me to come to your hotel, let me know. Please don't suffer in silence. I'm always here if you need me. x

She pressed send and then she got up, ready to begin her busy day.

By mid-afternoon she still hadn't heard from Dan and she'd become quite concerned. He normally messaged back straight away.

She'd tried to call him a couple of times but it had just

rang out. She couldn't bear the thought of him lying in a hotel room, all alone and probably throwing up relentlessly, whilst cursing Alice for taking him for that pie.

She'd checked his work calendar repeatedly to see if his meeting had been cancelled, but it was still there. And by now it should have been over with.

Maybe she could call the office to see if Dan had turned up? Maybe he'd staggered in asking for help in his sickly state and John had driven him straight to the hospital? No one would think to inform Alice.

She picked up her phone and quickly dialled the office number, now sure that something was very wrong.

'Good afternoon, Blooms Security Solutions. You're through to Alistair, how may I help?'

'Hi, could you tell me if Dan White has been in the office today?'

'Dan, our Business Development Manager?'

'That's the one.'

'I'm sorry, he's not based in the office. I can transfer you to his mobile, if that helps?'

'No, I just want to know if you've seen him? This is Alice Bloom and I know Dan hasn't been very well, so I wondered if he made it in for his meeting today?'

'Alice Bloom?' Alistair checked. 'As in the daughter of Norman Bloom?'

'Yes, that's me. Please could you tell me about Dan?'

'It's an honour to speak to you.'

'Thank you very much.'

'I've heard so much about your father. He did amazing things for this business.'

'Well, it was his business. You would hope he cared. Anyway, could you tell me if Dan has been in today?'

'Of course. No problem. Yes, he did come in today for his meeting. He looked fine. He left about half an hour ago saying he'd got a busy weekend. He didn't mention an illness.'

'Oh.' Alice felt quite thrown by this. Dan being fully in

action was the last thing she'd expected to be told. 'Well, that's good news then. I'm sure it was just a twenty-four hour bug thing. Good to know.'

'Can I help you with anything else? I know a couple of other people have called in sick today. Do you need to know about them?'

'No, it's fine. Dan and I are friends but I couldn't get him on his phone. I was just being silly and worrying, clearly over nothing. I'm glad to hear he's fine. Thank you so much for your help.'

'You're friends with Dan?'

'Yes. Do you know him well?'

'Oh yes. But I know everyone. Perks of being the receptionist.'

'Of course.'

'Is there anything else I can do for you today?'

'No, you've been very helpful, thank you. Have a lovely weekend.'

'You too!'

As Alice hung up she felt sad and a bit peeved. Why hadn't Dan responded to her messages?

She told herself there had to be a good reason. He'd probably got up late, then he'd had to dash to the office where he'd had his meeting, before he'd jumped straight back in his car to return to London. When was he supposed to message her?

No doubt before the day was out he'd call her and they'd share a funny story about it all. She just had to give him time. They were close friends; it wasn't as if he was ignoring her for no reason.

Having given herself a little break from her worrying, Alice got back to her programming. There were a couple of hours left and then she was going to start getting ready for her first proper date in years. The thought popped the smile back on her face. Although deep down she was still very anxious about Dan's sudden radio silence.

Alice was meeting Ethan that evening at the Wetherspoons pub in town. He hadn't offered to meet her for dinner, just for drinks at eight o'clock. She would have preferred to go for food. She thought a restaurant was a much better setting for a first date, but she had no desire to argue with him. She was, truthfully, just over the moon to be going on a date with him at all.

She entered the pub a few minutes early. She looked around, but Ethan had yet to arrive.

She ordered herself a glass of white wine and she found a table as near to the door as possible so she could spot him enter.

It was nearly quarter past eight before he swaggered in, and she was getting quite edgy.

'Hi babe!' he said, kissing her cheek. 'Can I get you a drink?'

'I've got one, but thanks.'

'Nonsense. What are you having?'

'I've still got half of this left.'

'What is it?'

'A Chardonnay.'

'No, like, what is it? Is it white wine?'

'Oh. Erm... Yes. White wine. A Chardonnay.'

'Cool. Back in a sec.'

Alice had forgotten how Ethan could make her head spin, and not in a good way. She told herself he was just nervous and she sipped at her drink while she waited for him to order.

She watched him as he chatted to the girl behind the bar for quite a while. He was clearly flirting with her, but Alice chose not to get jealous. What was the point? She was on a date with him, not that other girl. Ethan was just one of those flirty types, obviously.

He finally headed back to the table with a pint for him and a glass of rosé wine for her.

'Did they run out of white wine?' she asked.

'I don't know. Why?'

Alice's eyes swayed between the two different coloured drinks in front of her, but she decided to say nothing.

'How's your day been? Have you been at work?' Alice asked.

'Yes. I have to work every day. It's tough when you're at the top.'

'You work weekends too?'

'Oh yeah. I mean I get a couple of days off in the week, but it's hard. When everyone else is out partying on a Friday night, I have to be thinking about work the next day.'

'But you get a couple of days off in the week?'

'I like your attitude. You have a way of looking at the bright side of everything. You're very cheery. I like that. Too many girls are miserable or bitchy. I've dated quite a few girls who spend all their time bitching about their friends or moaning about their lives. You're not like that. It's good. It's refreshing.'

'I've done my fair share of moaning, believe me.'

'I like to think that I'm a positive person. It can get really difficult at times. You know, life. But you've got to look at what you've got, not what you haven't. See what I mean?'

'Totally. I mean look what you've got. You've got a great job, recently promoted-'

'Did I tell you about that? Yes, I completely transformed the Starley Green branch. They were begging me to take the promotion.'

'You said, yes.'

'Sorry, you were going to say something else. So rude of me to interrupt. You were going to tell me what else I've got going for me.'

Alice smirked, interpreting his words as flirtatious. 'Well... I was just going to say... You're quite good looking too.'

'You think so?'

'You know you are.'

'You know, when I die, I'm going to come back as myself. I really am.'

Alice burst out laughing, expecting Ethan to be joking, but his face didn't flinch.

'Seriously?' she asked.

'Do you not believe in reincarnation? I'm totally into all that shit. Coming back. Some people are definitely coming back as bugs. Tiny little ants that live for like a day. That serves them right. I'm coming back as me.'

Alice sipped on her drink as she tried to think of a response. She neither believed in the after-life nor could she get her head around his comments. Was it pure arrogance or cleverly ironic? She really wasn't sure.

She heard her phone go off in her clutch bag that was lying on her lap. Maybe it was Dan at last. She needed to check.

'When you say it would serve some people right to come back as an ant, what sort of a person are you referring to?' Alice asked. She really didn't care, she just wanted to ask him any question so she could subtly check her phone while he answered.

'Weedy little blokes.'

Alice was just opening her bag when she stopped. 'Weedy little blokes?' Had he really just said that?

'Yeah. You know the sort.'

'Why should being weedy mean you get punished in the after-life?'

'You're not getting punished. You're coming back as the thing that sums up who you are today. So like muscly men might come back as a rhino or something, and weedy men will come back as an ant. Do you see? That's how it works.'

'I don't think it does. Not that I believe in reincarnation, but I think those who do see it quite differently.'

'No. No. I am right. You know people say you are what you eat?'

'Yes,' Alice replied, cautiously.

'Well, when you come back, you are what you were, but... oh... what's that word?'

Alice shook her head. 'I don't know.'

'Metaphysically.'

'That seems deep.'

'No! Metaphorically. I mean metaphorically.'

Alice paused so she could properly consider his logic. 'You're saying that reincarnation is the act of coming back to life as a metaphor of your previous self? Like your physical self?'

'Yes.'

'What?'

'It makes perfect sense.'

'Does it?'

'Oh yes.' Ethan pointed to his temple. 'I'm not just a sexy beast, you know.'

Alice sipped on her wine again. She really couldn't work out whether he was incredibly clever and there was another plane to his thinking, or whether he was a complete stupid idiot. It could be either. She hoped it was the former.

Her phone went off again. She had to check it.

'A guy as good looking as you must have had a lot of girlfriends,' Alice said, trying to think of something that would get him talking while she checked her phone without seeming rude.

'Oh yeah. Hundreds. You lot can't resist me.'

Alice smiled and nodded. 'Tell me about your first ever girlfriend.'

'My first ever one or my first proper one? Because I was only five when I had my first kiss. Not a proper kiss, but we said we were boyfriend and girlfriend for like half an hour, until she fell over when we were playing kiss chase and never spoke to me again. Like it was my fault!'

'Your first proper girlfriend.'

'Oh right. Well there's not much to say really...'

Alice tuned him out, just nodding at periodic moments as she carefully slipped her phone out of her bag and checked it under the table.

Both of the notifications were marketing emails. There was nothing from Dan.

Where was he? What was he doing? Why hadn't she heard from him?

She checked her WhatsApp to see when he was last online. He hadn't been active since the night before. So maybe he wasn't just ignoring her. He must be busy. That Alistair had said Dan had got a busy weekend. He was probably out. Alice had to stop worrying.

She might be able to convince herself to stop worrying, but she couldn't banish her disappointment. It might only have been about twenty-four hours since she'd last seen Dan, but she was actually missing him.

She picked up her rosé and tasted it. She wasn't a fan of rosé wine but she didn't want to be difficult.

'...I've never met anyone like you,' Ethan continued as Alice tuned back in. She realised she really should be listening to him. 'That's what she said. She didn't know if she would ever get over me. But I couldn't be tied down to one woman. It's not fair.'

'Not fair?' Alice asked, trying to catch up with Ethan's epic story.

'Not fair on anyone. I wanted to sow my seeds. How could I do that in a relationship?'

Alice admired his honesty and the fact that he'd broken up with his partner rather than cheating on her. 'When you're young it's the best time to sow those seeds, I suppose.'

'Oh, it definitely is,' Ethan agreed. 'Do you like sowing your seeds?' He stroked Alice's hand. Despite his words always sending her head in a spin, his touch was titillating.

'I've been a bit out of practice lately. But I'm thinking it's time to change all that. At least let one man into my life.'

'One lucky man.'

Alice could feel the smile rise on her lips. 'A very lucky man.'

'Could I be that lucky man?'

'Are you feeling lucky tonight?'

'Oh babe, I feel like I'm about to win the Euro Millions.'

'Aww.'

He moved to sit next to her.

'No, seriously, it's a double rollover,' he said.

Alice fell silent but then Ethan laughed.

'Just kidding,' he said. 'I mean I have got a ticket, but I am pulling your leg too. Although imagine if I scored you and scored on the lottery. What a bloody good weekend that would be!'

'You're going to score me, are you?'

Ethan squeezed her hand. 'Being with you would make any man a winner. I see you as getting a hat trick in the FA Cup. It's something we all fantasise about, but imagine if that dream came true.'

Alice was starting to get confused. Was that meant to be a compliment?

He kissed her and she instantly forgot about the hat trick. Her body fizzed with delight at his touch. As he drew away, she saw a group of girls behind him all staring in jealousy.

In fact, as Alice scanned her surroundings, she noticed quite a few pairs of eyes looking on. She had never felt so visible and that excited her even more. Ethan was having an astounding effect on her.

'Shall we go back to yours?' he whispered.

'Now?' she said, already breathless at the idea of it.

'I want to get those clothes off and put my lips all over your body. I want to feel the heat between us and I want to hear you beg for more. I'm going to give you everything.'

Alice's toes curled up. She was very, very horny. It had been far too long and an incredibly sexy man was offering himself to her. She knew she'd be completely mad to turn him down, or even delay a second longer.

'Shall we get a taxi?'

TWENTY-TWO

The second that they entered Alice's bedroom, Ethan started tugging at her cardigan. They barely took breaths between the deep, fervent kissing and Alice's whole body was yearning to be touched. Intimately touched.

Ethan stepped back before spinning on his heel, stopping right in front of Alice's full length mirror. Alice used the moment to push Sammy on the floor.

'Oh baby,' Ethan said, admiring himself. He began unbuttoning his shirt in front of his own reflection.

Alice stepped forward to help him out when she heard her phone vibrate from her bag that she'd haphazardly thrown aside.

It could be Dan. At last. In fact, who else could it be?

She went to grab her bag when Ethan spun back around, hurtling his shirt across the room.

'Now it's your turn,' he purred, moving in towards Alice and slowly removing her T-shirt. He cupped her breasts as he kissed her again and she felt spasms of lust.

He pushed her to the bed and carefully removed her jeans before kissing her some more.

Her body began thrusting against his, like it couldn't get enough of the magnetic hold he seemed to have over her, but her mind kept flipping back to her phone. She had to check her phone. What if Dan needed her? He could have been in a car crash; he could be facing a serious problem. She had to find out why there had been such a delay in him messaging her back.

Ethan began moving down her body, nibbling at her in places no one had touched for a very long time. But she couldn't take her eyes off her bag.

Could she nip over there quickly? What could she say?

Ethan suddenly shot off the bed and popped back over to the mirror. He danced around a bit, seemingly for his own enjoyment, and Alice took her chance. She sat up and edged off the bed, but before she could reach her bag, Ethan flipped back towards her.

He carried on his little dance as he stripped off his jeans, although the striptease appeared to be for his own pleasure more than anything as he still had one eye on his own reflection. Once he'd thrust his jeans to the floor, he posed once again for himself, and then he whisked off his boxer shorts too. Finally he gave Alice his full attention as he outstretched his arms and flexed his muscles.

'I am the perfect specimen of a man,' he said, standing completely naked in front of her, with no hint of irony.

Alice scanned his body. He most certainly was attractive and definitely had nothing to be ashamed of. There was just something about his arrogance that was leaving a sour taste.

He turned around again to admire himself and she nipped quickly over to grab her bag.

'Do you like what you see?' Ethan asked. She wasn't sure whom he was talking to, and he seemed completely oblivious to the fact that she was now crouched on the floor yanking her phone out of her tiny black bag.

She had a text. She had a text!

She scanned her iris and her phone flashed up with the notification. This time she felt more than disappointment.

The message was from Karl.

I heard ur out with Ethan tonight. Ur a using bitch and nothing but a slag. I hate u & hope u die.

'Well?' Ethan said, turning back towards Alice. Surprised that she wasn't on the bed where he expected, he asked, 'Are you okay?'

Alice felt stabs of pain but she couldn't be sure exactly what they related to. Hurt from Karl's horrible words? Guilt that he might actually be right? Or perhaps frustration that she still hadn't heard from Dan?

Maybe all three?

'What is it?' Ethan asked, kneeling down to join her. 'Babe, what's the matter?' He wiped away a tear with his thumb. Alice hadn't even noticed that she'd started crying.

'I've just had a text from Karl.' She turned her phone towards Ethan so he could read it.

'What a wanker. Just ignore him. As if Bladder could ever really bag a girl like you. He needs a reality check.'

'Do you think he'll fall out with you?'

'He wouldn't dare. Not that I give a shit. He's just pissed off. Ignore him. You're not a bitch. Far from it. And you're certainly not a slag. You've kept me waiting long enough. And... well... it's me.'

Alice smirked. 'Yes it is. I never wanted Karl. Maybe I did use him. No, I definitely used him. But I didn't mean to hurt him.'

'He's got to get a life. He has no right to message you like that.'

Ethan grabbed her phone, and just as he did, Alice noticed her hand vanish. She quickly swiped it behind her back out of view. Her heart began pounding with the fear that she was about to disappear all over again. This would be the worst possible timing.

'He's all gone now,' Ethan said, handing Alice back her phone. 'That's all the message was worth. Ignore him.'

Panicking, Alice thought through what to do. But she was crouched awkwardly and it made it difficult to do anything.

Ethan reached out for her. She tried to back away, but quickly lost her balance. Instinctively she put her hand out to steady herself, before gasping at the realisation of what she'd done. Her eyes flicked down to see how bad it looked. She almost fainted with relief when she saw her hand fully in view again.

She sat back and took a deep breath.

'Why are you letting him get to you so much?' Ethan asked. 'Come on. You're about to get the best sex you've ever had.' Ethan flashed his devastating smile and Alice couldn't help but giggle.

Maybe it had been her imagination. She had to relax.

Alice took another deep breath and Ethan helped her to her feet. As soon as they were standing, their lips reunited. As the passion increased, Ethan removed her underwear with a swift glide of his hands, and they edged back towards the bed.

She grabbed a condom from her bedside table drawer, and between their kisses he mumbled something about how it might not be big enough. She sniggered as he climbed on top of her and she finally started to relax.

The sex was short but mind blowing. Alice lost herself completely as Ethan pumped hard against her, and it seemed no issue at all for either of them to climax.

As she caught her post-orgasm breath, Alice couldn't wipe the smile off her face. That had been worth waiting for. She desperately wanted to do that again.

'Thanks babe,' Ethan said. 'That was amazing.'

'I enjoyed it too. Very much.'

Suddenly her phone vibrated again. She could see it lit up on the floor. It had to be Dan. It had to be! Karl wouldn't be messaging again, surely.

She nipped across to pick it up.

'What are you doing? You're not messaging him back, are you? Do you seriously have a thing for Bladder?'

'What?' Alice replied, scanning her iris quickly. 'Of

course not. I'm just moving my phone from the floor so we don't tread on it in the night.'

'No fear, babe. Don't worry.'

Alice's head dropped with disappointment as she saw it was another marketing email. Since when did she get so many? That was just plain cruel.

'I'd better leave you to it,' Ethan said, standing up.

'What do you mean?' Alice asked, her attention now fully on Ethan.

'I can tell you're distracted.'

'I'm fine. Please stay. Please. I was hoping we'd have sex at least three or four more times.'

Ethan's sparkling smile spread across his face. 'Oh baby. You're looking to wear me out? Bring it on.'

They only managed to have sex once more before Ethan fell fast asleep. Snoring loudly next to her, Alice knew she was in for a restless night. And not in a good way.

All she could do was lie there and watch her phone. It sat on the bedside table next to her, and her eyes barely left it. She was ready to respond whenever the notification came through.

But by the time Ethan woke up, ready for more play at around seven o'clock in the morning, Alice's phone hadn't budged at all.

TWENTY-THREE

Ethan lay back on the bed with a sweaty glow.

'That's set me up for the day now, babe. Thank you very much,' he said.

Alice went to say you're welcome but she stopped herself. It somehow didn't seem right.

'You've got to work today?' she asked instead, propping her pillow up to get comfortable.

'Like I said, I work every day.'

'Except for the days you have off in the week,' Alice commented with a sly smile.

'If I get them. Sometimes I have to go in on my days off just to stay on top of things.'

'But I'm guessing mostly you don't go in if you don't have to.'

Ethan regarded her suspiciously. 'What are you trying to say?'

Alice hesitated. 'Nothing. Nothing at all. I'm just trying to get to know you better. Is that okay?'

Ethan got up off the bed and grabbed his shirt. 'I suppose.'

'Do you want to know what I do for a living?' Alice asked.

He shrugged. 'Sure.'

'I-'

'Don't tell me you're like a stripper or something?'

'What? Why would you think that?'

Ethan just shrugged again.

'I'm the Technical Director of a security solutions company, based here in Starley Green.'

Ethan glared at her but said nothing. He grabbed his jeans and finished getting dressed.

'Technical Director?' he eventually asked after he'd checked himself out in the mirror.

'Technical Director.'

'What do you do? Is it like security guards? Oh no, technical. So like robots?'

Alice rolled her eyes. She didn't understand where this obsession with robots came from. 'We design and manufacture all sorts of products. Day to day I... basically I just write code.'

'What does that mean?'

'It means I look after the software that goes with... our robots. Whatever. My job title is Technical Director, and I suppose I should be more involved in R&D, but... things haven't panned out that way.'

'Panned out?'

'I had a...'

'What?' Ethan seemed more in need for the conversation to end than actually being interested in what she was about to say.

'It's occurred to me lately that I don't quite know how it all happened. I thought I was doing the right thing. I was so young, and there was so much going on in my life. On paper, I'm still the major shareholder, but in reality I don't have much to do with the running of the company. They so easily accepted it. I was grateful at the time, but now I wish they'd put up more of a fight. They probably couldn't wait to get control.'

'Hang on,' Ethan said, sitting down next to Alice on the

bed. 'You're a major shareholder in a business? Like you own most of it? That sort of shareholder?'

'Yes.'

'Is it a big company?'

'I suppose. About an eighty million pound turnover.'

'Fucking hell!'

'What?'

'So you're like mega rich?'

'I'm comfortable,' Alice said, now feeling anything but comfortable.

'You're getting dinner next time, then.'

'Next time?' Alice asked.

'Yeah. Too right. I have to see you again, babe. You're a good laugh and a great shag. And believe me, I'm fussy.'

Alice sat back. It seemed like a compliment, whilst at the same time it also offended her. He was such a master of confusion. She really didn't know what to make of him.

'I'll have to shoot,' Ethan said, jumping to his feet. 'I'll message you. Let's do it again soon.'

'Maybe one night when you don't have work the next day?'

'Sounds good to me. I'll check the rota.' Ethan smacked a kiss on her lips. 'See you. I'll let myself out.'

'Okay,' Alice replied, but Ethan was already running down the stairs.

As the door slammed shut, Alice immediately grabbed her phone. There was still no message from Dan and now she was getting very worried. She was starting to question whether it was her.

By Wednesday morning, Alice still hadn't heard from Dan. She'd had a few texts from Ethan and they were having their second date that night, but Dan had seemingly disappeared off the face of the planet.

Alice had called and texted him every day, but nothing. Not one response. The only conclusion she could come up with was that he was deliberately ignoring her. Although she couldn't work out why. What had she done? It wasn't her fault he'd been sick on the night of Grave Annihilation. Maybe he'd really hated the band? But so had she. She'd admitted it.

Alice couldn't concentrate. She was sitting at her desk, trying to polish up some areas of her new Proximity Sensor, but her brain wouldn't engage with anything except for concerns over Dan. She'd begun to feel sick that she was about to lose her best friend. She needed to speak to him. She needed to see him.

In a flash, an idea came to her. She had no clue where he lived in London, but he frequently came up to the Midlands. She could speak to him then. She knew exactly where he'd be.

She opened his calendar up on her computer and she found herself pleading that he would be up again soon.

As if the universe had answered her prayers, she saw, in a striking green colour on her screen, that Dan was in the Midlands at that very moment. He was on an in-house training course and he was just a mile down the road from her.

She took a deep breath.

She hadn't been to the office since the day after the funeral. She hadn't been in nearly five years. Could she really just waltz back in there as if it were perfectly normal; business as usual?

She stood up with determination. It was her dad's company. On paper it was now her company. She could do what she liked. She had to face it again sometime. She might as well get it over with.

She raced to her bedroom. If she was going to face those people again then she had to look her best. She wriggled out of her jeans and put on a smart black dress, finishing the look with a cute pink cardigan. Professional but not overboard. It was perfect.

Next she brightened up her face with some make-up and she tied her chaotic hair back in a clip. She admired her look.

It was good. Not great, but a definite improvement.

It would do.

Butterflies tickled her stomach, although she couldn't be sure what she was more nervous about: going to the office or facing Dan? What was she going to say to him? What would he say to her?

She had to conclude that she'd offended him in some way. But it wasn't as if they hadn't had crossed words before. They'd argued about all sorts of things on the phone. Okay, sometimes it was superficial, like which was the best *Die Hard* film, but other times they'd debated bigger issues. Whilst they mostly shared the same political views, there had been times when they'd wildly disagreed. But it hadn't mattered. They'd enjoyed the fight and the next time they spoke it was all forgotten about. It was how they worked as friends.

But this was different. And she needed to find out why.

She grabbed her jacket and bag, slipped on her shoes, and made her way out the door before she could think any more about it.

A cool breeze chilled her as she walked up the street towards Starley Green. The office of Blooms Security Solutions was located on an industrial estate on the edge of the town; the other side to where Alice lived.

The journey should have taken her about twenty-five minutes, but she was marching on, desperate to get it over with.

She made it in nineteen, her heart pounding and her legs like jelly. She caught her breath as she stood on the side of the car park.

The car park was dedicated to her dad's company and it was packed full. It seemed far busier than the last time she was here.

Her mind flashed back to the day the building opened. It was one of the few times she'd seen her father emotional. He'd made a moving speech about how he'd taken developing cameras in his garage to a fifty strong team in just five years. It had been an exhilarating journey, and Alice felt the sting of tears herself as she considered how proud her dad would be now. It was such a shame he'd never get to see the company move from strength to strength.

She momentarily wondered where they would be if he was still in charge. Would it be doing even better? Had she made the right decision in stepping away from the board or could she have boosted business even more? Did a Bloom need to be in charge for the company to truly maximise success?

She sighed, realising it was all irrelevant. It was what it was. Whatever her dad may have wanted, she hoped that he would understand the decisions she'd made.

Her legs were still trembling as she cut across the car park to the front doors of the building. It looked different somehow. A lick of paint maybe?

She knew they'd updated the logo. She hadn't been invited to cast an opinion. Not that she had ever shown an interest. But she was coming to realise that maybe if they'd encouraged her she might have got more involved. Maybe it wasn't that she backed away, maybe it was that they had so easily let her disappear from sight.

She shook her head. She couldn't keep playing this over in her mind. It was what it was. Decisions had been made.

Her fingers were shaking as she pushed the glass door and entered the corporate reception.

It smelt of new carpet and her feet sunk into the plush navy blue pile. She immediately felt annoyed by how much the carpet must have cost. Was it necessary? Was money being wasted?

The enormous TV on the wall was showing Sky News. Sky? Why not Freeview? And there were cosy, stylish chairs in matching blue surrounding a classy glass table near it.

Last time she was here there had been no TV and just a small sofa in the corner. What was with all this expense?

'Can I help you?' the man behind the reception desk asked.

As Alice turned around, her mouth dried up. Who was she here to see? Did she need to declare it like a visitor, or could she just walk around wherever she wanted, as, technically, she owned the majority of the place around her?

'Hello,' she said, walking over with her hand extended. The man politely shook it. He was young and incredibly smiley.

'Do you have an appointment?' he asked.

'No. Actually... I'm Alice Bloom.'

The man gasped. It seemed far too dramatic.

'I'm Alistair! We spoke on the phone. What an honour to finally meet you.' He shook her hand again, his grin expanding.

'Oh yes. Hello, Alistair. Lovely to put a face to the voice.'

'You're here!'

'I am.'

'What brings you here? Not that you have to tell me. Obviously none of my business. But what brings you here?'

Alice took a breath. 'Curiosity. It's been a while and I believe that some of the sales team are in training today. I thought I might pop my head in and see what's going on.'

'The sales team?' Alistair asked with confusion.

'Yes.'

'None of them are in. Oh, except for Dan. Yes, I saw him earlier. And John, of course. But he's normally in. I don't know anything about training.'

Alice didn't know what to say. Although it didn't really matter. Dan was in the office and that was the only reason she was there.

'I might just head on up anyway. See what's going on.'

'Of course.'

Alice pointed to the door that led to the heart of the building. She felt she needed permission, even though she was technically Alistair's boss.

'Do you have a pass?' Alistair asked before he chuckled. 'What am I saying? Sorry.'

'A pass?'

'A security pass. It's kind of what we do here. As you'd know.'

Alice thought back. She'd never been given a pass before, but she'd also never wandered in on her own before. She'd always been with her dad or one of the other directors.

'I don't have a pass,' she said, feeling embarrassed.

'Oh.'

'I suppose I should get one arranged. Who would I speak to?'

'HR normally sorts them out. Maybe Vivienne could help?'

Alice nodded although she had no clue who Vivienne was. 'Right. Could you just let me up for now?'

'Of course I can. I'll just need you to sign in first.' This time it was Alistair who looked embarrassed. 'I'm so sorry. It's just health and safety and all that. I have to record all visitors. Not that you're a visitor. But anyone who forgets their pass has to sign in. I'll be in serious trouble if you don't. I'm so sorry.'

'It's fine. I totally understand.'

'I know you're not really a visitor. It's just the way-'

'It's fine.'

Alice signed her name and the date in the book, leaving out whom she was there to see. She placed down the branded pen (another unnecessary touch, she felt) and smiled at Alistair. He pressed his secret button and the door popped open.

'Thank you very much,' she said.

'Have a good day!'

She stepped through into a corridor and headed up the main staircase. The sales team had always sat near the back of the first floor, she remembered. She just hoped they hadn't moved.

She opened the door at the top of the stairs just a crack, and the hubbub of the office environment came rushing through. Phones were ringing, groups were nattering, keyboards were clicking and people were wandering about.

It was alive. So different to the silence of her home during the day.

She edged through the door, nervous that someone might spot her and make a big deal about it. But generally everyone was just getting on with their work. Which she was extremely glad to see.

She glanced down the office and she could see Dan right at the end. He was on the phone. A small smile tickled her lips as she watched him chat away to what she assumed was a client. He looked so confident and cool, like he owned the conversation. Like he was good at his job.

Like he was someone you could be really proud to work with.

Like he had this way of making your heart beat faster.

She placed very little emphasis on the fact that her heart was now throbbing dramatically. All other thoughts left her head as she focused on the one man that she was desperate to talk to.

Needing to limit who saw her, she walked towards the wall. Using some of the desks as barriers to hide her, she made her way towards him.

She stood to the side of his desk but he didn't seem to notice.

'Whatever time is good for you,' he said into the phone. 'That's perfect. Like I said, I'm free all day.' She watched him scribble "11am" on his pad. He was left handed. She hadn't known that before. How could you know someone so well, know someone for so long, and not know such a fundamental detail about them? Something about it made Alice warm and cosy, as if learning this about Dan somehow brought them closer together.

He glanced up, as if he'd noticed someone was standing next to him, and then he did a very sharp double take as he realised who it was. His eyes became larger as he took her in, his face full of surprise. She remembered that he had brown eyes, but they weren't as dark as Ethan's. They were light and friendly, and now they were staring right back into her blue irises.

'Yeah, sorry, I'm still here,' Dan said, turning away from Alice to concentrate on his phone call. 'No, it sounds great. You have a good day too. See you next week. Yeah. Cheers.'

He ended his call before his head turned immediately back to Alice.

'What are you doing here?' he asked.

'I came to see you.'

This seemed to totally throw him. 'You came to see me?'

'Why have you been ignoring me?'

Dan fumbled around with his mobile, like he was checking the call had properly ended. 'Why do you think I've been ignoring you?'

'Because you have. I can see your phone very clearly in your hand and so you must have received my messages. And calls. It's been nearly a week. We normally speak to each other all the time. Why have I not heard from you? I've been worried.'

Dan sat back in his chair like he was contemplating something deep and important. 'When was the last time you came to this office?'

'What?'

'When was the last time you were here?'

Alice took a second before replying. 'About five years ago.'

'Five years. It's been five years? You haven't been here for five years, but now, because I didn't call you back, you've come all the way down here just to speak to me?' He sat forward again. 'Or are you here for something else?'

'I came here for you,' Alice muttered, feeling instantly ridiculous. 'As I said, I was worried. I thought we were friends and yet since you walked off from me last week I've heard nothing. Are you mad with me?'

Dan shifted in his seat. He started fiddling with his phone again, as if he were checking for messages.

'Why would I be mad with you?' he asked, not looking at her.

'I have no idea. Are you mad that I made you sick?'

His head flicked up towards her. 'Sick?'

'You said you were sick. That's why you left me. You went really pale. Were you okay?'

Dan shook his head. 'Yeah. Fine. I was just tired or something.'

'I messaged you loads of times the next day. Why didn't you let me know you were all right?'

'Did you know I was here today?' Dan asked. 'Did you look at my calendar?'

'It was the only way I could get an answer. I was really concerned. I saw you had training and so I grabbed my bag and walked up here.'

Dan examined the screen of his phone, as if he were searching for barely visible hairline fractures.

'Did no one else turn up for it?' Alice asked.

'What do you mean?'

'That Alistair on reception, he said you were the only salesperson in today. But your diary said there was sales training.'

'There was training.'

'So did no one else turn up?'

Dan's eyes narrowed in on his phone as if he'd found the tiny imperfection that he'd been trying to locate.

'What's going on?' Alice asked. 'Why are you being so quiet with me?'

'There was sales training today,' Dan mumbled. 'Just not sales team training.'

'What's the difference?'

'It was just for me.'

Something about Dan's tone made Alice's blood boil. She grabbed the chair from the empty hot desk behind her and manoeuvred it so she was sitting next to him.

'What's going on?' she asked quietly. She could spot eyes across the room starting to notice her and she could detect faint whispering. She found it deeply uncomfortable, but Dan's welfare was far more important.

Dan hesitated before he edged his chair closer to her. 'John has had some concerns about my performance,' he uttered, his voice low and serious. 'I'm kind of on a warning. He thought it best to give me some sales training to help me improve.'

'What?' Alice screeched. The rage was now flaring through her.

Dan seemed to like her reaction. His tense frame relaxed. 'It's become a joke, Alice. No matter what I do, Emily is there. She's practically selling to every bloody company across London. I'm using every tactic I can think of and every contact I've ever made to get as many leads as I can, but it seems no matter where I go or who I speak to, Emily is five steps behind on making contact and then half a step faster at closing. It's all so blatantly unethical, but because she's raking in the customers and I'm barely bringing in pocket change, no one will touch her. I don't have a fighting chance. I've gone from being head hunted because of my talent to being patronised and barely keeping hold of my job. I don't know what to do.'

'Oh Dan, I'm so sorry.' Alice squeezed his hand. He had firm hands yet such soft skin. Everything about him was like a block of strength finished with a soft glow that melted her heart. She didn't know whether to give him a huge hug or a fighting pep talk.

Dan squeezed her hand back. Alice was all too aware of the audience that could see them chatting, but only she and Dan knew how their fingers were now interlocking. It was so intimate. She wanted the moment to never end, whilst also feeling the urge to hide under the table, away from the curious eyes that were peeking at them from every angle across the room. She could feel the intensity of the stares like a thick, claustrophobic gas, but she couldn't move.

Dan slid his fingers more tightly between hers, and Alice felt a surge of electricity shoot through her.

Was he now protecting her or was she still comforting him? The lines had blurred.

It was as if he could tell how uncomfortable the hushed gossip was making her, but his touch eased her concerns and gave her a strength she badly needed.

How did he manage to know her so well when she was still learning so much about him?

Well, she knew one thing for sure.

'You're a fantastic salesman,' she whispered so only he could hear. 'I know that for a fact. I also know that none of this is right. As soon as I heard Emily's charmless voice, I knew she was up to no good. It will all work out. Please have faith. My father would never let a good man like you go, and neither will John. She'll get caught out eventually. Just hang on tight.'

'You think I'm fantastic?' Dan asked.

'One hundred percent. I've never met anyone like you. You're quite simply amazing. That's why I was so worried. I couldn't bear the thought of anything having happened to you. And I couldn't bear the thought of us not being friends anymore.'

'Friends?' Dan asked.

'I hope so. Is that why you've been silent? Because you've been worried about work?'

Dan instantly let go of Alice's hand and wheeled his chair back so he was sitting properly at his desk.

'Dan?'

'Alice?' A female voice from beside them cut into their conversation. 'Alice Bloom?

Alice looked up to see the stern face of Linda, the company's Financial Director.

'Hello,' Alice mumbled. Her heart began racing again, but this time it felt heavier.

'I heard the rumours flying around, but I couldn't believe it,' Linda said. 'I take it you're here for the board meeting?'

TWENTY-FOUR

Alice didn't know how to respond. All she could manage was a weak nod of her head.

'Shall we walk together?' Linda asked, taking it that her assumption was absolutely correct. Her voice was kind but Alice could tell it was masking discomfort. Discomfort that Alice equally shared.

Alice stood up slowly. She'd never actually been to a board meeting and it really was the last thing she wanted to do. But she was in the office and there was no sound reason why she shouldn't attend.

'Yes, that would be great,' Alice said, sporting the best fake smile she could muster.

Alice turned to Dan. His eyes were bearing into her.

'Enjoy your meeting,' he said.

'Thank you,' she said, hesitating. There was so much more that she wanted to say to him. If only she could come up with a reason to get out of the board meeting, or at least delay her attendance.

There wasn't any rational excuse, though. A director of the company had turned up shortly before the start of the board meeting. It was hardly an odd conclusion for Linda to make that Alice was there to join them. It wasn't even as if Alice was at the office for business matters. Saying, 'I'll be along in a minute, I've just got to finish catching up on the gossip,' wasn't really a good enough reason for them to delay the meeting.

Feeling she had no option at all, Alice took a step forward to follow Linda.

'I didn't know,' she whispered to Dan as she made her way around his desk. 'I came here to see you.'

Dan opened his mouth to say something, but nothing came out.

'Are you coming?' Linda asked.

'Of course,' Alice replied as politely as she could. 'Speak to you soon?' she said to Dan.

'You'd better get to your meeting,' was all he could say in return.

Alice stalled again. Their conversation felt so unfinished.

'Alice,' Linda nudged, her eyes now piercing.

'Coming,' Alice said. She glanced back at Dan before walking with Linda across the office.

'You should have let us know you'd be in,' Linda said with a small laugh, as if it didn't really matter.

'It was a last minute plan. Very last minute.'

Before they reached the corner, Alice turned back one last time towards Dan. He was still watching her, but there was nothing more she could do.

They'd speak later. They could always speak later.

How she hoped they'd speak later.

Alice looked on ahead as they reached the boardroom doors. It was all exactly how she remembered it.

'The board will be very happy to see you,' Linda said, still trying to hide her lies.

'And I can't wait to see them,' Alice replied, joining in with the pretence.

Linda opened the door to reveal three men in suits. Alice immediately recognised the incredibly shocked faces, as if it had only been five days since she'd last seen them, not five years.

'Alice!' Kelvin said, coming forward to greet her. He was the current Managing Director. He'd been friends with her father for a long time and had invested heavily in supporting him when he'd decided to grow the company. Kelvin was now in place running things as the next largest shareholder under Alice.

'Hello,' Alice said, formally shaking his hand, all the familiarity between them a distant memory.

'The rumours were true then,' Steven said with the hint of a snarl, before he took his turn to shake Alice's hand. He was the Operations Director, although Alice had always been suspicious of exactly what he operated. She'd never particularly liked him, but he had a glowing track record and her father had needed his expertise.

'I can't comment,' Alice replied. 'I haven't heard any rumours.'

'It's wonderful to see you,' Charles said, swiftly grabbing Alice's hand and giving it a firm shake. He was the Marketing Director and had always been Alice's favourite of the senior team. He'd come highly recommended, and had proven his worth time and time again. Alice knew him only in a professional capacity, but she had a lot of respect for him.

'We weren't expecting you,' Kelvin noted.

'I already said that,' Linda replied. Linda had worked with Alice's father before Blooms Security Solutions had opened. She hadn't hesitated in taking a seat on the board when the opportunity arose. She could be harsh but Alice had always trusted her.

'It was a last minute decision,' Alice explained. 'I thought it was time I got back into the swing of things. But please, just pretend I'm not here. Carry on as normal.'

Unsure glances were cast across the room, but no one said a word.

'Can I get you a drink?' Charles asked, breaking the tension.

'I should get the drinks in,' Alice said. 'You start the

meeting. If you could just remind me where the kitchen is?'

'No, we're self-sufficient now,' Charles laughed as he pointed to the fancy coffee machine towards the back of the room, like he was showcasing a prize on a game show.

'What is that?' Alice asked. 'How much did that cost?'

'Far less than the time it takes for people to walk back and forth between here and the kitchen, meeting after meeting,' Linda chimed back with, still sporting her false grin.

'I'll have to take your word for that,' Alice said. 'I'll have a coffee, please.'

'But which variety?' Charles said, like he was the Willy Wonka of the coffee world.

'You choose,' Alice said, her pulse racing over the unnecessary expense that these directors had wasted on what was seemingly only for their own personal enjoyment.

Alice took a seat at the large table while Charles played barista. Alice guessed that the coffee machine was his idea. He was enjoying it far too much.

'I took the liberty of printing you off a copy of the board report,' Linda said, handing a thick wad of paper to Alice. 'Just in case you'd forgotten to bring a copy.'

Alice nodded. 'Thank you. I had indeed forgotten to bring my copy.' Alice was always emailed all the board reports and minutes of the meetings, but she couldn't remember the last time she'd even opened the email, let alone downloaded the report. She'd meant to. She'd wanted to. But ever since she'd taken a step back from the board, she'd felt it wasn't her place to interfere.

But she was here now and she was having no choice but to take part.

Her perfect coffee was placed before her and it smelt divine.

'Thank you,' she said. She grabbed her glasses from her bag and put them on so she could properly partake in the meeting. She looked at the document before her, with its tiny print. Even with her glasses on, she still had to squint a little to read it properly. A quick smile caught her lips as she realised she could finally go for an eye test. It was a small but wonderful feeling.

She began flicking through the pages when her smile disappeared. It was littered with jargon that she didn't understand. Her father may have brought her up to be business minded, but that didn't mean she was well versed in the lingo. She felt a sense that she was about to struggle deeply.

What on earth was EBIDTA?

'Can we all turn to the minutes from the last meeting?' Kelvin said, after all the coffees had been distributed. The whole room smelt like an Italian café.

Alice noted how all eyes were waiting for her to catch up, and she quickly flicked through to the page they were referring to.

Kelvin started to talk, but Alice was too busy glancing through the detail to pay any attention. She was hoping if she read ahead, things might start to slot into place. But it just left her feeling even more out of her depth.

She flicked on, ignoring the discussion that was now starting around her. About halfway through, she got to the budget and she stopped. This she was very interested in.

She focused on the numbers, trying to make sense of them. Trying to determine how much money had been wasted on frivolities.

'What?' she said. She wasn't really sure whether she meant to say it out loud or not, but she was glad she did.

'Is there a problem?' Kelvin asked, obviously irked.

'Is this right? Is there more budget for marketing than there is for research and development?'

'What's the issue?' Steven curtly replied. 'We are trying to run a business here.'

'Yes, a business that sells cutting edge technology. Our USP has always been that we're ahead of our competitors in terms of product development. How can we sustain that if we're focusing more on marketing?'

'It's all very well to have state of the art products,' Kelvin explained, 'but if we don't tell anyone they're available then no one will buy them. And then we'll all be out of a job.'

'There needs to be a balance,' Linda added with a softer tone, as if somehow that clarified everything.

'I'm not saying marketing isn't important,' Alice stated, 'I'm just questioning why the balance is so much in marketing's favour?'

'We've cut the R&D budget every year for the past three years and you've never mentioned it before,' Linda observed.

'Well, now I am,' Alice responded.

'I know product development is your remit, Alice, but as a board we have to consider all elements of the business,' Kelvin said. 'Customers buying our products is what equals success.'

'No. No it absolutely does not,' Alice argued.

'So you think we'd have success with no customers?' Steven mocked.

'It's not the fact that customers buy that has made us successful. It's why customers buy. My dad was always categorically clear about that. They can get cameras and access control from anywhere. We have dozens of very decent competitors. But we go further than any of them. We have the best tech with the best software supporting it. Our prices may be high, but the return on investment our customers receive is very fast and very real because we offer them unrivalled quality. It's not enough to have lots of glossy marketing campaigns saying these things, we need to actually be doing these things and proving our worth. Then the marketing will speak for itself.'

'I think that's a little naïve,' Steven stated.

'Did you think my father was naïve?'

This silenced the room.

'I may have lapsed slightly in keeping up to date with what's been happening since my parents' passing, but I knew full well what was happening when my father was in charge. I read his business plans and I know he put product development ahead of everything else. You said it yourself, you've only cut the budget since you've been in charge. It's not what he would have wanted.'

'Maybe not,' Kelvin immediately stated. 'But when he was here there was someone totally focused on product development. There isn't anymore.'

'I focus on product development!' Alice argued.

'Your new release this year was brilliant, and very worthy of the award it won. But we never see you. Glenn is good but he is not at your father's standard, and he isn't capable of doing what your father did.'

'Like you are,' Charles added.

'How are we supposed to push R&D if the person ultimately in charge of R&D isn't here to push it?' Despite Kelvin's gentle tone, his words cut deep.

Alice took a breath. Everything was changing around her. Her life had been on hold for far too long and it was about time she properly took control. She wasn't going to be a victim anymore.

'At a young age,' she said, 'I lost my family. Everything I knew and held dear. I told you back then that I wasn't the best person to run the company, and I was right. But you all so very easily agreed with me. You didn't fight me on it. You all happily let me take a back seat while you grabbed a hold of the reins. Well that has to end. Today. This company is not a seller of security products, it's a developer of high end technological security solutions. That's how my dad grew this business so quickly. He didn't care about fancy coffee machines and plush carpet, he cared about protecting people in the best possible way, and he used his technical expertise to make that happen. That's the company we will be finding our way back to. Do you understand? Enough is enough. I'm going to rework this budget and I look forward to meeting with you at the next board meeting where we will be discussing our new R&D led approach. I am sure no one has an issue with that. Thank you very much.'

Alice stood up. That had felt good. Very good.

'Where are you going?' Kelvin asked.

'To get on with the work.'

'Right. Okay. Erm... I have no issue with you preparing a revised budget for us to review. It has to be a well thought through plan, but you're right, Norman always wanted us to be open to change and to think progressively.'

'So we're all agreed then?' Alice said, trying to hide her triumphant grin.

'We agree that we'll discuss your proposal at the next board meeting, yes,' Linda said.

'Good.'

'But we have other things to discuss now,' Linda added. 'Aren't you staying for that?'

Alice felt her cheeks flush. She sat back down.

'Of course,' she mumbled. 'I guess my enthusiasm got the better of me. Please continue.'

Alice focused on her coffee, too embarrassed to look at her colleagues.

'Shall I add that to any other business?' Steven said.

'Yes. Please do,' Kelvin replied. 'There's no harm in jumping about, I suppose. But, for now, let's go back to the minutes from the last meeting. Is that okay?'

All eyes focused on Alice and she smiled sheepishly. 'As I said, please continue.'

She flicked back to the relevant section, her eyes burning a hole in the paper as she was too afraid to look elsewhere.

After the three hour, torturous meeting finally ended, Alice couldn't wait to get out of there. She hadn't contributed much else. Partly because she felt too stupid and partly because she had nothing else to add. It all seemed far too much like corporate nonsense, but maybe she'd get used to it.

She shook everyone's hands goodbye and there were murmurs of how much they were looking forward to her proposal next month, and then Alice dashed back to Dan's desk.

Only he was gone.

She thought about messaging him, but she didn't really know what to say. There was so much she wanted to tell him, but at the same time nothing felt right.

All she could do was hope that they'd speak very soon.

TWENTY-FIVE

By the time Alice got home it was too late to start working on her new business proposal. She had to get ready for her date.

She jumped in the shower and enjoyed the sensation of the hot water as it washed away the stresses of her day.

She stood, motionless, not feeling any energy at all. Shouldn't she be looking forward to her date with Ethan? She felt anything but excited.

But then she had just been through quite a big day. That board meeting had been epic.

As soon as she was out the shower, she put some uplifting music on, hoping it would perk up her mood. She slipped into her new blue dress, opting for the smart casual look, and she perfected her hair and make-up, trying to spruce up her forlorn face. Not that it seemed to work.

She rubbed her cheeks, desperate to spring some life into them. This was ridiculous. She should be thrilled.

By seven o'clock, Alice was slouched on her settee awaiting Ethan's arrival. She was playing a random person at chess since Dan still hadn't had his go.

She was focusing intently on her move when, like a flash, her hand suddenly disappeared again. She could see her phone, but it was seemingly floating in the air just by her wrist.

She threw her phone down and shook her hand, willing it to reappear. She couldn't go on a date like this!

The doorbell rang and Alice stood up, panicking. What was she going to do? It rang again.

Could she pretend she wasn't in?

She looked down, her heart pounding, and her hand popped back into view. It had just been another freaky blip. She'd have to keep an eye on it. This could get messy.

The doorbell rang a third time and Alice shakily raced over to answer it.

'Hello,' she said, trying to look composed. 'Sorry to keep you waiting.'

'Hi babe,' Ethan said. 'It's okay. There aren't many girls I'd wait for. But I'd happily wait for you.' He moved in and kissed her firmly.

As always, he looked incredible. His checked shirt was tight, enhancing his muscly physique, and his chinos flattered his strong, long legs.

He presented a small bouquet of flowers from behind his back, still with the Dobson's logo and price stuck to them.

'Thank you,' Alice said, telling herself that the gesture mattered more than the £2.99 price tag.

'I know all girls love flowers. And they're pink as well. Because all girls love pink.'

'Of course we do.'

'Are you ready?' he asked.

'Absolutely. I'll just get my shoes on.'

Alice popped the flowers in a vase quickly before she grabbed her ballet pumps.

'Where are you taking me then?' Ethan asked as Alice locked the door.

'What?'

'I said you'd get dinner this time. It's only fair.'

'Fair?' she asked, remembering the single drink he'd

bought her on their last date.

'Well, you're rich. So it's only fair.'

'I never said I was rich.'

'No, you said comfortable. Which is rich people's language for saying they're filthy rich. I mean look at this house!'

Alice didn't know what to do. She had no issue at all in buying him dinner, but she wasn't sure if she liked his attitude.

'Babe, don't look at me like that,' Ethan said. 'I'm just testing the water, that's all. Most girls only go out with me because they see a flashy guy who's got big muscles, a gorgeous face, a fancy car and designer clothes. I'm sick of gold diggers. I'm not after you for your money, don't worry. I just wanted to make sure you weren't after me for mine.'

'You have money?' Alice asked, her head spinning as always, trying to keep up with him.

'I'm comfortable,' he replied with a wink.

'Okay.' He was such a conundrum, but Alice decided that made him fun. 'I tell you what. Since we're both comfortable in our own ways, how about I get the food and you get the drinks. That seems fairer.'

Ethan hesitated. 'Depends on what you're drinking.'

'How about a cocktail before dinner, wine with, and then a beer or two after. You don't have work tomorrow, so let's make a night of it.'

Ethan considered his response. 'When you say "wine with" that's food-drink. Therefore you have to buy that.'

'Food-drink?'

'Yeah. Drink you have with food. It's part of the meal and therefore goes hand in hand with the cost of food.'

Alice chuckled. 'Fair enough. I'll get the wine and the food and you get the rest. You drive a hard bargain.'

'Oh babe,' Ethan said, wrapping his arm around her. 'Lots of things about me are hard.'

Alice laughed. 'Yes, I'm starting to see that.'

'You have no idea.'

'I really do.'

They walked on towards Starley Green, arm in arm.

'What fancy car do you drive then?' Alice asked.

'I have a Golf GTI,' Ethan replied full of pride. 'It's got silver paintwork with a black trim. Very classy.'

'A Golf?' Alice queried with surprise.

'I always wanted one. My first car was a Corsa. It was all right, but it didn't say anything. I wanted a car that made a statement.'

'You mean like a Ferrari would?'

'That's so predictable.'

'You're right. A Golf is more unusual.'

'That sounded like sarcasm. I don't think you understand. Let me tell you about cars.'

Alice wasn't able to get another word in during their entire walk into Starley Green. She was told the top twenty reasons why a Golf was better than any other car that existed today. Including supercars. She didn't listen to most of his lecture. She was instead still contemplating exactly how serious he was. Was this another challenge that she was supposed to unravel?

They sat down in Strikers, able to get a seat easily this early on a Wednesday evening, and Alice perused the cocktail menu.

'I think the surprise element is the best, though,' Ethan said, still justifying his choice of vehicle. 'You're at the lights, some jumped up Audi next to you, revving his engine like he's waiting for the lights to go out at Silverstone or something. He thinks I'm in a little car that's going nowhere. He's not aware of my 242 brake horsepower, the fact that I can go nought to sixty in six point four seconds, and that I'm driving it with my legendary skills. He thinks he's got it in the bag and then we go green. I leave him to choke on my dust. Wanker.'

'Who's in the Audi again?' Alice asked, even more confused than normal.

'What?'

'Is this someone you know?'

'No,' Ethan tutted, like she was an idiot. 'It's a metaphor. For people who think they're great but are really shit.'

'Oh. You're into your metaphors aren't you.'

'It's better than being into robots.'

'I quite agree,' Alice said. This seemed to stump Ethan and Alice enjoyed a moment of peace.

'Two Zombies then?' Ethan asked without even looking at the choice of drinks on offer. 'Hang on, am I buying these?'

'Yes, because these aren't food-drinks, are they?' Alice couldn't help her cheeky smile.

'No,' Ethan replied, chewing his lips. 'Fuck. What about a vodka and coke? Oh no, you girls prefer vodka and cranberry don't you.'

'I was thinking a Mojito actually. I've never tried a raspberry one.'

Ethan scanned the menu. 'Fuck that shit. You're having a vodka and cranberry.'

'I don't like vodka,' Alice stated, not best pleased with Ethan's tone.

'What's wrong with vodka?'

'Am I not allowed my own free choice? If cocktails are too expensive-'

'It's not that. It's not the money. It's the principle. I only ever buy them when they're two for one. Otherwise they're vastly overpriced and it's a complete con.'

Alice obviously knew this was utter rubbish, but she really didn't care that much to argue.

'If you'd rather we stick with a single spirit – if that sits better with your principles – then I'll go for rum, please,' Alice said.

'A rum and cranberry?'

Alice pulled a face. 'I think coke might be better with rum.'

'Fine,' Ethan said. Before she could say another word,

he was heading to the bar.

As she waited, she took out her phone from her bag to play a bit of chess. She'd barely even had a chance to look at it, though, when Ethan arrived back, placing two rum and cokes on the table.

'Thank you,' Alice said, taking a sip. 'I suppose a Cuba Libre is a cocktail too,' she added, trying to lighten up his sour face.

Ethan stared at her blankly. 'What?'

'A Cuba Libra.'

'What language is that?'

'What?'

'Are you speaking Cuban? Is that what you're saying?'

'You mean Spanish?'

'You were speaking Spanish? Wow. Say something else.'

'Paella, por favor,' Alice said with a giggle.

'Wow. What does that mean?'

'Are you serious?'

'How am I supposed to know? I never did Spanish at school. I did German. I hated it. I suppose you can't be good at everything. I mean, I was top of the class and all. I just wasn't very good compared to the other subjects I did. I was really good at Maths.'

'Me too. That was my favourite subject.'

'Yeah, like trigonometry and stuff. I loved all that.'

'Oh yes, me too. To maths!' Alice raised her glass to clink his. He clinked back and nodded.

'I've got to be in London tomorrow,' he said, 'so I can't go too mad with the drinks.'

'You said you didn't have to work tomorrow.'

'I don't.'

'What are you in London for then?'

'Training.'

'What sort of training?'

'I don't know. Stock rotation or something.'

'With Dobson's?'

'Yeah.'

Alice sighed. Conversing with Ethan was exhausting. 'So it is work?'

'No, because I'm not doing my normal job.'

'Are you getting paid for tomorrow?'

'Yeah. Too right. I told them I want everything on expenses.'

'Right, so it is kind of work.'

'What are you getting at?'

Alice paused. The truth, that was all she wanted. But it seemed like far too much effort. 'A day in London sounds fun,' she conceded with. 'I suppose you'll be visiting Head Office?'

'Yeah. I've got to go down and see how the factory works. Like the warehouse or something. They reckon me knowing how it all fits in together will make me better at my job. Or something like that.'

'That makes sense.'

'It's meant to be a massive site. I hope it doesn't go on for hours.'

'In London?' Alice asked as something clicked in her head.

'That's what I said.'

'A massive warehouse?'

'Yes.'

'Do you have security for it?'

'You mean like a security guard?'

'CCTV? Access control? Anything like that?'

Ethan shrugged. 'I don't know.'

'I would love to have a word with whoever's in charge. We'd have to see the site, but we might be able to save you money. I bet you anything we could improve security. Do you think you could put me in touch with someone? Think how good you'd look if you managed to increase security whilst saving the company money.'

Ethan seemed impressed. 'Yeah? You could do that?'

'If you get me a contact, I'll give you all the credit. Say it was all your idea.'

'Definitely! How about I ask them tomorrow, see if they're interested?'

'Just a call. Just a no obligation phone call. That's all I ask. I'll get one of my best sales people on the case. Just get me a contact and I'll do the rest.'

'You reckon I could save them money?'

'There's a good chance. People think buying cheaper equipment is the way forward, but it's about the set up. That's so often overlooked. But it's what we do.'

'Okay. Great. Leave it with me.'

Ethan reached out to hold Alice's hand. 'You're so hot,' he said and then he made a sizzling sound.

'Thank you,' Alice replied, trying not to laugh.

'How about we skip dinner and go back to yours?'

'Aren't you hungry?'

'Oh yeah. I'm hungry for you, babe. We could have a shag and then you could order in. What do you say?'

Alice wanted to argue. She wanted a date. She didn't want everything to come down to sex.

But she also found him incredibly attractive and she was still aching for human touch to make up for her drought.

'All right,' she said, her libido once again taking charge.

'Great.' Ethan knocked back his drink. 'Come on.'

Alice knocked the remains of hers back too, and then he grabbed her hand and practically dragged her home.

TWENTY-SIX

That Friday Dan was working from home. He'd spent the morning reluctantly trying to find new prospects, but his heart wasn't in it. He had this sinking feeling that whatever he did, Emily would just steal his hard work right at the very last second anyway. It made all of his efforts such a big waste of time.

An email came through from John. It was the latest sales figures. John emailed real time reports every Friday in a bid to incentivise the team into action. But all it did was make Dan throb with misery.

Dan opened up the attachment and his depression plummeted to an all new low.

Emily had doubled her target and he was at eighteen percent. Eighteen percent? It was shameful. In his previous job just getting one hundred percent had been a bad month for him. He didn't know what to do with himself sitting at eighteen. He'd never struggled like this in his life.

Although the truth was he wasn't struggling. He was making plenty of contacts and he was easily getting people interested in the products. He was even getting them to review his quotes, often favourably. Then just before they signed on the dotted line, Emily would somehow miraculously interfere and snatch the job for herself.

He was at his tiny table, which doubled as a desk during the day. He stared at the figures on the laptop. It wasn't just that he was doing worse than Emily, he was the worst performing member of the team by far. And had been now for the third month running. It was absolutely mortifying.

His phone rang and he saw it was John calling.

'All right, mate,' Dan said, answering the phone.

'How's it going?'

'I've just opened your email.'

'That's why I'm phoning. Don't worry, there's still time to turn it around. Remember what we discussed on Wednesday in the training.'

Dan felt utterly humiliated. 'I said it then and I'll say it again. The only issue I have is that Emily is forcing her way in to my deals right at the last minute and undercutting me. There aren't any smart sales tactics on the planet that can counteract backstabbing.'

'Dan, we can't keep going over this.'

'You're right. You need to look into it.'

'Maybe it's not sales training you need. What about some more product training?'

'I know these products, John. I know them better than bloody Emily. Test me if you don't believe me. Go on, ask me anything.'

'You need to stop comparing yourself to Emily. You have to find your own way.'

'I have been! She's the one who's constantly encroaching on my space. Not the other way around.'

'You keep saying this over and over, but you still haven't been able to come up with any evidence. Or even an explanation. How exactly can she be doing all the things you're accusing her of? I've even let you stop updating the CRM because you said she was obviously spying on you. I'm trying to support you, mate. I really am. But you're making it very difficult. You're hiding all your activity now, so the only way left that she can be doing any of what you claim she's doing is if she's got some sort of psychic link to you. Are you saying she's psychic?'

'Don't be stupid.'

'And I have spoken to Emily. She said she thinks the clients have been playing you off against each other to get the best price, and she always goes in slightly lower. She hasn't been bad mouthing you. Quite the opposite.'

'Doesn't it concern you that we're both constantly speaking to the same prospects?'

'Yes it does. It does greatly. London should be big enough for the both of you.'

'It would be if we worked as a team.'

'If you were making all these contacts and building all these relationships, just as you say you are, Emily shouldn't be able to swoop in and steal the deal. Should she? Do you see how it makes no sense to me?'

'It makes no sense to me either.'

'You have to stop blaming Emily. If you put half of that energy into building your client base, I'm sure you'd be at target by now.'

'Oh-' Dan bit his lip. He knew telling his boss to fuck off wasn't going to do him any favours.

'You know I like you, Dan. That's why I fought for you. But maybe you're out of your depth in this job.'

Dan felt a fiery anger ignite within him. He took slow, deep breaths, desperately battling with his urge to tell John where to stick it.

But he couldn't be out of work. He couldn't be a failure.

'Look, let's focus on next week,' John said. 'Emily has agreed that all the London leads gained will be split fifty fifty between you and her.'

'Isn't she generous.'

'She's not the enemy here.'

Dan scoffed as the burning anger pumped through him. 'The show's in Birmingham. I can't see us getting many London leads.'

'It's the biggest security exhibition on the calendar.

There will be London firms there, trust me. Two or three good leads will sort you out. It will give you your confidence back.'

Dan squeezed his pen firmly in his hand as he took more slow breaths, determined not to lose his temper with his boss.

'I've got a meeting. I'll have to go,' John said.

'All right.'

'Have a good weekend and I'll see you at the NEC on Tuesday. Eight am, don't be late.'

'It's in the diary.'

As Dan hung up, his body was shaking with rage.

His phone immediately rang again and he went to answer it before he saw it was Alice calling.

He stopped moving.

His rage slipped away as sadness and hurt flooded into its place.

A few weeks ago he would have been so glad to hear from her. He could have moaned about John and Emily and she would have said all sorts of supporting things. She always had this way of knowing exactly how to soothe him. Something no one else had ever managed to achieve.

But he couldn't speak to her now.

It wasn't that Dan had fallen out with Alice. He had no intention of never speaking to her again. He just didn't know how to speak to her at that moment.

Seeing how she'd been flirting with that Ethan bloke had shredded Dan's heart. She'd never flirted with Dan. Not really. He might have fooled himself at times into thinking their banter was flirtatious, but that night he'd seen the truth.

Dan was a friend. He might be a good friend, but a friend was all he was. And being a permanent member of the friend zone was the last place he wanted to be.

He just needed some time to come to terms with it. He loved Alice far too much to cut her out of his life. But then he also knew if he didn't get some distance he'd never get over her. He didn't want to constantly be taunted by something he could never have.

He focused on his laptop again, deciding the best thing to do was to get lost in his work. Then a WhatsApp pinged through from Alice.

Just calling to say hi! Call me when you're free. Hope you've had a good day? x

Dan shook his head. He couldn't keep ignoring her. Not only was it killing him not speaking to her, but she was so bloody persistent. He was sure it would piss him off if he wasn't so desperately in love with her. He replied:

Sorry, I was on a call. Got a really busy afternoon, then I'm out tonight with the lads. I'm actually away this weekend. Catch up next week?

The truth was quite different. Dan had cancelled all of his plans. Instead he'd decided to spend the entire weekend moping about and feeling sorry for himself.

This was deeply unusual for him. His weekends were normally jam packed. He'd make time to go to the gym, he'd often meet up with the lads, maybe go and see Watford play. If he wasn't spending time with his family, he'd perhaps meet his mate for badminton or go and visit his other mate up north. He might have even played a bit of chess.

But ever since he'd met Alice, his life had been thrown into turmoil. All he wanted to do was sulk about.

His phone pinged back a message.

Where are you going away to? Sounds fun! I'm not up to much this weekend. Looking forward to some time at home, it's been mad lately. Hope you have a good one. Definitely catch up next week. Speak Monday? x

Dan rested his head on his table. This was so difficult.

He hated having to lie, but he couldn't tell her the truth. If he said "I'm doing absolutely nothing at all except staying in bed and feeling sorry for myself" she'd be straight on the phone. He needed her to disappear out of his life for a while. As much as he hated it, it was what he needed.

He sat up and quickly replied.

Family stuff. Long, boring story. Hope you have a good one.

He hoped it was vague enough that she wouldn't message back. It invited nothing in the way of a response.

Setting his phone down, ready to get back to work, Dan once again pored over the sales report.

Eighteen percent? It was crushing.

TWENTY-SEVEN

By the following Tuesday afternoon, Dan's mood hadn't lifted at all. He'd spent the whole weekend in his pyjamas in a state of self-pity, and his Monday had been lived under a dark, gloomy cloud. He couldn't get Alice out of his head and everything about it hurt.

As he'd predicted, she'd called first thing Monday morning. She'd left a message saying she'd got exciting news and he should call her back as soon as possible. But unless it was to say that she was now single and pining for him, Dan really wasn't interested.

He couldn't escape a horrible feeling that she was going to announce a sudden, unexpected engagement. That might finish him off completely.

In reality, Dan had no idea what had happened after he'd left her with that Ethan bloke a couple of weeks ago. Whether they were now happily engaged or were in fact not speaking to one another was completely unknown to Dan.

As much as Dan would love it to be the latter, he was too afraid to ask. Being in the dark seemed like the safest option. Besides, either way, Alice had made it abundantly clear that she wasn't interested in him. Could she have been more adamant that they weren't on a date?

Feeling the missed call weighing heavy on him, Dan had replied to her via text. He'd said he was working long hours and would call her back as soon as he could.

He had no intention of calling her back at any point in the foreseeable future.

Now he was five hours into standing on an exhibition stand, representing his company along with his colleagues, getting absolutely nowhere and still feeling utterly wretched. The show had been extremely quiet until a couple of hours before, when suddenly a load of people visited them all in one go, not one being from London or anywhere near Dan's territory.

'Did we get a lot of London leads from this show last year?' Emily asked as they hovered around the display of cameras. 'Because I know John said it's the biggest show on the security industry calendar, but it's in the Midlands. I don't think London people travel.'

'Maybe if you looked in the CRM you'd get the answer,' Dan snarled. 'You do know that's where everyone else logs their leads, don't you?'

'Some of us are too busy making sales to be typing stuff into computers all day,' Emily replied, a sickly smile on her face. 'But I'm guessing you've had plenty of time to take a look. So do you know the answer? Are we both wasting our time here?'

Dan had started at Blooms shortly after the company had last attended this exhibition, but sharing Emily's concerns, he had looked in the CRM to see what his predecessor had logged. Unlike Emily, he'd viewed the task as a good use of his time.

The numbers weren't great: of the one hundred and sixty-four leads that were gained from the three day show, only seventeen had been from the London area. But still, Dan knew he only needed one or two of them to convert and he'd reach his target, so he'd concluded that it was well worth him being there.

He stood up straight. 'All right, I did look, and your

suspicions are correct. It is a waste of time. I just didn't want to tell you as I thought it would distract you from stealing all my leads. But if you want to tell John that you're heading back to London to see some clients, I'm sure he won't object. And neither will I. As much as I don't want you working, I also don't much relish your company here either.'

'Somebody's suffering from jealousy, I see.'

'I could never be jealous of someone using corrupt tactics to get ahead. But if that's the only way you can win projects.'

'As John said, the sales reports speak for themselves. I mean what is it you think I'm doing? Following you around London, jumping on your clients the minute you turn your back? I have better things to do.'

'I don't know how you're doing it, but you'll get your comeuppance. People like you always do.'

'And weak, poor sales people like you who can't hit their targets tend to lose their jobs.'

Dan felt a snap of anger but he couldn't let her win. 'Say I do lose my job. What are you going to do then? Because we both know you haven't been developing your own prospects. So if I'm not around to do the groundwork, how on earth are you going to keep smashing your targets?'

For the first time since Dan had known her, Emily didn't know what to say. She just stood tall and glared at him. Dan didn't know whether to cheer that he'd finally hit the nail on the head, or slap her for being everything he suspected she was.

Not that he condoned violence. Except maybe in very, very select circumstances. Like self-defence.

Could he claim this was self-defence?

Before he had a chance to properly acknowledge that he'd caught her out, though, she stormed off in a huff, mumbling under her breath that she was going to the toilet.

'And don't bother coming back,' Dan mumbled in return.

'Could you tell me, do you do 360° cameras?' a male

voice asked behind him. Dan turned around to find a casually dressed man, maybe in his fifties, studying the display of cameras over the top of his glasses.

'Yes, we do 180 and 360. In fact we pride ourselves on offering quite a comprehensive range to suit virtually all applications. Is this for your site?'

'I'm just doing research,' the man said. 'I don't think they're any good, these 360° cameras. I mean how can it really work? We can't see 360° so how can a camera?'

'We actually use a fisheye lens. What the camera captures and what we as people see are slightly different.'

'So it's capturing different footage?'

'No, not at all. It just adapts it so it makes sense for us. It's incredibly clever. And it's full HD, so you get pristine images. I can show you a demonstration if you like?'

'No thank you. I'll take your word for it.'

'What sort of projects do you work on?'

'I'm just doing research at the minute.'

'Would it help if I arranged for some more in-depth information to be sent to you? I could scan you to take your details, then get something emailed over?' Dan pointed to the barcode on the badge that rested on the man's beer belly.

He regarded Dan suspiciously. 'What are you going to send me? Something specific about 360° cameras or a load of marketing claptrap that I'm not interested in?'

'You've only asked about 360, so that's all we'll send you.'

'Okay then.'

Dan grabbed the scanner from the pop up counter at the front of the stand and pressed the button to zap the man's barcode.

'You're Daniel White?' the man asked, reading Dan's corporate badge attached to his lapel.

'That's correct. Can I ask where you're based?'

'Bristol.'

'Bristol. Are you just here for the event?'

'Yes. Nice to meet you.'

'You too. Enjoy the rest of your day.'

The man walked off and Dan stepped back over to the stand's counter where he took a sheet of paper and pen from the small shelves hidden at the back. He made a note of the man's details and a little memo for his Bristol based colleague that he was only interested in 360° cameras.

'Hello stranger,' a female voice said and it made Dan's whole body tingle with delight. He looked up to see Alice's beaming face.

'Alice. Hi. I didn't know you were coming.'

'No, neither did I. I didn't even know we were exhibiting. I really should read more of those emails from Marketing.'

'What are you doing here then?'

'I came to see you.'

Dan tried very hard not to smile. 'Have you been looking at my calendar again? Are you stalking me?' He wanted to be freaked out and mad. If it was anyone else in the world he'd be shivering with that creepy sensation, as if someone were invading his privacy. But all he felt was glee.

Some of the darkness dissolved away as hope crept in. Hope he knew he shouldn't be having. He knew this was meaningless optimism and it would ultimately end in more moping about and greater depths of self-pity. But he also couldn't help thinking that if Alice didn't care then why was she spending so much time checking up on him and worrying about him?

'I wouldn't have to look in your calendar if you ever bothered to answer my calls or call me back,' Alice replied. 'You're turning me into a stalker. You've only got yourself to blame.'

The smile forced its way onto Dan's lips. 'As you can see, I'm very busy. I can't be speaking to you when customers are in need.'

He didn't flinch as he watched Alice scan the very empty stand. Apart from a few fellow sales people, there was barely a soul in sight.

'I can see how you're being pulled from pillar to post here,' Alice said. 'You must be very stressed.'

'It was busy earlier. Well, a bit. So, how can I help you?'

'It's how I can help you. Did you not get my message? I have exciting news.' Dan's stomach churned with that dread again. He glanced at her left hand. There was no ring. That was a good sign.

'Sorry. Like I said, until this show is over with, I'm in demand, all day, every day.'

'Even after five o'clock tonight?'

'We're all going out for dinner together.'

'What if you got a better offer?'

Dan smiled again. He didn't mean to. 'Is Emilia Clarke in town? I'm sure I could make an exception for her.'

'This is an even better offer! How about *I* take you out for dinner. So few people get that honour. If that's okay with you, Mr I'm-proud-and-I-like-to-buy-dinner?'

Another agonising stab struck Dan's heart. He'd only insisted on buying dinner as he'd assumed it was a date. He wasn't going to be fooled into that line of thinking again. No matter how much he was begging for it to be true.

'I was just trying to be nice.'

'I know. You're always nice. And now it's my turn to be nice to you. So, dinner tonight. I'll meet you in Starley Green? Seven o'clock?'

'We're staying in Birmingham tonight. All of us. It's closer to here.'

'Oh. Okay. Birmingham it is. How about I come back here for five and then we leave together and go straight for a couple of drinks and dinner? Make a night of it. I've missed you so much. We have loads to catch up on.'

Dan didn't know what to do. She was saying all the right things, but he felt like he was teetering on the edge of more heartache and he couldn't bear it.

But the reality was, no matter how much it hurt, he could never say no to dinner with her. How can you say no to the love of your life?

'Sure. Sounds good,' Dan said. He had no idea whether it was the right thing to do or not. He'd never been in such a mess in all his life. Bloody women.

'Where are you off to now?' he asked.

'I'm going to check out the competition. The future of Blooms is all about cutting edge technology, so I need to make sure we stay cutting edge.'

'All right. Have fun.'

'See you at five.'

'See you.'

Dan watched as Alice virtually skipped away. She was so happy and full of life. Even when she was moaning, she had this way of making him smile. She was so sweet.

And interesting. She was always so interesting.

And sexy. Yes, incredibly sexy.

She looked fantastic in that black dress.

'Was that Alice Bloom?' The voice next to him made Dan jump. He wished people would stop doing that. It was Chris, the South West sales rep.

'Yeah. Oh, I've got a lead for you. Some bloke from Bristol was interested in 360° cameras. But only 360. He doesn't want to hear about anything else, and he made that very clear.' Dan handed his note to Chris.

'Cheers, mate. I'll get in touch. You and Alice Bloom, then. What's going on there?'

'What do you mean?'

'I heard the rumours that she was practically sitting on your lap in the office last week.'

'Don't be stupid.'

'It's not me. That's what everyone's been saying.'

'She was in for the board meeting and just came to say hi. That's all.'

'She didn't say hi to anyone else.'

'We're friends. We got to know each other at the awards a few weeks ago.'

'You were talking before that.'

'Is that a crime? She's helped me out with a few specs. Who else better to have on your side than the owner of the company?'

Chris shrugged, seemingly losing interest. 'Whatever. She's hot. I wouldn't blame you.'

Dan turned around to see Alice chatting with great command to a salesperson on a nearby stand. She had such authority about her. It was so alluring.

All he wanted was to be with her, as if she were this beaming ray of sunshine after he'd been kept in the dark for decades. She was his Vitamin D, and without her he was a brittle, broken mess.

Life was so unfair.

TWENTY-EIGHT

By five o'clock Dan was practically drooling with boredom. Most of the sales team had left a few minutes before. Only he, John, the Marketing Manager and the ever-keen Emily were still there.

'You can go as well, you know,' John said to Dan and Emily. 'It's been a long day. Let's hope it picks up tomorrow.'

'They've got the big keynote presentation tomorrow. I'm sure that will bring in the punters,' Emily remarked.

'I'm waiting for someone,' Dan said. 'You lot go. I'll help tidy up.'

'Who are you waiting for?' Emily asked.

'None of your business,' Dan replied. He grabbed a handful of brochures and piled them in the lockable cupboard at the back of the stand.

'Is that Alice Bloom?' Emily asked and Dan felt the nerves kick in.

'What's she doing here?' John queried.

'She's here to see you, isn't she?' Emily smirked in Dan's direction. 'Your little chess mate.'

Dan felt his face flush. He wanted his relationship with Alice (whatever that was) to be known about just as much as his secret hobby. This was horrendous. How on earth had Emily found out?

'Chess?' John asked as Alice approached. 'Hello, Alice. Are you still playing chess?'

Dan watched as Alice kept her cool. She didn't seem even remotely embarrassed about their clandestine adoration for the game.

'Hello, John. Yes. Why?'

John smiled. 'You were obsessed as a kid, I remember. Your dad bought you that electronic game and I think you wore it out.'

'My dad designed that electronic game. But it was far from perfect.'

'It certainly managed to beat you, though.' John laughed. 'I remember that day you threw it across the room because you'd lost three times in a row. You've always been a feisty one.'

'I was young. I think you'll find I'm a more gracious loser now.'

Dan scoffed. He shook his head with a wry smile as Alice turned towards him.

'I am!' she declared.

'You've been here all day?' John asked her.

'A couple of hours. I've been checking out the competition. There are a lot of good new products on the market. We've got our work cut out.'

'I heard you've been back to the office too. You're taking a more proactive role again. Good for you.'

Alice flicked her eyes quickly in Dan's direction. 'It was a very last minute decision. But I think it's for the best.'

'We're getting the train now. Are you heading back to New Street?'

'I am. Actually Dan and I are going for dinner.'

All eyes turned to Dan. He didn't know what to do.

'Are you ready?' Alice asked him.

'I'll just put these away,' he said, placing another pile of brochures in the cupboard. He could feel his face burning up. He took a few quick breaths before joining Alice. 'Shall we go?'

'Have a good night, you too,' John smirked. 'See you tomorrow.'

'See you.'

Dan walked away as quickly as he could. 'Did you tell Emily that we played chess together?' he asked Alice as soon as they were out of earshot.

'No. What was all that about? I thought it was our naughty little secret?'

'So did I. But she just called you my chess mate. How could she know?'

'Chess mate? Are you sure?'

'Yes. That's why John was asking you.'

'John! I bet John's said something. I used to play a lot with my dad.'

'She doesn't know I play, though.'

Alice thought for a second. 'You said she called me your chess mate?'

'Yes.'

'Well, there you go then. John's probably been reminiscing about the past, told a story about that stupid chess game and how my dad was always creating something, and now I'm your nerdy mate who plays chess.'

Dan felt his whole body relax.

'I know it's stupid, but I like it that our chess games are secret,' Alice said. 'It makes it more exciting.'

'I know! Chess is exciting,' Dan agreed.

'It certainly is. Although I've been starting to worry that you're going off it. You still haven't played your go. It's been like ten days.'

Dan sighed. 'I know.'

'Don't ever contemplate Fast Chess.'

'I've never played Fast Chess.'

'I can see why. It takes you forever to play your turn.'

'I'm busy. I'm not always looking at the game. But I'd like to remind you that it's thirty, eighteen in my favour.'

'I bet if we played faster, I'd wipe the floor with you.'

'Oh, bring it on. You still wouldn't stand a chance.'

'Right, next time you're up, we're having a chess evening round mine. I'm going to get one of those clock things.'

Dan stared at the floor. Was that a date she was arranging? No, it couldn't be. He was firmly fixed in the friend zone.

He absolutely loved the idea of having a night of nothing but chess. Chess and Alice. His perfect night in.

Oh, he was heading down a painful route. He needed to protect his heart better.

'Sounds great,' he said.

'What is it?' Alice asked.

'What?'

'You've got that tone again.'

'I haven't. I was just thinking about chess.'

'What aren't you telling me?'

'Is that your exciting news then?' Dan asked, changing the subject as fast as he could. 'That you think one day you might be better at chess than me?'

Alice chuckled. 'I think it's time for the truth, Daniel. If I'm honest, I've been holding back. I haven't been playing to my full potential as I thought if you kept losing you might not play with me anymore.'

Dan laughed. 'Really? I did think it was getting a bit easy. You don't have to hold back. I'd much prefer to know that when I constantly win, you're playing at your best.'

'Constantly win? I've still won eighteen of our forty-eight games, I'll have you know.'

'Maybe I've been holding back too. Maybe it's time we both brought our A game.'

'Yes!' Alice laughed. 'As soon as we finish this current game – if you ever get around to playing your turn – then on the next game it's time to be ruthless.'

'You asked for it.'

Dan and Alice were laughing so much, Dan almost walked right past the train station.

'Here,' Alice said before rummaging around in her bag. She pulled out a ticket. Dan followed suit, reaching into his jacket pocket.

They entered through the barriers and headed down to their platform.

'As much as declaring our all-out chess war is exciting,' Alice said as they found a quiet spot down the end of the platform, 'I do have other exciting news too.'

Dan felt that thud in his chest again. He re-scanned her hand, double checking she hadn't suddenly slipped on an engagement ring. She was completely ring-less, but he still wasn't feeling confident.

The train pulled into the station.

'I'll tell you everything when we sit down for a drink,' Alice said. 'I don't want anyone else to hear. This is going to be good for you.'

Dan nodded as he waited for the train doors to open. He had a feeling this news was going to be anything but good.

On the short journey to Birmingham New Street, Alice insisted that he play his turn at their latest chess game, so he pulled out his phone and caught up on his strategy.

He really wanted more time to think through his turn, but before he knew it the train was approaching their stop and he wanted to get his move done. He wanted to keep Alice happy. And, truth be told, he actually didn't mind if she won this game.

He moved his knight - not totally sure if it was the best decision - and closed the game down. 'Over to you,' he said as they stood and queued in the aisle.

'Thank you,' Alice nodded.

'So where do you want to go?' Dan asked. 'You must know Birmingham way better than me.'

Dan clocked a worried look in Alice's eye as they prepared to alight the train, but her body language didn't support the fleeting concern her face seemed to show.

'Somewhere close to New Street, I was thinking,' she said as they made their way up the platform. 'Do you have a bar you like to go to when you're up?'

'There are a few nice places up Temple Street that we tend to go to. But I'm happy for you to show me somewhere new.'

'Nonsense. Let's stick to what you know. That way you won't be distracted when I'm telling you my news.'

'Okay,' Dan said.

'In fact, you lead the way.'

Dan looked ahead up the escalators. He could sense there was something she wasn't telling him. She was being far too amenable. It made him even more nervous about the forthcoming "exciting news".

As they exited through the ticket barriers and left Grand Central, Dan was deep in thought, anticipating every possibility of what this terrible news was going to be. The only thing in the world he wanted was for her to declare her love for him, and as he couldn't see that happening ever in his lifetime, anything else she was about to say was surely only going to disappoint.

'Temple Street,' Alice said as they turned up into the road. 'So many great bars. Which is your favourite?'

'I'm not really in the mood for cocktails or anything like that,' Dan said. 'It's been a long day. I could do with a beer. A nice, cold draught beer.'

'Perfect. Here?' Alice asked, pointing to a pub on their left. Dan had never been in there.

'No, I prefer the place up here on the right. If that's okay? I mean we can go wherever you like.'

'Up on the right. I like it there too. Let's do it!'

Despite her confidence, Alice walked one step behind Dan. She was acting very strangely.

They headed into the pub. It was busy with an after work crowd, even on a Tuesday night.

'There's a table free at the back there,' Alice said. 'You

grab that, I'll get the drinks.'

'No, you said you were getting dinner. I'll get the drinks,' Dan replied.

'Do as you're told. Sit down. What do you want?'

'Are you sure?' Dan said, remembering how much he enjoyed her bossy side.

'Beer?'

'The strongest lager, whatever they've got.'

'Coming up.'

Dan made his way to the back and sat on a wooden seat. It wasn't exactly comfortable luxury, but after a few sips of beer he knew he wouldn't care.

He watched Alice chatting to the barman, asking about the lagers. No doubt running through each one to ascertain which was the strongest. Following Dan's request to the letter. She had such a good heart.

She brought over two pints and he immediately took a sip. His nerves were increasing with every passing second. He needed to know now and get this news over with.

'Go on then,' he said, the second Alice had taken her coat off. 'What's this news?'

'Ooh, you're going to love this.'

'Yeah?'

'I have a hot lead for you. Like a really hot lead. For a really big company. And you're the only one who knows about it.'

'What?' Dan said, utterly confused. He didn't know whether to be relieved or wait for the catch.

'It's with Dobson's Supermarket. Like the whole chain.'

'Dobson's? That's amazing. Where has this come from?'

Alice hesitated. She shifted in her seat and took a sip from her pint.

'I have a friend who works in the chain. I asked him about their security set up. Apparently they're spending a fortune and so they're more than happy to explore any way to save money.'

'Him?' Dan asked, not missing a beat.

'Yeah. Him.'

'Do I know him?'

'Erm...'

'If I'm going to speak to him then I should know who he is.'

'Oh no, you're not speaking to him. I just got the info from him. He's given me a contact at Head Office. Her name's Caroline. I've had a quick chat with her, just to make sure it's all legit. She's awaiting your call. She sounded very eager.'

Dan nodded. He sipped his beer. As good news as this lead was, it really wasn't his primary concern at that moment. 'It would still be good to know the full background, though. So, this man is?'

'It's Ethan. Do you remember Ethan?'

Dan's heart began to throb painfully and quickly.

He pretended to think about it.

'The guy who knew the really awful band?' he asked, as if he weren't quite sure. As if that whole night and that bastard's face weren't scarred into him forever.

'That's the one. Yeah.'

'You were meeting him for a date, weren't you?' Dan said. 'If I remember correctly.'

'Erm... yeah. Yeah. We've been out a few times.'

'Oh right. Good for you. Is it serious?' Dan took a gulp of beer as he waited for the news of their engagement. Maybe she'd be moving in with him. This was it. It was all over for Dan now. He'd lost to some slick loser who had far too much gel in his hair and who must spend every second of his free time in the gym. Slimy poser. Dan had a life, at least.

Alice shrugged.

'Do you play chess with him?' Dan asked.

'Chess?' Alice laughed. 'I don't think he's the chess playing sort of man.'

Dan liked that. Ethan obviously wasn't a good match

for her. What did Alice see in him?

'So what do you do together?' Dan pried, as casually as he could.

Alice shook her head. 'Not a lot at the minute. We're just getting to know each other. It's early days. It's no big deal.'

Dan felt a small reprise in his heartache.

'He works at Dobson's? In the security department?' Dan asked.

'No. He's manager of the Starley Green branch. At least I think he is. I don't really know. He's a bit of a conundrum really. One of those crazy clever people who always leaves you guessing.'

Bastard. Dan knew that Alice was also an insanely clever person that constantly left him guessing. It was something he absolutely adored about her. Maybe she had met her match.

'Anyway, he was going to Head Office for a meeting in London and I just had this light bulb moment. I got him to suss out their security situation and apparently this Caroline isn't very happy at the minute with their current setup, but she hasn't had the time to look into it. When Ethan said he had a contact who could take all the hassle away, she was apparently thrilled. So I'll email you the details, yeah? You'll contact her?'

'Yes, absolutely,' Dan said with none of the enthusiasm he should have been showing. 'Dobson's? That's huge.'

'And let's keep it just between us. There's no way Emily knows about this. They weren't even looking, and I know Caroline hasn't been speaking to anyone else.'

'I've now been allowed to leave my meetings off the CRM, so no one in the world should know.'

'I'm so excited for you! This could put you way past Emily.'

'Back to the top.'

'Where you belong.'

'Thank you so much, Alice. You're very good to me.'

Dan clinked his glass against hers. He wanted to kiss her so badly.

'You mean the world to me, Dan. You're my best friend. I've never had a friend like you.'

Dan's heart went into spasm again. He hated that word "friend". Unless it was going to have "boy" or "girl" preceding it then he just didn't want to know.

He focused on the wooden table, inspecting it for imperfections. Of which he found hundreds.

What was he doing there? This was far too painful.

He looked back at Alice, trying to conjure up a reason as to why he couldn't stay out late, when he spotted her almost in tears. She was staring across the room, horrified.

He followed her eyeline towards a couple kissing in the corner.

'What is it?' Dan asked. He couldn't make out who the people were.

'Nothing,' Alice asked. She stared down at the table, clearly fighting the urge to cry.

'Alice, what is it?' Dan touched her hand. 'Are you all right?'

'Yeah, I'm fine. I'm... It's...' She looked up at Dan and her face became fiery. 'Actually, do you know what, I'm not fine. I'm really not. That's Ethan over there.'

Dan's head snapped back over to the canoodling couple. As the man pulled away from the indecent embrace, Dan saw very clearly that it was indeed the same man he'd left Alice with on the night his heart broke.

Dan turned back to Alice. He didn't know what to do.

TWENTY-NINE

'Do you want to leave?' Dan asked. It was all he could think to say. She looked so distraught.

Alice took a few steady breaths.

'We can do anything you want to,' Dan added, squeezing her hand again. 'I can go punch him if you like.'

Alice was still breathing carefully, deep in thought.

She started shaking her head. Her face was tense; caught between fury and sadness.

She gulped back most of the rest of her drink. 'I think I would like to go. Would that be okay?'

'Of course. If we cut round that way, we don't have to see them.'

Alice stood up and put her coat on. She glared back over at the kissing pair and Dan could sense a battle raging inside of her.

'Do you know what, fuck it. He has no right to treat me this way.' Alice stormed off, right in the direction of Ethan, and Dan quickly followed. He couldn't resist seeing how this would play out, and he also wanted to support Alice in any way he could.

'Hello Ethan,' Alice hissed forcefully. Dan stood a couple of steps behind her.

'Babe!' Ethan said, not at all thrown that she'd caught him with another woman.

'Oh my God, it's Alice!' the woman said. Dan couldn't believe his eyes when he saw the woman who had been kissing Ethan throw her arms around Alice and hug her. From Alice's firm stance, it seemed as if Alice couldn't believe it either.

'Flick?' Alice spat with shock. 'What are you two doing?'

'We're celebrating!' Flick said. 'I've been for an audition today. Can you believe it? I've been talent spotted. I'm going to be on the telly. Well, maybe. Eventually. The stage first probably. Well, I'm someone's stand in. At least that's what I auditioned for. I can't believe it! I'm going to be famous. So Ethan said he'd come out and celebrate.'

'And kissing is part of that?' Alice asked fiercely.

'Are you jealous, babe?' Ethan said, attempting to hug Alice, but she pushed him away. 'I knew you were the jealous type. You're not going to cause me problems, are you?'

'This is the girl you've been shagging?' Flick said with delight. 'Oh my God! You've shagged my sister!' She started laughing.

'I am not your sister,' Alice stated, but all Dan could focus on was the fact that Alice had slept with this vile man. He felt dizzy and betrayed.

'Flick and I go back a long way. It's just a bit of fun. Who doesn't have a bit of a snog with their mates? You're out with him tonight,' Ethan said, pointing at Dan. 'Do you see me getting all jealous?'

'Dan is my colleague. We're talking about work.' Dan felt another sharp blow.

'Just the two of you in a pub after work?' Ethan remarked. 'Very professional. But it's fine. I'm not going to get all weird about it. We're not exactly serious yet, are we? If you want to shag him, you can.'

'Yet?' Alice spat.

'Look, we're young. I want to live life a bit before I settle down. I really like you, Ally, I do-'

'My name is Alice.'

'Woah,' Ethan took a step back. 'Where is the fun, chilled out rich girl I know? This is getting a bit intense. I don't need this shit.'

'You are getting a bit weird,' Flick said. 'We're just having a laugh. If you must know, Ethan was telling me all about you earlier, saying how much he liked you.'

'He was raving so much about me that you didn't even know he was talking about me?' Alice chimed back. 'And then you believed so much that he'd met the love of his life that you thought you'd snog the face off him to celebrate? How is it that you think I'm the weird one here? That somehow I'm in the wrong?'

'You need to calm down,' Ethan said. 'I think you need to go home and put this into perspective. I really like you, but we've just started dating. This is a bit extreme.' Ethan turned his attention to Dan. 'Will you take her home? Calm her down a bit?'

Dan didn't know what to do. His emotions were spiking all over the place. He felt hurt and angry at the same time as utterly protective of Alice.

'I'll do what I bloody well like, thank you,' Alice snapped back.

'Go home with him,' Ethan said. 'Get whatever it is you're doing with him out of your system. You have my blessing. Take some time out, and then when you've calmed down and you've realised what matters, give me a call.' Ethan's tone was deeply patronising and Dan felt his fists clench.

'I think *you* need to get some perspective, Ethan,' Alice replied, her voice so controlled. Dan didn't know how she was keeping her cool as well as she was. 'I think it's safe to say you won't ever be hearing from me again. And that really is your loss. We both know I'm the best you're ever going to get and you've just flushed it all down the toilet. Go and take your stupid ego, your stupid metaphors and your three brain cells and find a girl who actually gives a damn. Because you've just lost the best thing that ever happened to you. And I think I just got a very lucky escape.' Alice turned around. 'Dan? Are you ready?'

Dan nodded. He still wanted to punch Ethan, but he was so proud of how Alice had handled herself. He glared hard into Ethan's eyes before he followed Alice out onto the street.

She stood on the pavement and Dan looked at her. She was trembling with anger and her face became flushed.

'You did so well,' Dan said. 'What a bastard. But you did brilliantly.' As soon as the words left his lips, Alice broke down into sobs.

Dan quickly placed his arms around her and she wept into his chest, her body shaking at how upset she was.

They stood on the street and Dan just let her cry. People walked around them, some staring, some oblivious, and Dan held her tightly and warmly, not knowing what else he could say or do.

'Do you want to go home?' he whispered when her tears finally started to subside.

'Yes,' she nodded, still not moving from his embrace.

'I can see taxis at the top. Are you okay to walk?'

Alice nodded. She reached into her bag and grabbed a tissue. She tidied herself up, keeping as close to Dan as possible. As much as it broke his heart to see her so distressed, he loved that he could be there for her.

She wiped her face and then blew her nose before she pointed to Dan's chest. 'I'm so sorry,' she said. He looked down and noticed a couple of small black marks on his white shirt where her make-up had run.

'It's fine,' he said. It was more than fine. It was the most intimate moment they'd shared and he had a fleeting thought that he might never wash his shirt. Then he felt ridiculous.

'Are you ready?'

Alice nodded and Dan put his arm around her. They

walked closely together to the top of the street where they tracked down a small line of taxis.

'Starley Green, please,' Dan said as Alice climbed in the back of the black cab.

Dan sat next to her and as soon as the cab pulled away she rested her head on his shoulder.

The only words spoken were Alice's directions to her house. Other than that, they enjoyed a peaceful, content silence.

Dan quickly whipped out the cash as they pulled up outside her house, beating Alice to it.

'I'll give you the money back,' she said.

'Don't be stupid. You need looking after, so let me look after you.'

'Thank you,' she muttered as they stepped out the taxi.

The taxi pulled away and Dan got his first glimpse of her house. It was enormous.

'This is where you grew up?' he said as they made their way up the large gravelly drive.

'Yes,' Alice replied as she unlocked the door.

'You don't have a car?' he asked. 'You haven't left it in Birmingham, have you?'

Alice shook her head. 'No. No car. I sold my dad's just after... It was too hard. And I've not needed one since. Hard to drive around when no one sees you.' Alice's face suddenly changed, as if she'd just realised something really important. 'Oh God, your car's in Birmingham though, isn't it. I'm so sorry. I'll pay for your taxi back. I'm so sorry.'

'It's fine,' Dan said, soothingly. 'All that mattered was getting you home. You've had quite a shock.'

'Can I get you a drink?' she asked, taking off her coat and shoes and dumping them in the hallway.

Dan politely removed his shoes. 'If you're having one.'

'I have wine, beer, pretty much any spirit you can name. Take your pick.'

Dan followed Alice into her huge kitchen. She opened the fridge to reveal a large selection of beer and three bottles of white wine, and then she pointed over to the corner to where a small rack of red wine sat.

'Bloody hell, you do have quite the selection.'

Alice shrugged. 'I never used to go out. So I brought the party home.'

'Well, let's party like it's a Tuesday, shall we. I think we both deserve another beer.'

'Good choice.'

Alice grabbed two cans from the fridge and then two glasses from a cupboard, and then they both sat next to each other at the long dining table.

Dan took off his jacket and tie and neatly placed them on the back of the chair next to him before he cracked open his beer.

'You know, I don't know what I was most upset about,' Alice said, pouring the contents of her can into the glass. 'Was it that he cheated on me, or was it that he had the audacity to cheat on me? I'm actually not sure how much I really liked him.'

This grabbed Dan's attention. He sat silently, desperately hoping she'd elaborate.

'You know I said earlier he was a genius?'

'Something like that.'

'I don't think he is. I think he's a complete idiot. I wanted him to be clever because I couldn't bear the thought of dating someone so dense. But he really is dense. And unbelievably arrogant.'

Dan couldn't help but laugh a little. 'Sorry.'

'No, it's fine. It serves me right.'

'How?'

'I got drawn in by his looks. By his confidence.'

'You have loads of confidence,' Dan said. 'Why would you find his attractive?'

'I'm not confident.'

'You're the bravest person I know.'

'How exactly?'

'Look what you've been through.'

'Oh yeah, so brave. My parents died and I pushed the whole world away. That's what I do. I didn't leave the house for nearly five years.'

'You were suffering from depression. It's not surprising.'

'It was more than that.'

'Yeah, depression and grief.'

'I pushed everyone away.'

'Why do you always blame yourself for things? You know it's hard to push someone away who really cares.'

Alice studied her beer. She hesitated before speaking. 'You're the best friend I've ever had. Thank you for not leaving me.'

'I'm not going anywhere.'

'It kind of felt like you were. We've barely spoken since that night in Starley Green. When we saw the band. I know you've got your work problems. I understand. But you can talk to me. I'm always here for you too.'

Dan looked up at the ceiling, feigning deep interest in her crystal light fittings, while his head tried to formulate what he could say in response. More than anything, he wanted to tell her how he felt, but he had to concede that it was probably the worst time in the world. She'd just had her heart broken. She might be pretending that she wasn't bothered, but she clearly was.

She'd slept with that man. The whole idea echoed around Dan's head. Since he'd last been out with her, she'd had sex with another man. It made him bitter and jealous and he wanted to be angry with her, but she'd actually done nothing wrong.

He had to make peace with the fact that he was firmly seated in the friend zone. But at least he was comforting her after her break up. That was a step up from two hours before.

'Do you think it is all over between you?' Dan said, hating that he was asking, but he had to know.

'Oh yeah,' Alice said, nodding enthusiastically. 'He's not for me. Not at all. I don't know what I was thinking. I suppose he was just there when I needed someone. Right place, totally wrong bloke.'

Dan wished that he'd been there. It seemed timing was everything and he kept missing the mark.

'So, Karl and Ethan? You're getting quite the list of bad boyfriends. But as they say, third time lucky. I'm sure the next man who's fortunate enough to be your partner will be the one who stays.'

Alice scoffed. 'I think it's time I took a break from dating for a while.' Dan tried to control his sigh. That's all he needed. 'It's nothing but heartache and confusion.'

'Are you hungry?' Dan asked, needing to end that line of conversation.

'You know what, I am. Shall I whip us something up?'

'You're going to cook?' Dan asked with delight. 'I seem to remember you saying what a great cook you are. What's on the menu?'

Alice stood up to peruse her fridge and cupboards.

'I make a mean pasta sauce, if you're all right with just veg?'

'Sounds wonderful.'

Alice grabbed a chopping board from the cupboard and Dan joined her in the kitchen. They talked about nothing and everything as she whisked up a tomato based sauce, which she confidently threw on some penne.

Dan laid the table and took care of the wine, and it felt in every way like they were in a relationship. It felt normal and wonderful and he wanted the night to last forever.

Their joyful conversation continued over the food, and then after their bellies were full they moved the bottle of wine into the living room to flick through some Sky channels. Curled up on either ends of the sofa, they talked over all the TV, the conversation flowing more freely than the alcohol.

It was the perfect night and Dan was in heaven.

At around midnight, Alice started yawning repeatedly.

'I'd better leave you to get to bed,' he said, trying not to show his severe reluctance to leave.

'No, don't be silly. Please stay. I love having you here. You've cheered me up so much. I'd be such a mess without you.'

It took all of Dan's strength to resist punching the air. 'Are you sure?'

'Of course. I'm not having you travelling back now.'

'I'll sleep on the sofa.'

'You will not.'

Dan scanned his surroundings. 'Of course. How many bedrooms has this place got?'

Alice moved closer to him. 'You don't have to, but would you sleep with me tonight?'

'What?' Dan wanted to get up and dance. Had she really just said that?

'I don't mean sexually. Sorry, that came out all wrong. I just... I don't want to be alone tonight. I don't know what it is, but I've never felt safer than when I'm with you. I've never felt more cared about than when I'm with you. We've got a special bond, you and me, and I don't... I love you, Dan. You're the bestest friend I could ever hope for.'

Dan sat very still. All of his dreams were about to come true in all the wrong way. He'd fantasised about waking up next to Alice so many times. And now he'd be doing it probably fully dressed, without being able to kiss her, knowing that all she wanted was a friendly hug at the most.

It was one thing being shoved in the friend zone, but another having to play it out in the most intimate of situations.

'Is everything all right?' Alice asked as Dan still hadn't moved a muscle.

'Yep,' Dan said, thinking through his options. Any other night, this would be the perfect opportunity to tell her how he felt. But she'd just broken up with someone. He couldn't do it now. But how could he sleep in the same bed with her without being able to be intimate with her? That was wrong on so many levels.

'What is it?' Alice asked, now looking concerned herself. 'I just...'

'You don't have to sleep in my bed if it will make you feel uncomfortable.'

'No!' Dan said, without even meaning to. The thought of turning down this opportunity to be next to her was about as bad as having to sleep next to her as nothing but a friend. He couldn't win.

'What is it?' Alice said.

Dan decided to play it by ear. Maybe being in bed together would spark something between them. Maybe this was in fact the nudge they both needed. Or perhaps he could test the waters and then blame it on the alcohol if she flinched away? This could actually be the best idea in the world!

'Nothing,' Dan said. 'If you're sure. Sleeping together is a big step.'

Alice laughed and threw a cushion at him.

'I'm game if you are,' she said with playful eyes and Dan's body began to throb.

'I'm very game,' he said.

'Follow me, then.'

She locked up and led the way to her bedroom, thankfully not noticing the expression on Dan's face as it flicked between ecstatic and worried.

As she opened the door, Dan was immediately surprised by how pink and girly it was. It seemed so out of touch with Alice's sophistication.

'Are you sure there's room for me?' he said spotting the giant stuffed toy on her bed.

Alice laughed. 'Oh, that's Sammy. My second best friend in the world.'

'Sammy?' Dan asked. 'Named after your friend, Sammy?'

Alice sighed. She sat on the bed and cuddled the teddy. 'No. The truth is I don't have any friends. Just you. No one else. Everyone else walked away when the going got tough. Or maybe it's more accurate to say I made it incredibly difficult for anyone to be my friend. I didn't want you to think I was a loser. And Sammy was the closest thing I had to a friend... until you.'

'You don't have any other friends?' Dan asked, finding it hard to believe. 'But on your birthday, you said you went out with Sammy and the girls into Birmingham.' Dan shook his head as he computed what she was telling him. 'You took your giant stuffed toy out clubbing?'

Alice giggled. 'No!'

'Who did you go out with then?'

Alice paused. 'No one.'

'You said you met Karl that night.'

'Hang on, do you remember everything? And you say I'm the stalker!'

Dan sat down on the bed next to Alice. 'I'm just curious. I worry about you.'

'If you must know, I went out on my own. And I went into Starley Green not Birmingham. I really wanted to meet you.'

'You came into Starley Green? Why didn't you say anything? Could you not find us?'

'No, I saw you. And John. And all the others. I guess I chickened out. It was one thing to see you, but another to appear out of the blue to everyone else.'

Dan nodded. 'I can understand that.'

'Then as I was leaving, I bumped into Karl. He bought me a drink. That's when I first met Ethan too. Like I said, right time, right place, totally the wrong men.'

'You met them in Strikers?'

Alice nodded.

'So you saw me weeks before I first saw you?'

'Sorry. I didn't know how to tell you without seeming utterly ridiculous.'

Dan smiled. 'Alice Bloom, I could never think you're ridiculous.' Actually he just felt sorry for her.

Dan kissed her cheek. It was the most natural thing in the world. He waited to see if she would move in for a deeper kiss. It was the perfect time. This had to be the moment. Coming to bed together was surely the intimate jolt they both needed to finally get out of the friend zone.

They sat closely together, their eyes fixed on one another. Could it really happen now?

'You're going to need a toothbrush!' Alice said, jumping to her feet. 'Don't worry, I've got spares.' She shot off out the room and Dan slumped back on the bed.

This was a dream come true cum horrific nightmare. How had he managed to back himself into such a mess? This was going to be a long, torturous night.

THIRTY

'I'm so sorry, I'm going to have to go now.'

Alice was jolted awake. Her heart started pounding as she scrambled to remember why there was someone else in her bedroom.

'Are you okay?' Dan asked, sitting on the bed, curling her hair behind her ear.

She focused on Dan and the night before came back to her.

Then the impact of the sight of his body came back to her and she realised she was anything but okay.

'Alice?' Dan nudged for an answer. He had that worried look in his eye. Like he really cared. And she knew he did.

She nodded, sensing a fear inside of her that she had no inclination to rationalise. 'I'm fine. What time is it?'

'Six o'clock. I've got to get back to the hotel, get changed and then meet everyone for breakfast at eight. I can't have them thinking I've been out all night. The rumours are bad enough as it is.'

'What rumours?'

Dan hesitated before he shrugged. 'Any sort of rumours. You know the sort. I don't want to get labelled as a dirty stop out. That sort of thing.' He stood up and grabbed his shirt which was laid out neatly on a chair in the corner of the room.

Alice knew he wasn't being completely honest with her, but the butterflies in her stomach were far too distracting for her to question why.

She took one last look at his body and that terrified sensation intensified.

The night before, Dan had decided it best not to crease his suit, so he'd opted to sleep in just his boxer shorts. Alice hadn't thought too much of it, until he'd taken his shirt off. Then she'd completely sobered up.

It had been easy to tell herself before that she liked him no more than a really good friend. They had lots in common. It was all games and talk and a meeting of minds. But when she saw his lovely, mostly naked body, lust got thrown into the mix and it shattered all her pretence.

It wasn't that Dan was all muscly, toned and waxed like Ethan. She knew Dan was the sort who drove to the gym to walk on the treadmill and then drive home again. But it was the fact that he was more mainstream that she found so alluring. He had flecks of hair across his chest and soft supple skin that she'd accidentally melted into when he gave her a goodnight cuddle. He had little definition and not one sign of a six pack, but in every way he was manly and real, and she loved it.

All night she'd found herself fantasising that he'd kiss her. She had this new and wonderful desire for him to touch her, but she also wanted to explore every inch of him in return. She hadn't been able to look at him for the past five and a half hours without feeling flustered.

So how exactly was she going to live in denial now?

Because denial was exactly where Alice wanted to be. Dan was the closest friend she'd ever had. Their relationship didn't hurt, and she hadn't known that in a very long time. Everyone she had ever loved had left her, and she felt more afraid of losing Dan than anyone. She was petrified that even if he had feelings for her in return - which she was absolutely not even going to consider – getting together would change the dynamic of their relationship and would inevitably put them on the road to the end.

Remaining friends was the only way for it not to hurt, and therefore Alice was determined to keep it that way.

'How are you getting back to Birmingham?' she asked.

'I've already ordered a taxi. It'll be here in a few minutes.'

'Can I give you some money?'

'You most definitely cannot.' He buckled his belt and walked back over, taking a seat on the bed again. 'Thank you for last night. I had a really nice evening. I hope we can do it again soon. Don't forget, we need to have our Fast Chess competition, where I'm going to prove that I'm the true chess champion.'

Alice studied his face. He seemed far more gorgeous today than she'd ever noticed before. She'd always liked his looks, but suddenly all she could think about was taking all his clothes off again.

That was it.

She felt it.

She felt her common sense and strength being swiftly washed away as the most dangerous element in the world moved in to fill the void. It was love.

Damn it, she was in love with him.

This could only end in disaster.

'Maybe,' she said. 'I'll have to see if I can track down a clock. We can't do it before I get a clock. I think they're really hard to find.'

'Do you want me to look?'

'No! Leave it to me. Don't worry. You'd better get back to the hotel. Don't keep the taxi waiting. They charge you if they wait, you know. You need to get your tie on too. I think it's downstairs. Did you leave it on the table? And shoes. Don't forget your shoes. You don't want to leave them here. I mean you could if you wanted but then you'll be walking around in your socks. That will definitely end in some strange rumours. You can't be at an exhibition in just your socks!'

'Are you all right?' Dan said, rubbing her arm in a loving and attentive way.

'Oh yes. Absolutely yes. Don't worry about me.' She sat up to shrug off his tender touch without it seeming too obvious.

'I'll see you soon. Are you still okay to email me those details for Dobson's?'

'Oh yes. Of course. I'll do it this morning.'

'I'll let you know how it goes.'

'Please do. Like message me or something. Keep in touch.'

'I will. Sorry I've been a bit useless lately. There's been a lot going on.'

'It's okay. I know what it's like. Don't worry.'

'See you soon.' Dan kissed her on the cheek and Alice felt this new stirring passion radiate through her. She really had never met anyone quite like him.

He waved goodbye as he left the room and Alice slumped back down in her bed.

She listened without moving as he collected his things before exiting the house. She barely took a breath until she heard the taxi drive away.

She lay still for a while, letting her thoughts spin around her head at a million miles per hour.

Exactly when had she moved from seeing Dan as just a friend to falling in love with him? How on earth had this happened?

What did he feel in return? Anything?

She jumped out of bed at that thought. She couldn't bear it. If they moved from the friends zone then that would be it. There would be no going back and ultimately she'd lose him.

She couldn't have that. She didn't want to lose him.

She made her way down to the kitchen. She shoved a couple of slices of bread in the toaster and flicked the kettle on. She may as well start her day, although she felt like doing anything but work. She had never felt so edgy.

The memory of how much she looked forward to hearing from him echoed through her brain, as if she were mourning the end of an era.

She used to love their endless chats on the phone. Dan had never judged her, never got bored of her, never told her she was wrong. He accepted her just the way she was. Even when she was being stroppy, he just got on with it. Occasionally being stroppy in return.

They were a perfect match, but those wonderful days were in jeopardy. She didn't want their fun, regular conversations to be over. She had to find a way to preserve what they had. She had to hold on to the best thing she'd ever known.

She made her breakfast and then took it upstairs to her desk. Getting on with her job was what she needed to do. She couldn't keep going over these crazy new feelings. It was time to concentrate on her routine and surely everything would be back to normal by the time evening came around.

First things first, she texted Dan the contact details for Caroline at Dobson's, which only took her a couple of minutes, and then she decided to start tackling the proposed changes to the business plan, which she'd been putting off ever since the board meeting the week before.

It turned out it wasn't as easy as she had thought, and she was struggling to know where to start. But this was the perfect time to get lost in a challenge.

Before she knew it, her head would be straight again and all these silly fantasy ideas would be nothing but a distant memory.

That's what she needed. Just to get back into the swing of things.

* * *

How are you feeling today? Hope you're a bit better. xx

Dan pressed send on his message and put his phone back in his pocket. He picked up the wine menu, making the most of being able to peruse it before his sisters arrived and took over.

It was Saturday lunchtime and he was actually early to meet his sisters. His good mood was having a positive effect.

If only Alice was just as happy. He'd tried to call her twice the day before with no luck, and she'd eventually texted him back to say she was ill in bed and she wasn't up for talking. He was very worried about her, all alone and sick.

'Bloody hell, did we tell you the wrong time or something?' Mary said, kissing her brother on the cheek and taking a seat.

'Such wit.'

'You're even choosing wine?'

'I'm looking at what options I could have had before you tell me what I'm going to drink.'

'Am I late?' Clare said, greeting both her siblings with the customary cheek-kiss.

'I know!' Mary nodded. 'I suppose it had to happen one time.'

'Maybe I've been missing you,' Dan said. 'Maybe I was so excited to have our lunch today, I barely slept last night. Or maybe I thought if I got here early, I could leave early and suffer through less of your moaning.'

'We don't moan,' Mary argued. 'We debate, yes.'

'I don't think I've ever moaned about anything,' Clare added.

'Must be my hearing then,' Dan said, concentrating on the wine menu again. Before it was swiftly pulled out of his hand by Clare.

'It's getting cold outside. I'm thinking a nice warming Shiraz.'

'I didn't think you were drinking?' Dan noted.

'I haven't been,' Clare replied. 'But I figured that relaxation time was just as important as training, so I'm going to drink with my lovely siblings today. Is that a problem?'

'Not at all. I'm delighted to hear it. So what about a Chianti?' Dan suggested. Both of his sisters stared at him, clearly unimpressed with his choice.

'I didn't think you wanted another Shiraz at lunchtime?' Mary said to Clare.

'It was summer last time. I think that was the problem.'

'You're so fickle,' Dan gibed. 'What about a Merlot?'

'Fine, let's go with a Shiraz,' Mary stated. 'It's never bad wine in here.'

'What about we meet at the Wetherspoons next time?' Dan asked with a twist in his lips. 'I hear they pour wine on draught there. That might be easier.'

'How is the training going?' Mary asked Clare, carrying on as if Dan hadn't said a word.

'You're still doing the Marathon?' Dan added.

'It's going really well. I've been keeping a log and increasing my distance bit by bit. I'm not going to deny it's demanding, but anything worth doing is worth committing proper time to.'

'I completely agree,' Mary said.

'And the skydive?' Clare asked in return.

'I'm afraid it's going to have to wait until Spring now. It seems like such a long time away. I think I need a challenge for the Winter. It's so easy to fall into the laziness trap with the long dark nights.'

'I have good news,' Dan interjected, stopping the competitive talk before it started.

'Oh yes?' Clare asked. 'Have you worked out how to use the dishwasher?'

Dan flashed her a dirty look. 'I'm actually on the verge of scoring the biggest sale of my career.' Dan glanced around, just in case Emily was following him about. He couldn't see her, but he decided to drop his voice anyway.

'With Dobson's supermarket, no less.'

'Why the clandestine way of telling us?' Clare asked, mocking his low, hushed tone. 'Who's listening?'

'You never know,' Dan said, trying to make light of it. 'It's such a big deal, you never know.'

'Fantastic,' Mary said. 'Are they looking for a few security cameras?'

'They want a complete overhaul of all their security systems. Nationwide. It's massive.'

'Wow. Good for you,' Clare said.

'You said on the verge?' Mary noted.

'Yes. I went to see them yesterday and they were really impressed and extremely keen. I've still got to get the quote to them, which I'll send over on Monday, but all being well they'll sign the dotted line before the end of the week.'

'The star seller strikes again!' Clare smirked.

'How does one go about getting in with Dobson's supermarket?' Mary enquired.

'It was through a contact. A mutual friend.'

Clare instantly giggled. 'You've gone all coy! Did you see that, Mary?'

'I certainly did.'

'What can I get for you?' the waiter asked, appearing next to them.

'A bottle of the Shiraz, please,' Mary ordered.

'Very good. Are you ordering food too?'

'Just give us a couple more minutes,' Mary said, before turning straight back to Dan with inquisitive eyes. 'What is it about this mutual friend that makes you blush?'

'I'm not blushing.'

'You are. You really are.'

'Is our Danny in love?' Clare teased.

'Don't call me that.'

'Ooh, he is! Finally, after all this time, we get some girl gossip.'

'This is the exact reason why I've never told you anything before.'

'Well, it's too late on this occasion,' Mary stated. 'We know there's gossip to be had and we won't rest until we're satisfied we've got it.'

Dan sighed. Telling them about Alice was now going to be the far easier option.

'There's not much gossip really. There's just this girl at work. I quite like her.'

'Have you asked her out?' Clare asked.

'No.'

'What does she do? Sales too?'

'No,' Dan said after the smallest of hesitations.

'What?' Clare pushed, all excited. 'What is it? You went all weird then.'

'No I didn't.'

'What does she do? She's not your boss, is she?'

'You know a man called John is my boss. I've told you that.'

'Evading the question,' Mary noted. 'So is she John's boss?'

Dan couldn't have been more relived as the waiter appeared with their wine. They all pointed at Mary who eloquently tested a small sip and nodded appreciatively. Then he poured them all a small glass and left.

Dan really wanted him to stay.

'She's not really John's boss, is she?' Clare asked.

Dan shrugged.

'What does that mean?' Mary asked.

'She's a director of the company.'

'You're still not telling us the whole truth,' Mary said. 'We aren't going to rest until we're satisfied we get all the gossip. We've established this.'

Dan took a gulp of his wine. 'She owns the company. Okay. Her name is Alice Bloom. As in Bloom's Security Solutions.'

This shut his sisters up. Now they both just sat there gaping at him in shock.

'Technically she only inherited the company when her

parents died. She's never there. She's not really actively involved.'

'Are you allowed to have an affair with the owner of the company?' Clare asked.

'Who exactly is going to stop them?' Mary stated.

'We're not having an affair.'

'But you want one.'

'She's literally just got out of a relationship. We're just friends.'

Clare shook her head. 'Oh no. No no no. Don't go there, Daniel. This has disaster written all over it.'

'No it doesn't.'

'It does,' Mary agreed. 'She's technically your boss. Worse, your boss's boss. Add to that the fact that she's been handed the company after what sounds like a family tragedy, and she's just come out of a relationship, and it practically spells out no-go area.'

'They weren't together that long.'

'Dan, if you go ahead with this, you're going to get hurt,' Mary said. 'Trust me. This cannot end well.'

'You don't know her. She's lovely.'

'Aww.' Clare placed a caring hand on his arm. 'You must really like her. We know it's hard. But no good can come from this. The warning signs are there like fifty foot beacons. By all means stay friends with her, but if you tell her how you feel, you'll either be the gossip of the company for dating the boss, the rebound from her ex, or worse, the shoulder to cry on, as it sounds like she's got a lot on her plate.'

As much as Dan wanted to declare that his sisters were totally wrong, he had a sinking feeling there was some truth in their words.

Alice hadn't left the house in five years. Who does that? She'd refused to meet him for months. She'd invited him out just so she could meet another man.

She'd also admitted that Dan was her only friend in the world. He and a stuffed teddy bear. Something about it at the time had made Dan feel uneasy.

Maybe Alice Bloom was bad news. Maybe he'd been blinded by his intense feelings for her.

Maybe he was being given a very lucky escape.

THIRTY-ONE

By ten o'clock on Monday morning, Alice still hadn't risen from bed. She was wide awake and utterly distraught.

Since Dan had left her house the week before, things had progressively gone from bad to worse.

Her phone rang from the bedside table and she peered up with dread. It was Ethan. She ignored the call, just as she'd ignored his multiple other calls and texts over the past few days. His messages had gone from heartfully apologising to telling her she was a stuck up cow and she needed to get some perspective.

She had no intention of replying to him. Mostly because she just didn't care. Coming to terms with her feelings for Dan had made her realise how drastically insignificant Ethan was in her life. What had she been thinking getting involved with him at all? Her carnal desires had taken over all her senses.

Her phone pinged again. She peeked across and saw it was an email from Charles.

She sat up. She rarely got emails from any of the directors.

Dear Alice

I hope all is well and you had a good weekend?

How are the new budget plans coming along? As the next board meeting is only two weeks away now, I wondered if I could take a look at your recommendations before then. As you pointed out, a lot of spend has been allocated to marketing. If you're going to propose a cut to that then I need to know as soon as possible as we're already looking at next year's plan.

Any questions, give me a call.

Charles

Alice curled herself up back under the duvet.

That was her other huge problem. She knew her dad would want to spend more on research and development than on marketing and admin costs, but balancing budgets was proving to be much harder than she'd anticipated.

She'd been looking at it for days, but other than going round and round in multiple circles, she'd got absolutely nowhere. She just didn't know enough about marketing or finance to make any real suggestions.

The advertising and PR budget was huge. She couldn't believe that advertising in trade publications and online would be that expensive, and immediately she'd assumed either the numbers must be wrong or the company was over-spending. Then she'd researched a few of the magazines, found their rate cards and realised that Charles was getting massive discounts. It was shocking, but the prices they paid were sometimes fifty percent off.

Then she thought maybe they could cut back on stationery, or they could re-negotiate the astronomical phone charges. Or they could buy cheaper tea and coffee for the two office kitchens. But all of it seemed like such tiny ideas and she didn't know whether the board had already looked into this. And after her speech, she felt stupid asking.

She wanted to present them with some super cost saving ideas that would free up lots of budget to go back into R&D.

But with so many intricate threads to each area of the business, it was seeming like an impossible task.

That was when she'd taken herself to bed on Friday afternoon. After she'd contemplated how she was not only letting herself down but also her father - who would want her to take charge and stop the spending in the wrong areas – she hit a new low and buried herself beneath her duvet. And all she'd done since was either lay in bed or mope about the house, constantly in a state of depression.

She wanted to be able to talk to her friend about it. Dan had tried to call her but she couldn't face him. She felt herself flush every time she thought about him. She knew she'd be a wreck talking to him. It seemed he'd even got bored of trying now as she hadn't heard from him since Saturday lunchtime, adding more weight to her concerns. Had she upset him by not speaking to him? The last thing she wanted was for Dan to be mad with her.

She was very tempted to call him, but she'd seen in his diary he had a busy day. Although he was up in the office tomorrow. Maybe that would be an opportunity to speak to him.

She felt herself get flustered again as she thought about him.

It was so unfair. Everything had gone from being wonderful to absolute crap, and it had all happened in the space of a few hours it seemed.

Alice's phone went again. It was Glenn emailing her. She scanned it quickly. There were more problems with a client's software and, as usual, it was being escalated to Alice to sort out.

She exhaled with frustration. Was no one at the company capable? Or were they just lazy? She knew she'd have to deal with it, but she had more important things to do. She couldn't keep getting called upon to solve simple customer service issues.

She had self-pitying to wallow in, for goodness sake!

In a huff, she marched across to her office and flicked

the computer on. She'd get this sorted as soon as possible and then she'd raid the fridge for a fattening and indulgent lunch.

Alice didn't eat lunch. At seven o'clock that evening she was still in her pyjamas and all she'd done was nibble on biscuits for most of the day.

She'd solved the customer service issue in about four minutes and then had an email argument with Glenn demanding that the team got trained up better. He'd fought back, agreeing that training was an issue, but reasoning that they were understaffed and therefore had no time for training, so what was he supposed to do?

Alice went straight back to the budget. The salary spend seemed already high, but Glenn was right, they weren't solving customers' needs well enough.

Alice was now knee deep in note paper, trying to work out a new budget. She needed to somehow free up cash whilst at the same time ensuring she didn't sacrifice anything important.

It was too hard.

Too, too hard.

She took her glasses off and rubbed her eyes. She still hadn't gone for an eye test and they were getting sorer every day. She'd been too busy worrying about men and other stupid things. She hadn't got a grip on anything that mattered and now she was in a right mess.

She took a breath. Everything in her head told her she could do this. Numbers were her thing. But it wasn't the maths that was letting her down, it was her lack of understanding of the business. She was ultimately in charge but knew nothing about how to run it.

Her feelings five years ago that she was out of her depth came rushing to the surface. She was absolutely, totally, undeniably and drastically out of her depth and it terrified her.

She couldn't fight the tears anymore. She sobbed, quietly

apologising to her father for the mess she was making of everything.

The directors were spending on plush carpets and fancy coffee machines, not focusing at all on what mattered. She knew the budgets were all wrong. But she couldn't fathom how to sort out the issues.

Her phone pinged for what felt like the millionth time that day and she prayed it would be Dan. She had never needed her friend more.

He knew the business. He was there far more than she was. Maybe he could help?

She picked it up to find a message from Karl.

Her heart began to throb as she opened it.

I heard Ethans dumped u. Serves u rite. I guess he saw ur using ways to. Ur such a bitch. I hope u never find happiness.

The dam cracked. Tears flooded down Alice's cheeks. She buried her head in her hands and cried; the pain coming up from her broken heart. So much pain.

Karl was right. Not about everything. Ethan hadn't dumped her, but it was nice to know what he'd been saying. But Karl was right that she'd used him. She had been truly horrible to him, and the second he was no use to her anymore, she'd thrown him aside like garbage.

Alice shuffled back to her bedroom, wiping away tears with the sleeve of her dressing gown. She reached her bed and buried herself deep within in.

She cried into her pillow feeling like the tears might never stop.

It all reminded her of the days following her parents' death. Everything was still so painful. She hadn't moved on at all. She was letting everyone down, including herself. And everyone was letting her down too.

There was no one in the world she could rely on. Dan was her only friend but that had now been ruined. She could never be the same with him again. She'd even managed to mess up the best friendship she'd ever had.

She grabbed Sammy next to her. Sammy was the only strength in her life. She didn't know how she could have ever coped at all without Sammy.

She cuddled her teddy tightly as she cried herself to sleep.

She woke up in the middle of the night. It was pitch black and she really needed the toilet. She fumbled out of bed, her eyes only half open, and she made her way to the bathroom.

She quickly had a wee, not bothering to flush the loo, and then went to splash some water on her hands. She flicked the tap off, went to leave, when she stopped.

She looked down.

It couldn't be. It couldn't be!

She swiftly turned the light on - the brightness stinging her eyes, but she had to see.

She stood before the mirror and her worst fear was realised all over again.

She was invisible.

THIRTY-TWO

'Shit, shit, shit!' Dan said, speeding into the office car park and ramming his Audi A5 into the first space he came across, not even bothering to line his car up properly.

He grabbed his laptop from the boot and jogged to the front door.

'Morning!' Alistair greeted as Dan swooped by.

'Morning, mate.'

Dan swiped his pass, swung open the door and hurtled up the stairs to the board room. The Sales meeting had now started and he'd missed his chance to have a talk with John.

John had contacted him the evening before to request that Dan arrive well before the meeting as he wanted to have a word with him. Dan could only surmise that it was related to Dobson's and somehow John had found out. Maybe Caroline had called the office to query a couple of details and John had been informed about this huge new opportunity?

But Dan's hopes of having this satisfying discussion with John had all been crushed when his car ground to a halt on the M1.

He opened the door to the meeting room to find his colleagues milling around, grabbing coffee from the fancy machine.

'Sorry,' Dan said as he approached John.

'It's fine,' John replied.

'They closed the M1.'

'You said on the phone. It's fine. Let's just be grateful you weren't in the accident.'

Dan nodded. 'Yeah.'

'I came up last night,' Emily explained and Dan felt that urge again to slap her.

'Look, we still need to talk,' John said. 'Have you got a couple of minutes?'

'Have you heard the news?' Chris interrupted in his thick west country accent.

'What news?'

'I just need five minutes, Dan,' John said.

'Sure.'

'Emily has scored the biggest job this company has ever seen,' Chris said.

Dan stopped moving. He didn't realise it, but he'd even stopped breathing.

Emily stepped away, suddenly taking a great interest in the coffee machine.

'Can you believe she's got the contract for Dobson's Supermarket? Nationwide!' Chris said.

Dan felt the ground beneath him crack. He stared at her but she didn't take her eyes off the coffee machine.

'Dan, can we have five minutes.'

Dan couldn't speak. He just nodded and then followed John back to his office, over the other side of the building.

The second the door was closed behind them, Dan felt the rage kick in.

'That was my job!'

'Take a seat,' John said as he made himself comfortable at the table in the middle of his office. He gestured for Dan to sit next to him.

'That was my fucking job! How has she done this?'

'Dan, please sit down.'

'I only got the lead last week. I've kept it off the CRM, I've kept it as quiet as I can.'

'Sit down.'

Dan reluctantly took the seat next to John with a huff.

'They weren't speaking to anyone else. They hadn't even considered upgrading their system until I spoke to them. I only sent them my quote yesterday. There's something really shitty going on here.'

John sighed and shook his head. 'I've had enough of this now, Dan. You know I like you. You're a good lad with a great track record. But something's going wrong here, and you can't keep blaming Emily.'

'She's stealing my leads!'

'Okay. Prove it.'

Dan opened his mouth to tell John exactly how she was doing it, but no words formed. 'I don't know. She's up to something. She virtually admitted it to me at the show last week. Don't you think this is all a huge coincidence? That every lead I get, she ends up securing?'

'Or is it that every contract she gets, you claim you got as a lead first?'

'I'm not claiming anything. I'm telling you the truth.'

John shook his head again. 'Emily is the best salesperson this company has ever seen. That I've ever seen.'

'I'll take that as a huge compliment, since most of her sales should have rightfully been mine.'

'Dan, I don't know what's going on-'

'Tell me honestly, have you ever known two sales people clash like this before? There's got to be something in your head that tells you something's wrong.'

'There is,' John nodded. 'But it isn't telling me there's anything wrong with Emily. All I can see is that she's closing at a rapid rate. She's wiping the floor with everyone else. And all you're doing is bringing in a few scraps and moaning a lot.'

'For fuck's sake, John. Think about it. I'm the senior salesperson here. You brought me in for my experience. I was head hunted for this job. Emily doesn't have my training or background, yet she's somehow magically doing better than me? It doesn't make sense. Think about it!'

'Fine. Okay, she's stealing all your leads. I'll believe you if you prove it. If you're really telling me you didn't even know about Dobson's until last week and you kept it totally quiet from everyone, including me - weirdly enough - how exactly has Emily managed to mysteriously find out about it?'

'I don't know. Maybe she's following me? I bet she is. I was telling my sisters about this job at the weekend. I bet she was there spying on me.'

'Listen to yourself, Dan. Will you listen.'

'I'm not crazy.'

'Emily was in Wales at the weekend with her family. She's just been showing us the pictures. Were you with your sisters in Wales?'

Dan shook his head.

'Maybe she's got really good hearing,' John said. 'That will be it. Or maybe she's telepathic. Or maybe she legitimately got this lead just as you did.'

Dan opened his mouth to argue again when he felt a stab. Would Alice have told Emily about the job too?

Ever since his lunch with his sisters, Dan had been feeling cautious about Alice. As much as he felt like she was his soulmate, he also knew that she was knee deep in secrets. There was something cagey about her and it unnerved him.

Maybe she had been playing him all along.

But he couldn't believe it. Dan might have suspected that Alice was hiding things from him, but he didn't believe she was two-faced. She hated Emily as much as he did. She was the only one who could see Emily for the lying bitch she was, and he loved Alice for that.

So how had Emily managed it?

'Dan, we're about to go through the sales figures in the meeting. For the third month running, you're the worst performer. I've tried to cover for you. I've tried to give you extra training and give you a bit of leeway, but questions are starting to be asked. How can Emily, in the same territory, smash her target for the year in just seven months, but you can't even meet your target for one month?'

'Because she's stealing my leads! I keep telling you. She's getting her own pisspot work and then adding my work on top of it. How else could she smash her annual target so quickly? Who does that?'

'You've done that. You came here with the boast that you've smashed every target you've ever been given. Or was that a lie?'

'Precisely! Doesn't that prove it? Why is it I've never even so much as struggled before, yet suddenly I'm the worst salesman on the planet? It doesn't ring true. Think about it.'

'All I can think is that this isn't your forte. You were just selling access control before. Selling the whole system is obviously too much for you.'

Dan clenched his fists. He wanted to punch the wall. This was ridiculous. If John could just hear himself. None of this made sense, yet John was finding logic in the madness.

'I really am sorry, Dan. I really am. I will give you a glowing reference.'

Dan's eyes flicked up towards John. His anger subsided as panic kicked in. 'What are you saying?'

'I can't keep justifying things. Why have I got two London sales people, when only one is performing? I can't justify having you on the team anymore.'

'No. No! Give me another chance.'

'That's all I have been doing.'

'No! You'll see. You'll see. As soon as I step away, Emily won't bring the leads in anymore. You'll see. Can't I just go on a sabbatical or something? Just so you can see.'

'Dan, I'm sorry. I say this with deep regret. You know I do. But I'm going to have to let you go. There's nothing I can do about it. You're just not good enough.'

Dan stopped listening. Those words were the most painful words he'd ever heard. They cut him sharply and in that moment he felt himself give up.

Throughout Dan's life, that had always been his deepest fear: that he just wasn't good enough. Even when he'd been succeeding, it hadn't been easy. He'd always pretended it was, but in reality climbing up the ladder had nearly killed him. Truthfully, he wasn't naturally talented at anything. Blood, sweat and tears just to be even. He'd worked relentlessly at his previous job and he'd had quite a few lucky breaks. It wasn't talent, though. He had no talent.

'Are you all right?' John's concern cut through Dan's trance.

Dan didn't know what to do. He wanted to be gracious. To thank John for the opportunity and make sure that the bridges were still standing strong. But he had never felt so let down.

'Thanks for nothing, John,' Dan said instead. 'I wonder if Norman Bloom would be proud of you today?'

With that, Dan stood up, grabbed his things and swiftly exited, leaving the door purposefully wide open on his way out.

THIRTY-THREE

Dan left the building as quickly as possible. Faint words were echoing around his head. Had John said something about handing in his pass and how they'll have to sort out his car?

What was Dan going to do without his car? What was he going to do without a job?

He reached his Audi, slammed the door shut and then froze. He stared out his windscreen, totally lost as to what to do next.

As he tried to make sense of the fog building up in his head, he regretted storming out. He had a million questions and no way of getting answers.

He should probably go back in, but he couldn't bear the embarrassment. John would have returned to the Sales meeting and everyone would know that Dan had been fired. Dan, the star salesman, who turned out to be utter crap.

Emily would know that her devious ways had cost Dan his job. He doubted she'd feel bad. She was probably going to get a pay rise now.

How could he have let her get the better of him like that? Could he have done more? Should he have challenged her more?

Dan stared up at the company signage when another level of sadness hit him.

Bloom. Bloom's Security Solutions.

He wouldn't be coming here anymore. He wouldn't be coming to the Midlands anymore. He would have no reason to see Alice.

He hadn't just lost his job, he'd lost the love of his life.

Emily had cost him everything.

Dan picked up his phone. His work phone. He'd have to give that back too. He'd lose all those lovely emails and messages that he'd shared with Alice. It would all just be gone.

He had to contact her. He had to let her know. He had to say goodbye.

He felt sick as he dialled her number.

It rang and rang.

'Alice can't take your call...'

Dan hung up. Bloody voicemail.

He clasped the steering wheel tightly, his body charged with panic and confusion, topped off with anger at how severely he'd been let down.

He picked up his phone to try Alice again. He had to speak to her.

Once again it went to voicemail.

'Shit!'

For just a second the fog cleared and he had an idea.

Alice lived nearby. Very nearby. He'd been to her house. He didn't know where it was from the office, but he knew the street name.

He quickly opened Google Maps and typed in Alice's address.

It was about one mile away. That was all. He knew she'd be at home. She was always working from home.

He started the engine and took a deep breath. He had to see her one last time. He had to say goodbye.

He followed his Sat Nav and not a few minutes later he was pulling up outside Alice's house. He recognised it instantly. It was such a lovely road with well presented houses.

He was trembling as he stepped out and walked up her drive to the front door. He rang the bell quickly, before he changed his mind and wimped out.

After a few moments the door strangely opened, but no one was there.

'Can you just bring the bags in and leave them in the hallway,' Alice said.

'Alice?' Dan said.

Dan heard a gasp but then everything went silent.

'Alice? It's me, Dan. Are you there?'

Everything was very still and quiet and then the door slammed in Dan's face.

He was shocked.

'Alice? What's going on?'

Dan heard a vehicle pull up behind him. It was an Ocado delivery van. No doubt what she'd been expecting.

'All right, mate?' the man said as he jumped out the driver's seat.

'You're here for Alice Bloom?' Dan asked.

The driver checked his paperwork. 'Yep, that's the one.'

Dan rang the bell again. 'Alice, your shopping's here. You're going to have to open up.'

The man started to bring the shopping bags to the door. 'Is she in?'

'She's definitely in. I don't know what's going on. Alice!'

The door strangely opened again with no one on the other side.

'Alice?' Dan said.

'What do you want me to do with them? Shall I take them through to the kitchen?' the delivery man asked.

'No, just leave them in the doorway and I'll take them through. I don't think she's feeling very well.'

'No problem.'

Dan helped the man drop off the ten bags of shopping and then he bid his farewell.

'Alice, I'm bringing your shopping through,' Dan said, carrying half of the bags through to the kitchen. He scanned his surroundings on the way but no one was around.

'Alice?'

Dan placed the bags down before he returned to grab the remaining items. He knocked the front door shut with his foot and lugged the heavy shopping towards the back of house.

'You've got some frozen stuff here,' he called out, looking across the bags he'd placed in the middle of the kitchen floor. 'Are you going to put it away?'

Still there was no answer.

'Alice?' Dan examined the bags. There was a massive tub of salted caramel ice cream poking out of one of them. Should he do something? It would soon be melting. 'Shall I put it away for you? Where are you?'

'Thanks for your help, but would you mind leaving me to it now,' Alice said. Her voice seemed distant and edgy.

'Alice, what's going on?'

'What are you doing here?'

Dan opened his mouth to tell her the whole sorry story when something clicked in his head.

'Why can't you face me?' he asked.

There was no reply.

'Is it because you're feeling guilty?'

Again, no response.

'Come on, Alice. Just tell me the truth. Was it you who told Emily about Dobson's?'

'Emily?' she said, her voice seeming closer, but Dan still had no idea where she was.

'Yes, Emily. Was it you who stabbed me in the back?'

'Stabbed you in the back?'

'Yes! Emily got the job with Dobson's. They signed off her quote. She swooped in at the last minute and got the deal of the century. What I want to know is how she found out about it?'

'You think I had something to do with it?'

'We were the only ones who knew.'

'I gave that lead to you because I wanted you to get the job. I deliberately got that lead for you. I wanted you to do better than Emily. Why on earth would I tell her?'

'Then why can't you face me?'

There was no response.

'What is going on?' Dan could feel the frustration and upset starting to strain his voice. 'Alice, what the fuck are you playing at? If you've done nothing wrong then why can't you face me?'

Still there was nothing but silence.

'Well, you know what, if you won't let me see you, then at least take a good look at me. Because this will be the last time you see this face.'

Still no response.

Dan was struggling to control his emotions now. He felt broken hearted and let down by everyone. Even the one person he thought he could rely on.

'So I don't even get to say goodbye? Thanks a lot.'

'Why goodbye?' Alice asked.

'You won't see me again.'

'I haven't told Emily anything. How could you possibly think that I'd do that? You can't be mad at me.'

'I'm mad at everybody! And you hiding away from me for reasons I can't even begin to fathom isn't making it any easier.'

'I'm not hiding. I'm just not feeling very well. I'm in a bit of a state. I don't want you to see me like this.'

'I don't care about that, Alice. I don't give a shit about what you look like or what you're wearing. Can't you see? Are you really that dense?'

'Excuse me?'

'For fuck's sake, Alice. How is it that you're so intelligent but you can't see the one thing that's right in front of your face?'

'Why do you keep shouting at me? Please don't be mad with me.'

'I'm not mad with you. I'm in love with you!'

There was a gasp and some shuffling, but Dan was more focused on what he should say now. He never imagined for one second that he'd blurt it out like that, but he supposed he had nothing to lose. He'd lost everything anyway.

'I love you, Alice,' he continued. 'I've liked you since the first time we spoke, and I knew I was in love the second I lay my eyes on you. I love everything about you. You're all I think about all the time.'

'No,' she whimpered.

'Well, that tells me everything.'

'No, can't you see?' Dan could tell Alice was crying but he still couldn't see her. 'You can't love me. It'll ruin everything. We were friends. The best of friends. I've had the most amazing time playing our chess games and enjoying our endless chats. We could always spend so long talking about nothing and everything. But now we've fallen in love, it's all ruined.'

'What are you talking about?' Dan asked.

'Our friendship has gone. It's like this love has evaporated everything that was good. I mean you being here now. You're not the concerned friend you were. You're now feeling hurt because you think I've stabbed you in the back. There's too much emotion. It's destroyed the respect. We'll start getting jealous and every conversation will have meaning, and before we know it we'll resent each other and then never speak to each other again. It's starting now. You're already trying to say goodbye before we've even had a proper discussion about this.'

Dan shook his head. He didn't know what she was rambling on about. 'Okay, so we need to have a proper discussion. Fine. Let's go into your living room and talk about this properly. Face to face.'

Everything went silent again.

'Oh for fuck's sake, Alice, will you at least put away your ice cream,' Dan said. He needed to take control of something.

Dan grabbed the tub from the bag and opened her freezer.

'No! Please leave it,' Alice pleaded.

'You can't just leave your shopping on the floor like this!'

'Dan, stop it!'

Dan opened her freezer drawers, trying to find space.

'Stop going through everything. You'll mess it up,' Alice begged.

'You can move it later. I just don't want it to melt.'

'Dan, stop it!'

The freezer was packed full of Tupperware, vegetables, bread and tons of ice cream tubs. He couldn't find any spare space. He pushed some stuff aside, trying to find room.

'Dan, leave it! Stop it!'

He tried to force the tub into a drawer, his frustration now sky high.

'Dan!'

It wasn't naturally slipping into the drawer, but Dan was sure he could wedge it in. He just wanted something to work. He needed to be able to manage something.

'Dan, you're going to break it!'

Suddenly Alice's voice seemed very close. As he looked up, now sure she was standing next to him, the tub of ice cream flew out of his hand. It levitated through the air and carefully landed on the kitchen side.

'What the hell?' Dan said, jumping backwards.

The freezer door magically closed itself and everything went silent.

'What was that?' Dan asked, staring at the miraculous flying ice cream with horror.

Dan heard a heavy sigh. It was close.

'Alice?'

'You think you love me?' she said, her voice seeming so near. 'You think you love everything about me?'

Dan didn't know how to respond.

'Well, do you love this?'

Dan felt something touch his arm. He jumped back

again, fear and surprise shaking him to the core.

'It's me, Dan. Me. Alice.'

Something touched his hands. Something that felt strangely like fingers seemed to interlock with his fingers. Exactly as they'd done at the office a few weeks ago. He knew it was Alice's hands.

'What the hell is going on?'

'Do you want to know why I didn't leave the house for five years?' Alice asked, her voice directly in front of him. 'Do you want to know why I could never meet you, even though I wanted to so badly? Do you want to know why I've lost all my friends and I have no one? No one in the world but you?'

Dan couldn't respond. There were no words to describe this overwhelming situation.

'Dan, I'm invisible.'

THIRTY-FOUR

Alice concentrated on Dan's face. She was waiting for a response. Something; anything. She needed to know how he felt about the massive revelation.

But all he did was stare out ahead of him in shock. He was almost looking at her. He could almost see her with his wide and terrified eyes.

She could see his lips twitching, as if he wanted to say something but the words were somehow blocked.

She guessed the questions "why" and "how" were trying to find their way out, so she thought she'd help them.

She let go of his hand, knowing that any second he may turn invisible himself thanks to the temporary contagion of her condition. She feared that might push him over the edge completely.

'I wasn't like this before my parents died,' Alice began. She saw Dan move his head slightly, focusing in on where he could hear her voice.

'But their passing hit me hard. Not that I suppose that's surprising. I lost both my parents – my only close family – in an instant. I was so young, just about to finish university, and suddenly I'm all alone. After being part of a tight family unit, I had to find a way to tackle the world all by myself.'

Alice took a second as she acknowledged the pain of the truth. 'That was enough to deal with on its own. Then throw in the fact that the ownership of the company was passed down to me and you can see how I was pretty overwhelmed.'

Alice paused to see if Dan wanted to say anything, but he just listened silently, taking in every word.

'I was upset, scared and massively out of my depth. None of my friends had lost anyone that close. They couldn't understand. My boyfriend at the time was at first caring, but he soon became irritated. I suppose I'd changed. I was sadder and prickly, and I quickly became fed up with everyone telling me how to feel when no one in the world actually understood any of what I was going through. So I pushed them away. Good riddance. I didn't need the hassle, and I think they were glad to step away from me too.'

Again Alice paused, hoping that Dan would now utter something. He must have something to say. But he didn't so much as flinch.

'I became all alone. I stopped leaving the house, I stopped speaking to people, I stopped interacting with anyone at all. I came off social media and I switched off from the world. In every way I was invisible. And then I woke up one morning to find out I'd actually become invisible too. I couldn't see my body. I couldn't see me. I was lost from the world forever.'

Alice could see Dan's lips twitching again, as if questions were there but the words still wouldn't form. She desperately needed to know what he was thinking.

'I remember the day it happened so clearly. At first I was obviously shocked. I immediately blamed all the people who had let me down. I declared how I was mad at the universe. I wanted to be scared. I thought I should be scared. But after the shock had subsided, I realised that actually I was just relieved. It meant I could stop fighting. I'd hit rock bottom and that left only one direction to go in.'

Alice scanned Dan's emotionless face. What was he

thinking?

'All I needed was for somebody to make an effort,' she said. 'For just one person to be there for me in the way that my parents always had been. But when push came to shove, everyone was happy to walk away. Nobody really cared. Sad, depressed Alice was far too much like hard work for everyone. Except you.'

Alice looked into Dan's eyes but he was still giving nothing away.

'You are the only person who's ever fought for me,' she said. 'You never gave up. Never. Even though for months I couldn't meet you. Even after all the ridiculous excuses I made, you still kept trying. And it was thanks to you that I came back that day. I only went into Starley Green on the night of my birthday so I could see you. I wanted to know what you looked like. You meant the world to me and I hated that we couldn't meet in person. I stood right by you that night. It was fantastic to see you in the flesh. I heard John tell you all about how my parents died. I love that you've never mentioned it to me.' Alice hoped that Dan might now comment, but he still remained frozen and silent.

'It was just after I saw you that night that I met Karl. I stood next to him at the bar and he could see me. For the first time in years, someone could see me. It was mind blowing. As long as I was with Karl, I could be seen. And it stayed that way for a few weeks, until slowly I returned back whole and I didn't need Karl anymore.'

Alice couldn't look at Dan as she admitted the appalling truth. 'I used Karl. I was horrible to him. That's not the sort of person I want to be. But desperation made me nasty.' She looked up at Dan again. 'You make me good, though. You make me the best version of myself. I realise now that it was seeing you that night that spurred on my reappearance and brought me back into the world. It makes perfect sense. It was just deeply unfortunate that Karl was the next person I saw after you. Somehow everything seemed to get caught up with Karl. But I know that without you, I never would have come back at all. And that's why the thought of losing you has cost me everything again.'

'Why do you think you're going to lose me?' Dan said. Alice was so relieved. She took a breath to steady herself.

'Because ever since we've realised our feelings for each other, everything has changed.'

'Feelings for each other?'

Alice couldn't look at Dan again. Even though he couldn't see her, she felt a compulsion to hide.

'Alice?' Dan nudged. 'How do you feel about me?'

'Does it matter?'

'Yes.'

'I don't want anything more than friendship. I can't. If I say I love you then everything will be ruined. Things won't be the same anymore. It was suffering from pain that got me into this mess in the first place. Whenever I love anything it always hurts.'

'But you said me loving you brought you back.'

'No, it was our friendship that brought me back.'

'Alice, we've never just been friends. I've always been crazy about you. I used to dream about you and I didn't even know what you looked like. If you think me not giving up on you is just due to friendship then you're wrong. Very wrong. It's because I love you that I've fought so hard.'

'No!' Alice insisted. She couldn't believe that. She couldn't. 'I just need a friend. I don't need any more. I don't need heartache. I don't want any more heartache.'

'You were happy to have Ethan as more than just your friend, though.'

'And look what happened there! Even Karl who meant nothing to me. As soon as you enter the relationship zone, everything goes to shit. Everything!'

'Not if you really love the other person.'

'I loved my parents.'

'They didn't knowingly leave you.'

'But I loved them and it hurt so much when they went.'

'Alice, listen to yourself.' Dan put out his hands. 'Where

are you?'

Alice knew she should back away. She could just take a few steps back and he'd never find her. But she remained still. She felt compelled to see what he was going to do. She didn't want his love but she also couldn't not want it either.

He found her arm with his left hand, and then his right hand quickly found her other arm too. He slowly moved up her pyjama top until he reached her cheeks, and then he cupped them in his hands. His warm, safe hands.

'Alice, I love you. I'm never going to hurt you. I want to be with you. I want to help you. Even you being invisible doesn't put me off. It makes me want you even more. Everything about you has finally slotted into place and for the first time in my life I feel a true connection to someone. I might not have lost my parents, but I understand about feeling lost and alone. I really do. We need each other.'

Dan closed his eyes and Alice's heart began to throb. She knew what was coming and everything in her head told her to run. But she didn't move a muscle.

She closed her eyes too and Dan's soft lips met hers.

They wrapped their arms around each other as they melted into a loving kiss. A kiss they'd both needed so badly for so long.

They rested their foreheads together for a moment and Alice opened her eyes. She couldn't see anything in front of her, but she could feel Dan's breath against her. She could hear his heart pounding just like hers.

She stepped away, freeing herself from his embrace. She couldn't take the risk of him being freaked out by the catching invisibility.

'Alice,' Dan said, searching around for her.

'I can't take any more pain. I love you. I really do. But if I get hurt one more time then I don't know what it's going to do to me. Look at the state of me already. That's right, you can't! See! It's ridiculous. I need to protect myself. Can't we just be friends? Please?'

'I can't just be your friend, Alice. I feel too strongly for you. You say that you want to protect your heart, but in doing so you're breaking mine.'

'No. No!'

'Why can't we just give us a go?'

'No. I want to go back to how we were before.'

'Before I met you? Before I knew how beautiful you are on the outside as well as the inside?'

'Well, that's just got easier. You can't see me anymore. Doesn't that help?'

'Why are you fighting this?'

'I told you why.'

'You've got to... This is... Why can't...' Dan hit his fist against the kitchen worktop in frustration. 'You know you're not the only one suffering. I feel pain too. I think this invisibility thing is just an excuse because you're too afraid to face reality. Yeah, it's shit when you get hurt, but it's better to be hurt than have no life at all. All you're doing at the minute is wallowing. You're wasting your life in a ball of self-pity. You said you pushed those people away because you were fed up of no one understanding what you were going through, but maybe you pushed them away because otherwise it would mean making an effort. Being human.' Dan exhaled heavily. 'I love you so much. I couldn't love you more. Yet you're pushing me away too, because apparently that's easier. But you know what, that kiss was easy. It was the easiest thing in the world for both of us to do and it felt amazing. It's this fighting you're doing that's hard. Very hard. And it feels crap. So is this really what you want? Is this going to make you happy?'

Alice felt a flash of anger. Dan was making it seem so black and white when it was vastly more complex. He just didn't understand. He wanted to. He had the audacity to believe he did. But he didn't. Just like everyone else.

'Well, you know what Alice, you've got your wish. I won't be bothering you anymore. I meant it when I said this is goodbye. Do you know what happened today? I lost my job. John fired me. For some horrible reason that seems to defy all logic, Emily got the job with Dobson's. Caroline signed the contract with her, and they all think she's the best salesperson that has ever lived. And I got told today that I'm just not good enough. So I'm out. I'm heading back to London and I'm never going to set foot in this shitty little town again. So goodbye Alice. Have a nice life.'

Dan stormed out the kitchen, just missing Alice by a centimetre. Leaving her utterly in shock.

She flinched as the front door banged shut.

Dan was gone. Dan was gone forever.

What had she done?

THIRTY-FIVE

Alice felt the prickle of panic run through her. He couldn't mean it. She couldn't never see him again.

She raced to the front window. Dan was sitting in his car, his head rested against the steering wheel.

She wanted to run out. She wanted to run out and beg him to come back. He couldn't just leave like that.

But what could she do? Her front door would magically open of its own accord. She'd tap on Dan's window and he'd be in the street, talking to himself. What if anyone saw?

She couldn't do it. She couldn't. She needed her invisibility to stay invisible.

Dan might have accepted it. In fact he'd accepted it far better than she could ever have hoped for. Although, thinking about it, her revelation had probably answered quite a few questions that had been hanging over their friendship.

However, not everyone was as kind or as considerate as Dan. Alice knew that all too well. She couldn't take the risk of anyone else ever finding out that she was invisible.

She watched in hope that he would open his door and march back up the drive. She'd let him in. She'd instantly let him in. They could talk some more. Figure out a way forward.

Maybe they could kiss again.

No! No. It was the kiss that had messed it all up. Emotions had got in the way and it had sent Dan storming off.

Her heart cracked as she heard the engine of his car turn on. Within seconds he was driving away.

She felt her eyes sting as she realised that very moment might be the last time she ever saw him.

She waited and waited, hoping that he'd turn around. Hoping that at any second he'd reappear outside her door and they could put everything right.

She stood firmly by the window, determined not to give up.

But eventually she had to. He wasn't coming back. She knew he'd be on the motorway by now, darting back to London, never to set foot in Starley Green again.

She dragged her feet over to the settee where she flopped down in tears.

Dan was gone. Her closest friend was gone.

She sobbed, feeling the familiar ache of loss burning in the centre of her body.

Abruptly her tears halted as Dan's words clicked in her head. He wasn't gone because he didn't want to see Alice anymore. Dan was gone because he'd been sacked.

Alice's own company had sacked him. She'd lost one of the best sales people from her own staff.

How had this happened?

She sat up straight as thoughts started to bounce around her head.

She knew Dan was good at his job. She knew it. It wasn't a biased viewpoint because she loved him; she loved him because of his incredible attitude and diligent work ethic. Having been brought up in a world so focused on business, she couldn't help but find drive and ambition attractive.

Alice stood up. She had to do something. She couldn't let a talented employee go. Her dad would be turning in his grave knowing that his company had behaved so badly.

She raced up to her office and grabbed her phone, ready to call John and demand that he give Dan his job back.

She hesitated.

She couldn't do that. Not only would it undermine John, but Dan would be highly embarrassed.

An image of that day she'd visited Dan in the office flickered through her mind. Everyone had been staring. She hadn't properly considered it at the time, but what must everyone have thought? She was sitting closely with Dan, whispering with him.

No wonder Dan seemed so cautious about rumours. What had people been saying?

She placed her phone back down, deciding it would be quite unwise to demand that John give Dan his job back. It was one thing being close friends with someone in the office, it was another giving them special favours. Dan would never live it down.

Alice realised she only had one option. She had to prove that Emily was up to no good, and then demand that Emily be sacked and Dan get reinstated with a huge apology. If Alice was just handling the logistics then it couldn't be deemed as favouritism. Then it would be justice.

Alice knew the best place to start. She had to speak to Caroline. Unlike any other lead Emily may have stolen, Dobson's had come directly from Alice. Emily couldn't have known that. That one small detail that Emily had overlooked could finally be her downfall.

Alice flicked through her phone to find Caroline's number.

'Good morning, Dobson's. How can I direct your call?' the female voice on the other end swiftly answered.

'I'd like to speak to Caroline in Operations, please.'

'Certainly. Who can I say is calling?'

'Could you tell her it's Alice of Bloom's Security.'

'And will she know what the call's regarding?'

'Most probably.'

'Very well. Please hold.'

Alice waited for about thirty seconds until she heard the cheery on-hold music cut off.

'Hello, Caroline speaking.'

'Hi, Caroline. It's Alice Bloom here. From Bloom's Security.'

'Oh right, hello. You are a keen bunch aren't you.'

'I just wanted to follow up as I believe you've been speaking to some of my colleagues.'

'Yes. I've had a lot of interaction with your company over the past few days.'

'Has everything been okay?'

'Well, I think so. It's all been rather peculiar if I'm honest.'

'In what way? As I said to you before, it's my family's company and we couldn't be more thrilled to be working with such a great organisation as Dobson's. So if there's any feedback you can give to me on how we can optimise our relationship, I'm all ears.'

'Okay. Well, I was dealing with Dan, as you know. He phoned me up just as you said he would, and then he came to see me on Friday. A charming man. And very knowledgeable. I was quite impressed with some of his ideas as to how we could improve our system.'

'That's good to hear.' Alice felt so proud of Dan.

'But then it appeared he'd messed it all up.'

Alice stopped dead still. 'Messed it up?'

'Yes. I had a call from his manager and apparently he'd sent in the wrong quote.'

'Really?'

'Yes.'

'This was John?' Alice asked.

'Who?'

'John. His manager.'

'No, no, no. A lady called Emily. She was full of spirit but not very complimentary about Dan. It seemed he really had caused some issues.'

'What exactly did Emily say?' Alice asked, trying to keep her cool.

'That Dan had vastly overpriced the quote. She sent another quote to me and it was twenty percent cheaper.'

Alice's jaw dropped open. 'Twenty percent?'

'Yes. She said it wouldn't normally be that cheap, but as Dan had put on at least ten percent over their normal pricing, she felt she had to give me an extra reduction to make up for the inconvenience. But she said she could only honour the reduction if I signed the contract that day. Apparently she didn't want to cause a fuss, but if the quote stayed on the system for more than a day then the massive discount was likely to be picked up and questioned. But she really wanted me to have the discount. She was very persuasive. Very, very persuasive.'

'So you signed the contract then and there?'

'Well, I chatted to my team, but to be honest we were already going to sign. I was so impressed with Dan. I can't believe he tried to swindle us in the end. Such a shame.'

'You would have accepted Dan's quote?'

'Yes. I mean the price per camera was higher than what we already pay, but the overall spec that Dan quoted came out cheaper than our current supplier because he proposed such a clever approach. That's not to mention the fact that your equipment is far superior. So considering all that, Dan's quote was actually quite reasonable. Then to find out it should have been cheaper, and to get a twenty percent discount. We couldn't say no.'

Alice felt the rage fire up inside of her. She didn't know what Dan's quote was for, but she had no doubt that twenty percent off it was quite a substantial sum. And who knew what other large sums Emily had been reducing to steal Dan's clients. This could have cost the company millions.

'I'm pleased to hear that everything's been sorted out for you. And that you've got such a good price. As I said, we want to look after you. In that light, can I request that you no longer deal with Emily? She has given you a very generous discount and I'd like to investigate what happened. We will of course honour the discount, but as a director when customers are sent two competing quotes in a matter of days, it's good for me to look into why. I'm sure you understand.'

'No problem.'

'So you have my number, and I'll be dealing directly with you for the foreseeable future, until we can sort out our London territory and get just one salesperson contacting you. Would that be okay?'

'Fine. I suppose if you're going to deal with anyone, there's no one better than the owner of the company.'

Alice chuckled politely. 'Yes, indeed. Is there anything else that I can help you with at the minute?'

'No. No, it's all good. We were just waiting for the first invoice to be raised so we could get moving.'

'Great. I'll make sure everything runs smoothly. Any queries, please don't hesitate to contact me. But for now, I hope you have a very good day.'

'Thank you, Alice. You too.'

As Alice hung up, she was gritting her teeth with anger. The only positive was that she now had proof that Emily was not only undermining her colleague, but also doing the company out of money. Top salesperson indeed!

But Alice knew that wasn't enough. She still had to find out how Emily was managing it and expose her once and for all. How could Emily have possibly known what Dan was up to? How could Emily have known what was in the quote that Dan sent? Alice knew Dan had been especially careful to save everything locally. He would have taken no chances in putting anything on the shared server for her duplicitous eyes to feast upon. So how was Emily learning so much?

Alice span gently on her swivel chair as she cogitated the problem.

It seemed obvious to suspect that Emily had been tapping Dan's phone or listening in on his conversations another way. But that didn't explain how much she knew. The quote detail wouldn't have been discussed in much depth over the phone and Emily must have known the detail to requote it so convincingly.

Another little niggle started hopping around Alice's mind. Emily had revealed something else that she shouldn't have known about. Dan had spotted it but Alice hadn't given it much weight at the time.

Emily had known that Alice and Dan played chess. How had she found out? They'd told no one. They enjoyed it being their nerdy little secret. They only spoke about it on the phone or in the app game itself via the chat. Surely Emily hadn't been hacking Dan's phone?

Alice swung around to her computer, dismissing the hacking idea. Emily clearly wasn't stupid, but she was far from a technical genius. Instead Alice contemplated something much simpler. She opened her email and typed the word "chess" in the search box.

Seventeen emails to Dan came up. They'd emailed each other talking about the games they were playing. Nudging each other to make a faster turn.

Email. That's how Emily knew. She was somehow seeing Dan's emails. It had to be. It would explain absolutely everything. She'd have all his contacts, all his conversations with clients and all the documents he'd sent to them.

His emails gave Emily everything she needed to know.

Alice was sure she had the answer. If only she could prove it, they'd have to sack Emily on the spot.

Alice was very computer savvy, but she had to admit that she'd struggle to know where to start with hacking a colleague's email and not getting caught, so she doubted Emily would have any special skills in this area. There had to be a more straightforward explanation.

Ideas of how to catch Emily started rattling through Alice's mind. She could send Dan another email with a super-hot but very fake lead on it. Emily could phone Dan's sisters and they'd have her trapped.

Alice slumped back in her chair with sadness as she realised she couldn't do that. Dan had been sacked. He wasn't going to be getting any more leads to his email. He wasn't working for the company anymore.

Alice searched her brain for answers as to how she could corner Emily and prove her guilt, but everything Alice considered was either not possible now that Dan was gone, or far too time consuming.

If Alice left it too long, Dan would find another job. He was so talented, he'd be snapped up before she knew it. Alice couldn't bear the thought of Dan not being at Bloom's anymore. She had to trap Emily, and she had to do it now.

That left only one possible solution.

THIRTY-SIX

It was five to four and Alice sat poised by her phone. She'd messaged John to request that he and Emily join her on a conference call after the Sales meeting had ended. She'd said that she'd heard the news about Dan and wanted to discuss the new London territory moving forward.

John's short reply gave Alice the impression that he was less than happy about her getting involved, but it was tough luck.

Alice had one option and that was to trick Emily into confessing all. It was the only way to make sure that Dan was reprieved without a long-winded internal investigation that would leave them at risk of losing him forever.

She didn't know how she was going to manage it, but Alice was determined enough to bluff her way through until Emily caved in.

The clock ticked forward to four o'clock and Alice picked up her phone. This was it. Her fingers were trembling as she dialled the number. This was one of the biggest conversations of her life. She hoped she could pull it off. So much rested on this moment.

It rang for a short while before John answered.

'Alice, how are you?'

'I'm very well, thank you. Very well. And you? A good Sales meeting?'

'Oh yes. Lots to celebrate today. Emily's news has been a real boost to the team. It's made us feel like anything is possible.'

Alice smirked. 'Yes, Emily has shown us all how if you really put your mind to it, anything can be achieved.'

'Thank you, Alice,' Emily's voice cut through. 'Hello.'

'We're in my office on speakerphone,' John informed Alice.

'Great. So glad to speak to you both.'

'You wanted to talk about the London Territory?' Emily said, full of enthusiasm. Alice imagined her sporting a cheery grin as she hypnotised John with her eager eyes and can-do attitude.

'Yes. First of all I wanted to query how two people could clash so many times with the same leads? Surely London is a big enough city to find business without walking all over one another.'

'Exactly,' Emily said, much to Alice's disgust. 'But Dan and I just couldn't find a way to work together. It's such a shame. He's a nice man.'

'I think too nice,' Alice replied. 'He doesn't have an evil streak in him like some other people.'

'What does that mean?' John asked.

'The truth is, this call isn't about how we're going to move you forward Emily. It's about what we're going to do now that I've caught you out.'

'What?' Emily seemed surprised, but the confidence was still there in her irksome voice.

'I know you've been hacking his emails.'

'That's ridiculous,' Emily stated, sounding genuinely offended.

'And I have proof.'

'What?'

'One of the leads that Dan had been working on just happened to be a friend of mine. Dan didn't know it. No one did. But when I discovered that Dan had sent them a quote yet somehow you'd won the deal, I had to find out what had happened. I called my friend to find out that you'd phoned them up at the last minute with an alternative quote. A quote that was vastly reduced. You told my friend that Dan had priced his quote incorrectly. You implied that Dan was poor at his job and you offered them an extra discount to make up for it. But only if they signed then and there. Didn't you?'

'Which job was that?' Emily asked.

'You've done this several times, have you?'

'No, I just want to know which client has been saying awful things about me. Is it Carlton's?'

'You tell me.'

'How are you friends with Gordon Carlton?' John asked Alice. 'I don't think he's ever set foot outside of London.'

'Was it Price & Field?' Emily asked.

'It's worrying me that you don't know,' Alice said.

'I know Warren Price very well. He's never said you're a friend,' John stated.

'Well it can't be Hitchins,' Emily mumbled. 'They told me they'd never met you. It wasn't Caroline at Dobson's, was it?'

'Remind me again how you got the contact details for such a senior person at a national supermarket chain?' Alice asked.

'I cold called them. They were already looking for a new system. Good timing I guess.'

'Great. And when did you go and see them?' Alice asked.

'What?'

'Surely you must have visited Dobson's to give them such an in-depth quote.'

'I didn't need to go on this occasion,' Emily said.

'How can you quote for a job if you've never seen the premises?'

'They just wanted a like for like quote. They sent me their existing spec and I revised it.'

'But they've got fewer cameras on their new spec. I looked into it.'

'They sent me a floor plan,' Emily argued.

'I'm not happy you didn't visit such a big client,' John said. 'But if the spec meets their needs, I suppose it doesn't matter.'

'Why do you insist on defending her?' Alice asked, as her irritation starting prickling at her. 'How could you sack Dan when he's so good at what he does? How could you not realise that Emily has been hacking Dan's emails to steal his leads?'

'I haven't hacked anyone's emails!' Emily insisted, before she added, 'Was it Paul Lavender?'

'Oh for God's sake,' Alice replied. 'Doesn't that tell you everything, John? Rather than wonder what on earth I'm talking about, Emily is trying to work out which one of Dan's many prospects that she stole is actually my friend?'

'Alice, I'm very sorry, but so far all I can see is that you've had one phone call with a friend who's said some negative things about two quotes they've had in,' John said. 'How does that prove that Emily's been hacking Dan's email? That's a very severe accusation.'

'It certainly is!' Alice stated as she felt the cracks appear in her bluffing. 'Emily has been calling Dan's prospects up saying that she's his boss and then undercutting his quotes. What concerns me is how much genuine business has she brought into this company and how much was rightfully Dan's? I'd also like to know how much money she has cost us by going in cheaper to undermine her own colleague. Emily cost Dan his job and has cost my company potentially millions. Yes, these are very severe accusations indeed.'

'This is nonsense,' Emily said.

'Right then, you leave me no choice,' Alice said, getting desperate. 'I have Caroline from Dobson's waiting to join our call. John, you're going to love this.'

'What?' Emily said, still sounding confident. 'Whatever Caroline says, it's not what it seems.'

'So you didn't deliberately undercut Dan to win the job?'

'I was trying to save the job.'

'And how do you figure that?'

'Dan always quotes things really high. I was just trying to secure the huge contract for Bloom's. I was actually making the company money, not losing it.'

'But you have lost us money. Definitely thousands, if not millions.'

'That's ridiculous. Dan would have lost millions. His quotes were sometimes at sixty percent margins. No one would sign off that.'

'How do you know what Dan's been quoting?' John suddenly asked. 'I don't even know what Dan's been quoting. Not generally.'

Emily fell silent and Alice saw the first sign of hope.

'Because she's been hacking his emails,' Alice pushed.

'Emily?' John said.

'I haven't hacked anything,' Emily replied.

'How could you possibly know what Dan has been quoting?'

'I haven't hacked. I just happened to see one day.'

'Happened to see? Happened to see his emails?' John was finally starting to sound annoyed.

'It's not as bad as it sounds. When I first started, Dan was giving me some tips. I thought he seemed very good at his job and I was eager to learn more. I thought if I could look at what he's doing then I could mirror some of his tactics. So when he was at his desk one day, I peered over his shoulder and got his password. I only meant to log in once or twice. Just take a look at his approach. But when I saw his quotes and saw what he was charging people, I was gobsmacked. Like I said, he generally goes in at a sixty percent margin. It's not right. So I called one of his prospects up to see what they thought, and before I knew it, I was getting the deal at a cheaper price. It was my first big sale. It felt good.'

'It wasn't your sale!' Alice stated.

'Emily, how could you?' John said.

'He's been charging too much.'

'You think he should start at his lowest price?'

'Caroline at Dobson's would have paid the higher price,' Alice informed them both. 'She thought his quote was very reasonable.'

'It was really expensive!' Emily argued back.

'What gives you the right to make those judgements?' John stated. 'A good salesman goes in high and convinces the customer to pay it, always leaving room for negotiation. The client can always say no. Oh God, what have I done? You smashed your target at the lower prices. Imagine where Dan would be now? How many times have you done this?'

'You mean how many times have I secured a deal that Dan had put in jeopardy? Trust me, Dan was getting too greedy. He most certainly would have lost the jobs.'

'It was for Dan to negotiate!' John said, getting angry.

'At last!' Alice said, almost cheering. 'John, there is no place for the likes of Emily at Bloom's. She's been dishonest, deceitful and completely unethical. She had no right to look at Dan's emails. I'm going to leave it with you to sort out the logistics, but I want her gone and I want Dan reinstated. And any projects that he claims are rightfully his, I want them put against his sales figures. Unlike some people in this department, I can guarantee he won't lie. I also want to hear from Dan that you have profusely apologised to him. Do I make myself clear?'

'Alice, it's not what-' Emily started.

'Don't you dare, Emily. Don't. Dan is a solid worker and a very clever man. Your behaviour has been completely unacceptable. You should be ashamed of yourself. John, I want this dealt with in a manner my father would be proud of, and I want a full report tomorrow detailing everything that has happened. Do you understand?'

'Yes.'

'And John, next time a good worker comes to you to report an issue within the team, I want you to take it seriously. It didn't take much digging for me to find out the truth, so I'm guessing you couldn't have looked into it at all. I shouldn't have had to get involved, but for this company's sake I'm glad I did. Who knows how bad things might have got.'

'Thank you, Alice,' John said.

'I'll leave you to it. Speak to you tomorrow. Goodbye.'

Alice hung up. She took a few deep breaths before dancing around the room with delight. She'd done it. It was over. Emily was gone and Dan had got his job back.

Now she couldn't wait to tell him!

THIRTY-SEVEN

Alice immediately called Dan. She was buzzing with excitement. He was going to be thrilled.

The phone rang and rang and eventually went to voicemail.

'Hi Dan, it's Alice. Call me. I have news. News you'll be very happy to hear.'

She hung up and stared at her phone, hoping he'd immediately call back.

After about ten minutes of eagerly waiting, she considered how watching her phone might be having a negative effect on whether he would call. She couldn't help but feel as if her phone was deliberately preventing calls just to be mean. She'd always suspected that her electronic objects hated her.

She flicked into the chess app, at first just to fool her phone into thinking she didn't care, but then she realised the double whammy effect. Now, not only was her phone in the dark about her true motives, but playing her turn against Dan might jolt him into responding as well.

She pondered her move for a while. Dan always had the upper hand. He was definitely the better player. Not that she'd ever admit that to his face.

She focused on her pieces, getting drawn into the action. She'd been toying with the idea of moving her bishop. It might mean she'd have to sacrifice a pawn, but ultimately she was confident in her attack.

Her finger was poised over the bishop when she spotted that she could strategically move her knight to create a fork. How had she not noticed that before?

With a huge grin, she made her decision and she sent it off to Dan. She hoped he'd be impressed with her play.

Dan still hadn't called back and Alice was getting twitchy. She decided to try again.

This time his phone went straight to voicemail. That meant he was either in an area of no reception or, more horribly, he'd switched his phone off. How she hoped it was the former.

Coming to terms with the fact that her phone had no more power in this situation, she decided to do some work. She needed to take her mind off Dan. As soon as he got her message, he'd call back. Definitely.

She nudged her computer back into life and she opened the budget document she'd been working on. Her heart dropped when she remembered how she was still trapped in that cycle of doom.

The darkness of her depression loomed over her again. The joy of her recent win over Emily faded away and the harsh reality she lived in came into focus.

Her words about Emily echoed through her mind. She'd called Emily dishonest and deceitful. Alice suddenly felt like a terrible hypocrite.

Hadn't she behaved that exact way towards Karl? She'd been so cruel to him. Yes, the situations might have been different, but the motive was still about self-gain. Gain at the expense of another person.

Then there was the mess that was Ethan. She'd been so caught up in her fantasy world that she hadn't seen things for what they really were. How could she ever have believed that such an idiot was secretly a genius? His ego knew no bounds. It had been quite astonishing.

She had a flash of the night when they'd been to see Grave Annihilation and instantly she became nauseous.

Dan's declaration of love put the night into a whole different perspective. Had he thought it was a date that night? It was in every conceivable way a date. Except for the fact that Alice had been using him to get to Ethan.

No wonder Dan went back to the hotel feeling sick.

No wonder he didn't speak to her for days.

How could she be so naïve and stupid?

She grabbed her phone again. She needed to talk to him.

She dialled the number but once again it went straight to voicemail.

'Please call me, Dan. We need to speak. Please call me back.'

Alice felt queasy with guilt. Dan had been so kind to her. Dan was more than just a really good friend, he was the best thing that had ever happened to her. She was so incredibly lucky to be loved by such a warm, caring man. And she loved him dearly in return. They were perfect for each other.

What had she been thinking?

Light began to peer through the dark clouds above her as it dawned on her what a fool she'd been. The only pain she'd been experiencing of late had been of her own making.

Why was she fighting Dan? They were in love. That was amazing. And Dan had stuck by her no matter how many times she'd pushed him away. He'd kissed her when he couldn't even see her. Not many people would have been that understanding. He was a marvel. Wasn't that enough to prove he wasn't going to hurt her?

Dan had been right. If she kept going down this path then she would have nothing left. What would be the point of that?

Her parents had died. It was tragic and awful, but they wouldn't want this for Alice. She'd put five years of her life on hold, and even when she'd been given a chance to move on, she'd still done it with trepidation.

It was time for change. True change. It was time to get on with things.

If only she wasn't still invisible.

But that wasn't going to stop her. She'd call Dan every half an hour until eventually he answered. She'd find a way to get through to him. She'd find a way to fight, just as he'd fought for her. This wasn't the end.

She looked back at her computer with a new found strength.

Of course she couldn't tackle the budgets. She didn't know enough about the company. But wasn't that the point of a board of directors? That they all worked together as a team? Why was she trying to do it all by herself?

Since her parents died, she'd tried to tackle everything on her own and it hadn't worked. It had left her lonely and empty. It had left her invisible. Maybe it was time she gave teamwork a go.

All she had to do was lead her team in the right direction. She didn't need to have all the answers. They were supposed to come up with the answers together.

She quickly grabbed a pen and noted down some key objectives. The new year wasn't that far away, so if she could formulate exactly what direction she wanted the company to move forward in, then she could work with her team to get there in the right way.

And surely if they all worked together, she'd learn more and be respected more. It was hardly rocket science. She'd always thought of herself as clever, but she'd just realised that sometimes she could be really dim.

Alice did as planned and she called Dan every thirty minutes. She constantly got through to his voicemail, and she left messages on every other call. Surely he'd have to phone her back soon.

She went to bed that night feeling rejuvenated. She hadn't felt that good in half a decade.

How could being loved be so bad when it gave her this much clarity?

Alice slept very well that night. She had sweet dreams and when she woke up the next morning she felt refreshed and ready for the day.

She quickly checked her phone to see if Dan had called her back, but he hadn't.

Then she stopped. She put out her hands in front of her. She could see them. She could see them!

She jumped out of bed and ran to the mirror. She was back. Fully back.

Alice Bloom was back!

She called Dan straight away. It was eight o'clock and she hoped he'd be up. She hated the thought of him lying in bed feeling sorry for himself. That was where she'd been so many times.

It went straight through to his voicemail again.

'Dan, it's Alice again. Please call me back. I have so much good news to tell you. So much. Call me back. You won't regret it.'

Alice threw her phone on the bed and went to the bathroom. She was ready to have a shower and start her day. The first day of her new beginning.

She came out twenty minutes later to see she had a missed call. Her heart was pounding with excitement as she checked who it was from.

Oh, it was from John. She decided to get dressed and call him back.

'Good morning, John,' she said when he answered. 'How are you? How did things go with Emily?'

'We had a good chat after you left. It seems she wasn't the person I thought she was at all.'

'If it's any consolation, I think she had a lot of people fooled.'

'I should have seen it, though. I was so happy when Dan took the job. He's a talented salesman. I'm incredibly frustrated that I didn't see what was really going on. I want to thank you for what you did. I actually managed to get a hold of the quote that Dan sent to Dobson's. It was very impressive. Hard to believe he pulled it together in just a weekend.'

'He's good, isn't he.'

'Better than I ever gave him credit for. I made him feel small and stupid and I'll never forgive myself for that. I'm more than ready to eat humble pie.'

'I think Emily might have some sort of hypnotic force that Dan and I are immune to. She persuaded a lot of people of a lot of things.'

'Nevertheless, I should have known better. I've tried to call Dan this morning but his phone went straight to voicemail and his message box is full.'

Alice grimaced. 'Let me tell him,' she said. 'I have to speak to him anyway.'

'You were the one to bring the truth to light, it's only fair you tell him. I'd like to offer him a pay rise too. We can talk about the details, but tell him it's not just a straight return. I'm going to look after him to make up for the terrible way he's been treated.'

'I'll let him know. And I'm glad to hear it. I take it he'll be the only London sales rep now?'

'It turns out there was only one all along.'

'I'm sure that will make him very happy.'

'I can't believe we almost lost him. He's a true asset. That quote was brilliant. Emily was right, he went in at a sixty percent margin.'

'Sixty percent?'

'And you say the client was going to sign at that?'

'Yes. Yes they were. Were all of his quotes that good?'

'I'm going to find out. But it takes quite a salesman to get the client to sign at such a high price.'

'It certainly does. Do I want to know how much Emily cost us?'

'Probably not. Let's just be grateful we've got Dan back on board.'

'Not yet we haven't. But don't worry, I won't let him go without a fight.'

'Thanks, Alice. Thanks for everything. And for being understanding. It was quite a wake up call for me yesterday.'

'Let's just focus on the future now.'

'Keep me posted.'

'Will do. Speak to you soon.'

Alice ended the call with John and immediately tried Dan again. Still it went straight to voicemail, but this time it told her his message box was full. Crap.

She needed to see him. This calling was getting her nowhere. If only she knew where he lived. Wimbledon didn't really narrow it down that much.

Instantly an idea hit her. Technically Dan was still an employee. Her employee. And with employees came records.

She ran to her computer and switched it on. Her next call was to HR.

THIRTY-EIGHT

Dan took a deep breath. He stared at his phone. He had an important call to make and he was dreading it.

The day before, he'd driven straight home and hadn't hesitated in getting straight into his jogging bottoms. He'd then spent the afternoon flaked out on the sofa watching mindless television, eating indulgent food, drinking copious amounts of beer and generally feeling monumentally sorry for himself.

The second he'd heard his phone ring and he'd seen that it was Alice, he'd switched it off. He hadn't been able to face speaking to her. He couldn't face speaking to anyone.

When he woke that morning he wasn't feeling any better. He'd got up, had headed to the local shop to get a paper and some groceries, and then he'd cooked himself a full English breakfast. He'd been craving it anyway with his mid-week hangover, but when it had occurred to him that it didn't matter that he had a mid-week hangover as he had absolutely nothing else to do, he'd craved those fatty foods even more. What did he care? Everything had turned to crap. He might as well eat his body weight in hash browns and bacon.

Feeling sick with how full he was, Dan had then returned

to bed. He hadn't been able to sleep, though. He'd mostly stared at the ceiling wondering what he was going to do with his life. He wasn't worthy of another job and he doubted he'd ever get over Alice. He had never felt lower.

He'd scoffed down a pizza he'd found in the freezer at lunchtime, and that's when he knew he needed to get the worst part of all over with. The appetite wasn't just from depression, it was from the dread of telling his family.

He needed to tell his parents. As much as he wanted to hide under his duvet and pray for the world to go away, he had to face reality. Barely a day went by without some sort of chat on the family WhatsApp. If he didn't respond soon they'd all become suspicious anyway, and he knew if he lied, they'd know and just badger him even more. They always knew when he was lying.

When it came to his family, the only way to survive the torture was to get it over with quickly. He'd tell his mum and she could tell everyone else. That way no one would need to mention it to his face. His mum would insist on discretion and the whole nightmare would be over with.

He turned his phone on, waited for it to spring into life and typed in his PIN. It was then that his eyes nearly popped out of his head. He had twenty-two missed calls. Twenty-two!

He flicked to the caller list to find that the vast majority were from Alice, and one from John. Someone had left voicemails too.

He shook his head. He couldn't handle voicemails right now. He didn't want details from John about how he should hand his car and phone back, and he didn't know how to deal with Alice.

His anger at how she'd been behaving had quickly subsided during his journey home the day before. She was invisible. Invisible! He doubted anything else in his life would ever shock him more.

But ultimately he had to concede that his sisters had been right. Alice had been through hell. Her life had become so miserable, it had taken away her whole body. Perhaps she did just need a friend. Maybe he should stop being so selfish.

As he sat and reflected on Alice and her difficulties, it made him realise what he'd got. He might be useless at sales and he might have lost his one true love, but at least he had his family. Alice hadn't even got that. She truly was all alone.

Dan knew he needed to be a better man. He needed to find a way to put his feelings aside and just be there for her. The problem was, how? He loved her too much and it made it complicated. Maybe first of all he could just come to terms with his own life and then he'd drive up to see her. After all, he knew he couldn't help her until he'd helped himself.

Step one for Dan was to call his mum. He'd get this over with and then see how he felt.

He found his parents' home number and pressed to call.

'Hello,' his mum answered. He was so relieved it wasn't his dad.

'Hi mum, it's Dan.'

'Daniel? Are you okay? We don't normally hear from you at this time of day. Are you not well?'

'Sort of. How are you?'

'All is good here. Stop changing the subject. What's the matter? Have you been to the doctor?'

'It's not that sort of unwell.'

'What sort of unwell is it?'

Dan hesitated. 'I have some bad news.'

'Oh no. What's happened? Are your sisters okay? Clare's not had a heart attack overdoing that training, has she? They both push themselves far too hard. They're too determined, those girls-'

'Mum, it's nothing to do with Clare. Or Mary. As far as I know, they're both fine. It's to do with me.'

'What's the matter?'

Dan sighed. *Just get it over with quickly.* 'I lost my job yesterday.'

'What? Oh no, darling. What happened? Redundancy? They're making cuts all over. Peter's lost his job. And

Raymond. And Jennifer for that matter.'

Dan didn't know who any of those people were, which wasn't unusual. His parents had a lot of friends.

'Don't worry, darling. Even though you haven't been there that long, they still have to look after you. Were you on a month's notice?'

'It wasn't redundancy,' Dan said.

'What?'

'Let's just say it was a difference of opinion. They decided to cut back to one salesperson in the London territory and I wasn't performing well enough.' Dan took a deep, brave breath. 'Turns out I'm not very good.'

There. He'd said it. The truth was out. No more pretending. He was ready to take the lecture and this time he'd listen to it.

'What a load of nonsense!' his mother said. Dan had been wrong: there was something more shocking than finding out your friend was invisible. 'My son, not performing? You were head hunted for that job. They needed you. Now they're telling you you're not good enough? Exactly how high are their standards?'

Dan couldn't believe it. 'It's a bit complex. Someone was stealing my leads. I was outwitted and it cost me my job.'

'Someone was stealing your leads? How does that work?'

'I wish I knew. But it doesn't matter now. All that matters is I'm out of a job. Maybe I wasn't cut out for it.'

'Daniel, listen to me. You're very talented. You really are.' Dan was close to pinching himself. The conversation was so unexpected. 'You might not have an academic mind like your sisters, and I know that's always bothered you, but what you have is charisma. You have a way with people.'

'You think so?'

'Yes. You're just like your grandfather. Grandad White. He struggled so much with writing and maths, but he could get anyone to do anything. He was warm and kind and he listened. He found out what made people tick and it made them respond to him. That's what you have. You have his gift. You're so talented. You've just never believed it because you didn't ace it through school like your sisters. But if your sisters had to sell security equipment to big corporations like you do, how do you think they'd fare?'

'I don't know,' Dan mumbled.

'They'd be dreadful. They'd reel off the facts and figures and bore everyone to tears. You captivate people. I've seen you do it so many times. That time when you talked yourself out of detention, or when you got that shopkeeper to give you a discount on that computer game because I wouldn't up your pocket money. You're amazing. We didn't want to say how proud we were because we didn't want to reward what was actually naughty behaviour. But secretly we've always been proud. And that's why I know you're so good at your job. You were born to be a salesman.'

'I thought you hated that I was in sales.'

'What on earth gave you that impression?'

'You've never really asked me about it.'

'No, Daniel, you never talk about it. There's a difference. I don't know why at your age you still haven't figured it out. All your father and I want is for you to be happy. And when you were winning those trips abroad for being the top salesman, and getting all those huge bonuses, you seemed so happy. We couldn't be more proud.'

For a moment, Dan felt quite choked up. He couldn't remember his parents ever saying they were proud of him before.

'So if this stupid company thinks you're no good, then screw them.'

'Mum!'

'You don't need to be somewhere you're not appreciated. Life is too short. You have a real talent, and they obviously knew it once as they fought to get you on board. Now they're being short-sighted and, quite frankly, it's their loss. Life is a journey and you're about to start a brand new adventure. See this as a good thing, Daniel. Look at it positively.'

'It's pretty hard.'

'I do have to ask one thing, though. I'm sorry for my indiscretion on this matter, but I just need to know.'

'What is it?'

'Is this job loss any way connected to the fact that you've been trying to sleep with the owner of the company?'

'Mum!' Dan rolled his eyes with embarrassment. 'You've been chatting to Mary and Clare then.'

'They just mentioned that they were worried about you. There are plenty of nice girls out there. What makes this girl so special? She sounds very troubled with a great weight on her shoulders.'

'I am not going to talk about that with you. All you need to know is that it had nothing to do with Alice. If anything, she was the only one who believed in me. But she isn't involved in my department.'

'Are you sure?'

'Yes. Very sure.'

'Well, that's good. I just needed to ask. No judgement. It's just hard to see why someone as hard working as you is out of a job. Where's the justice?'

Dan felt touched.

'Although Peter was a manager. He'd built up the department from scratch and then they told him he wasn't needed anymore. What about that?'

Dan wanted to ask who Peter was, but he just didn't have the strength. It could turn into a very long conversation if he allowed his mum to elaborate. Instead he said nothing and his mum seemed to realise.

'What are you doing now? Are you wallowing in self-pity?' she asked.

'No.'

'Are you? How many films have you watched? I bet you ordered pizza last night. And don't drink too much.'

Dan hated that his mum always knew everything.

'What you're going to do now is get up off the sofa and find out the number of your local job centre,' she ordered.

'You need to look into that Universal Credit. You might be all right for money at the moment, but it's a tough world out there, so get what's rightfully yours. And your father and I can help you out too if need be.'

'You think I should contact the job centre?'

'Yes, absolutely. You've paid your national insurance and taxes for years and now you need the support in return. You have rent to pay. Jennifer said that because she lives alone she got a lot of extra help. Find out everything you can. Get some proper advice. And start looking for jobs. Moping people do not move forward.'

Dan was taken aback by his mum's attitude.

'Daniel, are you going to take action?'

'Yes mum.'

'Call me tomorrow?'

'Yes mum.'

'Because if you don't, I'll call you.'

'Okay.'

'Your dad sends his love. You've been robbed. Remember that. But something better is out there just around the corner to make up for it. Have faith.'

'I'll try.'

'Speak to you tomorrow. Take care. Love you.'

'Bye mum.'

Dan hung up and took a moment. None of that had gone how he'd expected, but it was great. His mum and dad were actually proud of him. He had no idea.

His doorbell went. Dan stood up, curious as to who it could be. His doorbell rarely chimed.

He picked up the intercom phone to see who was there.

'Hello,' he said.

'Dan?'

'Yes.'

'It's Alice!'

Dan nearly dropped the receiver. What was she doing there?

'Erm... come on up. Up two flights then on your left.'

Dan placed the receiver back before he darted quickly into his bathroom. He smoothed his hair down. He was looking a right mess. He hadn't even shaved.

He raced back to the door and opened it. Seconds later Alice appeared.

'Surprise!' she said, her face lit up with delight. She had a carrier bag in her hand and she was dragging a suitcase behind her.

'You're visible?' Dan said, full of confusion. 'What are you doing here?'

'I am visible. Very visible. I woke up this morning fully at one with the world again, and feeling better than I can ever remember.'

'And you came to rub it in my face?'

'No! I came to make your day. Since you refused to answer any of my calls or phone me back. Can I at least come in, since I've come all this way?'

'Of course,' Dan said. 'I wasn't consciously ignoring you. I've only just turned my phone on. I needed some space.'

Alice removed her coat, threw it on the side of the settee and made herself comfortable.

'Well, while you've been wallowing in your space, I've been dealing with Emily. You really should have answered your phone.'

Dan felt suddenly very engaged. He sat down next to Alice, eager to hear more. 'Emily?'

'I was spitting feathers yesterday after you left. I couldn't let her get away with it. So I called up Caroline at Dobson's to find out what was going on.'

'You called Caroline? What did she say?' Dan was getting excited.

'You're not going to like this, but Emily called Caroline on Monday saying that she was your manager and you'd given them an incorrect quote. She requoted them with a twenty percent discount and insisted that they sign then and there.'

'Twenty percent?'

'Yes.'

'No wonder they went with her.'

'Well, it's not that simple. Apparently Caroline was very pleased with you. She said your proposal was impressive and she would have accepted your quote. The full sixty percent margin that you sneakily tried to push through.'

'She wasn't going to negotiate?'

'You smashed it, Dan. Totally smashed it. John is also deeply impressed.'

'John? John knows?'

'He found out everything yesterday when I got him and Emily on a conference call. I backed her into a corner and left John to pick up the pieces.'

'Wow! So did she tell you how she was getting all my leads?'

'She found out your password and she's been accessing your emails.'

'My emails?' Dan was astonished.

'That's how she knew about everything you were doing. Including the fact that we have secret chess games.'

'Of course.'

'So Emily's out. I demanded it. If they were going to get rid of you for just not performing to their standards, they could hardly keep her when she'd behaved so badly. It was misconduct and then some.'

'She got the sack?'

'That's why John tried to call you. He wanted to offer you the role of sole London salesperson. With a pay rise, of course.'

'Bloody hell. I don't know how I feel about that. I mean obviously-'

'Before you say anything, though, I have a counter offer. Something you'll need to think about carefully.'

'What do you mean a counter offer?'

'I was chatting to John this morning and he mentioned how impressive your quote was. Not only how you pulled it together in such a short space of time, but also how you managed to go in at such a high price.'

Dan shrugged. Wasn't that the job?

'It got me thinking,' Alice continued. 'I pulled up some of your other quotes and I have to say they were all really good. Then I spoke to technical and found out that you do most of the quotes yourself, whereas a lot of the other sales people use the tech team for support.'

Dan shrugged again. 'I think you should take pride in helping customers by actually knowing what you're talking about.'

'Then I spoke to your old boss.'

'Neil?'

'Yes, Neil. I asked him what margins you generally worked to and he said more often than not you got the best margins across all the team. He said you had this magic way of getting clients to pay top price. Even when clients negotiated, you still outplayed everyone else. It seems he was gutted when you handed in your notice.'

'Bloom's gave me an offer too hard to refuse.'

'Then crapped all over you from a severe height.'

'I wasn't going to mention that.'

'The point is, Dan, you're amazing. And my father always believed in recognising and rewarding talent. He'd be very disappointed by what happened.'

'What are you saying? I thought John was offering me a pay rise anyway.'

'I don't want to offer you a pay rise. Well, there will be a pay rise, but with more responsibility.'

'What? Are you offering me John's job?' Dan chuckled.

'How would you feel about being John's boss?'

'What?' Dan virtually spat.

'I need more budget next year to increase our R&D, so that means we're going to need to sell more. I think we need a Sales Director on our team. And you, Daniel White, perfectly fit the bill.'

'Sales Director?' Dan stood up in shock.

'I'll need to run it by the other directors out of courtesy, of course. But I'll relinquish some of my equity. We can talk about the finer details. Will you accept it?'

'The other directors don't know?'

'Not yet. Although they're not really going to get much of a say. I get the casting vote and this is nothing but a positive step forward for everyone. Look, there are lots of little details, but there's no point in tackling any of them until I know whether you're interested or not.'

'John's boss? Like run the Sales department?'

'Yes. I was thinking John could still take day to day care of the team, but you'll be in charge of everything else.'

'Will that mean I won't be selling anymore?'

'It will mean whatever it means. You'll be in charge. Give yourself a couple of accounts if you want. If you've got time. You'll have the final say.'

A huge grin widened across Dan's face.

'Is that a yes?' Alice asked.

'I don't know the first thing about being a director.'

'Join the club! We can figure it out together.'

'Wouldn't it be more beneficial to hire someone with experience?'

'That's one idea. But my dad always believed in finding people with actual raw talent. And you, Daniel White, have that in abundance. So I'm thinking when you get into the job and you build that experience, you're going to be pretty unstoppable.'

Dan remained silent for a second, absorbing her words. 'Can I think about it?' he said with a small smile.

'Of course.'

'I mean, I'm very interested. I'm really flattered. I just need to let it digest. Ten minutes ago I was thinking of heading to my local job centre and now I'm being offered a director role. Big day.'

'And it's about to get bigger.'

'What?' Dan sat down again, ready for bad news.

Alice turned to face him properly. 'I was wrong yesterday. Very wrong. I love you, Dan. Truly love you. Yes it's a scary notion, and I can't deny the thought of losing you if it doesn't work out isn't a big concern. But what if we work? What if this is the real deal? Because it certainly feels like it is. You're all I think about too. All the time. Even when I was on a date with Ethan, I kept checking my phone to see if you'd messaged me.'

'Really?'

'I'm sorry for how I've behaved. I've been terrible to you. But I want to make up for it and I want to give us a go. Will you be my boyfriend?'

'What?' Dan felt like he was getting hit with a big, bright, happy ray of sunshine. It was surprising but very satisfying.

'I love you, Dan. Please be mine.'

Alice moved in to kiss him. Quickly at first, as if to check it was okay, and when he didn't resist she came back for a more passionate second try.

He loved the feel of her, and he couldn't resist running his fingers through her hair. He had never desired anyone more.

She backed away a little breathless. 'Is that a yes?'

'Alice, I could never say no to you.' Dan's face started to ache under the strength of his smile. 'My girlfriend?'

'Yes. Definitely. Your girlfriend.'

They kissed again, warmly and deeply.

Dan moved back to take a good look at his gorgeous girlfriend, to make sure it really was all happening, when he spotted her suitcase again in the corner of his eye.

'Are you moving in too?' he asked, not exactly sure how he felt about that just at that moment.

Alice giggled. 'No, don't worry. But it's good to know you want to take things slowly. That's that conversation dealt with very quickly.'

'I didn't mean-'

'Shut up. I'm only winding you up. No, I'm not moving in. I just needed a back-up plan. It's a fair trek back to Starley Green.'

'It's about two hours.'

'Precisely! My plan was to camp outside until you let me in, and then maybe get a hotel if it got late and it had all gone horribly wrong.'

'And if it all went terribly right?'

Alice flushed. It was so cute. She shrugged and turned away from him. 'I thought maybe I could stay the night,' she mumbled.

Dan wanted to punch the air. This day was getting better by the second.

'Well, we have some serious games to get through,' Alice said as she grabbed the carrier bag she'd brought in with her. 'I wasn't thinking of sleeping much tonight.'

'Neither was I,' Dan grinned.

Alice handed him the bag.

'What's this?' he asked.

'Take a look. I've just bought it. Turns out there's a shop not far from Euston.'

Dan opened the bag and immediately laughed. He took out the chess clock. 'You got one!'

'Now where's your *Lord of the Rings* chess set?' Alice asked eagerly.

Dan couldn't believe how happy he felt. Life had literally never been better.

'All in good time,' he said. 'I don't say this often, but chess can wait.'

'Chess can wait?'

'Oh yes.'

'Wait for what?' Alice asked.

'You'll see,' Dan smiled, and he kissed her again.

ABOUT THE AUTHOR

Lindsay is a British author who lives in Warwickshire with her husband and cat. She's had a lifelong passion for writing, starting off as a child when she used to write stories about the Fraggles of Fraggle Rock.

Knowing there was nothing else she'd rather study, she did her degree in writing and has now turned her favourite hobby into a career.

Lindsay is also the author of:

- The *Bird* Trilogy, a supernatural love story full of magical twists and turns.

- *Emmett the Empathy Man*, a comic tale about a superhero who comes to life with disastrous results.

- *In the Blood*, a science fiction love story about two people who could never have possibly met yet know everything about each other.

- *Shape the Future*, a science fiction love story about a girl who is told that her boyfriend is cheating on, only to realise that the truth is far more shocking.

All of her books are available on Amazon.

To find out more about Lindsay and her books, visit www.lindsay-woodward.com

INVISIBLE